1973

THE
EVENING
OF THE
GOOD
SAMARITAN

THE EVENING OF THE GOOD SAMARITAN

by Dorothy Salisbury Davis

Charles Scribner's Sons   *New York*

for Harry

CONTENTS

THE
EVENING
OF THE
GOOD
SAMARITAN

PART
ONE

1936

ANDERS HALL was dated 1887, the year Midwestern University was founded. Built of gray stone, Gothic in structure, and darkened by the soot and smoke of the seven hundred trains which daily converged on Traders City, it looked much older. In the bleak cold of mid-January, its lights remote behind the high mullioned windows, it stood as dark and formidable as a medieval stronghold, and seemed especially so to the students who were that night forbidden its proximity. Despite their banishment, they came together in threes and fours within sight of the building and talked softly among themselves. Whenever a group grew larger a uniformed policeman ambled through its midst. "Break it up, boys." "All right, boys and girls, on your way."

And not so much because they were policemen as because they wore uniforms and when unoccupied with the dispersal of the students mingled and joked with the militant Legionnaires who were allowed to gather at will, they were bitterly resented by the students. The Legionnaires were out five hundred strong, "wearing their medals and their limps and their bleeding purple hearts," determined that the red flag of Russia would not run up that night in Traders City.

"*Amerika über alles,*" a student jeered, and in the black of night a legionnaire saw red. He grabbed a policeman's stick and brought it down on the first bare head he could swing at. It was a glancing blow he struck but the man who caught it shouted:

"For Chris' sake, look who you're crackin', will you? I'm a reporter on the *Dispatch*."

A hoot went up from the students. The *Traders City Dispatch* was Judge Phipps's paper, the world's greatest by the Judge's own admission, built on comic strips and sports news, advice to the lovelorn and vox populi; it reached, they said, its height of wit and wisdom in The Bright Comments of the Children. But over a million people read it and by and large they probably took Judge Phipps

3

4

no more seriously than most Midwesterners took, say, Hitler or Mussolini at the turn of 1935.

The police moved warily along the campus walks. Sometimes a man of them would thresh his way through the bordering shrubs while his partner stood watch in the open. It was the absence of demonstrators now that bothered them: so few in sight seemed to portend the collecting of a multitude in some undiscovered place. That the students might be simply obeying orders they could not credence. There had been a riot on the campus a few nights earlier, between—roughly speaking—the extremes of right and left among the student body although some of the boys arrested had no previous history of political activity. They had come to sustain a teacher whom they liked, they said, and had then been outraged at the invasion of the student meeting by the vigilant legionnaires who had scarcely even an "old grad" among them.

That night in Anders Hall the annual banquet tendered the faculty by the trustees was taking place. No announcement had been made, but a definition of University policy was expected. The issue was not new, nor was it confined to Midwestern, but when during the Christmas holidays the parents of a boy had withdrawn him from the school and had publicly charged that the faculty was "rife with Communists," it came flaring into the open. The state senate ordered an investigation, the newspapers coaxed from the boy the name of at least one teacher he believed a Communist although, lawyer-bidden, the boy himself qualified, "Communist, that is, with a small 'c'."

The pitch of tempers, however, had soon gone up to high C. More than once the racial issue was introduced: Midwestern admission records did not require the statement of religious affiliation, and many had long thought that a mistake. It was the smallest of comfort to the harrassed administration but some, nonetheless, that the name of the professor cited was Jonathan Miles Hogan. By no stretch of the imagination could it be said that all Hogans were Communists.

A solitary figure, bare-headed, his coat collar turned up against the wind, the constant wind of Traders City, walked back and forth in the shadow of Anders Hall. Keeping to himself, he had escaped police detection. When he paused and lit a cigaret he drew attention to himself. He was neither well-dressed nor shabby and a little old for a student by the calculation of the policeman who shone his torch in the young man's face. The face was strong, already lined at the mouth and eyes. The mouth was dominant, large and firm, but with the hollows of easy humor at the corners. His dark brows were drawn over eyes as blue as the policeman had ever seen in a man. It would have hurt him somehow to discover that this lad was an agitator. But that was his fear.

"Let's see some identification." He waited for the man to bring out his wallet. "What are you doing here?"

"Waiting to see if my father comes out."

"Isn't that touching," the policeman said. Meanwhile the reporters were crowding in, six or seven of them, a press card in the hat, carte blanche. The policeman read the identification out loud because the names amused him: "Thaddeus Marcus Hogan . . ." His tone changed. "M.D. . . . Why didn't you say you were a doctor in the first place?"

An answer would have been lost. The reporters had picked up the name.

"It's Jonathan Hogan's son."

"Hey, doctor, do you think your old man'll get fired?"

A dozen questions came in rapid sequence, most of them prefaced by "hey."

"Hey, doc, have you got any kids yourself? Are you married?"

"Change the order of the question and I might answer it," Marcus Hogan said and the men who heard him laughed.

"Is the professor really a red, doc?"

"He doesn't think so. That's what's important, isn't it?"

"Would you say he's a pink?"

"No, sir. I would not say my father is a pink." It was said with humor. Again the reporters laughed. Hogan himself kept looking toward the great doors of Anders Hall.

"Doctor Hogan—is your father going to come out and speak to you?" The voice was very young and very polite for a reporter. The policeman asked him for identification. "I'm editor of the *Daily Orange*," the reporter said. The *Orange* was the University paper.

"On your way, sonny," the policeman said.

"Leave him alone, Clancy," one of the reporters said. "He's got credentials."

"My name isn't Clancy," the cop said.

"Goldstein," the newspaperman amended.

"Shut up, you bum, or I'll run you out of the park."

"Up . . . the rebels!" The reporter jerked his thumb in the air.
The policeman cursed him aloud.

Seen suddenly but having come up in an unhurried manner, students were all around them, not milling, just there, but an ominous crowd of them by the surprised policeman's calculation as he flashed his torch over their faces. He fumbled for his whistle.

Marcus Hogan caught his arm just before he got the whistle to his lips. "I'm sorry, officer, but isn't that a sure way of starting trouble?"

The policeman dropped the whistle, but he said: "You're under arrest for laying hands on an officer."

Startled, Hogan hesitated an instant. Then he said quickly, raising his voice as though there was absolute logic in his words: "It's all right. I'm a doctor. Let us through." And he took the cop's arm.

A way opened for the two men and behind them the small crowd gradually fell apart, the students seeking information of one another as to what had happened. Before even the reporters realized it, Hogan was gone. One of the reporters shouted, baiting the students: "What's the matter? You all chicken?" But they refused to be provoked.

Several yards away the policeman said, "Get off the campus, doctor. That's all."

"No arrest?"

"Your old man's trouble enough for the police department."

Marcus Hogan stood a moment staring back at Anders Hall. It was almost nine by the pale-faced clock in the tower. He had come on the chance that if he were not upheld by the University, his father was unlikely to have stayed on to the feast among his peers.

Bon appétit, he thought, and hunching his shoulders to raise his coat collar to where it might cover his ears, he said, "Good night, officer," and walked off trying to remember where he had parked his car.

In the withdrawing room adjoining the banquet hall an impromptu meeting which had lasted far too long was drawing to its climax. Donald Hawkins, president of the University, was both counsel and, insofar as his administration was on trial, witness for the defense. He was by some years the youngest man present, and by some millions the poorest. He was as well the only self-made man among them with the possible exception of Alexander Winthrop.

Dr. Winthrop's wealth like that of the other trustees was inherited, but by choice he devoted himself to politics and public health. It may be said in passing the two endeavors were not merely compatible but indivisible in Traders City. Winthrop liked Hawkins. He admired both scholarship and the law. It was Hawkins's foundation in the latter that was going to win the day for him, not so much in the persuasiveness of his argument which was considerable— he had reduced the issue to a university's responsibility for the teachings within its walls, not the avocations of its teachers, a remarkable achievement considering the charges against Hogan—but in the confidence he evoked without directing himself to it at all that, legally, the University was on safe ground.

It was a time in the history of the country when confidence made the man: witness (however reluctantly in present company) the success of the President of the United States. He did not call attention to it, but Hawkins was known to admire him, and something in the toss of his head made Winthrop think he more than admired, he sought to emulate him. He was almost defiantly self-confident.

Having won his friends, albeit the vote was not yet taken, Hawkins addressed himself to the one man present who might be considered a spokesman for his enemies. Alexander Winthrop conducted a daily column in Judge Phipps's *Traders City Dispatch*. "Dr. Winthrop," Hawkins said, smiling, "if Judge Phipps were among our number, how do you suppose he would vote?"

The wily young devil, Winthrop thought, to probe at that moment the well known inconsistency of the publisher. It was Phipps's *Dispatch* which had first put the "red" charges into headlines.

"I'm hardly a better spokesman for Phipps than Phipps himself," Winthrop said, "but I'll say this: many's the time I've heard him speak out for academic freedom."

A murmur of dry, ironic laughter passed among the men around the table.

The chairman called for a vote.

In the banquet room itself the long tables were still pristine, row upon row of them, the linens gleaming, the silver neat, but the water in the glasses was turning beady. The smell of roasted turkey which had pleasantly smitten the nostrils of the guests arriving had now taken on the savor of left-over gravy. Cigar and cigaret smoke webbed the rafters. The faculty of Midwestern University, six hundred thirty men and women—about twenty men to every woman of them—waited restlessly. They were tired, irritable and nervous. The floors were drafty and the monastic benches along the walls chilly respite to those who had to get off their feet. They could not very well go to table ahead of their hosts.

Few of them were principals to the controversy, no more than a half dozen members of the faculty had been mentioned—and only Jonathan Hogan consistently—but all of them were inevitably having to take sides, to defend or deny the right of a university teacher to political activity outside the classroom. The definition was likely to be that broad—political activity—to those defending the right. To those who denied it, and some did openly, confident of vindication by the University trustees, it narrowed down to Communist influence in the classroom. That the loudest condemnation came from certain Catholic teachers in a school oriented toward Presbyterianism tended to make liberal partisans of otherwise conservatives. Practical men on both sides were thinking of the school's endowment.

Everybody knew that Jonathan Hogan was a prime mover in something called The League Against War and Fascism. They were all against war—in the Midwest most people were against foreigners as well as their wars—but a man did not have to share the rostrum with Communists to prove it: so went the majority thinking.

Jonathan Hogan himself yellowed his fingers chain smoking. He felt an invisible *cordon sanitaire* around him through which his friends broke now and then to bring him cheer or ease his nerves. Someone—friend or enemy, he wondered afterwards—said, "Look here, Hogan, I shouldn't worry. There are several universities in the East that'd be glad of a man of your calibre."

That had the calibre of a shotgun, Hogan decided and winked at the man, though unintentionally. He had a tic that worsened under strain.

Finally the massive carved oak doors swung open and the president of the University came in, all amiability and apology, and followed by a jovial dozen of the most influential men in Traders City. A general air of sheepishness hung over the guests as they moved toward the tables.

A trustee headed each of the twelve tables and on the dais President Hawkins greeted the professors emeriti who were especially honored on this occasion every year. He stood a moment before taking his place. A hush fell over the hall. He tossed his head, his characteristically youthful gesture, and said, "I've been asked to say a word of apology and welcome—I shall say a good many more words later—but on behalf of the trustees and myself, I bid you, every man and woman, welcome and good appetite! But before we go to table, I want to read to you a release I have just handed to the press: 'For immediate release: The Board of Trustees of Midwestern University, by unanimous vote, tonight reiterated the University's belief in its responsibility for the teachings within its classrooms, and in the right of its members, outside the classroom, to any activity consistent with moral rectitude.

" 'The University regrets the violent partisanship recently agitating the campus; the students have been reprimanded and have subsequently shown every intention of confining themselves to peaceable demonstration.

" 'Accordingly, President Hawkins has respectfully requested the Commissioner of Police to withdraw the men on special assignment to the University campus.

" 'Classes will convene at the usual hour Monday morning.' "

He turned, eschewing the dramatic possibilities of the moment, and addressed himself to the dean of theological studies: "Doctor Stoneham, will you say the blessing, please?"

Jonathan Hogan did not eat very much; he was not a man who ever ate heartily. But there were those, eating crow along with their turkey or fish, who enjoyed the meal far less than he did. Such a man was Walter Fitzgerald. After the president's address—it would be called in the morning papers one of his most notable speeches: The Purpose of a University—when the formal seating was abandoned, men of natural affinity drew together with an ease impossible before the dinner. Camaraderie prevailed. Professor Fitzgerald felt himself a lonely man. He was profoundly shaken by the outcome of the trustees' meeting: that the opinion was unanimous he found hard to believe.

Standing apart, he fell easy prey to a woman who had wanted all evening to tell someone of a new project. The head of the library school was preparing a bibliography of sources . . . on God knows what. Fitzgerald would have liked to get away from her. It was said she could always find a cripple in a room on whom to lavish the charity of her attention. He half-listened, his eyes straying from her round, eager face in pursuit of a way of escape. Suddenly the woman inquired after his wife and his daughter. "I wonder if she will be as beautiful as her mother."

Having discomfited him by the intimacy, she shot a smile up into his face and walked away, leaving him in no greater admiration of women certainly than he had been before her company. He turned and found himself in company he wanted even less.

Jonathan Hogan seemed to be taking the president's words as a personal vindication, accepting congratulations all around. If it occurred to him to regret his part in bringing notoriety upon the school, he was not showing it. Yet he was not arrogant. Even Fitzgerald would not say that. And when, as Fitzgerald had observed, the chairman of the Board of Trustees had not merely shaken hands with him, but had put his arm about him, he himself could scarcely do less now than offer Hogan his hand.

"Well, Fitzgerald?"

Fitzgerald said as they shook hands, "The important thing is that we trust one another. That's the important thing." He did not mean to be hypocritical. He said what he thought had to be said.

Hogan understood him better, perhaps, than Fitzgerald understood himself: he was a man who fell so pitiably short of his own ideal he needed constantly to strike a pose; he reminded Hogan of an Elizabethan priest—all voice and no sacrament. His life was one long ceremony. Fitzgerald, an associate professor of philosophy, had come into Midwestern University with the present administration. His teaching background was fifteen years at a boys' preparatory school where eight out of ten students went on to study for the priesthood. He was not a scholar, not in terms admissible to Hogan, for, his being a Thomist, Fitzgerald's logic was proscribed; he believed in absolutes of truth. But it was typical of this administration that students wishing to study scholastic philosophy would be taught by a scholastic. Fitzgerald was the next best thing to a Jesuit. And there were times, such as the days just past, when he reminded Hogan of one: he was a lovely mixture of caution and righteousness.

"That's the important thing," he said. "There you have it."

Fitzgerald looked sharply at him to see if he were speaking his own mind or trying to provoke him. It was hard to tell from Hogan's face. His eyes were not unkind, but the lines at his mouth were perpetually sardonic, his smile always suggesting skepticism or, worse, mockery, an attitude Fitzgerald envied even while he condemned it. Hogan's head nodded a little almost constantly, a tic of

some sort pulling at his eye. That a man as frail as he should remain an atheist and a radical was to Fitzgerald incomprehensible.

Hogan considered himself far less than a radical in his chosen
field. He taught economics and identified himself with Keynes. He
had been one of the men tapped by Washington in the early days
of the New Deal. The economics suited him: he believed in capital-
ism if labor were strong enough to strike a balance in the bargaining;
he thought its control until that time the proper province of government. But Washington politics appalled him, the maneuvering for
power destructive of the whole ideal. He had not stayed there long.

The library woman, making the rounds of several coteries, trying
to find an opening for herself, unintentionally wheeled back to them.
"There you are again!" she cried, shot her smile at them, and made
off in another direction.

"Damned woman," Fitzgerald said.

Hogan chuckled. He felt almost giddy with relaxation, benevolent
even unto Fitzgerald.

Fitzgerald cast a quick, scrutinous gaze over the company. Hogan
forestalled his escape. "I have a favor to ask of you, professor. On
the surface it may seem presumptuous, but I assure you in the end,
it won't be."

He was interrupted by the arrival of a short, stout, balding man
who came up to them shaking his finger in anticipation of what he
had to say. "There is a man! Ach, a man like a god, our Hawkins.
Did you ever hear such words before? A poet. He should be an
emperor. And a man of God, of religion. You hear me, Jonathan?
The man is of God, I say. Do you deny it?"

Hogan laid his hand on the shoulder of his friend. "Professor
Fitzgerald, do you know Doctor Mueller?"

The two men, already acquainted, merely nodded for Mueller was
talking again, his accent coming through the more strongly the more
rapid his speech. Its being Austrian, there ran through it a steady
sound of buzzing. "Once I knew one other man like him, my good
patron, the archduke, Otto, God preserve him. It is the only hope
for Europe, a man like him. Cultured, liberal, a patron of music,
of science . . . and yes, of women. His mother, the Empress Zita,
what beauty! There now, I spit on Hitler!"

Hogan smiled wryly and gently patted the back of his friend. Long
and thin, short and thickset, they made a curious pair, a proper

study in the variations in human anatomy. "Would God your Archduke Otto would do the same."

Mueller very nearly jumped up and down. He gave the effect of so doing even though his toes did not leave the floor. "He will! You will see. You will see."

"I am much afraid," Hogan said softly, "it will be Hitler who will spit on the Archduke."

"Oh, that man," Mueller said, shaking his jowl like a mastiff. "He is the greatest bastard in the world."

"Easily that," Hogan said.

Fitzgerald said, "The trouble with men like Hogan, Dr. Mueller, they think they are the only ones who hate Hitler."

"We are. At least, we are the only ones who hate him enough."

"And you are not even a Jew," Mueller said, and gave him a hug. "It is wonderful. I love this man."

Fitzgerald cleared his throat. He was distinctly embarrassed. Foreigners were much too emotional, especially Jews.

Hogan, also embarrassed, grinned, which made him look boyish and thus closer to his actual age than his infirmities ordinarily allowed.

"I have interrupted you?" Mueller said.

"Nothing that can't wait," said Hogan.

"Why should it wait?" Mueller took from his pocket, leaving the pocket gaping, a paper bag. "I have here the sweets and the nut-meats, and biscuits I have already made into crumbs. My girls will be waiting at home like mice to collect them." He shook Fitzgerald's hand heartily and then took Hogan's hand in both his own. "Jonathan, I am very proud of the President of this University, like the President of the country . . ."

"So am I. Good night, Erich," Hogan said affectionately.

Mueller rollicked off, pausing soon, having something to say to almost everyone he passed.

Fitzgerald said dryly, "He's generous with his comparisons."

"With everything. He has a young wife and four girls, did you know? A confident man obviously—in America." He glanced at Fitzgerald from under drawn brows. In his own way he was baiting the man who often baited him.

Fitzgerald said, "A physicist, isn't he?"

Hogan nodded.

"I envy him," Fitzgerald said. "Oh, not the four daughters. God knows one's trial enough, but that abstract world of his, dabs of light on a black screen, a multiplicity of mathematical equations, a kind of music of the spheres and all so marvelously removed from responsibility in this unhappy world. How fortunate a refuge!"

Hogan denied himself contemplation of the man's fatuousness. "You have a touch of the poet, professor."

"My Irish origins."

Hogan doubted he was that proud of them.

"You wanted to ask me something, Hogan. Do. I don't care for crowds like this. You're accustomed to crowds, of course."

"I've grown accustomed to them, yes," Hogan said blandly. "Why, I have a son, professor, the younger of two—the older boy's all right. For that matter, so is Marcus—all right. But this may amuse you, I'm a little fearful of where his social conscience may lead him." To a man like Fitzgerald the words would have distinct political coloring. "I'm father enough, you see, to want certain of the solid opportunities for him. He's a doctor of medicine. Wants to be a surgeon. What he needs is further residency in a good hospital."

Fitzgerald was stunned that Jonathan Hogan should come to him for help. If he had had his way, Hogan would have been dismissed from the University. He had made no secret of the opinion. It was a peculiar irony that it was he who was now silenced in effect, not Hogan, and the obligation of sportsmanship put upon him. And yet, the more he thought about it, he found an odd satisfaction in Hogan's having come to him.

"Where did he go to school?"

"Rodgers University."

"You've always looked to the East, haven't you?" He could not resist the barb. "May I ask where he interned?"

Hogan named a small hospital on the west side of Traders City. "He's had a couple of years' residency there, too. But their surgery is, shall we say, conservative."

"And what is he doing now?"

"Trying to get the tuberculars out of the county jail into the county sanatorium."

Fitzgerald gave a short laugh. Hogan's directness was disarming. "I suppose you'd like me to speak to Winthrop. Is that it?"

"I thought you might like to talk to the boy first. See if he's worth your intervention."

Few men, and especially Walter Fitzgerald, can resist doing an enemy a kindness. Hogan had chosen his moment well, and only a little cynically. He suspected, as did a number of people, a relationship to exist between Alexander Winthrop and Fitzgerald's wife. Presumably Winthrop would be indulgent of Fitzgerald in other matters. Fitzgerald, the unfortunate ass, continually boasted of his and Winthrop's friendship. Hogan did not know Winthrop except by reputation. He was on the University Board of Trustees, he was City Health Commissioner, a man of politics, money and enormous influence in Traders City medicine. He also conducted, and it was curious that a man in his position should, the medical column in *The Dispatch*.

"Let me be blunt, Hogan. Is your son political?"

"Not since his undergraduate days. Sacco and Vanzetti was his last cause. He just about tolerates me."

Fitzgerald looked at him sharply, suspicious again, afraid of having his leg pulled. It prompted Hogan to wonder if his recommendation might not do the boy more harm than good. Yet in the end, Marcus must recommend himself. The problem was to get him Winthrop's attention. "Of course, it's a wise father that knows his own son," he added.

Fitzgerald said, "Have him come round to my house tomorrow afternoon. Do you know where I live?"

Hogan nodded. He had come to know quite a lot about Walter Fitzgerald this semester, including the fact that along with ontology, cosmology and metaphysics, Fitzgerald lectured his students on atheistic communism and how to detect its disciples. He said, "Many thanks, professor," and again shook hands with him.

Fitzgerald was already at the cloakroom, surrendering his tab to the attendant, when he realized that the encounter with Hogan had so improved his sense of well-being that he was no longer eager to go home. He would not go back, however; he abhorred indecision in a man . . . and rather admired it in a woman. He did have work to do, and he too had a family although they were certainly not waiting up for him like mice; Mueller was a sloppy man to be a scientist. The cloakroom attendant came out and helped him on with his overcoat. He was surprised. He did not expect such courtesy in young people any more. He would have laid odds this lad was no radical.

"Walter, let me drive you home."

Alexander Winthrop had come up quite unbeknownst to him, a rare and gratifying occurrence. He generally knew where Winthrop was in a room. "Have you time to stop for a nightcap?"

"Why not?"

Fitzgerald took Winthrop's coat from the boy's hands and held it himself. "I'll be glad of the ride. It's a bitter night."

"In more ways than one, eh?"

"I'm glad to hear you say it." He had suspected unanimity to have been hammered out of the board as out of a jury.

"Don't mistake me, Walter. I like that young upstart of a president." Winthrop shrugged himself more comfortably into his coat.

"Oh, so do I."

"You should. He hired you. But I'm pretty sure I shouldn't." He took a folded bill from his pocket and proposed to give it to the attendant.

The boy demurred. "No charge, sir, thank you."

Winthrop said, "Do I insult you?"

"No, sir."

"Then don't insult me." He tossed the money on the half-door ledge, and taking Fitzgerald by the elbow, steered him to the side door where his chauffeur was waiting.

The Fitzgerald house on Oak Street was not far from the campus and would in time be absorbed into it as were already most of the gray stone houses in the neighborhood. With their ample lawns and gardens and the great tall trees, these were the homes built before the turn of the century by the professional elite of Traders City, lawyers, architects, engineers, whose children now were likely to be raising their families in the north shore suburbs. The Fitzgeralds had bought the house soon after their marriage when they had come to the Midwest and largely with money provided by Elizabeth's Boston aunt. Elizabeth had chosen the neighborhood because of the University and seeing further into her husband's future than he himself dared look. She had kept the twelve-room house herself until he had grown used to the place so much beyond his own concept of their means. Then she had hired a maid and set herself to the earnest study of music. In the early days Walter had had to ride the streetcar an hour each way to the seminary where he taught and through slums as drab if not as old as those in which he had grown up in Philadelphia.

"I like the smell of this house," Winthrop remarked, drawing a deep breath. He often said these words, for the moment he opened the closet door to hang up his own coat he caught the pungency of cedar. And often there were flowers in a vase beside the hall mirror. Elizabeth Fitzgerald had a small greenhouse in the garden where she cultivated plants and blooms in all seasons.

Fitzgerald thanked him. Mention of the smell of a house always carried for him the association of cooking cabbage which had seemed ever prevalent in the hallways of his youth. Rubbing his hands together he crossed the hall to his study, but Winthrop, instead of following, strode directly to the sliding doors of the parlor where, from outdoors, he had seen the light. With the softest of knocks and not waiting at all, he admitted himself. Fitzgerald followed him, having no choice. But he was very much aware that Elizabeth disliked being burst in upon. However, she looked over her shoulder and smiled, seeing them. She gave Winthrop her hand across the back of the sofa and drew him around to the fire.

"I've sent Michaelson out to the kitchen," Fitzgerald said, speaking of Winthrop's chauffeur. "Has Annie gone upstairs?"

"If she has, she'll soon come down again. She can tell the minute a man comes into her part of the house." Elizabeth was about to rise. "Will you want tea or drinks, Walter?"

"I'll attend to it myself," he said, and she sat back. "Brandy, Alex?"

"That'll be fine, thanks." Winthrop stood, his back to the fireplace, his hands in his pockets, springing up and down a little on his toes. The room seemed smaller when he was in it, restless, generally impatient with the prospect of either small or precise talk. An evening among scholars, for all that he admired them, set his nerves on edge. He belonged, he said, among railsplitters, not hairsplitters. Nonetheless, no other honor had so gratified him as election to the Board of Trustees of Midwestern University.

"Sit down for a little while, Alex," Fitzgerald said.

"I will, I will—thanks." He was a large-boned man, a shade under six feet, solid but not fat. He had a square, tough jaw and a mouth not quite strong enough to go with it. He often, in determination, had to shoot out his lower lip by way of satisfying that inner demand for an outward show of purpose. His eyes were black, though sometimes in direct light—or seen in a moment of affection—they seemed to be a dark, limpid purple. Neither lotion nor brush could keep order in his soft black hair; at forty-eight he showed not a trace of gray in it.

Fitzgerald started out of the room. "Shall I close the doors?"

"Do," his wife said. "There's a draft when they're open."

And remarking that the drapes across the garden windows should be heavier, he went out and rolled the door noisily closed behind him.

Winthrop's lips still bore the amused, tolerant smile he often gave Fitzgerald in Elizabeth's presence. "Can *you*?" he said.

"Can I what?"

"Tell the minute a man comes into *your* part of the house?"

"I knew you were here," she said, and picking up the book she had been reading, turned its pages idly.

He stared down at her, observing the heightened color in her high-boned cheeks. It quickened the course of his own blood. "Do you mind that I came like this?"

"It's rather tortuous, isn't it?" Still she did not look at him.

He broke his hands apart, and moving with the pent vigor of someone doing one thing when he wants to do another, shifted a chair around and then back to where it was and finally sat down in it. "Was there a point to his closing the doors, do you think?"

"I doubt it."

"The only time my conscience bothers me is when I think the least of him," Winthrop said. "Who the devil else would close the doors on us like that?"

"Sometimes I think he knows—has known for some time."

Winthrop gave a short, dry laugh.

"I don't suppose it really matters—except for Martha. I will not have her scandalized."

"What are you reading?" he asked, but not caring, wanting only to change the subject.

She did not answer. "Did it go against Walter tonight?"

"Haven't you got it backwards, my dear? It wasn't he that was on trial."

"It was . . . in his own mind."

Winthrop did not have much humor; therefore he was often more direct than even he would have preferred. "That's a mighty small place for a man my size to get in and out of every time."

"He worships you, Alexander."

"What does it mean, you saying that to me, Elizabeth?"

"Only that Walter hoped your vote would justify him among the trustees."

"I assure you, his name never came up."

"And Hogan—what happens to him?"

"Unless something treasonable shows up in his record—and I'm sure it won't—he stays. I voted with the rest of them. I don't give a damn about Hogan. I think it's a good thing we'll know what he's up to for a while. But to tell you the God's truth, Elizabeth, I don't think he's any more dangerous than your husband."

She looked at him frankly and smiled. It crossed her mind that he had himself got a liberal education that night from whatever source. "Some new poems," she said, indicating the book. "They're very nice."

He glanced at the door for there was the sound of footsteps in the hall. "May I see you tomorrow?"

She nodded. "After two." They would meet in her music studio downtown as was their custom.

The steps receded, Walter apparently having forgotten something. "Elizabeth . . . look at me."

She lifted her head and steadily they gazed at one another across the untraversable few feet between them. She could see the strength and tenderness of him, the dangerous weakness, for the lidded desire all but spilled from his eyes.

"I have never wanted you more than at this moment," he said, meting the words out slowly to watch them affect her.

She cast her eyes down and spread her strong hands like wings upon the book.

"Elizabeth . . ."

She got up then and went around the couch away from him. Only then did she meet his eyes again. "I am going upstairs now, if you will excuse me, Alexander," she said.

And still he looked at her. "I love you," he said, but no louder than a whisper.

"I know," she said, and briefly pursed her lips to him before turning and moving with unhurried grace from the room.

Fitzgerald was coming with the tray from the kitchen when she reached the hall. "Good night, Walter. I'm going up now."

"Good night, my dear. I'm sorry it took me so long." To Winthrop he said, going into the parlor, "it's too bad Elizabeth went off so soon. You mustn't mind, Alex."

"She said good night to me," Winthrop said.

Fitzgerald took this to mean that his wife had been brusque. "God knows, she's not an easy woman. All temperament. But she soon gets over it. They say there's Spanish blood in her family—a lot of it in the part of Ireland she comes from."

"She looks Spanish," Winthrop murmured, as though the subject had just come up. Even Walter had told him this many times before. Elizabeth did look Spanish, with her dark hair parted in the middle and tightly drawn to a bun at the back of her head, the long neck, the oval face with olive coloring, the black eyes and heavy lashes.

"You're coming to dinner all the same on Sunday, aren't you, Alex? It is your Sunday and she'll be expecting you."

"For God's sake, let's have the brandy," Winthrop said.

· 2

NOT long after Winthrop and Fitzgerald had left Anders Hall, Jonathan Hogan took his departure also, going out alone and past the porter's desk at the main entry. How quickly the hounds of notoriety had given up his scent. A few hours earlier the reporters had followed him into the building, the porter unable to restrain them. Now good news was no news where he was concerned. He took a short cut cross-campus to the streetcar line. There was in the southern sky a trail of stars that vanished into the yellow smoke over the steel mills. Snake-quick tongues of flame flicked into the night. They would be after him again, of course, the yellow press: they would watch his every move.

He boarded the first streetcar south. The car was overheated, the brass-barred windows mud-brown still from the last thaw, the straw seats lumpy. He caught the disinfectant smell associable with public lavatories so that he supposed the women talking together in a Slavic tongue were coming off their cleaning jobs downtown. Most of the male occupancy would go on the midnight shift at the mills. One could thank God, of course, that there was a midnight shift. One could be grateful for a number of things this night if he were Jonathan Hogan. But he could also be realistic, and there was nothing like a southside streetcar ride to sober a man giddy with too easy a triumph. He had been exonerated, true. But he had also been rendered impotent outside the classroom for a long time to come if not for the rest of his life.

Men like Winthrop had sustained him. The president of United States Copper had put his arm about him. A killing kindness: was this the intention? They could not care very much, those men really, about his anti-Fascist, antiwar activities; only the Walter Fitzgeralds, the pious and the patriotic, cared about them. The trustees almost to a man were *laissez faire* capitalists, and it was doubtless known among them, though not likely to have been discussed that night with Hawkins, that he was economic advisor to a group of labor organizers about to go to work in the steel industry. The best service he could do them now would be to withdraw from their council. He had been defended and isolated. But what could they have done? Suppose they had fired him? They would have not merely brought him down then, they would have compromised Hawkins and the University. They had acted honorably. Who could gainsay that? It fell to him now to be as explicit in his loyalties.

Adieu, gentlemen, he thought, leaving the streetcar.

"Good night, professor," the motorman called after him for they had long been friends on the same run.

He turned and waved his hand.

The newest thing about the house he shared with his unmarried son was the sign at the walk: T. M. HOGAN, M.D. The house itself was set a distance back from the street unlike the other buildings in the block. It afforded a garden in front. Otherwise from the parlor and from Marcus's office there was a fine view of the neighborhood's back porches. Frontside, the houses were ugly enough. The area was changing fast. Mrs. Turley, the Negro woman who kept house for them, often said, "Mr. Hogan, you ought to go and live among the white folks now and sell this place for money while you can. It all going to be colored people soon."

She was right: he hadn't much inheritance to leave his sons. As he climbed the steps he could see Marcus sitting forward on the sofa, his shoulders hunched. It occurred to him that the boy was waiting, had probably been waiting for word for some time.

"Dad?"

He looked in at the living room door.

"It's a wonder you wouldn't phone a man," Marcus said.

The older man put away his coat. He took off his collar and tie and hung them on the banister. "I'm sorry, Marc. I thought you'd be at the clinic. It all came out fine: they voted me everything but a raise."

"I heard it on the radio finally," Marcus said. "Complete exoneration."

"I feel let down all the same," Jonathan said.

Marcus laughed and shook out a cigaret from his packet, offering it to his father.

"Thanks, no. I'll have my pipe. I've smoked too much tonight." He went to the mantle and filled his pipe from the jar there. "You know, the chairman of the Board of Trustees came up and put his arm around me. Think of that: United States Copper."

"I don't suppose any of it rubbed off," Marcus said.

Hogan sat down wearily and struck a match on the bottom of his shoe. "I'd be a great fool to think this restored things to where they were. And yet . . ." He shrugged. "Even Fitzgerald shook me by the hand. The important thing is that we trust one another: that's what he said." He puffed the fire into his pipe.

"Who's Fitzgerald?"

Hogan started to explain. Suddenly he was very tired, and he could feel something hard, numbing, running up through his head. "He's in the philosophy department."

"Isn't he the one who was after your hide?"

"One of them. Ah, but he's Irish, Marc. That's the difference."

"Meaning what?"

The numbness eased off as he rubbed his forehead. "Oh, just that. He's sentimental. If his victim doesn't die of the blow he struck him, Fitzgerald'll be the first man out to congratulate him."

"The damned hypocrite," Marcus said, for he had watched his father age these last few weeks.

Hogan pulled at his pipe, thinking, and then laughed. "You know, I shook him up a bit tonight though. The minute he stuck out his hand to me, I said to him, 'Professor, there's something you can do for me, now.' 'Anything, anything at all, Jonathan,' he said. In fact, I think he said, 'Jonathan, my boy.' And I said, 'I want you to speak to your friend Winthrop about my son. Like Winthrop,' I said, 'he's interested in public health. He's got some fine ideas on chest surgery, but what he needs is a good residency.'"

Marcus grinned. He sat, finally relaxed himself, his hands dangling between his high, bony knees, the cigaret smoke trailing sensuously up the back of one hand. "What did he say?"

"He wants to look you over himself tomorrow afternoon."

"I'll be damned," Marcus said, and sat for some seconds thinking about it. His father had spoken lightly, but it was in Marcus's mind that he might very well be judging his own position by the extent to which Fitzgerald was willing to go now to make amends. "Let's have a beer." Marcus got up. In the kitchen he opened two bottles.

"Will you go to see him, Marc?"

"Why not? Any nurse can do what I'm doing in the clinic—and downstairs here. At the rate I'm going, it's going to take a war to make a surgeon of me."

Jonathan frowned, the pulse starting up where it sometimes appeared at his temple; together with the tic, it distorted a face that ordinarily was handsome.

"I'm sorry I said that. It wasn't necessary. I didn't like what I saw on the campus tonight. I was over there. There was a meanness in the police."

"There always is, Marc, among men who would rather obey than think. Self-discipline is one of our more recent luxuries."

"I'll say," Marcus said and both men laughed.

Marcus touched his glass to his father's. "Skoal," he said.

"Skoal."

· 3

Martha Fitzgerald was always of two minds about week-ends: most of the girls who lived within fifty miles of St. Cecilia's College went home on Friday afternoons. It was a lonely moment for her after they had trooped down to the North Shore station, watching until the train pulled out. At home she could herself go to a play or a concert, or even to a dance if somebody's brother didn't have a date of his own making. And she could gorge herself on Annie's cooking. But after the hollow moment of watching, she generally went off on a long walk with one of the lay faculty or with classmates, and had tea in the village—tea consisting of raisin toast sopping with butter and a chocolate milk shake. And staying, she could spend all of Saturday morning in the studio—without the boondogglers. Sometimes she thought she was the only one in art class who took it seriously—except for a girl called Genevieve Revere of whom Martha was in awe, and vaguely, a little afraid. Genevieve was always talking of Paris and how she expected to be there soon. Once she suggested that if Martha could spend her junior year abroad they could run away from school together and have an apartment in the Latin Quarter. Martha had been appalled at the idea.

Sister Mathilde was already in the studio when Martha arrived, herself working, her black sleeves turned up to where the white undergarment showed at her wrists. She was young and she painted beautifully despite an almost palsied shaking of her hand. She had had a nervous breakdown, it was said, and most of the girls considered that quite as important an accomplishment as her painting.

Martha put on her smock and went to work at her own easel after the merest exchange of greetings. They were accustomed to silences in the studio. Even out of it, she had little to say to Sister Mathilde. There was in the nun's way of looking at a person a sort of probing as though to discover deep, important things that made Martha fear saying something trite in her presence. She soon forgot Mathilde altogether and gave a start when the nun, standing beside her, said, "Come here a moment with me, my dear."

Martha followed her to an easel near the window which the nun then turned around to where the water color propped up on it caught the full morning sunlight. Martha thought at first that its subject was something anatomical or biological—like intestines, except that they were green; snakes, she decided, curling around a barkless tree. By then she had glimpsed the name on the easel: Genevieve Revere. Her first reaction was one of shock, realizing that the nun was looking at and showing the girl's work when she was not there. Martha did not say anything. She could not. The nun, who was several inches beneath her in height, turned to look up at her. Her eyes were moist, glistening, and she was even paler than usual. Martha could never tell whether she was pleased or angry because of the set of her mouth, the lips perpetually curved upwards ever so slightly at the corners.

"Isn't it extraordinary?" the nun said then. "Isn't it wicked?"

"I like most of her painting," Martha said in feeble defense of someone she did not really care for as a person.

"Oh, my dear, the girl is wonderfully talented. She can paint like an angel. She's done this deliberately, you see. She wants to get even with me."

"For what, sister?" Martha said, but she did not care at all. She was shocked discovering that the nun was trembling, the dark veil over her white coif aquiver. She would have given anything for the nerve to move, to run. One expected anger in a nun, laughter, reproach . . . but never this . . . whatever thing it was, so personal.

"For loving her soul, and trying to save it, while she makes riot of it. I do penance for her every day of my life. I know what sin is, Martha. My father and mother were divorced when I was thirteen years old. My brother hanged himself in the hallway of our house, and now I have to do penance for her, too, this wicked, beautiful child."

Genevieve Revere was not a child, Martha knew. She was nineteen years old, and another of the reasons Martha feared her was that she dared to say out that she hated Sister Mathilde; she made fun of her, called her a Puritan witch, a creep, a ghoul. She would stand at the blackboard before art class started, this tall, violent, vitriolic girl, and draw voluptuous nudes on which she would deftly stroke swatches and sweeps of clothes against the metronomic rattle of Mathilde's beads as the nun came up the stairs. Only Mathilde's breathing could be heard in the instant of her entry and then the plunking sound of the chalk as Genevieve dropped it ostentatiously onto the blackboard railing.

Martha felt herself leaden, bound head and foot, chained as ever was Prometheus, and as gnawed at as was he. Sister Mathilde was looking up into her face as though herself in an ecstasy of pain. "Can you tell that I'm weeping?" the nun asked. Martha shook her head. "I am. The tears are running hot and scalding down my throat. I love that child. I want her for God."

Martha could not look at her any longer, and yet the nun's eyes clung to her own, drawing, sucking back her gaze. Then Mathilde turned to the painting, the green water color, the bare tree bound round with snakes, and lifted a trembling finger which she pointed at the tree. "You understand her allegory, don't you? You can see the tree is meant to represent me."

"No," Martha said.

"Oh, yes. I can see it quite plainly."

Afterwards Martha could never remember the impulse, or the

sound she made; she always thought it must have been a scream, but no one answered it. What she did remember was the impact in each of the five fingers on her right hand as they struck the drawing board, and she recalled the scrape of her fingernails, and the sound of the tearing and crumpling of paper. The nun, she knew, turned away to the window, and Martha, throwing down the destroyed water color to the floor, managed at last to move toward the door, faster then, and then faster, almost away.

"Martha!"

She paused on the threshold and looked back.

"Thank you, my dear," Mathilde said and bowed her head over her clasped hands, the knuckles of which she pressed against her mouth.

Martha ran down the back stairs so that she might encounter no one, tore off her smock and escaped outdoors wearing a borrowed coat. She walked to the lake alone although it was forbidden, but even the cold wind sifting snow about her face could not drive out or make orderly the tumult and revulsion. She tried to pray a little, and then to understand. To understand without feeling. She was eighteen and suddenly she remembered an older friend now on the faculty telling her of having been kissed by a priest once when she was eighteen. She had not been able to take Holy Communion for months and months afterwards, compounding her own sins thereby, and unable to account the reason to anyone, or for that matter, to herself. "It just wore off—like most things do," her friend had answered her query. And remembering it now, Martha was oddly comforted.

She walked along the crisped sand where the water had come up in a slow eddy and had been caught and transmuted to ice. She thought then of Hans Christian Andersen's *Snow Maiden* and the devil carrying the mirror up to heaven that he might mock the angels. She had never altogether understood the story as a child, but something like that seemed to have just happened to her. Bits of driftwood lay among the dunes, the color of flesh, and shaped by the constant wash of the lake, some pieces, to the delicacy of an elbow or a shoulder or a breast. She took her hand from her glove, for it was cold, and with only the remotest consciousness of an association, warmed it beneath her coat at her own breast.

She walked to within sight of Dr. Winthrop's mansion, high on a bluff to the north. He was her father's friend, not hers. Martha turned back. In the school basement she lingered at the radiator until she was warm, and then went upstairs and knocked at the door of the dean's office. She asked permission to go home for the rest of the week-end.

Mother St. John bade her telephone home and if they would expect her, she might go, of course. A wise woman, the nun did not even ask a question. But after Martha had gone, she thought a moment on the girl's usual Saturday morning activities, and then wrote a note on her calendar pad unmeaningful to anyone except herself. She wrote: "Leonardo da Vinci."

·4

MARTHA had attended convent boarding school through high school and into this, her second year of college. It never occurred to her to wonder why she, an only child, was sent away to school. She was only a little happier there where she had practically no time to herself than at home where she was left very much alone. Her mother was away a good part of most days. And Annie's care, as far back as Martha could remember— beyond food, her insides, a clean head and an occasional Irish fairy story—consisted largely of saying "Don't" to things she was unlikely to have done more than once in any case: Don't go too near the lily pond; don't climb the rose trellis; don't eat the snow berries. Her mother maintained music rooms in the International Building on Lake Front Avenue where she taught piano and voice. Martha very nearly stopped there that Saturday afternoon on her way home. She did not do it, however, knowing her mother did not approve such surprises; she liked to have everything prescheduled. Martha dearly loved houses where people just dropped in.

Her father was not to be interrupted either, she discovered when she got home. He was in his study, "talking very serious with a young man," Annie said. "Just change your dress and come down to the kitchen. I have a surprise for you."

Martha no longer needed to change her dress whenever she came into the house, but it was one of the things Annie simply could not understand. Whenever Martha tried to explain it, after the whole rigamarole Annie would say, "All right. Just this once, put on an apron and come down the way you are." Martha took her overnight case upstairs, trying not to feel sorry for herself. She had begun to feel sorry for Sister Mathilde, although she did not think she could ever again walk into her art class. She took from her suitcase a small black notebook in which she was in the habit of writing down impressive passages from her reading. She turned to a line from Galsworthy which she had recently entered: "Peace? There is no peace. There is life and there is death." How true! How cruelly true. And what was to be said to Genevieve Revere about her horrid water color?

She was distracted from her melancholy by the wafting up from the kitchen of the smell of fresh spice cake. Before she had finished washing her hands the aroma was fairly irresistible. She went down the stairs at a giddy clip, and very nearly collided with a man coming out of her father's study.

"I'm awfully sorry," she said. "I didn't mean to run you down. But there's kind of a blind spot here when you come from upstairs."

He looked at her, surprised but unperturbed. His smile was more courtly than warm, she thought, and that she admired. "It is a busy intersection," he said gravely. With a nod he proceeded toward the front door. He was tall and seemed to her rough-hewn, his features being so pronounced—almost squared off, like a modern painting. He moved at an unhurried pace, but he was going away nonetheless.

"I'm Martha Fitzgerald," she said proudly and loudly, having to say it to his back.

He turned, his hand on the knob of the front door. "I'm Marcus Hogan, and if I weren't already ten minutes late to an appointment, I'd not be guilty of running away from the scene of an accident like this."

Martha gave him a wide and sudden smile, so ingratiated was she with his way of saying things, and he lingered a second or two just looking at her. "I wish it weren't such an important appointment," he said. Then with a little bow, he turned and was gone. There was in his manner something almost supercilious, a quality she by no means despised, being taken at the moment with *Pride and Prejudice*.

From behind the lace curtains she watched him down the steps and into his car, which was old and noisy when first he started it. Before he drove off he tipped his hat in the direction of the house. Martha drew back quickly, the color flaming into her cheeks.

She hesitated outside the study door, then tapped lightly and opened it. Professor Fitzgerald scowled. He half-expected young Hogan to reappear on some pretext or other, just by way of catching him off-balance. Hogan, he supposed, had his father's skepticism of the motives behind all charity—even when he had himself applied for it.

"May I come in, papa?"

"Oh, it's you, is it? Of course, you may come in. When was it otherwise?" He stood up to greet her, but waited for her to come around his desk and kiss him. He sat down again and motioned her into the chair recently vacated. "Sit down, my dear."

Martha was aware of the warmth where Marcus Hogan had been sitting. "Annie said you had a serious engagement."

Professor Fitzgerald made a non-committal noise. "Not all that serious. What brings you home of such a sudden?"

Martha shrugged. "Restless, that's all. You've had a haircut."

Her father smiled and smoothed the hair about his temples and at the back of his head. It was almost pure white. "Yes, but a bit too short this time, I'm afraid." He was always inordinately pleased when she noticed a fresh haircut, and never entirely satisfied with the haircut itself.

"Is he a student of yours, papa—the person who was here?"

"No."

"Is he very nice?"

"I never saw him before today in my life. I shouldn't want to say."

Martha smiled in the sudden, deep way she had, as though something irresistibly amusing had occurred to her. "What did he sell you, papa?"

Fitzgerald leaned back in his chair and laughed. No one in the world could relax him except this child, this girl, this maiden. "A bill of goods, I shouldn't wonder. But I mustn't be too hard on him. The hardest thing for any man to sell is himself. He's a young M. D. trying to get started. He wants a recommendation from me to Dr. Winthrop."

"But you don't even know him."

"I do know his father," Fitzgerald murmured.

"I think I could give him a recommendation," Martha said airily so that her father knew she was not being altogether serious.

"On what grounds, pray?" There was the lushness of Irish rhythm in his voice whenever he made a joke or teased her.

"Personality."

"Oh-ho." Her father nodded his head. "Personality—that will take him a long ways with Dr. Winthrop. He'll be here to dinner tomorrow, by the way." Martha lifted her head. "Dr. Winthrop," Fitzgerald added quickly.

But the color had leaped again to Martha's face. It irritated her father. There was something very nearly indecent about growing up. He had thought his daughter had blessedly escaped the "boy crazy" phase. Now it would seem she was merely retarded in reaching it. "You'll be home, won't you?"

"Of course," Martha said, but this was one more thing which seemed to have gone awry. Ordinarily she would have contrived to return early to school, discovering it to be Dr. Winthrop's Sunday, for she did not enjoy his visits; nor did she like to ride out to the North Shore with him afterwards in the back seat of the limousine. It was reasonable that he propose to drop her at St. Cecilia's, passing there on his way home, but he was always trying to find out what went on inside of her, as though he were someone to whom she should tell her inmost thoughts. "Now that we're alone," he would say, or, "Now that I've got you to myself . . ." And he was forever trying to cheer her up while most of the times she felt perfectly cheerful already.

"I'm glad," her father said. "I think it hurts him sometimes, the way you manage not to be here for his visits. The amenities are the least of our obligations. I know you don't like him, and that hurts me, too, you know."

"I've never said I didn't like him, papa."

"There are a number of things your mother never says to me, also, but she makes them amply plain all the same." He regretted saying that. It was not relevant. Martha he knew to be completely unlike her mother in temperament, in character. The girl was open where her mother had turned in upon herself years ago, leaving him no more than an observer of something he nominally possessed. And yet he would have sworn Elizabeth was not a cold person. Early in their marriage he would have said she was rather too passionate for a woman.

Martha did not say anything, merely looking at her hands which she clasped in her lap. Her throat felt as though they were clasped inside of it.

"For example, I'm about to recommend this young medic—who seems to have beguiled you with a charm which utterly evaded my

powers of observation. I shall recommend him against every personal inclination. He's untidy, he's arrogant—and he's cocksure of
himself. He's too old for that. Self-assurance becomes very young
people and the old folks in whom we have to tolerate all the follies
left to them."

"Why do you—recommend him?" Martha said.

"Noblesse oblige. Do you know what that means?"

Martha nodded. She knew what it meant, but she did not see how
it pertained.

Fitzgerald pulled his high collar away from his throat. "Besides,
I suspect he's a good doctor."

Martha smiled just a little and he saw that her lower lip was
trembling. She was very near to tears.

"I'm not scolding you, my dear," he said, trying to keep the severity in his tone lest too abrupt a change bring on the deluge.
"You're not in trouble at school, are you?"

She shook her head that she was not.

"Out of money?"

She started to shake her head "no," changed her mind and nodded
in the affirmative. It was always the easiest way out, to pretend that
everything could be fixed up by a supplement to her allowance.

Fitzgerald laughed as the phone on his desk rang. It was Winthrop,
returning the call he had put in to his office while Hogan was with
him. "It's nothing that can't wait now, Alex. I had a young doctor
here wanting an introduction to you."

"Quite a number of them do. What's his name?"

"Marcus Hogan." Fitzgerald took his wallet from his pocket and
motioned to Martha that she was to take five dollars from it.

"The name's familiar," Winthrop said.

"Jonathan Hogan's son," Fitzgerald said.

"I'll be damned."

"I thought it a bit thick, myself."

But at the other end of the phone Winthrop was laughing heartily.

"I don't often presume to intervene, Alex," Fitzgerald said when
Winthrop's laughter subsided.

"It strikes me as a damned funny exception."

"I think the young man has something to offer."

"Do you, Walter? Why didn't he come to me in the first place?
I'm not exactly inaccessible. I'm beginning to think I'm one of the
most accessible men in the city."

"He doesn't know you, Alex."

"Knows you well enough, however, doesn't he?" Winthrop said dryly.

Martha was taking an unconscionable amount of time to get her money and leave him.

Martha felt herself to be taking too long, also, but she did not want to go until she could catch his eye and whisper her thanks, at least. Finally she arose from the chair and leaning over him, brushed his cold, moist forehead with her lips. He drew away from her, or from the distraction of her hovering over him, Dr. Winthrop still talking on the other end of the phone. But Martha felt the repulsion. There were times one wanted to kiss someone, anyone almost. She went out of the room without looking back.

At last Winthrop said, "Have him set up an appointment with my secretary then."

"Thank you very much, Alex . . . By the way, Martha will be home to dinner with us tomorrow."

"I know."

"All right, Alex. We shall expect you at two." He hung up the phone, thinking that Winthrop could not possibly know, Martha's having called and asked her mother if she might come home only that morning. Fitzgerald put it down to Winthrop's unwillingness to admit there was anything he did not know. That was the kind of ego the man had.

·5

ALTHOUGH Dr. Winthrop was her father's friend, it was Martha's opinion that the person who gave him the full measure of devotion in their house was Annie Moran. She read his newspaper column every day—it was entitled simply ALEXANDER WINTHROP, M.D.—and was forever quoting it as the living gospel on the arthritis, or the whooping cough, or rupture, or measles. Now and then she even wrote in to him. He would answer questions on "any decent disease," Annie said in one of the peculiar distinctions of hers which made Martha wiser if not specifically enlightened. Annie would scour her kitchen to the gleaming point and pronounce it fit for Dr. Winthrop himself, a reference, presumably, to the public sanitation for which his office was responsible. A word of praise from him at the dinner table was enough to turn Annie's face beet red.

Annie came from the same place in Ireland as Professor Fitzgerald's parents. In fact, she was on visiting terms with a number of cousins whom he himself never saw. Whenever she was put out with Martha's mother, she would speak of the cold wind from the north. "We've both felt the cold wind from the north now and then," she would say in the wake of a quarrel between Professor and Mrs. Fitzgerald, allying herself with the professor. Martha at such times felt a stronger loyalty to her mother. Otherwise, she was almost afraid to love her, giving herself up more to a sort of worship. She loved to watch her, a dark, graceful woman whom Martha in no way resembled, and to listen to her play the piano. She often looked at Martha with an expression of love in her eyes, but she rarely touched the girl, and never, never kissed her, offering always her cheek to the girl's kiss and with her eyes closed as though the moment were altogether painful. She had been born in the north of Ireland into a family which had shown a Spanish strain from the days following the flight and wreck of the Armada, and she had grown up at the time of the Gaelic revival and of the Young Gaelic League, her home the gathering place of poets and rebels. The tales of such young men filled Martha's childhood with strange contrasts, for she liked also Annie's West Country peasant lore. Her father was almost completely silent about his youth. There had been a great deal of religiosity in it, Martha gathered. Her mother, while a Catholic, only occasionally went to church, and almost never to the Sacraments. Her father said it was due to Jansenism in her part of Ireland. Her mother was a woman of great reserve and a sharp wit and was admired, Martha knew, in the University circles where her father was merely tolerated. She could tell it in the occasional gatherings in the house, and it hurt her the more because her father seemed not to see it, to think, rather, that people came primarily on his account. It was torture, afterwards, to Martha, hearing him say, for example, "I don't think it was necessary, Elizabeth, the way you cut poor old Duff to ribbons."

"He'll not bleed, Walter. He's too fatuous." (Her puns ordinarily delighted Martha.)

"A wit like yours is unbecoming in a professor's wife. Frankly, I was embarrassed."

"Were you? And for me, Walter?"

"Yes, for you, damn it. I don't want people feeling sorry for me."

Martha wished at such moments she might leave the house and not come home again. She could not remember ever having loved both her parents at the same time. That Sunday, sitting opposite Dr. Winthrop at the dinner table, she tended to feel more strongly drawn to her mother, perhaps because her father had his friend. They talked of everything, the two men, except Marcus Hogan, a subject Martha had dimly hoped might come up. Suddenly, then, she became aware that without her knowing it the subject had come up, and in a dreadful way because Martha's father didn't really know what Dr. Winthrop was talking of either.

He was saying: ". . . And this fellow is so puffed up with his own importance—an importance that doesn't mean anything to him unless he can make sure other people see it—that he goes around like a peacock exploding his tail."

Elizabeth Fitzgerald said, "Exploding his tail; that's an extraordinary image, Alexander."

"Damn near good, isn't it? Where was I?"

"Exploding a tale," she said.

"Elizabeth, for heaven's sake," Fitzgerald said.

"Exactly," Winthrop said. "You never get him on the phone that he isn't talking to somebody else at the same time. He'll get me on the wire for some damn fool thing. It won't make sense to me. Then all of a sudden I'll realize he's got somebody sitting next to him he wants to impress with his own importance. That's taking advantage, let me tell you."

"There are people like that," Fitzgerald said. "May I cut you another slice of beef, Alex?"

"Thank you, Walter," he said expansively. He even winked at Martha when their eyes met.

Having been in her father's study when Dr. Winthrop returned his call the day before, she knew very well he was talking now about her father and to her father. But before her father would understand—or maybe it was just before he would admit understanding, for she could remember the cold sweat on his forehead and it was glistening again now—Dr. Winthrop would have had to name the subject of the call, Marcus Hogan. She looked down at her plate and loathed the man opposite her as never before. A cat got that kind of satisfaction out of pawing a wounded mouse.

She glanced then at her mother and caught there a truly withering stare in Dr. Winthrop's direction. Martha had never loved her mother more. Dr. Winthrop caught the look of wrath then, too, for he said, speaking to no one in particular, "He's out in California now, this fellow I was talking about, by the way."

"A good place for him," Fitzgerald said. "California's the land of fourflushers. Let me have your plate, Alex."

Afterwards, when Martha was packing and her mother brought up her freshly laundered blouses, Martha said, "I don't like Dr. Winthrop much, do you, mother?"

"He's one of your father's closest friends."

"I don't think he's a friend of papa's at all. I think he's making fun of him all the time."

Her mother looked at her a moment across the white counterpane. Then she said, "You haven't lost your gold cufflinks, have you?"

"I can't wear them. Do you like him, mother?"

"I don't see that it matters at all. Why can't you wear them, Martha?"

"Mother Josepha says they're too ostentatious."

"How extraordinary!"

"You don't like him, do you?"

Her mother lifted her chin ever so slightly. "On the contrary, I like him very much."

Martha pushed her clothes into the suitcase; what odds if they were wrinkled? The only important thing was to get out of the house, even if it meant the long drive with Dr. Winthrop. Her mother had lied to her, a deliberate, calculated lie. And worse, she must know that Martha knew it was a lie.

"I suppose I could get you a pair of mother-of-pearl links—such as your father has for his dress shirt. Could you wear them?"

"That would be fine, mother."

"I've never thought gold especially ostentatious, except possibly in teeth."

Martha did not even look at her. She closed the suitcase and took it from the rack. If it were not a lie, she thought, it would be even more terrible.

Dr. Winthrop was waiting at the foot of the stairs. Reaching him, she gave her suitcase into his hand and watched him pass it along to the chauffeur. She wished she could ride up front with Michael-son. He had been a coachman before automobiles were popular, and he loved to talk about horses.

But on the drive north, Dr. Winthrop brought up the subject of Marcus Hogan. "I suppose you've met the young man your father's taken a shine to?"

"Dr. Hogan? Yes, I met him."

"Were you favorably impressed?"

"It was a casual meeting, but I thought he was very nice."

"Not arrogant?"

"More aloof, I'd say."

"Whatever that means."

"Reserved."

"Ah-ha. That's a woman's distinction for a man who doesn't make love to her on first acquaintance."

Martha did not say anything. This was typical of the things Dr. Winthrop said to her when they were alone. She was aware of being watched out of the corner of his eye.

"A good looking fellow, would you say?"

"I think so."

"I'd take your opinion for gospel any day." He reached over and took her hand in his, lifting it from her lap to the seat between them. "What does your mother think of him?"

"I don't think she has met him."

"You don't think?—Didn't you even talk about him together? I thought that was what women talked about all the time—men."

Martha said nothing.

Winthrop added, "She thinks his father's a handsome old coot."

Martha doubted her mother had ever used those words in her life. She withdrew her hand on the pretense of having to blow her nose.

Dr. Winthrop said, "I suppose every father doing a young man a good turn is looking to the future of his own daughter."

"I'm sure papa didn't have that in mind," Martha said.

"The bigger fool he, then."

"My father is not a fool, Dr. Winthrop."

Winthrop moved again to better look at her. "You're every bit as pretty as your mother."

"My mother is beautiful," Martha said, intending it as contradic-tion. 'Pretty' seemed such an insipid word.

Dr. Winthrop gave a brief, impatient shake of his jowl. "Your mother is beautiful and your father's a wise man. You're the luckiest girl in America."

"I think so." Martha knew her retort to be rude, but she did not care.

"Well, you're right on half the count anyway."

Martha, contemplating his meaning and sensing the contempt in it, felt the sudden sting of anger. "I love my father very much, Dr. Winthrop."

"And don't you think I do? How else could we put up with his vanities and inanities?"

She looked directly into his eyes. "I don't like you."

He gave a short laugh, a sound more of surprise than of mirth. "You've got courage, girl. I'll say that for you. You're your mother's daughter."

"And my father's."

"Oh, yes. Perversity's child out of patience."

Anger quicker than any other emotion brought Martha to tears. She could not hold them back, but she muffled the sound of them for some time. At the first sniffle, Dr. Winthrop began to fuss, making all sorts of horrible noises meant to soothe her. "Dear girl, I was only teasing you. I always tease you, I'm afraid."

He put his hand on her thigh and gently patted it, quite truly forgetting himself. Martha plucked his hand up and flung it off like something alive. "If you touch me again . . ." she said, and caught her breath. She had no words with which to finish such a thought.

Winthrop was upset with himself, but retreat or apology was impossible. "What will you do? Tell your father?"

Martha said, "God damn you."

"Well, well," he said, feeling relieved—almost justified—"I've heard a lot of things to recommend a convent education, but this is just about the best one of all. Yes, indeed." He maneuvered himself forward in the seat and tapped on the window separating them from the chauffeur.

Michaelson slid open the panel and said over his shoulder, "Yes, doctor?"

"You will stop at the next North Shore station, Woodland Park, is it? Miss Fitzgerald wishes to take the train from there." He sat back. "Yes, indeed, the best one of all."

Martha interlaced her fingers and closed her lips tightly lest she say the word. The closer they came to the station, the surer he was, she thought, that she would apologize.

Finally he said, "You'll have to explain to the sisters . . ."

She said nothing. Nor would there be any need for explanation. She would not be late.

Then as they parked at the station and the chauffeur took her case, Winthrop said, "Your father will not thank you for your heroics, Martha."

She stepped out of the car and then turned round and said to him, "I'm sorry if I offended you, Dr. Winthrop." But she took her suitcase from the chauffeur and went quickly into the station.

·6

DR. HOGAN scowled, taking the infant's hand in his and separating the fingers so that he might draw enough blood from one of them to put under the microscope. He saturated the cotton and wiped the finger clean. The smell of alcohol in its purest form had a great deal to recommend it, for his office was heavy with the smell of humanity in a far from pure condition. The scowl was intended to concentrate the attention of the parents on their sick child; they tended, once in his office, to give the child over to his concern so that they could devote themselves to the abuse of one another. He hoped to get them out without having to share in their family recriminations. He had neither the energy for it, nor, he sometimes feared, the love.

"Now, young fellow, this is going to hurt you more than it does me. That's because I know it's for your own good." To the mother he said, "We'll hear from him now."

"Oh, doctor, if only he'll squeal, it'll be music to my ears."

It was a hoarse rasp, the baby's sound of protest.

Marcus quickly drew his specimen into the pipette. He was his own nurse and technician. "Brave lad," he said.

"Sure, what can you tell from that? Take some blood, man," the father said.

"Don't be telling the doctor what to do, Donel. The child needs all the blood he's got, poor thing."

"He's an O'Shaughnessy, damn it! Full-blooded, every man child of the clan!"

Marcus grinned and stored his specimen. If he had taken a milli-litre more, O'Shaughnessy would have passed out at the sight of it. "Wrap him up well, but not until you're ready to go out. I'm going to write a prescription for you."

O'Shaughnessy, following him to his desk, watched him, frowning more deeply at every symbol. "Is it expensive, that medicine, doctor?"

"Not very."

"What you'd think was cheap 'ud bankrupt the likes of us, sure."

"I'll give you a requisition on the clinic pharmacy," Marcus said.

Mrs. O'Shaughnessy, a pale, undernourished woman who was somehow nourishing—at Marcus's last count—six children, said, "Oh, I don't think you'll need to do that, doctor. I'll manage, Donel."

"She has the devil's own fear of charity, doctor, and getting it all her life without knowing it."

"It isn't the charity offends me. It's them social workers—you'd think it was coming out of their own pockets."

"I don't think a bottle of cough medicine will bring them down on you," Marcus said.

"But he's working now, doctor."

"Working? Oh, I'm working, true enough, but you'd never know it from what they pay a man—ninety-six dollars a month."

"He's on the W.P.A."

"Good," Marcus said.

"Ninety-six dollars a month," O'Shaughnessy repeated. "And you know what it says on the check? It says: 'The Treasury of the United States,' it says. Wouldn't you think they'd be ashamed to write a check the size of that on the Treasury of the United States?"

Marcus laughed and gave the prescription and requisition to the mother. "Bring the child to the clinic next Monday unless the fever kicks up again. In which case, you'd better call me."

"Thank you, doctor."

He went to the outer door with them. They had come a long way by streetcar—from the West Side downtown and to the South Side—to offer a child into his care that might die without ever saying a word to prove he had speech, or who might live to become, by grace of his oratory, mayor of Traders City. The near West Side was no-

torious for those extremes. They had come to him because, he supposed, of a momentary meeting of his eyes with the mother's over a
child at the clinic: she had seen there something she must have taken
for compassion. He had meant it for no more than reassurance. But
people take what they must have to live.

"Will we pay you now, doctor?" Mrs. O'Shaughnessy said.

"Don't be insulting the man," her husband said. "He's not like
the quacks in our neighborhood, setting up to bleed the poor in
more ways than one. Economic royalists—of an international complexion—if you know what I mean." O'Shaughnessy began to warm
to his own rhetoric. "They're the first to vote for the spending of
millions, but the last to pay their own taxes. I've a book I'd highly
recommend you read, doctor. It'll open your eyes to what's going
on in the country today. I'll bring a copy along to you the next time.
Well, good day to you."

"That will be two dollars," Marcus said quietly.

"Eh?"

"You heard the man and he's right. If you've money to be sending away for books, you've the money to pay him his fee."

"Two dollars," O'Shaughnessy said, subdued. "And seven cents
each, both ways, it'll cost us twenty-eight cents carfare besides."

"You could have gone to one of the quacks in the neighborhood
and saved the carfare," Marcus said evenly.

O'Shaughnessy took several folded bills from his pocket and separated two of them from their sparse companions. Marcus's sarcasm
was quite lost on him. "I'd rather pay twice the amount to an Irishman." He handed Marcus the money with a flourish. "God bless
you, Doctor Hogan." He slapped his hat on his head and walked
proudly out of the office in front of his wife who followed after him,
carrying the baby.

Marcus swore softly, locked the office door and returned to his
desk long enough to put the two dollars into a tin box, and to enter
the amount in his cash book. He scanned the week's entries, totaling
them almost simultaneously.

"By God," he said aloud to himself, "this week I made more than
O'Shaughnessy." His good humor restored, he picked up the phone
and called Dr. Winthrop's secretary for an appointment.

·7

THE office of the Health Commissioner of Traders City was in the basement of City Hall, and it was scarcely more elegant in *décor* than the furnace room, the door to which was only a few yards away. The hickory benches and tables, at which were filled out complaints, petitions and justifications—those on the level not to be settled across a luncheon table, that is—were yellowed with age and pocked with marks of indelible lead. The only decoration on the pale green wall was a large calendar provided by a purveyor of ice, lumber and coal. One would not have been likely, appraising the office, to suppose that the man who ran it owned an art collection recently estimated to be worth six hundred thousand dollars. Winthrop himself was more at ease in the office than in the midst of his art collection, if truth be told. He loved politics and where better could a man keep his ear to the ground than in the basement of City Hall?

Nor, after all, did Winthrop spend so much time in the office. He was a useful public servant in any administration. He had served under three mayors, and under the auspices of both political parties. He was a pursuasive speaker, a good arbiter, and there were few better expediters in the city. He had been drafted into the civic service by a "reform" mayor who had a very simple measure for integrity in public officers: it seemed to him indisputable logic that a rich man was incorruptible. *Per se.* Traders City was, in fact, very proud of its simplicity and of its size: the population was almost three million.

Alexander Winthrop would have preferred the law to medicine, and he often pointed that out as though certain shortcomings might be justified by the admission. Not that he ever explained his mistakes: he did not even admit them: but that too was as much a characteristic of the city as of the man. Until the Depression there had always been so much of everything—building, new industry, transportation; the key word was always "progress"—mistakes were construed as lessons. Any school child could tell you, for example, that Traders City could not have a subway system, the sand beneath the city being virtually "quick" when it came to driving the sup-

40

porting piles. Any school child could tell you because very few of their fathers questioned the canard despite the fact that almost every administration floated a new subway bond to make sure their predecessors had not hoodwinked the people.

Dr. Winthrop's fortune came primarily from patent medicines. Over the years his father—whose picture was on every bottle of "Winthrop's Remedy"—had had a great deal to do with The Law, and curiously, the more respectable he himself had become at its hands, the more disreputable he had thought The Law itself. He had been absolutely immovable on his son's profession: he made inheritance contingent upon his finishing medical school. It was one of Winthrop's sardonic jokes on himself that having managed that, he ought to be able to do almost anything. He belonged to that first generation of Traders City men born into money. Other family fortunes were largely in farm machinery, meat packing, steel, grain and lumber. He was welcome in any club in the city, and was easily within reach of an invitation to any celebration he wanted to attend. Nonetheless, he never did escape the feeling that his money was not quite respectable. And he knew very well this was an opinion shared by Traders City society. He would have said he did not have time to think of such nonsense. But because he thought about it at all he did not have time to think very much about it. He made certain from the very beginning of his career that he became as nearly inexpendable in his own right as any man ever is: he was a trustee of the Art Museum as well as of the University; he wrote the newspaper column himself—although it was largely researched by his staff; he was on the council of every important charity, on the board of several industries and a director in the County Medical Association. And he was Health Commissioner of Traders City: he could close any hospital, any nursing home, any restaurant, any hotel. He could even condemn real estate. He had a very great deal of power.

All these things were in the mind of Mike Shea, County Democratic chairman, when he began to think of tempting Winthrop with high elective office. An accumulation of powers was not the same thing, Mike reasoned, as a concentration of it. And the vanity of some men took ascendancy after a surfeit of power. He had the feeling that Winthrop was getting near surfeit.

Mike himself had never held an elective office higher than alderman, but at formal dinners he sat next to the mayor's wife, provided, of course, the mayor was his man. In thirty years Mike had put quite a number of his men into City Hall. The present mayor was in office, however, by an act of God, his predecessor having died at his desk. Now he proposed to run on his own. Mike had no objection; the mayor was a pious man, noted for his good works, and Mike was very much in favor of good works, public or private.

Indeed, it was a matter of public works that set Mike Shea to thinking of Alexander Winthrop. Mike had got a severe shock when the governor of the state refused to approve a proposal to build an airport in Traders City, largely out of federal funds, and over the appeal of the mayor. Mike was shocked and then furious. A conservative Democrat, he could not begin to understand the New Deal. Emergency spending would never bother him—in fact, he had thought Traders City would profit by some of it with the airport, but measures like Social Security and Workmen's Compensation, for example, filled him with suspicion. He did not begrudge the poor people its meager aid, God knows, but something that permanent, it seemed to him, drained the party of its political treasure, and mortgaged its future for the day's abundance. He prophesied that a decade hence the working man would be voting the Republican ticket because the Democrats had no more issues. And now, if the governor had his way —and him a Democrat, albeit a New Deal variety—Traders City was not even going to get a share of the day's abundance!

The restaurant at which Mike Shea proposed he and Winthrop meet was itself suggestive of conspiracy. Ordinarily, Mike did his entertaining at the Athletic Club although he was about as athletic as a cart horse. Nor could he resist having the tables turned on him when Winthrop would propose that they go instead to the Union League Club. Whatever his public opinion of "bankers, manufacturers and trusters," Mike dearly loved entrance to their secluded chambers. But this time he was adamant: Patsy's Steak House on Dearborn. When Winthrop got there, Mike was already settled in one of the private dining rooms.

"I haven't been in this place since Prohibition," Winthrop said, taking the hand Mike offered across the table. Mike had an interesting handshake: he gave an intimation of a clasp, and then quickly, before a man got hold of it, he collapsed his hand; it was all much in the way of a boxer's feinting and then riding with a punch.

"It's a quiet spot," said Mike, "and you know, the older I get the more willing I am to stay out of the main stream." Mike had always stayed out of the main stream; but invariably he was to be found under the bridge.

"If you've some good lager beer," Winthrop said to the waiter.

"The very thing I had in mind," said Mike. "There's nothing goes with steak like a glass of good beer. Are you sure you wouldn't like a little neat whisky first, Alex?"

They talked of a number of things having no great importance, Winthrop aware of Mike's gentle probing. Mike often spoke of "the whole man." "You've got to take the whole man into consideration," he would say, and it amused Winthrop to watch the old kingmaker scratching together bits of information about himself. They talked of baseball, the Traders City teams having gone south for spring practice. "I go down myself every year," said Mike, "except elections." He sighed and immediately veered away from the subject of politics so that Winthrop doubted that was what he had in mind. "I've a locker in the Lions' clubhouse, you know, and they've given me a cap that sits down on my ears like the old Jew's derby."

Winthrop laughed.

Mike took a long pull at his beer. "My God, the Germans know how to make beer, don't they?" He brushed the foam from his lips with the back of his hand and then wiped his hand with the napkin.

"A queer business, that, at Midwestern University, wasn't it?"

Winthrop noted with some gratification the past tense. "Ah, it's the same thing all over the country these days, Mike."

"I'm glad to hear you say that, Alex. I don't like to see us standing out from the crowd for something like that. Mind, a little rebellion's a useful thing, as somebody said. But enough's enough. You wouldn't say that Hogan fellow's a Communist, eh?"

"I don't think so."

"But he's damn useful to them sometimes, wouldn't you say?"

Winthrop said, "So is the American Legion, Mike."

Mike looked startled for a moment, so startled, in fact, that Winthrop got his first intimation that Mike had been thinking of proposing him for elective office. "Well, I suppose there are times when the Lord God Almighty gives the devil a hand, if it comes to that," Mike said slowly.

"That's just what I meant: it takes two to make a fight. Those kids didn't want a riot, but when the Legionnaires marched in to lay down the law to them . . ." He shrugged.

Mike sent his tongue on a quick tour of the dry, craggy lips. "It's a fine organization all the same, Alex."

"Sure it is. I'm a member myself."

The flesh crinkled up around the pale blue eyes. "I'm glad to hear you say that, Alex. Shall we have another bottle of beer and tell them to put on the steaks?"

Winthrop was, thereafter, careful not to overstate his views. He had nothing radical to say, and his remark about the Legion had been made as much to shake Mike up just for fun's sake as to affirm conviction. It was a dangerous bit of play to indulge in with a politician, and when the steak was finished and the apple pie before them, and Mike had not yet come to any issue worth the luncheon check, Winthrop wondered if he had not pulled a boner. But instead of becoming conciliatory, he allowed his impatience to mount and to turn, not on himself, but on Mike: what was so important about a machine boss that he could command a public servant's appearance for two hours of babble in the middle of the day?

"I hear we're not getting the airport," he said when a moment lay open in the conversation, and he said it by way of dusting Mike's wounds with salt, for he knew that the Democrats were counting heavily on Public Works to ingratiate the incumbent mayor with the voters.

"Oh, I wouldn't say that," said Mike. "It's all a matter of negotiation among the right people. The criminal thing is—the time it wastes."

Winthrop was amused at Mike's calling negotiation a waste of time, but Mike himself was in deep earnest. He went on while he unwrapped the tinsel from a cigar, "I tell you, the willful practice of politics, unless you're a politician, is a terrible waste. It's no good having to spend all your time if you're mayor, say, making up to people for having rubbed them the wrong way. For me, it's different. I'm a politician. I've been carrying coals to Newcastle all my life, just to make sure the fires never go out."

Winthrop took a box of safety matches from his pocket and handed them to Mike across the table.

"Now take yourself, for example," Mike said, having lit his cigar, and his hard blue eyes penetrated the smoke he sent up between them, "you're a natural politician. You know when to palaver a man, and you know when to strike a match on his behind."

"I suppose I've never had to be on the beggary end of things, Mike.

It makes a difference. If there's not been one way to something, I've always found another."

"Aye, but the point is," said Mike, "you're a natural. When you go into a room, it's not long before a man knows whether he can do business with you or he can't."

It was as good a moment as any. Winthrop folded his arms, an amused, patient smile stretching the corners of his mouth. "What have you got in mind, Mike?"

"Oh, this and that," said Mike with a limp gesture of his hand. He took his cigar from his lips and examined it. He looked up at Winthrop suddenly. "Do you think the governor was altogether wrong, Alex, when he put his foot down on the airport?"

"No," he said without hesitation, but the God's truth was that until that instant he had not given the matter any critical thought whatsoever. "After all," he proceeded carefully, "he's not running for reelection this year himself, and the man running for mayor is an absolutely unknown quantity—politically speaking."

"But I'm supporting him," Mike said in a tone more mischievous than aggrieved.

"I was looking at it from the governor's point of view."

Mike sat chuckling for a moment. The governor had been elected two years before on a Democratic landslide the basis of which was the early New Deal popularity. Mike had had nothing to do except pass the cigars the day after election. "Tell me the truth, Alex—if you were running for mayor yourself, would you want my endorsement?"

Winthrop shot out his lower lip, as much to discipline the lip itself as to hedge for time. "I'll put it this way, Mike: a man can disown his son without offending nature, but neither you nor I would give two cents for the kid who spits in his old man's eye. Would we?"

Mike's shoulders shook although not a sound of amusement came from him. "That reminds me of the Irishman getting off the boat." And the old man told a story the merits of which Joe Miller himself would have likely doubted. But Winthrop was caught. He settled his eyes on Mike's and put a grin on his mouth, but all the while his mind was searching the possibilities. To what extent Mike was committed to the incumbent mayor he did not know, but Mike himself was certainly in the saddle for the time being; his only trouble occurred when a mayor of the city got so strong a vote he could virtually take over the party from Mike, and this fellow in office had never been tried. It was a bad omen for him, surely, that the governor had cold-shouldered him so soon. In a way, of course, it might be Mike Shea and the city machine the governor was "nixing." Oh, and did not Mike know that, the wily old fox!

In almost the same voice he settled the Irishman in America, Mike asked, "Alex, what would you say to having a run yourself in the primary against the mayor?"

For once he was silent, looking from Mike to the spoon he picked up and turned round in his fingers and then to Mike again.

"It's the greatest sport of them all," Mike said, temptation in his voice. "It's something every man in public service has the right to experience—the voice of the people crying out their approval."

Something in Mike's fervor and choice of words had the opposite effect on Winthrop to that intended: there was something disturbing as well as exciting in the voice of the people; they could shout a man down as soon as up; they went through his life, turning it over page by page, and even the illiterate of them could read between its lines. Winthrop shook his head, and at the moment meant it.

"I wouldn't embarrass you with my endorsement," Mike said. "After all, I'm expected to see which way the frog jumps before placing my money."

"It isn't that, Mike."

Shea ignored the protest. "As a matter of fact, to make the run more exciting, I might put my tag on the mayor still. It would not be the first time I bet against myself."

Winthrop put his elbows on the table. "Mike . . . you want a winner, no matter where the bets are."

Mike wagged his head in affirmation. "My mother, God rest her, knew me no better. And that, Alex, is why I'd like to see you run—to try your strength. You may not win at all, you know. The people are notoriously ungrateful." Mike could reverse himself with the ease of an eel. "You couldn't just run on your record, fine as it is. You would have to present yourself and make a few promises. You cut a beautiful figure on the speaker's platform—you know that, Alex? There's the look of the boy about you—the All-American who grew up to be mayor of Traders City and God knows what next in this grand country of ours. You're a young man, Alex."

"I'm not far from fifty."

"Fifty! Holy Mother of God! I swear to you, if I was fifty again, I'd run myself." Shea talked a bit of the man who had died in office; he spoke devoutly, for great things had indeed been expected of the deceased. But in any case, Mike always spoke highly of the dead.

Winthrop had surrendered entirely to thoughts of himself. There was no escaping the truth that he wanted elective office at this moment more than anything in life . . . more even, God forgive him, than the thing that might very well stand in his way: his relationship with Elizabeth Fitzgerald. He knew of no one who actually was aware of the relationship, but he was sure that a number of people suspected it.

"I'm not a family man, Mike, for one thing," he said in tentative protest.

"You're a bachelor! Sure, the men will envy you and the women covet you. That's an asset in these times. Many's the poor gob who's wished himself without a family having to put them and himself on relief."

"And I wouldn't want the muckrakers poking around in my private affairs," Winthrop said, coming as close to putting the fact before Mike as he intended to.

"Isn't that the beauty of being a bachelor?" Mike cried. "The people make allowances. I tell you, whether or not allowances are needed, the people make them. The man you don't have to allow anything to just isn't human." Mike gave himself a thump on the chest. "My own heart is a Pandora's Box."

Winthrop tilted his chair back and laughed heartily; it was a great, booming laugh that seemed to bounce off the ceiling. He put his hands in his pockets. "Let me think about it for a day or so, Mike. I'll let you know."

"You'll have to file before the end of the week."

"If I file at all."

Mike studied the nub of cigar that had gone dead in his fingers. "You might find, Alex, that a good man to have in your corner—he might even run things for you, and I'd say he's a comer himself, having got his start with the New Deal in Washington—young George Bergner. You know him, don't you? Sure, you must, he lives in Lakewood. And you must know his father?"

Winthrop nodded. The elder Bergner was one of the top surgeons in Traders City and a friend. Young Bergner was a lawyer . . . which, Winthrop supposed,—but with no great bitterness—could happen when father was a gentleman.

"That's up to you, of course," Mike said. He put out his hand across the table. "I'm glad we had this little talk, Alex. I know you're a busy man, but I'm glad you thought of old Mike at a time like this."

Winthrop grinned and gave a good squeeze to the bag of bones which seemed to collapse in his grasp.

Mike massaged his knuckles. "You'll get over that handshake after a few thousand rounds." He looked up then and puckered his face. "If you don't mind, Alex, I'm going to stay and talk a while with Patsy. I'm thinking of getting a storage locker, and I'd like to buy my steaks where he does—if I can get his price."

Winthrop took his coat from the old-fashioned stand. He did not wear a hat if he could help it. His foot trod against a brass spittoon, tucked under the stand. Patsy's was equipped for all comers. He glanced for an instant at the pictures around the walls—signed, in one case, up the dancer's leg, the signature scratched among the mesh of the stocking—"Texas"—all the nightclub entertainers of the twenties had left their love with Patsy, who in those days called himself "The Dago Kid" and had managed to scratch his own name on the fat underbelly of Traders City.

"So long, Mike." Winthrop saluted him from the door.

"Alex." The old man beckoned him back, and waited until he had his full attention. "As we used to say at home . . . Mind, I said nothing."

·8

WINTHROP, instead of returning directly to his office, turned up his overcoat collar and began to walk; apple pie was not the best solace for a nervous stomach. But with the food before him, he ate as some men smoked, to ease the tensions. He belched, wind into the wind. Inhaling then, he got the taste of soot in his mouth. They were poisoning the city with their smokestacks and their steam engines. To burn hard coal, they said, would mean economic ruin. He wondered. The city was ringed with elevated steel rails on which ran electric trains—power generated, of course, by coal. But the plants could be moved out of the city . . . and with them a population of voters. And downstate the only industry was coal—soft coal. He stood a moment at the foot of Marquette, the Wall Street of Traders City. The skyscrapers were fewer—and newer—and there was room for a great many more. The feel of the prairie was still to be got at the heart of the city; there seemed a reluctance to build up. For mile after mile, the city clung to the ground and groped, when it moved, aimlessly into the flats, leaving the sky to the winds. It was a great shame that a city of such promise should wallow on the ground because its generation of pioneers had given way to their politician sons and businessmen, to corporate bigness, where little men were allowed authority and big men hamstrung in the chain of it.

He found himself outside the McCormick Building, on the thirty-first floor of which were the law offices of a firm that included George Allan Bergner. Bergner would be either there or in Washington, or in the state capital; but he was not wallowing in the flats of Traders City wherever he was. George had got religion: the New Deal, hallelujah: the great day a-coming. Government not just of the people, by the people, but government *for* the people: the NRA, the AAA, the CCC, the PWA and the WPA *ad nauseum*—or *ad glorium?* Alexander Winthrop was not prepared to say. He was not prepared, that was the trouble. For the first time in his life he was not prepared to take full advantage of an opportunity.

This was not entirely true, he realized, turning reluctantly back toward his office. What was true was that for the first time his course of action in a given opportunity was not his alone to determine.

He made it a practice not to look around the waiting room, going into his office. Too often a friendly glance to the wrong person at such a moment discovered him half-committed before he ever got into negotiation. Normally a man of high spirits, he rather enjoyed acting glum and preoccupied pushing by the oak railing and into his milk-glassed inner office.

When Winthrop got to his desk and his secretary reminded him that he had a date with a Doctor Marcus Hogan, he was for the moment puzzled. Then he remembered, and threw back his head in laughter. He laughed with the deep physical gratification to be got from the ironic. But when the laughter passed, all he could feel was the sharper edge of his own problem.

"Is he here?"

"He's been waiting for almost an hour, doctor."

Winthrop smiled and his voice was nastily silken. "Then why didn't you call me, my dear? He's a friend of Professor Fitzgerald's."

Marcus had not minded the wait. He envied men whose days were more crowded than his own. And Dr. Winthrop's secretary had provided him with a fine collection of medical journals. She had got a faint scent of the dispensary from him and had hoped to tell him of her own pains—but at the last moment failed of courage.

"I'm sorry to have kept you waiting, my boy," Winthrop said, and gave him a lingering handshake that bore Marcus down into the leather chair at the side of the desk.

"I caught up on some homework," Marcus said, "thanks to your library."

"So. You're a friend of Professor Fitzgerald's. High recommendation, that, you know. How long have you known him?"

"He's a friend of my father's," Marcus said.

"Oh, is he?" Winthrop said pleasantly. "Well, now, tell me about yourself."

Winthrop, however, scarcely listened. From the moment he had laid eyes on the young, big-boned, long-limbed visitor, Winthrop wondered how he had got to Walter Fitzgerald, why, and what had prompted Fitzgerald to say a good word on his behalf. He was struck with the puzzle Walter Fitzgerald was to him still. He knew him as little now as when he had first met, misjudged, and all but hero-worshiped him, the very reverse of their present positions. Fitzgerald had been a handsome man fifteen years before, his features finely wrought in the way of a piece of high-style art: he had looked to Winthrop then like a Roman orator; he carried himself with grace, a man fond of walking, and his voice was finely modulated, his phrasing elegant; everything about him had proposed a man magnificently self-disciplined, cultured; and at that point in his own life, Winthrop had not yet seemed able to discipline the movements of his own body: his legs would sprawl, and as his father had often pointed out to him in his youth, he used hands the way a seal used its flippers. In time, of course, it was Elizabeth who had rubbed some of his edges smooth. She, more than any one person, was responsible for whatever polish, whatever depth there was to him. She had been patient with him in so many, many ways . . .

Marcus doubted very much that Winthrop wanted to hear any such recital as he had asked for, or indeed that he had the intention of listening, although he had lapsed into what might be called a benevolent silence, his eyes not quite focused on the speaker. Winthrop roused himself to say, "Go on, man, don't be bashful. You must have a litany of recommendations that Walter put you through.

He's careful, my friend Walter is. I imagine you've come well rehearsed."

"It wasn't a matter for much rehearsal, doctor. I've a limited repertoire." He accounted his training and experience. "I'm working now at the Brandon House Clinic on the West Side."

"Where did you get the name Marcus?"

"It's a family name. It's Thaddeus Marcus, actually."

"Thaddeus Stevens," Winthrop mused. "Who was he now?"

"I'm not sure—a Civil War general? Or was he a senator. I think that."

"No relation, I presume?"

"Not to my knowledge," Marcus said.

Winthrop nodded as though there had been sense to the exchange. "Brandon House Clinic—mostly Irish out there, isn't it?"

"Yes."

Winthrop appraised him frankly even to the cut of his clothes. "Hogan—that's Irish, too, isn't it? Is your mother also Irish?"

"No, sir. She was a New Englander."

"Wasn't *Mayflower* stock, was she?" Winthrop grinned.

"The *Fortune*," Marcus said.

Winthrop cocked his head questioningly.

"The next ship after the *Mayflower*," Marcus said.

Winthrop ran his hand through his hair. "Really? I wonder now what prompted me to ask."

"My father and I find it amusing. My brother has made the most out of it."

"Your brother has better sense than both of you, if you don't mind my saying it. A family tradition, whether you like it or not, is an asset, especially in medicine. Doctors pretend they don't have time for snobbery. But they make the most of what time they've got." He gave a short laugh. "The wives work out the details, you see. You're not married?"

"No."

"How are your prospects?"

"Limited, I'm afraid, but perhaps that is also an asset just now."

Winthrop gave a grunt with the sound of amusement in it. "What does your brother do?"

"He's in the diplomatic service. He's in India now."

Winthrop nodded. "That's the place for it." He lapsed into silence again, having meant, Marcus supposed, the place for snobbery.

Marcus knew he was not waiting for him to say anything, for his eyes were blinking rapidly, in the way of someone thinking out an idea. Suddenly he asked, "Would you like to hear how I came to be Commissioner of Health?"

Marcus said, "It never occurred to me to wonder," which was cutting the truth as close to the margin as he dared.

Winthrop was looking directly at him—or through him—his dark eyes absorbed, eager—onto something. The energy of the man was enormous. He said, "Do you think I've done a good job at it?"

Marcus opened his mouth for a second before speaking. He then took a deep breath and said, "I never thought my ignorance would stand me in good stead, doctor. But the actual truth is, I don't know. I've heard things I wouldn't say are complimentary. And there's a situation of my own knowledge which I'd say is not good. But whether or not you could do anything about it—I don't know. And I suppose if I did know, I'd try my damnedest right now to find a way of not saying it."

"What is it you think is bad?" He waved his hand. "I'll beg responsibility, so you'll never know." His voice was persuasive, a sound close to a purr in it.

Marcus reached for a cigaret. Saying something derogatory at this moment would guarantee a long ignorance, he thought. "I feel as though I've just had an invitation to a hanging, and I'm not sure it isn't my own."

Winthrop smiled broadly. He handed Marcus a packet of matches. "Tell me: what's the situation?"

Marcus lit his cigaret. "Well, sir, it concerns a disease I know a little about—tuberculosis. In two years I've watched the infections multiply and the facilities to isolate the carriers stand still. There's a crying need for a new sanatorium, and I can't help thinking how much more important that is than the downtown airport for which our mayor has proposed to go to Washington for money. Is it your fault? I shouldn't think so, sir. Not likely." Marcus shook his head and took a long pull at his cigaret.

Winthrop sat a full moment without speaking; what a remarkable coincidence that Hogan should mention the airport. He did not know, of course, that the governor had vetoed it. "Tell me, Dr. Hogan, who do you think is going to be the next mayor?"

"I shouldn't be surprised if it were the man who's in the office right now, doctor."

"And do you think it would make any difference to his being elected whether he proposed a sanatorium or an airport?"

"I'm afraid not very much. He'll probably do better with the airport. It's very dramatic."

Winthrop nodded. "I imagine that's what he thought, too."

They talked for a time about a new sanatorium, which Traders City did indeed need. Winthrop called in his secretary for statistics and asked Marcus's opinion on their accuracy. Winthrop said then, "A county project. Everybody says it ought to be a county undertaking."

"It won't make any difference to the patients," Marcus said, "only to the politicians."

Winthrop looked up sharply and clamped a sudden smile on his mouth. He had been about to say that if it were county sponsored, it would be out of his jurisdiction. "I suppose you see yourself some day heading up a sanatorium such as this, Doctor Hogan?"

"No."

"Oh, come, man."

"I haven't got the makings of an administrator," Marcus said blandly.

It was almost beyond Winthrop's credulity that a man who could see the need for a sanatorium should not see himself as its administrator. His own vision invariably reflected self-aggrandizement.

"What did you say?" Winthrop wanted to hear him say it again.

"I said I haven't got the makings of an administrator."

"What have you the makings of?" He was abrupt of speech, impatient, as though suddenly aware of urgent work.

"A surgeon. What I want is the surgeon's residency in a good hospital."

"Ha! Do you know what the waiting lists are?"

"Yes, sir. I'm near the bottom on quite a number of them."

"Are you near the top on any of them?"

"No. And I don't think I'm moving up."

Winthrop shook his head. "I'm not a juggler. And a recommendation from me may not do you as much good as some people seem to think. These men don't admire me. Some of them are afraid of me—for reasons better known to themselves than to me—they may thank God." He talked on, going over in his mind the while those places where he might have power. He began making notes on a desk pad.

Marcus knew that in spite of his protests, Winthrop was going to help him: he had somehow got through to this ambitious man, whom he liked despite having come prepared not to. He believed Winthrop above all else a politician, and he had the contempt of the young for all politicians.

Winthrop looked at him from beneath lowered brows. "It's the chief surgeon has the say in most places, you know. And, of course, you don't know any chief surgeons?"

"Not well enough apparently."

"How old are you, Hogan?"

"Twenty-eight."

Winthrop pushed away from his desk and got up. His energy was almost palpable, and Marcus once more envied him his multiplicity of jobs. "Can you take orders and keep opinions to yourself until you're asked for them?"

"I think so."

"You'd better *know* so. I suppose you've heard of Albert Bergner?"

"Yes, sir."

Winthrop frowned, thinking, but there was a play of excitement about his own mouth. "You admire him, don't you?" he said impatiently.

"Very much."

"Then for Christ's sake, say so."

"I admire him in surgery, doctor."

Winthrop whirled around and stood over him, a towering wrath: "That's all of him that needs your approval, boy. Who the hell do you think you are to have an opinion on anything else in a man like him?"

"I think Doctor Bergner is a truly great surgeon," Marcus said. Winthrop was right; he did not try to defend himself.

"You're damned right he is. Fortunately, the view is shared by men of even greater distinction than yourself." He moved to the door of his office, hunched down a few inches in order to see out of the clear glass near the frame: a nervous habit, merely. The venting of his own sarcasm, so far as Winthrop was concerned, always purged its victim of whatever offense he had given. He turned back to Marcus. "What was the name of that boat?"

Marcus was a second or two making the connection. "The *Fortune*."

"Write it down and give it to my secretary. It's too late for me to start learning history now. And your mother's family name, give her that too, if you don't mind." He stuck out his hand. "That's all for now, Hogan."

"Thank you, doctor," Marcus said.

The handshake was brief and not another word was exchanged between them.

That night when Marcus was going over for his father as much as he could remember of what had been said, he felt a certain reluctance about mentioning Dr. Bergner, but if anything at all were to come out of his interview with Winthrop, it seemed likely to be contingent on the famous surgeon. Bergner still lectured once a week at Midwestern.

His father did not say anything for a moment, but the name affected him; his hesitancy averred that. "I don't suppose there's anyone better in your field," he said finally.

Marcus said: "He's got some peculiar ideas for these times, doesn't he?"

"You may have put that just right, Marc. I don't like some of his ideas—on the scientific breeding of men, for example, toward the select, the superman. But there ought to be ways of improving the species. And the issue should not be confused with Fascism."

"You wouldn't say he was a Fascist?"

"Not I, knowing as little of his work as I do. It may well be scientific."

"Are you afraid of science, dad?"

"I like to think I am a scientist of sorts. Not like Mueller. Erich's very patient with me. You know, Marc, I think in the end that's how I'd have to judge Bergner, too—by his patience. A patient man is humble. A humble man is patient. Arrogance is the real enemy."

"I wonder what Winthrop's connection is with Bergner," Marcus said after a moment. "Or maybe there isn't any connection. It was just a name that came into his mind. There was a number of *non sequiturs* in that conversation."

"There won't be any of them in the superman." Jonathan took his pipe from his pocket. "I'm talking nonsense." He scraped the bowl of the pipe and knocked it out in the fireplace. "And it ought to be said before we get off Bergner, he's well thought of by quite a number of Jewish people."

"Speaking of *non sequiturs,*" Marcus said slyly.

His father thought about it and then laughed. "I suppose it is at that."

THE day was ominous, the sky a slow whorl of grey clouds out of which escaped occasional flurries of snow. It was not a good day to drive into the dunes. Nor was it a good day to wait in the wind. Elizabeth Fitzgerald, standing before her own pale image in a Lake Front Avenue window felt as shabby as any walker in the street. She considered these the worst moments, waiting, except for those alone afterwards when there was no emotion left, only the dull ache of guilt. Once there had been a kind of ecstasy to the waiting. But that, too, was muted. Only his presence satisfied her, awakening and putting to rest all passion in an afternoon.

And yet she loved him. Long ago, she had thought of him as a lover before it had come to pass. She had from the beginning felt his presence in a room before even their eyes had met.

She stared into the drugstore window, determined to see beyond her image in the glass. Was there anything uglier, she wondered, than a cheap alarm clock? A pyramid of them had been built in display. She counted them, and re-counted them until she caught sight of Winthrop's car a half block away. She moved quickly to the curb so that he need stop no longer than it took to shift gears. They always met at the beginning of a block, never at its end lest a traffic light delay them and expose them to chance recognition.

"You're not dressed very warmly," he said. He had thought she looked frail, forlorn, awaiting him, almost a stranger from the robust woman he had so long been in bond to. He had even speculated on her course if he had driven on and never come to her again. Remembering this fleeting thought, and having her beside him, he grew soft with tenderness. He removed his glove and put his hand into her pocket, closing it upon hers, cold and buried there.

"Would you like a drink, my dear? I've brought a bottle."

"I don't suppose you managed a straw?" She flashed him a sidelong glance.

He laughed, the moment's awkwardness dispelled. "I was thinking just the other day—they've stopped putting window shades in the new cars."

"And they're going to build houses of glass. Alas for all sinners."

He drove in silence, unsure of her mood which could fall dark as sudden as the change of pitch in her voice. He needed to brake the car quickly on South Lake Front Avenue, for the wind had caught up dust and debris and dashed it against the windshield. The once elegant buildings of the neighborhood were all condemned now, but only half torn down, the insides stripped of marble, chandeliers, and often of plumbing fixtures, good items for salvage. They were occupied nonetheless by a squatter population, the unfortunates who could not raise money for rent but somehow managed enough to buy off the police inspectors.

"By God, the city is filthy. We've got to clean it up."

"You'll have to begin with an ax," Elizabeth said.

The words, so characteristic of her, moved him to an even greater tenderness, and he resolved with childlike naïveté to be a better man for Traders City than anything which he had done heretofore gave warrant of his likely being.

She said, "There are twenty-three alarm clocks in the window of the Walgreen Drugstore. Would you buy an alarm clock, Alex, if you didn't need it?"

"No."

"There comes a point in all advertising, I think, where they cross from the reasonable to the ridiculous without ever realizing it."

"I started to collect clocks once," he said.

Quick of wit and tongue, she said, "There are twenty-three of them in the window. Shall we go back?"

He turned his head and smiled at her.

They came soon to the lake's edge, passing the site, a parking lot since the World's Fair, where the present city administration had proposed to build an airport. The waters of the lake were gray-green, white-capped. The rocks along the shore line were crystaled with ice.

"It won't take me long to build the fire," Winthrop said.

The cabin sat a long drive back from the highway and a short walk up from the lake among the dunes. The only neighbor at any time of year was a man who raised goats and cared more about their way-wardness than that of man or woman. Elizabeth had never met him, but she knew the goats fairly intimately. Once on an autumn afternoon, she had coaxed enough milk into a cup from one of them to color her tea. As was Winthrop's habit, he stopped for a can of water at the man's house. In that way he forestalled curiosity that might arise with the appearance of smoke from his cabin chimney.

There is in every clandestine relationship a moment which especially portends disaster, whether or not disaster ever befalls it. With Elizabeth and Winthrop the moment occurred—curiously never when they met in her studio—but in this sanded wilderness, at the instant of the door's closing. They were helpless before one another, much less before the world in their headlong abandon to the first embrace. The act of love made them scarcely more each other's prisoner.

Elizabeth wrapped herself in a quilt until the room was warm. She would carry the smell of dampness for some hours, and there would be no joy in the consciousness of it. More and more the future seemed to encroach upon them. Nor was it merely that they were not young any longer. She had never been young, not romantically in the way of most girls, of her own daughter who, she was sure, dreamed of one young man or another. She herself had been a child and then a woman. Exported from Ireland at the age of fifteen to a wealthy aunt in Boston, she had felt the hand of a man upon her aboard ship; the purser had made love to her and she had liked it. Oh yes! Now and then, for a fleeting instant, she would remember his face, the red cheeks, the white teeth, and the soft, almost wistful mouth. Her aunt, unaware of the purser, of course, had not been long nonetheless in deciding that the best way to cope with so high-spirited and bold a child was to see her married soon. She committed her to a quick finishing at the hands of the Sacred Heart nuns, and set about finding a suitable husband.

Winthrop looked round from where he was fanning the flames. There was sound stirring in the kettle, and the wind was moaning in the flue. She had been watching him, but seeing beyond him, looking into the fire.

"I was just thinking of the sailor who made love to me on the boat when first I came to America," she said.

"Handsome, I'm sure."

"Very."

"I'm sure he had a wife and half dozen children he didn't tell you about."

Elizabeth smiled. "Or perhaps a child and a half dozen wives as they say about sailors. But he put me on the way, I was thinking, to a quick marriage. I don't mean that I slept with him. But I would have liked to. Is that a terrible thing to say?"

"Was Walter the first man you slept with?"

"Yes."

She said no more. He came and sat beside her on the sofa, but holding his hands up and away much as a doctor might, preparing for surgery, except that his precaution was due to the dirt he had got on them. "Will you turn up my cuffs, Elizabeth?"

"And the only one—else." She pushed the cuffs up to where his wrist bones showed.

"This hasn't been a very satisfactory life, has it?"

"I can't think of our not having had it, Alex. But there are times it troubles me a great deal, how much it must have hurt you."

He frowned, uncomfortable that her concern should be for him at the moment. "And you?" he said.

"I've not been hurt by it. Sometimes I think I've been saved by it. I had every right to pay for a bad marriage."

"I'd better wash my hands," he said.

"Alex." She kissed him deeply, but with only their lips touching, until he felt her cold hand upon his flushed cheek. He took the hand in his own and kissed the palm of it.

When, later, they were having coffee laced with whisky, and both of them staring into the fire, Elizabeth said, "Ah, but it's not at all too late for you, really, Alex. Time, but not too late."

He did not attempt to dissemble. He found himself soon telling her of Mike Shea's proposal.

She nodded now and then soberly, and put her hand on his, sometimes squeezing it, a message he tried vainly to interpret. Nor did he understand quite what she meant when presently she asked, "Is he a trustworthy man, Mike Shea?"

He could not bring himself to ask her to be more explicit. "All politicians are trustworthy—in politics," he said off-handedly.

"In some ways, Alex, you are too good a man." She went no further. She could not force him to meet an issue he did not want raised.

"I hope you're always my only jury," he said.

She laughed and brushed back the strands of her black hair with the heel of her hand and then tucked them into the braid.

"I wish now I had studied law," he said, thinking again of his prospect.

She said, "Walter will be so proud of you." The association arose because Winthrop, when first he had met Walter Fitzgerald, had thought him a lawyer; he had heard Fitzgerald talking about the Scopes trial, his tongue acid, scathing, picturesque in the way of trial lawyers, in the way, in fact, although Winthrop had not known it then, of William Jennings Bryan, the prosecutor, whom Walter had admired to the point of imitation.

"I'm not so sure," he said. "If I run, I'll have the New Deal behind me, and you know how Walter feels about them lately."

"What about Judge Phipps?"

Winthrop ran his hand through his hair. "I think I'll be able to sweeten up Walter before him."

She leaned her head back on the sofa. "Ah, Alex, you will be very fine for Traders City. I shall have to register now so that I can vote for you."

"I have a hurdle or two to jump over first," he said.

"Your Lakewood society friends—what will they say?"

"I don't give a damn what they say. I never have."

She glanced at him, smiled, and said, "Good," although both of them knew it was a lie. He cared very much, but he also knew that no amount of his caring would make any difference. And that, in turn, contributed to an independence that bordered on the stubborn in him.

"Elizabeth, there's always the chance . . ."

She interrupted, pouncing as though she had been waiting for that beginning: "Always . . . there has been the chance, Alex."

"It never mattered before. What I mean is—it was never worth anyone's while . . ."

"I know what you mean, Alex."

He felt uncomfortable nonetheless, the words having come closer to the truth as he first said them than he liked. In spite of everything, intended frankness, a persistent love between them, her understanding that was almost foresight in its depth—in spite of all, however, he felt the guilt compounding. Nor did it help when Elizabeth said: "Martha will just have to take her chances, now, too." He got up and tinkered with the fire tongs, kicked at the logs. He stood then, looking at her, his back to the grate, his lip out so that his expression was one of perplexed hurt.

"I said that, Alex, because it had to be said, and really it's the *only* thing that does have to be said. We must start back soon. The wind sounds worse."

"I'd give a great deal to have your daughter like me, Elizabeth."

"Someday it may happen quite naturally."

"I always say the wrong thing with her." He flung his hands in the air, that curiously awkward gesture of his which had put his father in mind of a seal. "She makes me feel like an oaf, a bumpkin."

"What I suspect you feel, Alex, is that she's looking through to your very soul. She has that way about her, but I assure you she's not. There is an innocence beyond the dream. We are not all alike despite what these psychologists say." She drew the quilt more tightly about her. "If you will go about your business now—I'll dress."

It was strange, he thought, and on that day it was chilling, to realize that she always undressed but would never dress before him.

He stood a moment longer. "Elizabeth, you haven't stopped loving me?"

A smile crossed her lips, so sudden and brief he could not say if it were sweet or bitter. "No. Not yet."

· 10

A MARVELOUS thing about parliaments and politicians is the haste with which they can do something if it cannot be done at all otherwise. When history will wait, legislators quibble. In three years the New Deal had got through Congress a mountain of legislation, some good, some bad, but all aimed at national recovery on the level of everyman. There had been fervor before in Washington in living memory, the first Roosevelt's administration and Wilson's, surely, but it lacked the scope, the reach the New Deal had into far cottages and urban industry. Virtually no one who lived by the sweat of his brow was unaffected by it, and by 1936, those who lived by investment or on the managerial level, were also affected, for as of January 1, all industrial payrolls registered Social Security withholding payments.

It could not be said that there was a large-scale crossing of traditional loyalties, particularly in the Lakewood suburb of Traders City. It may well have been there that Roosevelt was first called "a traitor to his class." But here and there the younger scion of a moneyed family tended to go along with the President's social philosophy even if neither he nor the President could precisely identify it. There was not time to precisely identify anything: too many people over the nation had little more by way of identification than their hunger.

George Allan Bergner had grown up in Lakewood society, had married fashionably, but had taken early to the New Deal. He had virtually graduated into it from Harvard Law School. That reaction to his father's conservatism was partially responsible George knew, but was unlikely to admit lest it seem to diminish the independent image he wished people to have of him. He and his father quarreled with the relentless zeal of religious partisans. Dr. Bergner thought equalitarianism a mischievous nonsense, and never missed the opportunity to point out to his son the ingratitude of the masses.

"What have they got to be grateful for?" George would cry.

"True, true," the old man would say. "They'd be much better off never to have been born at all, most of them."

What George could not or would not understand was that half the time his father was deliberately overstating his own views by way of provocation. It was a compound of mischief and contempt on the old man's part, and scarcely less reprehensible than bigotry. All this Alexander Winthrop understood very well. He had seen its origins in George's school days when Dr. Bergner's first impatient wrath was wreaked on John Dewey and "his damn fool pragmatism." Nor had George ever been an honor student. Winthrop's friendship with Doctor Bergner had developed over the years when George was away at school and then at Washington, and it was one of those contradictory attractions between men: Winthrop, himself the son of a tyrant to whom he had not been able to stand up, accepted on more or less equal terms by Dr. Bergner who failed to see the possible coming resemblance between Winthrop and his own son when he reached Winthrop's age.

That Winthrop understood the Bergners, father and son, made it no easier to spend an evening in their company. He arrived at the house, expecting to have dinner alone with Dr. Bergner. It was the evening of the day he and Elizabeth had gone to the dunes, and he had looked forward to it, by no means at ease with his own conscience. He had hoped to set things somewhat right with himself promoting young Hogan with the old doctor.

George gave him too ostentatious a welcome for comfort: Winthrop knew he must have already got the political bug in his ear. From the outset he was playing to his father, even while speaking to Winthrop. Winthrop doubted he had played to Louise since the day he had asked her to marry him. Louise had a pale, ethereal quality, blonde and quite pretty, and Winthrop had often thought that if only she would keep from talking, she would be excellent company.

Over their first drink in the "small room" between the parlor and the conservatory, George said, "I signed that petition for you today, Alex."

Winthrop looked at him questioningly.

"Draft-Winthrop-for-mayor."

"Oh, that," Winthrop said, unwilling to admit he had not known such a petition existed. For a man who worked behind the scenes, Mike Shea was quick.

"How wonderful!" Louise cried. "I didn't even know Lakewood had a mayor."

"Mayor of Traders City, dear," her husband said coldly.

"I sometimes live there too," Winthrop said to soften her embarrassment. Dr. Bergner was going through the faintly audible "putt-putt-putt" which always preceded his wheeze of laughter. Louise might be pretty, but she was remarkably stupid, and Winthrop observed not for the first time the satisfaction this seemed to give the old man.

"Where do you think the county chairman will stand?" George asked.

"Squarely behind the winner of the primary. It's my opinion he'll stay off his feet till then."

George gave a snort of amusement.

Dr. Bergner said, "Who? Who's that you're talking about?"

"Mike Shea, county Democratic chairman."

"He's never run for office before in his life, has he?" the old gentleman said.

"He's not running now, father," George said. "We were speaking of his support, whether Alex would have it if he runs for mayor."

The old man grunted and tipped back his head to drain the last of the sherry from his glass. He was ferocious looking, white-haired, but his brows and mustache were still almost black. Louise had once confessed to Elizabeth Fitzgerald after a party that she had nightmares about her father-in-law.

He said derisively, "Doing business with a man like that—and you call yourselves progressive."

"Politics are practical, if they're anything, father," George said ponderously.

"*If* they're anything. It's politics, not religion that's the opiate. Give everybody a piece of paper on which to mark his X—Why? Be damned to everybody. Form without substance! Ballots for the masses. A fraud, that's what it is. Do they know any more what you're doing for having put their mark on a piece of paper after your name?"

"At least, we tell them, father."

"And do they know any more for *that,* I ask you?"

"I think it's rather beside the point," George said. "The important thing is that we tell them."

"Important to whom?"

"All right, father, important to us!"

"Ha! One would think I raised him a papist." The old man looked around to find his daughter-in-law. "I want a drop more sherry." He took her arm. "You and I understand one another, don't we, my dear? You would vote for me, wouldn't you? It makes a man proud we enfranchised the women, let me tell you . . ." His voice faded as he led her to the buffet.

"The bastard," George said under his breath. George was fair complexioned, his cheeks now as ruddy as a schoolboy's, his eyes watery with anger, frustration. He could be no more than thirty, but he was going bald, and what hair he had circling his head was curly. He looked more like a tonsured boy in a pet than a man in wrath.

"Can't you see, he's deliberately provoking you, George?" Winthrop said.

"Of course, I see!"

More than once while they were talking Winthrop questioned in his own mind the wisdom of putting his campaign in the hands of a man who could be maneuvered into purposeless fury. Still, no one knew better than he the helplessness of a son in the presence of an autocratic father. And George had the contacts: he made that plain at once, describing the predilections of a dozen influential men, and how they could be got round—a curious recital for a man who had just sanctified the universal ballot.

He and Winthrop agreed to meet the following morning.

After dinner Winthrop went upstairs in the elevator with the old gentleman to his study, George having taken his wife home early. Louise complained of a headache, and small wonder, the tensions between father and son. Once they were gone, Winthrop started to enjoy himself. He liked the house as he did no other except possibly Elizabeth's—and there were rooms there he had never seen, and rooms he wished he had not seen—but here he recognized a house which had been built by a man who knew exactly what he wanted and brooked no compromise. The style was Georgian, the rooms high-ceilinged, not large but sometimes breaking into one another as the parlor into a small sitting room into the conservatory, giving at once a sense of space and intimacy. Not a piece of furniture in the house, Dr. Bergner had told him once, that was not rosewood or cherry, and not a piece that was not signed or, in the case of antiques, authenticated. "But you'd never know it, would you, Alex? That's the thing. It isn't the crown that makes the king now, is it?"

Alex always considered it an education to come here. He regretted that the old gentleman took him upstairs in the elevator with him. The walls along the stairway were hung with family pictures, starting with daguerreotypes and ending with a tinted photograph of a young girl sitting stiffly on a wrought iron bench as though tightly corseted. A fine oil painting of her hung in the parlor. In the days when they had walked up, Dr. Bergner would say, "That's my late wife. You didn't know her, did you?"

Winthrop had not even known his own mother. He had grown up in the care of many nurses, one after another of whom took a tearful departure of the child, having quarreled with his father. From his childhood he remembered the scent of many bosoms where he doubted a man had ever laid his head.

Dr. Bergner gave him a brandy and then settled himself in an old platform rocker. It was the only ugly chair in the house and, perversely, the old man preferred it to any other. "Well, Alexander. Mayor, is it? Why not Governor? Or President?"

Winthrop cupped the brandy glass in his hand. "Because nobody asked me," he said.

The old man snorted and reached a palsied hand for his glasses which, when he wore dinner clothes, he carried on a black ribbon. It was a firm hand with which he set them on his nose, however. He still spent three days a week in surgery. "I'm glad you're not a fraud—but I wish you were a practicing man," he said. He took off the glasses, having looked at Winthrop. "Selfish of me. Old people are. But I was selfish as a young man, wasn't I? You would suppose so, wouldn't you?"

Winthrop said nothing. He inhaled the fumes of the brandy and then sipped it. Most of Bergner's questions were statements.

"What's the name of this youngster again? The one you want me to take on?"

"Marcus Hogan. Thaddeus Marcus Hogan."

"Interesting name, isn't it?" the old man said, nodding. He liked a flourish in names which made it seem peculiar that he had named his own son George. George Allan, to be precise. He spoke of and to him always as George Allan, which in the boy's childhood had been an ignominious distinction among his fellows. "What was it about his family, Alex? Oh, yes." The doctor generally remembered things he asked himself aloud. "True, you know, the part about the *Fortune,* and the mother's family. Very old stock. I looked it up. Who did you say his father is?"

Winthrop waited, hoping vainly he would answer that question for himself also. Then he said, "He's the professor of economics at the University who's been in the news lately."

Dr. Bergner nodded a vigorous understanding. "Oh, yes, yes, that one. I remember."

Winthrop said: "I hope you won't hold that against the son."

Bergner lifted his head and squinted at him, unable at the moment to get hold of his glasses. "On the contrary."

They did not speak much more of Marcus Hogan that evening. Winthrop promised to provide Bergner with information on him. When he rose to leave, the old man asked, "Are you having that usual March madness of yours this year?"

Winthrop knew he referred to the ball he traditionally gave on the first of March. "Especially this year, Doctor Albert."

"Tell you what you do: invite young Hogan. I shall come and look him over."

· 11

WINTHROP'S parties were always lavish. Knowing that he would be criticized by the matrons of North Shore society in any case, he chose to err on the side of opulence: it might not stop them from talking, but neither did it stop them from attending. He could tell from the jewelry out that night, a number of legended pieces, that he rated a high place on the season's calendar. Some people were away for the winter, of course, but it so happened that this was one of the greatest years in the history of Traders City opera, and one of the customs demanded of fashion was its support.

Winthrop received alone. One of the virtues of bachelorhood was that by it he was in an ancient tradition remembered only, but distinctly, by the family dowagers. They never failed to tell him on such occasions of the fine unattached gentlemen, now seemingly a vanished breed, who had made romantic their own youths. Winthrop supposed it due in part to the permanence of attachment in those days. Even now, however, divorce was not common in Lakewood.

Now and then a man arriving would murmur surreptitious congratulations on his candidacy. He did not expect a numerous vote from among his guests: a few might cross the line in the primary since the Republican was running unopposed, but what he did find gratifying was the attitude that even Traders City politics might, by grace of men like him, become respectable. He guarded himself against reading too much into a cordiality that might be founded on mere boredom.

One old gentleman, who shouted because he was himself deaf, pulled Winthrop down to where his ear was next to the old man's lips and then said loudly enough to draw good-humored applause from half a dozen people standing nearby: "I'm going to vote for you to help you break that damned machine."

Winthrop smiled and pressed the man's hand, and thought the while that, unfortunate though it might be, he could not win without some damned machine. The governor was full force behind him; but he was haunted by the probable truth in one of the *Dispatch's* venomous cartoons: it described Mike Shea as a lean and hungry tiger ready to leap, but undecided which of the lambs he wanted, the incumbent mayor or the challenger. Winthrop had found it humiliating to be cartooned as a lamb. But as George Bergner said: "Politics *are* humiliating."

He waited. He could not deny to himself the eagerness with which he waited a first glimpse of Elizabeth. She saw him now only in her own home with Walter present or on such an occasion as this. And yet he waited. Other guests arrived. The women went up the south stairs to powder and dressing rooms. The gentlemen were provided a private drinking lounge up the north stairs, which Winthrop called the Trophy Room. There were certain of their number who did not believe it proper to drink whisky in the presence of ladies. Or, to put it more exactly, they did not believe ladies should be allowed in the presence of gentlemen drinking whisky. Balance in all things, Winthrop thought, observing the dichotomy. A string orchestra was playing in the drawing room all but unattended. Balance in all things; life is a budget. The ridiculous phrase ran through his mind all evening thereafter.

Winthrop's estate, Tamarack, named after the great tall trees, sparse and stately guardians of the lawns, ran from Deerpath Road to the lake, almost the distance of a mile. The mansion was a pale pink stone fashioned after a Roman villa and built early in the twentieth century; it sat on the bluffs high above the water's edge. In the afternoon a fresh snow had fallen upon the four-inch layer crusted beneath by a sudden freeze. The air was stinging sharp, clear and dry, so that the snow sifted gently like sand. The sky was electric with stars.

One might pray for such a night if he were host, Marcus thought, but it was rough on a man who didn't know his way. He had to stop twice to adjust the chains on the back wheels of the car, driving out from the city, and he suspected the Lakewood streets to have been deliberately laid out to confuse strangers. Actually, they followed for the most part the topography of the ravines. When he reached the stone gates of Tamarack and turned in after a chauffeured limousine, he patted the steering wheel and said aloud, "You and I are going to be the only Chevrolets present tonight." In front of the house he gave it up to a red-cheeked Irishman in a fur cap with whom he thought the car at least might have a rapport.

Listening to his name announced, he tried to remember when last he had heard himself called out from a crowd. On a Saturday night in the barber shop. Winthrop shook his hand and suggested that he go up and have a quick whisky to warm him.

Marcus thanked him, but alone, he stood a moment admiring the foyer in all its ornate grandeur. The staircases, describing roughly the shape of a horseshoe, were pure Italian marble, the balustrade running up one side, round the balcony, and down the other with each baluster an individual carving. He could not resist putting his hand to a cupid's buttocks, for there is a sensuousness to marble akin to that of delicate flesh. Nothing he could do would conceal the fact that he was out of place, so Marcus stood and stared, almost defiantly. He could feel the constriction of a dress suit that no longer fitted him well. He was just at the point of belligerent self-consciousness when a lean-necked, jeweled woman, nearing forty, he supposed, goodlooking in a horse-womanish way, came up to him and said,

"You look like someone I ought to know."

"I feel like someone somebody ought to know," Marcus said, and introduced himself.

"I'm Sylvia Fields. You're not one of the governor's bright young men, are you?"

"I voted for him, if that's what you mean."

"How vulgar of you to use that word," Miss Fields said mockingly. Marcus knew who she was: an heiress with leftist politics, a maverick if not a horsewoman. "Come in next to the fire," she said, again with a trace of mischief. She drew him toward the drawing room, a servant opening the double doors as they approached. It was from here, Marcus realized, the music had been coming. A few people were listening, as the quartet deserved, but most of them were gathered in small groups at either end of the room. Miss Fields' rather metallic voice carried above the music and the murmur of conversation. "I've just had a fabulous conversation I'm dying to repeat to someone. I don't suppose you know Eleanor Gluck?"

"No. The opera singer?"

"That's Alma Gluck. No relation, I'm sure. But the place is swimming in opera stars."

"Floating, don't you mean?" Marcus said, for he had observed several buxom and dramatic-looking women.

Miss Fields laughed. "What were we saying? My conversation with Eleanor. I shan't even try to describe her to you except that she's got an upper lip that's pure gristle. D'you know what I mean?" She stiffened her own by way of illustration.

Marcus nodded and smiled.

" 'Oh, Sylvia,' she said to me," and Sylvia swished two imitative fingers on Marcus's sleeve, " 'what are you and I doing here at all, will you tell me, in the house of a man campaigning to be mayor? *You,* of course, do do extraordinary things—but nothing common.' I said something about the office of mayor not having to be common, and she said, 'Oh, but it *does.* It's like the House of Representatives. They all seem to me *so* uncouth.' I said, 'Abraham Lincoln was in the House of Representatives.' And she said, 'That's *exactly* what I mean, darling.' "

Marcus laughed. "I wonder what would happen if I were to shout: 'Three cheers for Roosevelt!' "

"You'd be killed," she said amiably. "Shall we have a drink?"

"Right now I'd give half the night for one," Marcus said.

"Don't be profligate. You may find something worth saving it for." She looked at him frankly, in such open appraisal that Marcus could feel a tingle in the back of his neck. Then she said, "I know who you are! You're Jonathan Hogan's son."

Marcus nodded.

She hooked a bony hand through his arm. "I adore that man." She led him across the drawing room to a small bar camouflaged among the potted plants. There she introduced him to her brother, Anthony, two other young men, and then to George Bergner and his wife who joined them at that moment.

Bergner corrected her introduction from Mr. Hogan to Dr. Hogan, which gave Marcus the satisfaction of being identified on his own. He had assumed there was purpose to this invitation: he knew inquiries had been made about him, but so far as direct communication from Winthrop after the January interview, he had had none. Also, so far as his career was concerned, he had put the name Bergner out of his mind. Now he began to pick up all sorts of fantasies. A man he might safely assume to be the surgeon's son had recognized him. He kept trying to think where he had heard of George Bergner himself.

"Fellows, let's invite Sylvia and the doctor," young Tony Fields cried. "You, too, Bergners."

"To what?" Sylvia said. "Whenever I'm included in Tony's plans it means I've got to take the blame."

Fields was a handsome boy, many years younger than his sister. "We want to borrow the Wileys' sleigh and horses. They won't call dinner for an hour. Wouldn't you love a gallop along the lake?"

She shuddered. "No!"

"Come on, Syl. You're getting old."

"Some day I'll admit it. What am I supposed to do?"

"Get permission." Tony smiled ingratiatingly.

"What do I say to him? 'Excuse me, Wiley, my brother and I would like the keys to your horse'?" To the bartender she said, "A large scotch and a little water, please." When they were served, she touched her glass to Marcus's and then went off in search of the owner of the sleigh.

Marcus was aware the while of being under Bergner's scrutiny. Finally Bergner said to him, "Have you met my father yet?"

"No, not yet."

"He's here," Bergner said, a remark that seemed to put Marcus right back on his own again.

It was some moments later, when Bergner said, "I met your father in Washington, Hogan," that Marcus realized his present political job: Winthrop's campaign manager. "It's too bad he didn't stick it out. They needed him."

"He didn't think so," Marcus said.

"The only way you know you're needed down there is when they refuse to accept your resignation. I'm on a sort of reverse loan myself just now." He volunteered the latter information, Marcus supposed, lest it be thought his own resignation had been accepted.

"To elect Winthrop?" Marcus said.

"It'll be a feather in my cap if I do." Bergner gave a short laugh. "And I'll be up to my ass in tar if I don't."

His wife was the only woman within earshot, and she seemed not to have heard. She smiled when Marcus glanced her way. He thought she wanted terribly to be included.

"Tally-ho," Sylvia said, returning.

Marcus had no desire to go sleigh-riding. It was something one did with a girl when both were very young. He was himself between ages, neither envying youth nor finding in it yet a challenge, as apparently Sylvia Fields did.

"You'll have to be my date for the time being, Dr. Hogan. Utterly safe. I've promised to drive the horses. But somebody's got to remember—I always forget—'gee' is for left and 'haw' is for right, isn't it?"

"The Gees and the Haws," Marcus said, "stand up and be counted. What side are you on?"

"Marvelous!" Sylvia cried. "The Gees and the Haws."

"Actually," Marcus said, "it's the Haws and the Haw-nots."

He was groaned over and howled upon and carried off, going far more willingly than he had anticipated a few moments before.

The sleighing party careened off the driveway and across the lawn at the approach of an automobile. Everyone shouted, "Gee!" and then in the car's wake, "Haw," although it was the hand on the reins to which the horses responded.

Within the car, Martha Fitzgerald looked out the back window after the sleighers, a little sad that they were going away. She was pleased to have been invited to the ball, and surprised, considering her flare-up at Dr. Winthrop when last she had seen him. Everyone at school was envious, the nuns disapproving because it was Lent, all of which had but spiced the anticipation. Now, however, her natural shyness was tempering the pleasure.

Dr. Winthrop came across the foyer to meet them. Martha could hear the clack of his heels on the marble floor. She had never seen such elegance although her mother had told her of this house. It belonged, Martha felt, somewhere back in history, say, the days of the Congress of Vienna. There was even chamber music playing somewhere nearby.

"Elizabeth," Dr. Winthrop said and took her mother's hand.

"You look well, Alexander."

"Now I am," he said, and Martha wondered if he had been ill. He extended his hand to her. "And so you've come at last to visit me, Martha."

She put her hand in his. He released it at once for which she was grateful and a little ashamed for being so. He spoke as though she had been avoiding his house, and, of course, she had been, but she did not think he knew it. She could feel the tightness of the skin upon her forehead and knew the vein was showing in the middle. "Thank you for inviting me, Dr. Winthrop."

He turned to her father. "Walter, at least a dozen ladies have been asking where you were. I've promised you to all of them. Get out of that, my friend."

"Wouldn't I be the great fool to try?" Fitzgerald said, making the others laugh. Martha felt proud of him.

Her mother was speaking with friends whom Martha did not know. Nor did she sense any special welcome for her and her father. They were probably musical people. She and her father went into the drawing room, her mother waving after them. A manservant passing an enormous tray of champagne stopped before them.

"May I, papa?"

He nodded and they both took glasses. "Have you not had champagne before?"

"Not out of a glass of my own," she said.

He toasted: "To my daughter, who is as beautiful as any woman present tonight."

Martha smiled broadly, and then, self-conscious, cast her eyes down and sipped the wine. She supposed she was rather pretty. She wore a new formal gown, green silk taffeta, tight-bodiced, the skirt wide and a little noisy when she walked. Now and then she glanced at her father over the rim of her glass. His eyes were searching around the room, presumably for some of the ladies of whom Dr. Winthrop had spoken. No one came up to them, and she supposed he was handicapped by her presence. She could never think of anything to say at the moment conversation seemed most necessary. She sipped again from the bubbly glass.

Then she said, "Did you ever read *Handy Andy*, papa?"

"Never."

It was a book Annie had read aloud to her over and over, often at Martha's request, Annie laughing until she had tears in her eyes which had made Martha laugh more at her even than at the book.

"There's a very funny passage where he opens a bottle of champagne and puts all the candles out with it."

"And hits the lord and master in the eye with the cork, does he?"

"Yes," Martha said. "How did you know?"

"I know how they write an Irish fool," he said coldly.

"But it was written by an Irishman, I think," she said after a moment's thought.

"I'm sure it was, more's the shame."

Something has discomfited him, and whatever it was, she had unintentionally aggravated it. He was always open to hurt but never to consolation. She had been rebuffed too often to try now to discover him. They stood for what seemed a very long time silent and privately miserable. In a way they were like prisoners bound to each other by invisible chains—at once resentful and sympathetic of the other's plight, loving and abhorring.

Martha broke the bond, her voice too loud: "I want to speak to mother. You don't mind, do you, papa?"

"Of course, I don't mind. I think I'll go up to the Trophy Room myself."

He was gone from the drawing room before ever she found her mother so that she did not need to carry out the pretense. Instead she found a chair apart and listened to the music.

The sleighriders returned just as the announcement was made that dinner was about to be served. They dispersed to repair the disorders of the wind and reassembled in the hall as other people began to converge there, moving toward the dining hall. Marcus had assumed the sleighing party would dine together, supposing he would go in with Sylvia Fields, but something happened which he did not understand until some time later. At the moment he was about to speak to her, Sylvia turned and called out, "Tony!"

Her brother grinned and shrugged a little, waited, and gave his arm to his sister. To Marcus she said, "I expect you to ask me to dance later. You will, won't you?"

He said, "I'll ask, but you'd be well advised to refuse."

"I am reckless in many things, Marcus." And her eyes lingered a moment on his as though she craved understanding of the unexplained.

She and her brother proceeded toward the dining room. Marcus glanced at Bergner, who was watching them, a tight, wry grin on his lips.

"I feel as though I'd been jilted," Marcus said.

"How do you think she feels?"

Marcus did not answer, not understanding.

"She's been in love for years with a man who can't see it."

"But not her brother," Marcus said.

"No. Not her brother. But sitting above the salt, she's in a better position for suffering." Bergner put his hand to Marcus's elbow. "I understand my father expected you to be brought to him before this. I'd just like to be the one to make that introduction." To his wife he said, "Louise, wait here for me. I shall be right back."

"Give your father my love," she said after them.

"I know where to find him," Bergner explained, steering Marcus into the drawing room again. "I need only follow the music."

Marcus saw the old man in the distance. At least his white hair would make one suppose he was old. Almost everyone else was at the doors on their way to dinner. Only the old gentleman sat content, the old gentleman and, apart, a very young girl. Passing, Marcus glanced her way and stopped, for at the instant of their recognition of one another, her quick smile would have stayed him on his way to the moon.

He murmured a word of excuse to George Bergner and went up to Martha, knowing himself to be also grinning, and feeling a pleasure that seemed inordinate to have been derived from a girl's smile. He wondered if she could possibly be as glad to see him as she seemed, and indeed, as he hoped. He noticed the height of her forehead and the blue vein of shyness.

"You wouldn't by any chance be waiting for me?" he said.

She shook her head no, and then at a turn in his expression, affirmatively, smiling again.

"And will you go into dinner with me?"

"Thank you, Doctor Hogan."

"Your eyes are green," he said. "I thought they were blue."

"Sometimes they are," she said. "It's the dress."

"Don't go away. I shall come right back here for you."

He rejoined George, suddenly more confident, much more confident than he had been at any time since entering this house.

"Father," George said when they reached the old man, "this is Marcus Hogan."

Dr. Bergner put on his glasses with a trembling hand that Marcus noticed steadying as the glasses touched the nose, and then very slowly, the old gentleman looked at him from shoes to pate. "You go a long ways up, don't you?" he said. And only then rose from the chair and shook Marcus's hand. "I thought your name was Thaddeus."

"It is on the record, doctor," Marcus said, "but I was called 'tadpole' too often as a kid and I didn't like it."

The old man gave a spurt of sound which had the effect of fluffing his dark mustache. "George Allan here did not care much for his name either. But I think, given the wisdom of his—how old are you? —thirty-two years, he would say now it was about what he could have expected from his father. Louise got a headache?"

"No. She's meeting me in the hall. She sent you her love."

Dr. Bergner grunted, and said then to Marcus, "I want to speak to you after dinner." And to George: "Is there a place we can go to talk, Hogan and I?"

"Why don't you try the Trophy Room?"

"Not till I'm atrophied!" his father cried, and with an air of self-pleasure, he asked Marcus, "Do you like puns?"

Marcus nodded slowly. "I'll trade them, blow for blow with you, doctor."

The old man took his arm and squeezed it slightly, a gesture Marcus noted was not lost on his son. There was not the best of feeling there, he realized.

Dr. Bergner, his hand still on Marcus's arm, and starting them toward the doors, said loudly, "Where the hell is that Fields woman? She was supposed to fetch me in to dinner."

"Sylvia's mother," George explained. "We're an inbred lot out here."

A highly powdered woman of seventy or so, a tiara of jewels on her head, came toward them. Marcus was thereafter to think of her and speak privately of her as "The Dowager."

"Where have you been?" Dr. Bergner demanded.

"Where the king goes on foot," the dowager said without trace of a smile. "George, Louise looks desolate out there, like a cat at a crossroads."

The elder Bergner said, "I want you to meet Doctor Hogan, Alicia, a young man from whom I just might accept assistance one of these days."

The dowager looked at Marcus scrutinously. "Do I know the family?"

"You will, you will," the old gentleman said, and turning to the musicians who were now putting their instruments away, he called out quite as though he were about to castigate them, "The andante in that last Schubert, gentlemen . . ." He shook his head so that his jowl and mustache quivered, ". . . never heard it played better."

Marcus, with a gesture to Martha to be patient, waiting for him, asked, "Doctor Bergner, where will you want to see me after dinner, sir? We didn't settle it."

The old man put the question to his son.

"There's a library on the second floor. You won't be disturbed there for years," George said.

"But I like to be disturbed," Dr. Bergner said, with malice in his eye. He released Marcus and gave his arm to Mrs. Fields to whom he added, "Especially by Alicia."

George waited for him although Marcus did not ask it while he went for Martha, and when Marcus introduced her, George said, "How marvelous!" It was a remark Marcus did not like even if it were a gratuitous bit of praise and this he somehow doubted. There was, he suspected, a meanness in George Allan Bergner which perhaps came of having a father too big for him. The truth was, Marcus was feeling protective of the tall, fragile-seeming girl whose fingers rested lightly on his arm as they moved toward the dining hall. Therefore, when Bergner suggested that Marcus take Louise in and allow him to take Martha, he resented it fiercely, the more so because he could do nothing but oblige.

Martha said, "I should think we'll all be together at the table, won't we?" Something within herself made her want to withdraw just a little from Dr. Hogan the very instant of coming close to him, not because she in any way feared him—and she had liked him from the very first sight of him—but rather because she feared the disquiet in herself.

So Martha went into the dining hall on the arm of George Bergner. Passing her father who had a rather plump and operatic-looking woman at his side, she gravely nodded to him, and he looked pleased. His face was flushed so that she was sure he had had a drink or two, sufficient, she hoped, to soothe whatever ailed him. (Annie, no matter what she administered, be it feast or physic, would always say, "Take it. It's good for what ails you.")

George Bergner said, "Do you like Lakewood—from what you've seen of it?"

"Very much."

"In spring it's much nicer. Trillium everywhere and apple blossoms."

"I know," Martha said. "I go to St. Cecilia's College."

"Ah! One of their Marriageable Daughters?" Bergner said.

Martha laughed. His reference was to the placards in the village store windows advertising the school play: they were doing a version of *Pride and Prejudice* and the placards read: "St. Cecilia's College presents *Marriageable Daughters*."

"That's rather blatant advertising, I'd say," he went on teasingly. "And are you all really marriageable?"

"Yes. Only some more than others, I guess."

To Marcus, Bergner said, "Below the salt for us, wouldn't you say?"

"Well below," Marcus said. "I shall be lucky if I'm not put out in the yard."

The table seemed to stretch from one end of the long room to the other, set for two hundred people and with three wine glasses at every place. Actually, there were ten tables, each far enough from the other to permit servers to pass between, but the shimmering whiteness of the linen sustained the illusion of unity. At either end of the hall a stone fireplace was bright with the blaze of six-foot logs, the glow of which, along with that of myriad table candles, reflected in the crystal chandeliers and gave the effect of prismatic, changing light.

Bergner asked to choose their seats, remarking that they would see why presently. It seemed a curious choice he made, to face—beyond the people opposite them—an enormous dark velvet drapery. The other walls were hung with tapestries. Then when everyone was seated, the overhead lights were extinguished, leaving only the candlelight, and the draperies were drawn. They had concealed a dais where presumably dinner was served on lesser occasions, but beyond that there was a series of twelve French doors, permitting the diners this night the vista of a splendid sweep of untrammeled snow.

"My God!" was Marcus's awed tribute.

Martha said, "I wish there was a rabbit—or something alive."

Dr. Hogan looked round at her, amused. He did not say anything. Indeed they said very little to each other throughout dinner, the Bergners on either side of them equal to every silence, intruding upon it, but in a way—at least to Martha—leaving it undisturbed. She could not remember ever having felt so perfectly at ease among strangers.

Marcus, too, was occupied largely with thoughts and emotions which Louise's amiable chatter did not disturb. She had a fund of unmalicious gossip quite suitable to first acquaintanceship. She was really a very gentle girl, her accent Southern, and after a time she told him she had come from Richmond, Virginia. Marcus, meanwhile, anticipating his post-dinner talk with one of the great surgeons in the country, could not help going over in his mind the Traders City hospitals in which, doubtless, Dr. Bergner had the last word: Metropolitan, Mount Clement, and Bishop's, to Marcus's knowledge. Surely, room for T. M. Hogan, M.D., would not overcrowd the staff of one of them. Was a residency too much to hope for? A toast was proposed and drunk to the health of their host.

"Wouldn't it kill them here to drink to his election?" Bergner said, directing his remark to Marcus across Martha.

"Bad manners, do you think?" said Marcus, remembering Sylvia's appraisal of the company.

"Where I come from," Louise said, "only gentlemen go into politics."

Bergner said, "Where you come from, dear, there *are* only gentlemen. Gentlemen and squalor. That's almost a pun, isn't it? My father would be proud of me." He laughed unpleasantly.

Marcus, addressing himself to Bergner, asked, "Who is the dark woman at Dr. Winthrop's right?"

"That's my mother," Martha said.

"Is it? She's very beautiful." He was grateful that the girl was too shy to more than glance at him for the moment, and he deliberately avoided meeting Bergner's eyes which he knew to be waiting his. The fact was he had been startled at the discovery, and he was for some time thereafter preoccupied with it. He could not escape associating it with what he knew of Sylvia Fields, and her proximity with her brother, Dr. Bergner and her mother, to the head of the table. It was not entirely unwarranted to suppose the man with whom she was in love was Winthrop. But Mrs. Fitzgerald sat on his right, and in some remote corner of his memory, Marcus had registered a bit of University gossip.

Martha asked, "Mr. Bergner . . ."

"Please call me George," he interrupted. "I'm not that old despite the recession." He pointed to his hair line.

"George," she amended. "My father is the man down fourth from my mother. He has white hair. Do you know who the woman is sitting on the far side of him?"

Bergner, having looked, said, "Why, that's Gertrude Milgrim, the opera singer."

"How wonderful!" Martha said. "But poor papa! He can't even carry a tune."

Bergner laughed aloud, an inordinate burst that angered Marcus and prompted Louise to lean across the table and ask, "What did she say?" Then to Martha, "What did you say, honey?"

Marcus answered. "She said her father was unmusical and isn't it strange that he should get an opera singer as his dinner partner."

"That's what I like best about Alexander," Louise said. "He mixes just all sorts of people."

Martha, having observed that Marcus did not repeat precisely what she had said, sensed something to be remiss. It occurred to her then that her father might be under the pall—in George Bergner's terms—for being several down the table from the top. His own father was sitting across but one from her mother. She said, meaning that a friend is not compromised by a mere seating arrangement, "Dr. Winthrop is my father's best friend."

"So I've heard." Bergner touched his wine glass to Martha's. "To friendship."

Had he looked at Marcus then he would have seen the color of wrath and he might not soon have forgotten it.

Well over an hour later as they left the table, Martha asked Marcus, "Would you like to meet my mother?"

"I should—very much," Marcus said, and deliberately abandoned Louise to her husband. And as they moved among the intermingling guests, he murmured, "A deserving couple."

Martha said, "What did you say?"

"Something nasty, I'm afraid. But not nasty enough."

And so he met Elizabeth Fitzgerald, a woman whom her daughter resembled only in height and a certain proud bearing. He supposed Mrs. Fitzgerald to be a person of great passion and deep reserve. That her daughter worshiped her was plain, and it was likely too that she craved more love of her mother than was allowed her . . . if he were right in the other matter.

Professor Fitzgerald came up to him and shook his hand. He said, "I'm glad to see you here." But he did not even mention the young doctor's name.

Marcus observed Sylvia Fields watching him, and as soon as the chance came, he introduced Martha to her and her brother. Sylvia, even bitter in love, he felt, would be a far kinder person than George Bergner. He tended, of course, to romanticize in his appraisal of all women.

Something with which Marcus had not reckoned was Tony Fields' readiness to take over the only person as young as himself present. George Bergner, who had by then caught up, was the first to see it outside Marcus. Elaborately he set about repairing the damage he knew he had done to any possible friendship between himself and Marcus. It was, though Marcus did not know it then, the pattern in all his relationships: his was a long history of amendment, restitution. In fact, he got on toward his goal with people by overcompensating to them for an earlier and deliberate affront: not to accept him at such a moment would be tantamount to rejecting an apology. His way to Marcus's heart was to be won, it seemed, by hacking down young Tony Fields. He began a loud recital of Tony's athletic achievements; the implication plainly was that Tony was a playboy. To Fields himself he said:

"Isn't this your time of year to be off somewhere skiing, Tony?"

"I'm working," the boy said.

"Oh. A marvelous experience, isn't it?"

"It's a loathsome experience. Work is a Puritan notion, the only thing out of all the tenets of Christianity they hung onto and the one thing guaranteed to keep the human being on the level of the jackass."

He was talking nonsense, but everyone within earshot was amused, Marcus observed.

Tony, his handsome face flushed with excitement and the pleasure of hearing his own voice, elaborated: "What the devil difference is there in me sitting at a desk behind a stack of Poor's industrial ratings on the one side and a stack of Moody's industrial ratings on the other, and the donkey chasing after the carrot in front of his nose? By heavens, the donkey at least cares what's in the carrot!"

Bergner said, and then abandoned the defense, "Tony, you'd better care, old boy. You'd better care."

"But I care very much," Tony said. "I'm rather fond of carrots."

Martha turned that sudden and wonderful smile of hers on the boy, and Marcus thought that with Bergner to defend him he would not need a prosecutor.

Martha was no more than a little amused by Tony Fields, and she gave him more attention than she truly wanted to, but it occurred to her the moment he introduced them that Marcus wished to disengage himself. She supposed he thought her very young.

Then, just as he was about to go off with Dr. Bergner, Marcus looked around. "Please don't go far," he said. "I shall be back."

Marcus strode self-consciously alongside Dr. Bergner. It was hard to keep step with him, especially on the highly polished floors, for he had the habit of pulling up suddenly every few steps to draw several deep breaths before proceeding. High blood pressure, likely. The servant guiding them threw open the library door, and then touched a switch which lighted several milk glass sconces along the wall as well as the reading lamps. Marcus's first thought was that the room had remained unchanged, possibly undisturbed, from the day a decorator had put his imprimatur on it. The servant lighted the fireplace and told them where the bell cord hung if they should wish anything.

Bergner was rubbing his hands together, looking round the room. "Well, well," he said, "sixty feet of red vellum, twenty of blue. What's that?" He trembled a finger at a row of white leather bindings, gold-tooled, near where Marcus stood.

Marcus said, "Dickens, of all things." He took a volume from the shelf. "I got my Dickens in six point type and paper as rough as an elephant's hide. These aren't even cut."

Dr. Bergner took his glasses from his pocket and put them on, tilting his head back then to look at Marcus through them. "Wouldn't it offend you to see grubby little finger marks all over that exquisite paper?"

"Not much," Marcus said and put back the book.

Dr. Bergner gave the gutteral explosion which in him passed for a laugh and put away his glasses. He chose a chair in front of the fire and indicated the one in which he expected Marcus to sit. "Why don't you have some brandy, Hogan? I'd like to see that—that tassel in operation. I shouldn't be surprised if it plays 'Swanee River.'"

"Will you have something yourself, doctor?"

"No, damn it. Doctor's orders, ha!" He scowled. "Who's this man Fitzgerald?"

Marcus told him.

"He's an ass. I listened to him prate all through dinner. 'Ma-*teer*ialistic scientists.'" He mocked Fitzgerald's accent. "He's an Irish bigot. I supposed till now he was a politician—one of those indispensables to a man who wants to be mayor of our metropolis." Again Dr. Bergner groped for his glasses. He did not keep them on for any length of time ever, merely needing them when he wanted to take a good look at a man, as he did now at Marcus. He said abruptly, "What qualifies you, Hogan—aside from the fact that your mother's grandmother's grandmother's grandmother missed the first boat to America—to become an associate of mine?"

Marcus grinned. He supposed a number of people were afraid of this old tyrant, and he had no doubt that Dr. Bergner was tyrannical. His daughter-in-law, Marcus was sure, lived in terror of him. Marcus did not say a word; he stretched his hands out in front of Bergner, palms downward, fingers separated, the hands absolutely steady.

Bergner looked at them, his lower lip shooting out a bit presently so that it pulled down the corners of his mouth. "Well, well," he said at last, and drew a deep breath. "Well, well."

Marcus dropped his hands.

After a few seconds, Bergner said, "All right. We'll see what's in those hands, we shall, but not until we've seen what else is in you. I shall pay you a small salary, doctor . . . and since I have a son a lawyer, he'll draw up the contract."

"A salary, doctor?" Marcus said, his confidence diminishing.

"A small one, to be sure." He found his glasses with no trouble this time and looked at Marcus. "I'm hiring a servant, doctor. Oh yes, that's what it amounts to, hiring a servant."

Marcus felt something like a slow crumbling inside of him: his dream of residency in a good hospital. It was not a new experience, but the events of the night had not prepared him for it.

"An indentured one, at that," he said.

"You do not like it, doctor?"

"Not much, sir."

"Well, well." The old man leaned back. "Perhaps you would like me to assist you, Doctor Hogan?"

"I can conceive of the day's coming when that might happen," Marcus said in quiet bitterness. He had had no right, of course, to the vision he had got of himself among the glitter of the night's company; he had been conjuring success in spite of himself. He had been thinking of position or his pride would not be suffering as it now was.

Bergner said, and his jowl and mustaches shook with the vehemence of his words, "So can I, but I do not look forward to it, doctor. And I will not look backward in the company of an untried cub."

His words touched Marcus to the marrow. He said, "Can I live on the salary, Doctor Bergner?"

"If you live alone you can manage. Oh yes."

"I live with my father."

"Ah, yes, yes. Jonathan Hogan. Does he measure himself, I wonder, by the amount of money he gets for what he does, eh?"

"I don't think my father has ever measured himself, doctor. Or for that matter, any man."

"Well, well." Again Bergner's lip shot out, pulling down the corners of his mouth. "Shall we meet next Wednesday then, say, in my office, and draw up the contract?"

There was no use pressing on the amount of the salary even, Marcus thought. He was destined, it seemed, to a life of apprenticeship. "Yes, sir."

"Be there at twelve then. Now, doctor . . ."

Marcus looked at him, for he paused, waiting full attention.

"Put out your hands to me again the way you did a few moments ago."

Marcus held out his hands, palms downward, and saw himself the tremor in them: his emotions and his nerves had responded badly to the interview.

Very slowly, Dr. Bergner brought his palsied, loose-skinned hands to the level of the younger man's, and as Marcus watched, all but mesmerized, he saw them grow steadier, steadier by far than his, and then all but still. And looking up he saw the hard lines of discipline, the act of will, showing upon the old man's face. The watery gray eyes under the dark, jagged brows proclaimed a fierce triumph. Marcus was already the master's servant.

Winthrop traditionally opened the dance by taking into it the grande dame of Lake Shore society, Alicia Fields. She had been judge, jury and jailer to him in Lakewood, at first resenting his buying Tamarack, then condescending to advise him on his household, not always wisely, and sometimes with deliberate malice. He sometimes wondered if her tolerance of him did not begin and grow commensurately to the aging of her unmarried daughter. It was only a year ago that she had said to him, "Alexander, I think you may call me Alicia now." He still reverted sometimes to "Mrs. Fields." Now the old lady could scarcely dance a step, and in her old age she was becoming a bawd. It amused him only in that he remembered how diffident he had been in her staid presence some fifteen years before.

They walked onto the ballroom floor, arm in arm, and that sufficed to satisfy tradition. He guided her then to a chair at the wall and sat with her through the first dance.

"So at last you're on the road to fame, Alexander. It's the way you've always wanted to go, via politics, isn't it?"

"Yes, though I didn't always know it."

"You knew it. I knew it. And now I'm glad. Shall I tell you why?"

"I think I know, Alicia."

She darted her eyes at him without turning her head very much. "And you don't want me to say it?"

He merely shrugged.

"It's all over?"

He frowned, not because she had said the words, but because it seemed not irrevocably so, their not having been said by anyone till then. He nodded slightly in affirmation.

"Then what is she doing here tonight?"

"It's better," he said, meaning that it was better not to make conspicuous an absence.

The old lady leaned toward him and said, "I shall be watching you when you dance with her, Alexander."

"Do!" he said sharply.

She gave a dry laugh. "I thought so."

"You have a dirty mind, Alicia."

"Its cultivation is one of the few pleasures left me. Go. I can see your impatience."

He shook his head and smiled down at her. "You're wrong." It was a lie, but it was the kind of lie he had to tell himself also, assuming that in time he would not know it from the truth.

"Alexander, do you know what would be a genuine boon to your candidacy? A wife. You could even do it for the newsreels."

"I'll think about it, Alicia," he said, humoring her.

"Do. It's the only way to seal things off, to stanch the wounds. Don't you think I know? I lost a husband when we were still in love. I have a boy to prove it, twenty years his sister's junior, and a child of passion. Don't you believe me?"

"You were fortunate in love, Alicia," he said, uncomfortable always when people spoke frankly of the intimacies of their own lives. He took her hand for a moment, using the show of affection to facilitate his escape. "I shall be back."

"Too late, too late," she cried, and waved him off with a delicate hand.

In calculated time he danced at last with Elizabeth, so dearly familiar that night and yet distant now as a virgin nun. They did not speak until the music stopped, the players changing songs. He said then as they touched hands again, "I don't know how much I could bear of this."

"There is not so much to bear, Alexander. And you're going to be mayor of Traders City. Isn't that enough?"

"I don't know. Before God, I don't know. There's something about trying for office I think must spoil a man before he has a chance to prove himself worthy of it."

"You've grown already, Alex. And there is something about high office, so I've heard, that raises even little men to greatness. And you have never been a little man."

"I hope to God you're right, Elizabeth." Then, when he began to ache anticipating how soon this dance would end, he said, "I shall love you always . . . and be grateful."

She threw back her head and looked at him from beneath the dark lashes he had felt so often brush his cheek. Her smile mocked him. "Ah, Alex, Alex, you do love sad songs."

"Don't you?" he said, sensing her doubt of his sincerity—or maturity.

"Not any more," she said, her brows arched—if he had but known it—to help hold back the tears. "I'm feeling almost gay these days."

"I'm glad," he said, hurt to the core.

And, mercifully, the dance for them was ended there.

In the course of a half-hour Martha and Tony Fields came to know a number of things—at once important and not important—about one another. For example, they learned that she preferred Verdi to Beethoven and he Beethoven to Verdi, an order of preference which in not many years would be reversed for both of them. Verdi opera being so popular that season of opera in Traders City, it was scarcely fashionable of her to admit a taste for it; that she did admit it Tony professed he found refreshing. Martha supposed she should be flattered. But after that she kept watching for Marcus's return.

She saw him as soon as he came into the ballroom, but when he stood so long outside the dance and if he saw her at all did not acknowledge it, she wondered if she had not imagined entirely his interest. She danced with George Bergner, and Bergner, seeing Marcus, contrived for reasons of his own to end their dance in his vicinity.

"Hello," Bergner said, "the interview is over, is it?"

To Martha, Marcus said, "I was thinking, standing here."

She felt the color rise to her face: he must know she had been waiting.

"Yes, George, the interview is over. I've just put your father in his car."

"Did you make a deal?" George asked directly.

Marcus looked at him. "He seems to feel the need of legal counsel. We three are to meet Wednesday morning."

George laughed. "I kind of hoped you'd tell him to go to hell. Somebody should some day."

"I should think you're in a better position to do it than most people," Marcus said, and turned to Martha. "May I?"

She nodded, and Bergner left them. Martha said, "You don't really want to dance, do you?"

"No, and I'm not very good at it. I don't know what I'd like to do—get drunk, run barefoot in the snow. How would you like to go on a grand tour of the establishment? I understand there's an art gallery somewhere."

"I'd prefer that to the other possibilities you mentioned," she said.

He smiled and they moved away from the dance. They had to go through the drawing room, on a servant's directions; there several older people had gathered in quiet talk before the fire. They suspended their conversations and peered around, some of them eerily from behind the tall chairbacks, as the young couple passed: it was one of those pictures which fasten upon the mind forever.

Martha whispered, "Do you see them?"

"Yes."

"Someday when I'm painting, I'll remember. Except that I seem already to have seen a painting of them."

Marcus stopped. "Say that again."

"I don't know just what I said. Only that as soon as I was seeing the picture of those people in my memory—it seemed I had first seen it long ago."

"What happened to me tonight is a little like that," Marcus said, and they went on. "I got my comeuppance. But I hadn't really earned it. But then, I haven't earned more than I got either—not in Dr. Bergner's terms." He wet his lips. "I didn't have that foolish sort of dream—the famous surgeon saying to me, 'My boy, you will be the greatest . . .' You know, that sort of thing? I just wanted a little place of my own in medicine—but with a title to it. There's the rub. I wanted the title, didn't I?" He looked at Martha but answered himself. "Resident, resident surgeon at Mount Clement, I wanted to hear them say. And who did I want to hear say it? Not my father. My father, if anybody, knows that titles have no meaning."

They went along and came then to a tiled passageway; the door from there opened upon a separate building, a wing built especially to house Dr. Winthrop's collection of paintings. Marcus read the instructions for lighting the gallery.

"Have you been here before? Have you seen the collection?"

"No," Martha said.

"And you paint, yourself?"

"Yes, but not very well."

He looked at her, his hand upon the door. "Do you know that you don't paint well?"

"No," she said tentatively.

"And you don't believe it for a moment, do you?"

"Perhaps for a moment," Martha said.

"I'm glad I caught you in that one," Marcus said, and grinned at her. "It makes me feel much better."

He held the door and they entered a large room, the ceiling of which was lighted through smoked glass. The windows were of medieval stained glass, lighted from outside by spotlights.

"I never saw the sun at night," Marcus said, looking from one window to the other, and then in paraphrase of the "purple cow" poem, "I never hoped to see it." He let it end there, unable to think of another line.

"And so loud, too," Martha said.

"The sun at night?" She nodded, and he said, "You have a nice way with words."

They turned to the paintings, thirty-seven of them, individually lighted, masters all, or the work of masters, but neither Martha nor Marcus had anything to say as they moved from one picture to the next, and when they had circled the room and were again near the door, Marcus said, "Say in one word—how you feel about all of these: one word, that's all you've got."

"Dead."

And it came easily, the word, for she had never had an experience quite similar. She would not have felt that way about two or three such paintings—after all, her awe of the great names in art would have bade her see what life there was and more—but the accumulative effect was numbing. And having said the word, she thought of being sealed within a tomb, the gorgeous crypt of an ancient monarch. "Aida," she said, as they left the gallery. "I should have said Aida."

"Very apt," Marcus said. "I was afraid at first that I was jaded."

"I wonder how Dr. Winthrop feels about them. I've never heard him talk about them at all."

"Maybe he doesn't know they're here," Marcus said. He turned off the gallery lights. "Now where shall we go? I think I want a drink. Do you mind?"

"I think I'd like one, too."

When they reached the marble hall again, he took her hand for a moment, and with his other hand pointed a shaking finger at the north staircase. "I thought I was going to come down those stairs owning half the world because I'd found a place in it."

"And you didn't."

"Oh, didn't I, though? That's exactly what I found—a place. He's hiring me at a salary."

Martha took champagne again while Marcus had a double whisky brought him, and they sat in the hall on a marble bench somewhat concealed beneath the arch of the stairway.

"I'm behaving badly," Marcus said, "and I know it. I've just re-membered something my father said when all this first came up—after I'd seen Winthrop—you know?" She nodded. "We were talk-ing about Bergner, Dr. Bergner, and he said I'd have to judge him by his patience, that a humble man was patient . . ."

"You admire your father very much, don't you, Marcus?"

"Yes. He's fine."

"How do you think he'll feel about it?"

Marcus gave a short laugh and then turned that question over in his mind. "You know, I don't suppose he'll think it's bad at all. He has a great deal of confidence in me."

Martha held to the idea she was building on. "And it won't mat-ter to your father, Marcus, will it, that it came about in a way through papa?" She felt almost ashamed when he looked at her for having contrived the shaft. She had become a little enviously aware of Marcus's regard for his father. This, together with her almost articulate realization that no one admired her father, prompted her to use that particularly feminine way of distracting a man: the in-sinuation of herself and an ailment of her own.

"Of course not," he said. And when he saw the color rise, he real-ized that he had hurt her. He finished his drink, and it was a hard swallow.

"It's all mixed up, isn't it?" Martha said, and putting down her glass on the floor beneath the bench, she sat, her hands in her lap.

"When I saw Dr. Bergner's hands shaking that way, I think I could have guessed that he would hurt you."

Marcus frowned: it was a strange observation.

"I knew a nun," Martha went on, "whose hands shook like that. She was an artist. She's in a sanatorium now, they say." And she told him then about Sister Mathilde and Genevieve Revere's painting. "I've not been able to tell that to anyone before. I don't know why I've told you. There's something a little wicked about it—not just morbid—isn't there?"

"A little," Marcus said. He was wise enough to hold back any glib explanation.

"But do you know what it is that I remember most about it, Marcus? The way she looked at me, so proud of being able to cry without the tears coming out of her eyes."

"Self-discipline," Marcus said, and his own thoughts leaped immediately to Dr. Bergner and his steadied hands.

"But in a wrong sort of way—like a cripple that's stronger than most people who aren't crippled. I suppose that's cruel of me, isn't it?"

"No, it's much the truth," he said.

"But why did I destroy the picture? That's what troubles me. It was a terrible thing to do."

He drew a deep breath. "God help us, Martha, when our consciences put us at the mercy of cripples."

"That's the difference between mercy and pity, isn't it?" she asked after a moment.

"You insist on going to the heart of matters, don't you?" He looked at her until she met his eyes. "Do you know, you've taken a great burden from me?"

Her smile was sudden. "I'm very glad."

"Someday I shall tell you about it," Marcus said, "but not now."

"I suppose we should go back to the dance now," Martha said.

He shook his head, but got up. "There's a view I want to see, and I know with whom I want to see it." He held out his hand.

She took it, rising, and they crossed the hall to the dining room. The long tables were already down, the velvet drapes drawn. They walked through the room hand in hand, and if the servants working there saw them, they never let on. Marcus parted the drapes and they stepped up on the dais, the darkness closing behind them.

The trees, the snow, all outdoors was whisper-still as they gazed out. Suddenly a deer came out of the woods, right up to the terrace.

"I ordered that for you," Marcus said.

"From Santa Claus?"

"There isn't any Santa Claus," he said. "But don't you worry." He put his hand to her cheek and turned her face to his and kissed her very gently, but lingeringly, for he felt the tremble of her lips. He wondered if she could hear his heart beat as he could hear it. "Now we had better go back," he said a moment later.

"Yes." The deer, when she looked, was gone. "Poor animal. I hope there's something out there for him."

"And for me," Marcus said, parting the curtain so that a shaft of light shone upon them. "There's nothing in this kind of living for me, Martha. You know that, don't you?" He indicated with a toss of his head the house within.

"Nor for me. I know that, too," she said, and went in before him.

• 12

ON MONDAY of the first week in April—the week before the primary elections—the tiger made his leap. Mike Shea declared all out for the mayor. Winthrop admitted that he was not altogether surprised, and only a little hurt; while he needed the regular party vote, he had come to the point where he was not going to be willing to pay for it; he had no intention of packing City Hall with men who could deliver votes but not much else. He even confessed to George Bergner on the afternoon the news broke that Mike could not very well have been expected to support a man who all but promised the destruction of his machine.

Bergner was sitting in the Winthrop headquarters, his back and backside aching from too many hours on a folding chair, his elbows slivered from the raw wood table top that rested on two sawhorses, and wondered if the time had come to give Winthrop a broadside of the truth. It was incredible to him that a man in Winthrop's position could be so naïve. He was also convinced that he had been duped himself.

"It was my understanding, Alex, when I took on your campaign, that Mike was keeping hands off right down to the wire."

Winthrop shrugged impatiently. "It was mine, too, for that matter."

"How did you happen to pick me—out of all the politicians in the state—for your campaign manager?"

Winthrop hedged, getting then his first intimation that Mike, instead of merely testing Winthrop's strength, had been probing his enemy's weakness. "I knew your history. Your father's a friend of mine. . . ."

"My father never put in a good word for me in his life. It wasn't by any chance Mike Shea's idea, was it?"

"And if it was?"

Bergner laughed unpleasantly. "I'd like to know, that's all. I think you owe it to me, Alex, to play square now, at least. You've got a fortune to fall back on. All I've got is my wits, and after this debacle, I don't think much of them myself. What are you going to do now, Alex?"

"Wait a minute," Winthrop said. "Are you quitting? Is that what you're saying?"

Bergner got up from the squeaking chair. "No, I'm not quitting. It's too late for that."

"Then what are you getting at? You know what I'm going to do—fight all the way to Tuesday. After that, I don't know yet."

"Let me try a little prophecy: you'll shake hands with Mike Shea and go back to the bargain basement, the Health Department, the *pissoir* of City Hall."

Winthrop, sitting at the end of the table, pushed away from it and looked to see who was present. "I must seem like a dead duck, George, if you're willing to take out my innards." He called out to two campaign workers folding handbills at the front of the room: "Ladies, take the afternoon off! Right now!" He did not smoke often, but a package of cigarets lay on the table. He got up and lit one, waiting for the workers' departure. When they were gone, he said, "Now, then, George, spit it out."

Bergner, faced up to, struck another tone. He had had his moment of pleasurable venom. "For Christ's sake, Alex, do you know what we've done between us? We've brought the governor of this state down to the size of Mike Shea. If you don't win, the governor's through. He gave you full endorsement. Let's face facts, political facts: if Mike's man wins the primary, when fall comes Mike Shea will be doing business directly with the President of the United States, not the governor. F.D.R. is going to be running for re-election himself, and if Mike's the boy who's got the votes, let me tell you, Alex, the President is the greatest politician of them all."

"I know, I know," Winthrop said. "That's why I've never altogether trusted him."

"I never altogether trust any man, including myself," Bergner said, thumping down in the chair again. "Why the hell couldn't we have had some decent chairs in this place? You could afford them . . . I can't say I didn't suspect something, the half-assed way some of the wardheelers sashayed in and out of here."

Winthrop went over in his mind that first luncheon conversation with Mike Shea. The place—Patsy's Steakhouse—the very timing of it, should have forewarned him: it came on the heels of the governor's veto on the Traders City airport.

"It's a wonder I didn't see it myself," he said at last. "I'm so used to people coming at me with the damnedest ideas, the most outrageous, damn fool schemes . . ."

"That's because you're a rich man," Bergner said.

Winthrop said, "I had a fellow come in with an idea for a water purifier; for twenty-two million dollars he could put one in every home in America."

"Cheap at twice the price."

"I expect frankness, don't you see?" Winthrop went on, convincing himself. It was Shea's duplicity that hurt.

"That's what made you a perfect setup."

"A pawn," Winthrop said, "a god-damned pawn, that's what he used me for." He was always slow to anger.

"That's about it," George fed the anger. "We're to be off the board before the real game starts."

Winthrop crushed out the cigaret. "A filthy habit, smoking. Bad for the heart, too. Did you see my column last Thursday?" He had continued throughout the campaign to contribute his regular piece on health to ALEXANDER WINTHROP, M.D. in the *Dispatch*.

"I must have missed that one," Bergner murmured. He had never read one in his life.

Winthrop began to pace the room, the length of the table and sometimes around it, the energy fairly oozing out of him. He looked healthy, fit. He was like a breath of fresh air on the political scene:

that was what people said at the grass root level. Not that there had been any grass roots for many a year in the part of the city where the vote was heavy. They had long ago been stamped out by the wardheelers. The people might cheer for Winthrop, but they would vote for Mike Shea's man. It was a great shame, Bergner calculated, that the Republicans hadn't run Winthrop: the man they had was no dynamo, the mayor would beat him handily.

It was curious, how closely parallel the two men's thinking ran. When Winthrop turned and asked his question, Bergner would have sworn he was about to say the same thing.

Winthrop said, "Is there any reason I can't file as an independent candidate if I lose in the primary?"

Bergner moistened his lips. "None. Look at La Guardia in New York."

"This is Traders City, not New York, thank God."

"Hear! Hear!" Bergner said, his mockery concealed. "Ten thousand signatures on a petition—very simple."

Winthrop sat down and pulled the telephone over to him. He called the *Traders City Dispatch*, and getting the switchboard, said to the operator, "Put me through to the tower, Jean. Winthrop speaking."

Judge Phipps had been very decent, arch-Republican that he was. As soon as Winthrop had told him he was running in the primary, the *Dispatch* had struck a sort of plague-on-all-your-houses tune. It was just possible Phipps would back him all-out as an independent.

Bergner watched and listened, his response a mixture of admiration and doubt. While he admired a man who could go directly to the top dog for what he wanted, he regarded such procedure a handicap in some instances, dangerous in others, particularly to a politician. In a democracy, the wider the span of influence, the better. There was a place for every man—so long as every man knew his place.

On the thirteenth of April, the day after primary elections, Mike Shea ambled into the office of Health Commissioner at City Hall. He went the round of the clerks, shaking hands, and then tapped on Winthrop's door and stuck his head in.

"Can you give me a minute, Commissioner?"

"Come in, Mike."

Shea gave him the hand that was neither live nor dead fish. "Ah, Alex, you did a fine job, a fine job."

"Thanks," Winthrop said. Knowing himself to be no actor, he resolved to say as little as possible.

"The mayor will be calling you, Alex, but I wanted to be the first to say it—he wants you to stay on as Health Commissioner."

Even as Bergner had prophesied.

"That's very generous of him," Winthrop said, as hollow a sentence as he had ever got off.

But Mike wasn't listening for echoes. "I'll say this for you, Alex, you played it for keeps. There was a while there, I thought you had it."

"I thought so myself."

"Close, close," Mike said, and he sat back and chuckled. "It was a good fight, a real good one. It's good for the people, you know, once in a while, to put on a fight like that."

Winthrop said, "Mike, did you ever really think I had a chance?"

"I don't mind telling you now, Alex, if I hadn't thought so, I'd never have come out for the mayor when I did."

"And you don't consider that to have been a breach of faith, Mike?"

"Alex, let me put it this way to you: There are times a politician has to make a choice between faith and survival."

Winthrop said, "God and Mammon."

Shea chuckled, his tie clasp catching the light as it quivered on his belly. "Very good, Alex, very good. I'm glad you didn't use that one on us. Oh, it was a grand fight. You had no idea now, did you, how popular you were with the people of Traders City?"

Winthrop shrugged. He had not been popular enough by some six thousand votes.

Mike, his eyes half-closed, broached a new subject, for it was a way of Mike's, this lidded watchfulness, as though he could better see through a man, his own eyes half-concealed. "This fella, Bergner, of yours—how would you like to pay him off with a good party job?"

Winthrop could not bring himself to say the word "generous" again. "I'll have to put it up to him, Mike."

"We'll be needing a liaison man 'twixt here and Washington—and I understand he knows his way around down there."

The wily bastard, Winthrop thought, and deliberately put down his own gorge which was slowly rising at the way Mike had, and was now continuing to play him for an absolute fool. Bergner had had him dead to right. Winthrop looked at his watch. "I'll talk it over with him, Mike."

"Do, do. You know, Alex, that sanatorium you were harping about in the campaign? I wouldn't be surprised if the mayor would go along with you on that now. If Washington does their bit, that is. I was thinking, that might be a good project for Bergner to start on."

Winthrop was genuinely uncomfortable. Judge Phipps and Bergner would soon be waiting for him. Within the afternoon Mike would know he had made a mortal enemy. Or within the afternoon, he was going to make one of Mike, and the truth was, neither man liked enemies, whatever their opinion of one another.

"I'm sorry, Mike, but I have an appointment."

"Well, when you've got to go, you've got to go." Mike got up. "No hard feelings, Alex?"

"No hard feelings." He took the hand that fell away having met his own.

"And you'll stay on as Health Commissioner?"

"It's a while yet to November anyway," Winthrop said. He put on his overcoat.

Mike walked out with him. On the sidewalk, he said, "And maybe along toward summer, you'll do a little campaigning for the mayor, a speech here and there?" Winthrop looked at him. "Sure, it's only your pride that's hurt, man, and you'll be over that soon. And I know in my heart of hearts, Alex, that whatever else you are, you're a good sport. And a wonderful campaigner. Sure, you blow over this old town like a breath of spring."

Winthrop walked the scant mile between City Hall and his town flat. No conveyance would have borne him as satisfactorily as his own legs, for the rhythm and the power he felt in them suited the headlong drive he was bound on. Only once before in his life had he felt anything like this exuberance: when he was a boy and astride a runaway horse from which he would not—and could not—be thrown.

George Bergner and Judge Phipps were waiting for him, Phipps with a dummy layout of the extra edition of the *Dispatch*. It bore the headline:

WINTHROP TO RUN AS INDEPENDENT

Phipps pointed to his front page editorial, an appeal to the voters of both parties. "Over a million readers, Alexander."

"I wish you were running it on the sports page," Bergner said bluntly.

Winthrop looked from one to the other of the men, arch-Republican and New Dealer. The strangeness of their fellowship added to his gratification. "Let it roll, Judge," he said huskily. He was surprised to discover that he was hard put to get the words out for the sudden pounding of his heart.

Phipps picked up the telephone. Listening to him talk to the make-up man, Winthrop went to the window and looked down upon a hundred or so rooftops, then up to the Prudential Building, the Traders Mart, the *Dispatch* Building, on the top floor of which was a radio station where he would be spending a lot of time from now on. Traders City: she had been called many things. The most elegant hogpen in the world, Queen of the Lakes . . . A man got to know a woman, making love to her, he thought, and he got to know himself, showing off for her, and in the end he had to be as good as she made him think he was. Far down on the Lake Front Drive, he could see a blue-green strip of roof: the International Building where, he supposed, this being Wednesday, Elizabeth Fitzgerald would be teaching music until four. By four o'clock the special edition of the *Dispatch* would be on the street, and at four o'clock, he would be speaking to a group of men and women who soon would be known as "Responsible Citizens for Winthrop."

• 13

For all that Marcus had chastised himself for seeking place, it was remarkable, having it, how quickly he came to take it for granted. He saw with awe, that spring, his name go up on the callboards of three hospitals as a result of his association with Albert Bergner. But it was no time at all before, looking at the board to see who was in, he did not even glance at his own name.

It was true, Bergner had him under contract, a signed agreement that for five years Marcus was, exclusively, to assist him. Whether the document would stand legal testing soon became a no more than academic issue with the younger man. Nor did Bergner advertise the contract. He brought Marcus in simply as "my associate." And if Bergner had died the next day, Marcus fully realized, he would himself have been even further "out" than before if that were possible. Too many men a good deal his senior knew themselves to be better qualified and, some felt, in actual line for the association. Would any of them have been willing to sign a contract at the wage of a PWA laborer, he wondered. All the same, he came to feel himself incalculably lucky—when he could feel anything. He worked night and day. Bergner appeared at each of the hospitals only on his one morning in surgery. Marcus was charged with the pre- and post-operative care of all his patients, as well as attendance on Bergner on surgery. There were times when he suspected, having to hasten from one place to the next, that his apprenticeship to Bergner was going to qualify him better as a taxi-driver than a surgeon. But the day came before spring was over when, during an abdominal, Bergner suddenly lifted his head, scowled at Marcus, nodded and stood back. Marcus took over and closed the wound. The old man never again finished an operation by his own hand.

There was little occasion in their relationship for the amenities although Marcus spent a good deal of time with Bergner. Once a week he was expected to dinner at Lakewood. It was the one night in the week he arrived anywhere on time for dinner. And afterwards he was expected to read abstracts he had made of articles from the scientific journals: anything relating to anesthesia, to blood clotting, to respiration during surgery. Most of it the old man proclaimed nonsense, but now and then he would say, "Ah-ha. Watch that, watch that, Hogan. It may be something. Now, read me the pedigree of the man who wrote it."

Marcus had all but forgotten Bergner's reputation as a social philosopher—possibly because he wanted to. He preferred to know no more about his theories than that he was looking for a "perfect" man, whatever that was. Therefore he got a mild sort of shock, discovering that the old man had put a researcher on his, Marcus's family tree.

"Have you any objections?" Bergner snapped when Marcus mentioned it. "I shouldn't have done it if I didn't think you worth it, let me tell you. Researchers come expensive. The damned government's got them all digging in courthouse basements." Then he added, contradicting himself, "About time, too. What are we but the sum of our ancestors? What are we? You're one of these sentimentalists, I'll wager: environment. Blame everything on environment, eh? Perfume the piggeries and you'll raise gazelles."

"Are gazelles clean?" Marcus asked.

"Don't be facetious with me. Answer my question: do you mind a search of your family?"

Marcus said dryly, "I can bring you a Bible that should save you two hundred years."

"I'll see it, happily. I don't suppose they had the foresight to enter the unbaptized also?"

"Beg pardon?" Marcus said.

"The premature births, stillborns and the like. Very important to my work, and information almost never available."

"I don't really know," Marcus said.

"I'll have you look into my book one of these days, Hogan, when it's done. A major contribution, I think. Mine, anyway. When the living are dead, some of them would only have been dead the sooner but for me, eh? And for you. Taking out little bits of them that's gone rotten. But give us a man that doesn't rot . . ."

"That'll be the day," Marcus said quietly.

"Pure-bred stock . . . why not?"

Marcus got up and put his coffee cup on the tray. "I've got to go, doctor."

This might have seemed abrupt to another man, but Bergner was by then so deep in his own thoughts, he was anxious to get upstairs to his study. "I know, I know. Alike, all of you, the new humanists: you go round forever on the treadmill of political equality, eh? Profound believers in the perfectability of man, the part of him you can't lay hold of—you can't even prove is there—the soul, the over-soul. But I, who propose to find out what makes a good body, my own son calls a Fascist. What do you think of that, eh? What do you think of that, Hogan?"

"I think you must have goaded him into saying it, doctor," Marcus said in George's defense, although he cared little for him.

The old man gave his single spate of laughter. "Of course, of course. But a man is what he's goaded into as well as the picture he poses for, isn't he?"

And it was true, true, Marcus thought. In the end, one had to account not for his best, but for the worst he could be provoked into doing. He waited until the old gentleman had gone upstairs in the elevator. Hearing its door open and then close on the next floor, and the tread of the old man's footsteps, he let himself out at the front of the house. The housekeeper would come presently and lock up. It was hard to feel sorry for George; he was moderately successful, although his success must always hang on that of another man—one saw that, knowing him better. It hung now on whether or not Winthrop won as mayor. But George was a chronic malcontent. So many things in his life, even his marriage, seemed to have been contrived to aggravate his dissatisfaction with his own lot. He was in a number of ways like the worst of his father: the same streak of cruelty was in them both, the need to hurt the better to mend. But there is something terrible in a son who imitates the worst things in his father because he cannot match the best.

Marcus drove from Dr. Bergner's to the Fields's where Martha was waiting for him: they practiced an amusing sort of duplicity on the nuns in this arrangement in that he was seeing much less of her during the evening than they had approved. They assumed, Marcus picking Martha up at six-thirty, he was taking her to dinner—dinner, to be sure, served in candlelight and elegance, for she was not expected to sign in until ten-thirty. Instead, Martha dined with the Fields's where Marcus joined them at nine-thirty or so. At that hour she would not have been allowed to leave the campus: thus the duplicity in order to meet at all.

He found the young people, Sylvia, Martha and Tony, having iced coffee on the patio overlooking the lake. A three-quarters moon had risen not long since, throwing its long white shadow across the dark and shimmering water.

"There never was such a night," Marcus said.

Perfumed oil was burning in an urn, driving off the insects.

"Never," Sylvia said.

Marcus drew a chair up near Martha's and stretched out his legs. Presently, in the darkness, their hands met and hung clasped between them, as indeed their lives needed to hang now: nothing said, nothing promised, the future undefined, the present a precious all and yet itself all promise. Melancholy intruded upon their happiest moments: Martha talked of Europe, not often, but inevitably, her parents having determined that she take her third year of college with the nuns abroad. Already the pangs of anticipated separation made more poignant their every meeting—as would have something else had not these circumstances so quickly smitten them. There is no falling in love without retreat upon discovery, pursuit and wilder flight, done all in a fearful, joyful expectancy of love's rapturous captivity.

"Poor Alex," Sylvia said, "having to spend all his time in the city."

"And what about you, poor you, Syl?" her brother said. "He's going to be mayor when he gets through. What are you going to be?"

Marcus answered for her, the word coming easily to him: "Tired."

Sylvia was working hard at Winthrop's headquarters. "Isn't it odd," she said, "that Tony should be so annoyed with me? And this is the only politics I've ever pursued with mother's approval. The day Judge Phipps came out for him, Alexander became a new man in her eyes."

"And an old one in mine," Tony said. "Old Fogy Winthrop."

"Cut it out, Tony," Sylvia said.

"What he gets away with by not combing his hair." Tony ran his fingers through his own in imitation.

Marcus thought he was showing off, but Martha sympathized with Tony although she failed entirely to see that Sylvia Fields was in love with Winthrop. But then she was accustomed to her father's excessive loyalty to the man.

Martha said, "You don't like Doctor Winthrop, do you, Tony?"

"Not much," the boy said.

"Do you know why?"

"Yes!" Tony tossed his head. His handsome features, the long nose, the high, curved forehead, shone as the lantern light caught his profile. But his one word hung with no amplification.

Martha said, "I don't either, and I wish I did know why."

Marcus groped in his pocket for a cigaret.

Sylvia said, too quickly and rather too loudly, "I called on your father today, Marcus. I thought he might give us something—a few words of support. There are a lot of votes coming of age this fall."

"There are a lot of votes never come of age and never will," Tony said, "and I shouldn't be surprised if old Alexander gets at least half of them."

Marcus said, "Tony, I've had my Bergnerisms for tonight. You're not old enough to spout that kind of stuff yet. I agree with Sylvia. Cut it out." He shook a cigaret out of the package. "Have a crushed Camel."

"Thanks," Tony said. He grinned sheepishly when Marcus held the lighter for him.

Marcus winked at him, saying to Sylvia, "What did my father say?"

"He was gracious as usual, but he said that he was very much afraid he might sink the boat, jumping aboard it."

Marcus nodded. His father thought Winthrop would make a

pretty good mayor; at least, he would be susceptible of good advice, and if he made it, he would be beholden to forces which would automatically cancel each other out. Marcus groped again for Martha's hand. "Hadn't we better go?"

"I think we should," Martha said, and held her watch to the lantern light.

Ten minutes' drive, a long kiss in the car, and a short good-by on the convent steps. Mother Josepha, that night's portress, would be waiting to hear exactly what she had had for dinner. Martha would exaggerate the menu and probably the nun would know it, for she would say, "Oh-ho?" and her brows would arch clear up to her coif. She would turn out the vestibule light then and say good night, and she might even volunteer that she would pray for Martha's intention, although Martha had never asked it. She would go in the nun's door of the chapel and Martha would get her veil and enter by the students' door, and at least one of them—probably two—would say a prayer for Marcus's conversion. Martha would leave the chapel first, and putting her veil away, she would hear the lights being switched off. Pausing to genuflect at the open door on her way to the students' wing, she would see the red glow of the vigil lamp in the darkness and perhaps the glint of the long gold chain by which it hung from the ceiling, and she would murmur quickly, "Good night, Sweet Jesus, my Savior. Good night, Sweet Mary, my Mother. I give Thee my heart, my soul and my life. Keep me from sin this night and forever."

Seeing it all in a sweep before her, she came back in mind to the moment, and squeezing Marcus's hand, said, "Now?"

Marcus found his father playing chess with his friend Mueller, their heads fairly floating in the smoke of pipe tobacco. Marcus looked down at the board and watched for a minute or two. Mueller winked at him, confident, and Marcus laughed. It had suddenly occured to him to wonder how Dr. Bergner would feel about a homely, dynamic little man like Mueller who had begot four daughters in a row.

"How are the girls, Dr. Mueller?"

"They are blooming," the physicist said, starting off the sentence with the buzz of his accent. "They send you their love and ask if you are still waiting."

"For all of them?" Marcus said.

"For the choice," Mueller said. "But no dowry. The dowry I am saving for the one who goes last."

"Sensible," Marcus said.

"Check," his father said.

Mueller threw up his hands and then clapped them together. "Oh, my friend," he said and made a solicitous sort of clucking, "checkmate."

Jonathan Hogan turned around stiffly in his chair. "Now, what was so damn funny when you first came in?" He spoke, of course, as though Marcus had thrown him off his game. It was so common a routine it did not even require an answer.

Marcus said, "Coffee, anyone?"

"All you have to do is warm it up," his father said.

"How many times has it been warmed up already?"

"Once or twice, that's all."

"I'll make a fresh pot," Marcus said.

His father was putting away the chess pieces. "The joy of physics," he said, "of German physics. Did you see that in the paper the other day?"

Mueller grunted.

"What was the difference now—between it and Jewish physics?"

"The German physicists are happy—the Jewish physicists are sad, that's all," Mueller said facetiously.

"I wish that were all," Jonathan Hogan said.

Mueller reached for his pipe. "That makes as much sense as what was said, let me tell you. The German researches for the joy of observing the reactions. The Jew makes physics a purely mathematical thought construction—propagated in characteristic Jewish manner."

"What does that mean?" said Marcus.

"I think it means the German works for pleasure—the Jew wants to be paid. What does it mean? Everything. Nothing. It means what they want it to mean."

Marcus, going into the kitchen, thought of Martha's father and his periodic tirades about materialistic scientists.

When he returned with the coffee, his father asked, "Did you have a decent supper, Marc?"

He thought for a moment. Bergner was not a gourmet. "Probably. I can't remember."

"You are in love, Marc!" Dr. Mueller cried. "And me with the four girls."

Marcus laughed, knowing that he was indeed in love. It gave him deep, deep pleasure to sit as he did now, cup in hand, his legs stretched out, and to think of Martha—to conjure her wide, frank eyes, serious, innocent, curious, changing as their color seemed to, and the sudden smile which fairly went through him every time.

"When I was your age, I was in love. Oh, my God, I was in love!"

Jonathan Hogan said, "Erich, when were you not in love? Tell me that."

But Mueller had grown quite serious. "Have I been in love since? My friend, I tell you the truth, I do not know. I am so hurt, so . . . dead when my first wife died. And the little French girl, Julie, she was so pretty, and she liked me, and now the children they all look like her . . . and sometimes I wonder who I am." He sat, quietly fondling his empty pipe. "There is a man I would like to see in this country—I would like him to come out soon, before it is too late. He is a doctor of medicine—a surgeon, Marcus . . . Nathan Reiss. He stayed with my wife night and day and him a young man! He operated twice. Are we not the strange creatures, my friends? If my wife had lived, sometimes we should have spoken of Dr. Reiss. Perhaps. But she died and I remember him more clearly—almost—than I do her."

Marcus went upstairs very soon. It was not a comment on human nature that Erich had made at all. As many people blame the death upon the doctor who cannot save a life as honor him for trying to save it. It was simply a comment on Erich Mueller.

· 14

BECAUSE Martha very much wanted him to attend the annual St. Cecilia Bazaar, Marcus managed it. In the midst of some fairly gawky youths, not a few of whom still bore the scars of adolescence on their faces, he felt a remote sense of tolerance he supposed was paternalism. In his own pre-medical days at Rodgers, he had been a very serious fellow. Gin and politics had been his only vices, and he had now put both of them behind him. The girls one knew in college he had always considered quite apart from the girls one talked about academically. And that afternoon, roaming the lawns and pausing at the raffle booths of St. Cecilia's, observing the students in their wide, calf-length skirts, he remembered the invasion of the Rodgers campus by the girls from what he and his chums called—in mockery of their fathers who had been even more formal in their fraternization—the female academy nearby. In his day, hemline and waistline had very nearly met. Remembering, feeling the warm June sun upon his back, aware of the high and aged elms and of the solid brick of which the nuns had built their college, hearing laughter near, and somewhere off during a sudden hush the tinkling of a bell, he thought of the way one generation cycled into the next, perpetuating each what became its heritage. Here nothing changed but to better match that which had endured before it.

Marcus stood among the outdoor exhibit of paintings. He was trying to guess which of the canvases was Martha's, when a girl said to him, "That's Martha Fitzgerald's," and indicated a landscape with some extraordinarily ominous clouds hanging over a meadow.

"Oh, very nice," he murmured.

"Those clouds were supposed to be light and fluffy—like dumplings," the girl said. She was herself plump and wonderfully open-faced, the sort of girl he would have expected to see in a meadow, a peasant's blouse over her large bosom and her brow damp with honest sweat. He would probably discover she was third generation St. Cecilia bred. "It was really a very nice day," she concluded in critical comment on Martha's painting.

"Well," Marcus said, "dumplings have a way of turning out like that sometimes, don't they?"

The girl giggled and fled, but now and then as he moved on, he was acutely conscious of her eyes upon him. He suspected that for a time he was going to show up in her dreams. And if she were to show up in his, it would surely serve him right for such conceit.

"Marcus . . ."

He turned when Martha spoke, and saw the nun with her, a small, bright-eyed woman whose rimless glasses sat on the bridge of her nose so that she had to cock her head back to look up at him. She had a nice smile, her lips closed, and his first opinion was that here was a woman in control of herself and at peace with her world. He knew Martha greatly admired her.

"Mother, may I present Doctor Hogan? Marcus, this is Mother St. John."

She gave him a small hand, her own grasp brief, firm. "I'm so glad you could come, doctor."

"Thank you." He knew from the way Martha had introduced them, from the tone in her voice, that this meeting was the reason Martha had most wanted him to come. Mother St. John was the dean of St. Cecilia's. His experience with the religious hitherto had been entirely among the nursing orders who tended, on the whole, to have been recruited from working class families.

"Shall we find a place to sit for a few moments?" the nun said. "Have you had refreshment, doctor? Martha will bring you tea, perhaps?"

"We are to have tea with my mother in town afterwards," Martha said.

"Oh, yes. I'd forgotten." She led the way among the trellised roses to where the garden furniture had been set out. "Please smoke if you wish, doctor. You don't smoke, do you, Martha?"

"No, mother."

"So many of the girls do. I am going to recommend a smoking room one of these days—not because I wish to encourage the habit among them, but if having to walk a mile in the dead of winter to find a place of concealment does not discourage it, one might doubt that a smoking room would matter one way or the other—except to the dignity of the college."

She would be very strong on dignity, Marcus supposed, and modern in her outlook. Martha had said so, but he had nonetheless felt that a medieval aura hung about all members of a religious community, and vaguely he approved it—as most assuredly Mother St. John would not, he soon discovered. She remarked in the train of a conversation Marcus immediately forgot, alert as he became to her meaning, "I should not think anything done solely for its own sake to be entirely good—whether it be art or prayer, philosophy or the study of ancient Persia. So many people, I am told, study and translate among the ancients today because they cannot abide the superficialities of our times. I think this rather terrible: one must use the past as a guide, not a crutch. Don't you think so, doctor?"

Marcus rubbed the back of his neck, thinking. "I think—Mother St. John—that anyone who needs a crutch is going to find one. I realize that is not a direct answer to your question."

"When I was a child," the nun went on, her hands in her lap, loosely one within the other, and with the sun catching the glitter of the small gold crucifix on her ring, "I had a teacher—a sister of another order—" Marcus caught the twinkle this brought to her eye; it disappeared quickly, "—who always used a pointer in class. It must have been several feet long and at least an inch thick at one end. I remember she would say, 'Now, look at the blackboard, and I shall go through it again.' "

Martha and Marcus laughed.

"Something else she would say in that vein:—she was a rather bad-tempered woman, I am afraid—'If you do that again,' she would say, 'I'll give you a straight zero.' And she would describe it with the tip of her pointer." Mother St. John herself illustrated with a finger. "Then one day she broke the pointer over one of the student's heads. The child sustained no permanent ill effects fortunately, and I remember that Sister Joanna was a much better teacher without the pointer."

It was an entirely pleasurable ten minutes Marcus spent in the nun's company, and when she rose to leave him and Martha, she said, "We shall miss Martha next year, shan't we?"

"I haven't got used to the notion of her going yet," Marcus said.

"It will be quite time enough when she is gone," the nun said, matter-of-factly, and gave him her hand. "Come and see me sometimes, if you will, Doctor Hogan. I very much admire your father. He behaved with such dignity through his ordeal. I have sometimes thought that if our curriculum allowed such refinements as political economy, I should be tempted to ask him to give the course." She glanced away from him for an instant, and then back, the twinkle again in her eyes. "Perhaps it is as well we are so small a school."

She padded away from them, her footfalls muffled in the grass. In the classroom corridors, Martha recognized the footsteps of almost all the nuns.

Marcus said, "What a remarkable woman! What does she teach? You told me once."

"Psychology and English poetry."

"Not ancient history."

"No. Mr. Cummins comes out from the University. He's very young." He had been appointed although Martha's father had recommended someone else. Martha's father did not entirely approve of Mother St. John either, and he was a little offended that he had not been proposed as a trustee of St. Cecilia's. He was, after all, a prominent Catholic layman, an educator, and had a daughter in the college. Martha thought now that he would hit the roof when he heard St. Cecilia's was to have a smoking room. She decided it would be one more of many tales which she did not carry home.

"Marcus, if we were to leave now, could we go down to the lake for a few minutes? I'd love to see it a last time and I shan't have a chance tomorrow. It's commencement."

"I wish you would stop speaking with such finality. You're neither gone yet, nor forgotten."

But later, as they sat upon a log at the bottom of the ravine and watched the green-blue water come up time and again and stretch itself upon the sands, she spoke again in somber words: "If I should die this very day, Marcus, I would have had more happiness, I think, than most people—and almost all of it this spring." Marcus merely squeezed her hand. She went on: "I feel deeper, more mature. Maybe I'm not, but I think I am. Marcus, I love you very much."

He looked at her then, both frowning and smiling, and getting up, drew her into his arms and held her until they could feel the sands running out from beneath their feet.

Whenever Marcus drove Martha back from school they stopped at the studio and her mother had tea sent up from the second floor restaurant. There were two rooms, one the music room in which were a grand piano, a music rack and two chairs. The other room was cluttered and overfurnished, almost gaudy, in somewhat heady contrast to the very proper house near the University campus. A bowl of red roses filled a corner table.

"I was always told as a child in Ireland," Elizabeth Fitzgerald said, as she gathered up several books and put them on the shelves, "of the Spanish part of my ancestry, but as I look around this room, I wonder if it wasn't their explanation for a visiting gypsy."

"Aren't they called tinkers in Ireland, mother?"

"Indeed they are, and they're not dealt with in nearly so romantic a fashion as here, let me tell you. It would have had to be a kidnaping."

After a second's pause, Martha said, "The roses are lovely. They're the first you've cut, aren't they?"

Her mother glanced at Marcus, amused, and said to her daughter, "Do I embarrass you?"

"Of course not."

"I used to embarrass your father. I think that's why he married me

—to put the cloak of respectability about me." It was, she knew, why her aunt had fostered the marriage. "They are slow with our tea today, aren't they? Perhaps we should have gone home for it. The garden is lovely now. You must come one afternoon soon, Marcus. I don't suppose you get to spend much time out-of-doors, do you?"

"It depends on where I have to park the car," Marcus said in his dry way. "If I have a long walk to it, I'm allowed to breathe fresh air on the way."

The tea was brought up by a waiter Elizabeth Fitzgerald had not seen for some time; he had been off ill and she was most solicitous. Marcus was, quite by chance, watching her at the instant she discovered the man had brought service for two only. A change as severe as a mask passed over her face. The color drained from it except at two points where her skin drew tightly over the cheekbones.

"You have made a mistake, Peter," she said, her calm voice belying entirely the change in her face. "Tea was ordered for three."

"Oh, madame, pardon me. I have forgotten."

"I suppose you had better take it all down and start over." She turned to Marcus. "You can wait a little longer, doctor?"

Their eyes met and held in an exchange he did not suppose he would ever forget. The color returned to Elizabeth's face. Marcus moistened his lips and said, "Of course," although he knew he must leave within ten minutes.

She looked up at the waiter. So did Marcus; he could not help himself. The man's face was a bulging red. She said only, "Please, Peter," and he was gone.

Marcus took a cigaret from his pocket and lit it. He did not offer one to his hostess, and he could not bring himself to look toward Martha. She had been at the window when the waiter came. Nor was it likely she would have understood anything, seeing. One needed a certain curiosity, an experience. Possibly one needed to be a man and to have felt, as he admitted to himself now that he had felt, the sexual attractiveness of this dark, proud woman and her gypsy haven. He had known, he was sure, from the night of Winthrop's party. That was one thing; but Elizabeth Fitzgerald's confirming that he knew was something else. It was something between them now. He got up and went to the window where he put his arm about Martha and brushed her temple with his lips. He had never before touched her in her mother's presence. And he had never felt such tenderness toward her as now when she pressed his hand between her arm and her ribs.

"Will you come to Sunday dinner at our house?" Marcus said. "I'll invite the Muellers—and it's time you met my father."

"I should love to, Marcus. May I, mother—Sunday?"

"I should think so," Elizabeth said.

She got up and left them then, going into the music room. She played some very dark Beethoven, but Marcus and Martha smiled at each other through it, and kissed deeply, searchingly as not before. Marcus was on the very edge of saying the word, of proposing that they marry soon. But he held back—not from the obvious considerations of her youth and his poverty—but because somehow there was a curious, knight-errant sort of feeling to his emotion, as though he were doing it to save her, or to do right by her—as God knows, she did not need have done. So he talked of Sunday and of all the Mueller children, whom, he hoped profoundly, they would leave at home.

Martha and her mother went out into the garden almost as soon as they reached home that afternoon. It was always her mother's habit, even if it were raining, to walk in the garden when she got home. But this was the poet's sort of June day. The oak trees were shedding seed pods, dropping them down like clusters of dragonfly wings, the peonies were blowzy, but the roses were in high glory. The garden was entirely her mother's. As a little girl Martha had always had a patch of her own to cultivate, but she did it less from love of the garden than from the desire to please her mother. Her father rarely came beyond the terrace, but he would often come out there and look down, nodding approval. He liked to boast among his colleagues of his wife's garden: "All her own work. I've never lifted a hand in it. She has a boy to help sometimes, and he'll be a gardener when she's through with him."

"I remember the roses at home always this time of year," her mother said. "They run right up to the cottage near the manor. We used to sit on the wall at twilight—it doesn't get dark until after ten in the summertime there—and watch the sheep. It was so still at times you could hear them munching the grass. And their bleating was the loneliest sound."

"What's a linnet?" Martha asked. "You know, 'Full of the linnets' wings.' "

"It's a bird—fairly common in Ireland. It feeds on the seeds of flax . . . You're very much in love, aren't you?"

"Yes. Terribly."

"You're so young, Martha."

"Am I? For what?"

"To be so serious."

"I'd be serious even if I weren't in love," Martha said.

"Do you talk about marriage?"

"No."

Her mother laughed a little. "I sounded like your father. I didn't quite mean it that way. I don't propose to question the honor of Marcus's intentions."

"Does papa question them?"

"He considers it part of his duty, being your father."

"Marcus and I understand why we don't talk about it. We should have to say all sorts of things we didn't really mean—to explain something that doesn't need explaining as long as we don't talk about it. I don't suppose that makes much sense to you, does it?"

"I'm always on the side of reticence. But I'd never thought it possible for people in love." She plucked a leaf and turned it between her eye and the light. It bore an insect's perforations. "Oh, dear—and so soon. I shall have to spray tonight. Martha, I want to ask a very great favor of you, my dear. That's not how I should put it either." She laid her hand on Martha's, one of the rare times she reached out to her, for that was implicit in the gesture. "I want us to go abroad together this summer—you and I."

Martha was too stunned to speak for a moment. She glanced at her mother, and then away quickly; her mother's eyes were a well of longing, full of tears, reminding Martha again of Sister Mathilde. Never, never before had her mother allowed anything so personal between them. It was inexplicable to Martha, and although she tried to resist it, the resentment in her grew quickly.

"I don't want to, mother, not if I have to go to school there in the fall."

"I see." Her mother withdrew her hand.

"If we were to go this summer, could I go back to St. Cecilia's in the fall?"

"No, Martha, that part is quite set. Our going this summer is entirely up to you."

Martha felt herself disarmed by the responsibility. It was her own impotence that angered her. "It's because of Marcus, isn't it?"

"No."

"And you know I'm helpless. I've just told you we were not making a lifetime of plans. If we weren't so sensible, so honest, you wouldn't be able to take this advantage, mother."

"You're not making any sense at all, Martha."

"I know I'm not. It doesn't make sense to me to go to Europe this summer. None! None!"

"I didn't expect it to," her mother said quietly. "If you will remember what I said to you . . ."

Martha interrupted: "Is papa willing that we go? He didn't even want me to go this fall."

"Until you met Marcus. Do you think he has taken easily to the idea of your being in love with him—with Jonathan Hogan's son—a Protestant, a man ten years your senior?"

"I know he hasn't. And I know you've made that easier for me, mother. I grant that."

"I've not made it easier or more difficult, Martha. Understand that."

"But now you've made it impossible!" Her voice broke on the word.

"Martha, listen to me for just one moment, please." She spoke then, very carefully: "If I were in the position with your father to make things easier—or for that matter, more difficult—to have any deep influence with him whatsoever—I should not need to ask that you and I go abroad together this summer. I said in the beginning it would have to be a favor you did for me. I hoped not to have to explain it to you."

"You don't, mother." Martha was now having to do battle with her own tears. Her mother had won over hers, and she had won over her daughter, too. Martha was already beginning to feel the distance spread between her and Marcus. And this the happiest day: so she had proclaimed it.

When Martha wiped the tears from her eyes, her mother said quietly, persuasively, "You are very young—you have a lifetime—and it isn't practical, let alone possible, for you to get married soon anyway. The religious issue between you and Marcus is going to take a great deal of time and tact."

Martha nodded, hoping her mother would stop. These were the very things she and Marcus avoided saying. She had thought her mother understood.

"I don't pretend it will be easy for you, Martha. You and I have never been—close, as they say. I've always felt it my duty to encourage a more intimate relationship between your father and you—since I was failing both of you in so many ways."

"You don't have to talk like this, mother. I was surprised, that's all. I agree to go."

"I don't want you just to agree. You see, Martha, I owe your father a great deal . . . In twenty years, we have done some rather cruel things to each other. People do, you know."

"I know," Martha said.

"Your father is also ten years older than me. You'll find the distance lengthens as you get older."

Martha did not say anything.

They had reached the tool shed at the end of the garden and turned back. "I just wonder if there isn't time for Walter and me to find a happier life together—before we're left to it alone, happy or no. I expect that would please you, wouldn't it?"

"Yes," Martha said, but she did not have any feeling about it at all. In fact, she much preferred being with her mother when they did not talk. There was something more "giving" about her when she seemed to be holding back, or doling out her communication. Martha sensed now, her mother having mentioned the difference in hers and Martha's father's ages, that she was in some way referring to their sexual relationship. Martha had occasionally thought about it, but not very much; she did not really know what happened to people in that way when they got older.

"I want to try a couple of months' separation from Walter—and then when I come back and we have the year alone together . . ." Her voice stopped. She was looking straight ahead at the house, and Martha, glancing sideways at her, saw the straight, hard line of her mouth. Then she threw back her head and opened her mouth, breathing deeply. "We shall visit your uncle in Ireland. We shall have a glorious summer, Martha. I promise you!"

It was an agonizing commingling of feelings Martha and Marcus went through about one another after that; the sense of parting hung over their every meeting. Sometimes an impatience to have it quickly accomplished came upon them and then a refusal to believe it was happening at all. "The moment is all," Marcus said more than once, and afterwards mocked himself for its melodrama. It was indeed much better for them that she go abroad this year, and going, that she go quickly: a year should greatly clarify his own future at the rate he was getting on now with Bergner. They would come to agreement on this at every meeting, he and Martha, and then crash into each other's arms for the moment that was all.

Marcus was not able to be home for the Sunday he had first invited Martha, nor the Sunday following, so that when finally he was able to arrange the dinner he had proposed it turned out to be a farewell party as well as one of introductions.

Mrs. Turley, the Hogans' housekeeper, fussed and polished. "You got no business bringing that elegant girl down here, Dr. Marcus. You ought to get your father to sell this big old house."

It was an old complaint. The house was not very old and not very big, but it was the house in which Marcus and his brother had grown up, and from which his mother had been buried when Marcus was twelve and Trent seventeen. It had seemed a very big house to him then, for Trent at the time had been a freshman at Rodgers. Because of the flu epidemic, he had not been allowed home even for the funeral.

"Our guest is not that elegant," Marcus said.

Marcus brought Martha himself, timing it that they might have an hour or so before the Muellers arrived. His father was waiting on the front porch, and came down the steps to meet them.

Martha complimented him soon upon his garden. Marcus had never mentioned it and, to be sure, it bore comparison to her mother's only in that whatever was growing took root in the ground.

"It runs rather heavily to carrots this year," the elder Hogan said. "I have a feeling that if I'd put in the radishes, I'd have found them by now. Don't you think so?"

"If you'd put in any more carrots," Marcus said, "we'd be hard put to find the house."

Martha laughed. "I like carrots," she said.

"I wish I could say the same," Jonathan Hogan said. "I like the idea of carrots. How is your father?"

"Well, thank you. He sends you his very best regards."

"Shall we go in?" Marcus said. Fortunately it was a cool day, the wind off the lake sufficient to make it more comfortable indoors than out.

Martha stood a moment in the hallway, looking at the pictures hanging there, of old-fashioned people in various styles of clothes and poses. Then she looked into the living room. "You don't mind my exploring, do you?"

"No. That's what we're here for," Jonathan Hogan said, "to stand inspection."

"You sound just like Marcus," Martha said.

"More and more, the older he gets," Marcus said. When they were in the living room, he asked, "Is it what you expected?"

"Very much. It's so—lived-in looking."

Marcus nodded. "It gets lived in now and then." He grinned and glanced at his father, more than a little self-conscious. "When my brother and I were youngsters, the whole neighborhood lived in it."

"It reminds me of mother's studio."

In the wake of the little silence Marcus let hang, his father said, "Well, I guess we've passed muster, Marc. When do you sail, Martha? You don't mind my calling you that, do you? I don't know exactly what you'll call me. Some people call me the Red Jonathan. It makes me feel like a pope, which I doubt is what they have in mind. Do you go to Italy?"

Marcus was amused. He sat back. His father was trying to put forward the worst and the best of himself at once. He must feel this ordeal rather keenly. It was quite some time since Marcus had brought a girl into the house, and on those few occasions his father had felt it incumbent on him to make himself scarce rather than personable. Martha sat in the middle of the couch, very erect and yet relaxed in manner at least, her hands limp in her lap. There was a serenity about her that gave him much pleasure in observing, almost the quality of a painting, an inner stillness.

"We sail on the third," Martha said. "Paris first, then Rome."

"French boat? You'll be fortunate if they don't strike before you've landed. I can't just figure out what's happening over there now. The Communists are throwing their weight around. It's the first time they've got anywhere near the government. Presumably they're supporting the coalition, and yet they seem to be doing their best to hobble it."

Leon Blum had just come to power in France, heading the government known as the Popular Front.

"Papa says it may be dangerous for me to go to school there next year. They closed all the convent schools in France once, the government, you know."

"The French have a way of doing things once they would never do again, and which no one else would do even once. They are culpable, violent, wretched. But their revolutions are always their own."

"Do you admire them, Mr. Hogan?"

"No, I don't admire them. Not at this stage anyway. But I love them . . . and I don't think the convents will be locked up again. It is thirty years later. And, you see, a good number of French Catholics, particularly the intellectuals, are quite a ways to the left these days."

Martha said, very seriously, "You wouldn't consider my father left, would you?"

"I'm afraid not," Hogan said gravely. "Left of Herbert Hoover, perhaps." And they both smiled.

Martha soon decided that she liked Mr. Hogan. She tried not to be distracted by his tic. He spoke to her as to an adult, and he did not explain something unless she asked him to. Marcus was not at all interested in politics, not even in world affairs.

The Muellers were not at all what Martha had expected. He was a jolly man who talked with a buzz, as Marcus had said, but his wife was so young—at least twenty years younger than him. And their language was remarkable. Mrs. Mueller generally spoke English, but as soon as the conversation got any way complicated, she lapsed into French, begging an explanation from her husband. His French, with its Austrian accent, Martha decided, was another language altogether.

Every once in a while that afternoon, Martha and Jonathan Hogan found themselves looking at one another, and when their eyes met, they would smile, both feeling rather shy, but curious—and engaged. Martha thought of the word, not meaning it to have any relationship to a promise of marriage. They were engaged—*with* one another.

Mrs. Mueller kept talking about Paris, the places Martha must go, the people she must see. "So many friends, they will take you under their wing. Jonathan, that is right? Under their wing?" She cocked her right elbow in the air and fanned her left hand beneath it. She was all gesture when she talked, all vitality.

Hogan smiled and nodded. "Very good."

She tossed her head. "I am speaking American, Erich!"

"Whatever you are speaking, darling, it is music."

"Ho! You hear, everybody?" The Frenchwoman laughed and again addressed herself to Martha. "At our house everybody talks. Four little girls. And me. Erich says I am number five little girl."

Dr. Mueller nodded gravely and, without speaking, made the shape of little moving mouths with his fingertips bunched together. Everyone laughed.

His wife said, again to Martha, "You are an artist, no? Marcus says you paint very good, very nice-ly. I have some friends I will write to—Montparnasse, Erich? You remember Henri and the others?" She turned to Marcus. "They are a little bohemian. Only a little."

"I also want to give you an introduction," Mueller said. "I want to give you the name of a doctor, Miss Martha."

"That's much better," Marcus said.

Mueller shook his head. "No, I am serious. It is very important to know a doctor when you are a stranger in a country. The nuns are very dear ladies. I admire them. But they are more sentimental than any other women. If the doctor has the nice beard and kind eyes—that is all they have to know about him. Doctor Reiss is some- times in Vienna and sometimes in Paris. I think you said your mother is with you this summer?" Martha nodded. "Good. You will visit socially first. That is always the right way."

So many things within the compass of that afternoon were strange to Martha, marvelously strange, because this was Marcus's house, these his family friends, this his way of life. She looked earnestly on the portraits, on the old French prints in the dining room, the books, "medical and unmedical," Jonathan Hogan said, "poetic and unpoetic, knowledgeable and nonsensical—a library got together by random scratching at the cribs of learning." Making the speech, he had in hand a highball glass, and when Martha smiled her appreciation, he bowed gallantly, and without spilling his drink.

And Martha shook hands with Mrs. Turley when Marcus introduced them. She had heard him speak often of her with great affection, but it was the first time in her life she had ever touched a Negro.

Then there came a moment at dinner, with laughter and talk around them, when she and Marcus looked at one another across the table, and saying nothing said all there was to say: their love, their good-by, and then looked down to their plates and went on eating. Nothing after that had any reality for Martha: it was all like a ceremony, like getting a medal, or like the May procession in which one walked with many but thought apart. She felt no thrill, no pang thereafter; it was all ritual, the good-byes here and at the railway station. And her memory would go back always to that moment; whenever she wanted Marcus most before her, all her life, it was that moment she tried to conjure.

· 16

"WE SHALL not play any truth or consequences, you and I, on this trip, Martha." They were in their first full day at sea, and the gulls still pursued the ship, reminding Martha of Marcus, and the poem he often misquoted—so beautifully—about the white birds flying. The sun was warm and yet it was comfortable to have the deck blankets over their knees. In all directions there was only the undulating sea, whitecapped, opaque, endless, fathomless. "We are two women on a voyage of discovery," her mother went on. "We might have met at the dining room table. We shall do absolutely nothing on this trip, either of us, that we don't want to do. Agreed?"

"Agreed," Martha said.

Her mother laid back her head. Already the sun was burnishing her cheeks so that her dark eyes seemed to glow the more. "We shall probably do a number of things neither one of us wants to, only because Thomas Cook thinks we ought to. But it's best. Everyone knows Mr. Cook is very respectable."

"Is there really a Mr. Cook?"

"If there isn't, let us not tell your father."

Martha laughed.

"I don't expect to have any flirtations, do you?" her mother said.

Martha thought for a moment. "I should not like to commit myself on anything so theoretical."

This time her mother laughed and laid her hand for a moment on Martha's where it rested on the arm of the deck chair between them. "When I was a little girl, we used to be taken to the continent at least once a year, nurse and all. Only the older people seemed to enjoy it. I loathed it. None of the parks in Paris that I remember had any grass in them. The green grass is terribly important to the Irish. I don't suppose you remember your Uncle Philip?"

"Not very well." She could remember his taking her, during his visit to Traders City when she was very small, to see a rodeo but what she remembered most about it was that he wore his carpet slippers, having walked a blister on his heel. "Mother, do you feel that you're going home, because we're going to visit Ireland?"

"I suppose I do. It will all be changed, of course, and so am I. But in a way, I'm going home. What did I just say about truth and consequences?"

But in the cathedral city of Chartres, less than a week later, where the Fitzgeralds stayed an extra day, omitting Versailles, Martha came to realize how much more there was to this journey for her mother than she had begun to understand. They were having dinner at the hotel and with it a bottle of wine. Her mother was eating very little, a piece of bread with the wine. She would smile at Martha if their eyes met, more to ward off intrusion, the girl thought, than to welcome anything she might say.

Suddenly she asked, "Do you miss Marcus very much?"

"Yes, in a way."

"But you enjoy writing to him?"

"Oh, yes. I look at everything in a special way so that I can tell him about it."

"It makes things more beautiful, doesn't it?"

Martha nodded. She wondered if her mother were not wishing she was in love, herself. How terrible not to be in love when love was yours to give. She had danced on shipboard and been very gay; she had led the Grand March with the captain at the farewell ball. But now that they were alone her gaiety was not spontaneous. Both of them started to speak at once, and stopped.

Her mother said, "Would you mind if I were to leave you for an hour or two? Take your time and finish dinner. I want to go about a bit alone. We agreed to that, didn't we?"

"Of course," Martha said. "I like to be alone sometimes myself."

And with that her mother left the table. Martha ordered cheese, even though she did not like it very much, and then dessert. Marcus liked cheese, and she thought about ways to describe it to him. She began to enjoy herself enormously, a sort of exhilaration at being for the moment quite on her own. She even speculated briefly that perhaps her mother was meeting a gentleman whose acquaintance she might have made on the boat. Martha numbered the possibilities: they did not come to much. But she was not shocked at herself.

She was sitting near the window. The sun had set but the street lamps had not been lighted yet. She wondered if a man would come around with a torch. She saw her mother leave the hotel, wearing hat and gloves, and walk without a backward glance down one of the narrow, cobbled streets that angled, as did most of the streets of the town, toward the cathedral. She walked out of Martha's sight.

Martha finished her dinner, signed the check for it, and left the dining room. People were just beginning to come in, tourists who made the most of daylight and observed the French habit—while they were out of Paris, anyway—of lingering over dinner until bedtime. She went outdoors and walked down to the river where a little boy was fishing. They both waved at a passing barge. A woman was doing her laundry aboard it. A party of ducks swam up and started scolding the fisherman. He scolded them back. Martha understood one about as well as the other. She returned to the hotel and went up to her room, climbing the winding staircase rather than go up in a birdcage, as she presently wrote to Marcus. "The elevators all look like birdcages and I'm always afraid of being hung up in one like a parrot . . ."

Her mother returned before she had finished the letter, and did not interrupt. After making her toilet, she sat down herself to letters and accounts while Martha made ready for bed. When she was propped up there with the guide book to Avignon, their next stop, and a French *roman policier* which she could read with the help of a dictionary, her mother came to the side of the bed and looked down at her as though she had news to tell which she could no longer contain. At Martha's invitation she seated herself on the edge of the bed.

"Martha, I thought I should tell you—you will know it in the morning anyway—I've been to confession tonight."

Martha could not precisely remember when she had last been aware of her mother's going to confession. It was a long time ago. She said, rather startled and startlingly, "In French?"

Her mother burst out laughing. Then very quickly, the laughter turned into tears. Martha drew her into her arms—she was not reluctant—and held her until the weeping was past.

"I'm very happy," she said then. "Thank you, my dear." Getting up, she put her hand beneath Martha's chin, lifted it, and bending down, kissed her low upon the cheek so that the edges of their lips just touched.

It was not the best of summers in which to travel Europe, nor yet the worst. Some tourists were given to sudden, frantic activity, as though it might soon be too late to see or do some things, and this despite—or perhaps because—of the urgent reassurance of the natives. But rebellion had broken out in Spain and was within the week called civil war. In Avignon, the Fitzgeralds overheard an American priest, who was conducting a tour just re-routed out of Spain, tell all within his hearing that there was such a thing as a just war. The Republican government of Spain had—to say the best word for it—tolerated the burning of convents, the sacking of churches. (Republican in the Old World sense of Red Republican, he explained, not the Kansas-Alf Landon variety. Everyone laughed.) Martha, for some reason, kept mixing up the Italian Marshal Balbo with the Spanish General Franco.

They had not seen many towns in France, of course, when they reached Avignon, but both Martha and her mother took a special liking to the people. They marked what they supposed a Spanish influence—color, bullfight advertisements, the sharper, less nasal sound of language, and the prominent bone structure in the people's faces. As was becoming their habit, the two of them broke away from their camera-toting comrades, forsaking to them the austere castle of the "captive" popes, and walked the narrow, winding side-streets. The children stared at them frankly and generally without smiling, pulling back into darkened entries as they drew close.

A vendor of oranges called Elizabeth Fitzgerald "señora" and spoke to her in Spanish until she replied in French that she was not Spanish. To which he cried, "Oh, American!" which comment on her mother's French made Martha giggle. They bought an orange apiece.

"I wonder if he thought we were refugees," her mother said afterwards. They had heard there were refugees crossing the border, but had not seen any, at least to recognize.

Martha supposed a refugee did not necessarily wear rags.

"I have a feeling they are not very sympathetic here with the rebels," her mother said.

"But look at all the churches, mother."

"I was looking at the poverty. And they don't beg—isn't that interesting?"

In Italy they came upon beggars who begged as a way of life, a trade, beggars suddenly arrogant if one refused them, boastful of an empire, the Ethiopian jewel now secure in the king's crown. And in Rome, Martha first heard the marching. She awoke one morning in her hotel room, high above the Via Veneto, to the sound of cheers and rhythmic clomping—the hard, fierce footfalls of tens of hundreds of military boots. Her mother was already at the window, gazing down.

"They're so ridiculous—looking at them from here. One should always look down on soldiers. It puts them in proper perspective." And she went back to bed, trying first to ring for breakfast, but no one was answering bells anywhere.

Martha could see the white-jacketed staff on the steps below, the boys saluting over the heads of one another. All up and down the street, as far as she could see, the same scene was re-enacted, the cafe tables and chairs thrust back from the sidewalks, and the laughing crowds tumbling outdoors, half-dressed, half-awake, waving, saluting, many of them in the Fascist manner.

And when the soldiers were gone, the tables and chairs came out again, and the multi-colored umbrellas were opened to the sky. Martha loved Rome. Even the beggars were handsome. The romantic Christ seemed to be everywhere. But it was in Rome that she was for the first time really homesick.

They reached Vienna toward the end of July, going up from Venice through Trieste on the overnight train. Several members of the tour predicted Martha would love Vienna best of all. She and her mother somehow belonged there: it was the happiest city in Europe. Elizabeth was amused: of all the characteristics credited to her over the years, gaiety was not among them. Martha, riding from the station behind a fat-necked, talkative driver, and looking out on wide boulevards, the baroque-fronted buildings, rows upon rows of trees, remarked, almost wistfully, "I do love to waltz."

It sounded like a small girl's counseling of herself that despite its strangeness there was bound to be something at the party she would like. And it did seem from the outset that all Vienna had determined this also. It was not merely the charming manners the good hostelers managed for visitors. There ran that week through much of Austria a festive spirit, rejoicing sometimes near hysteria. Chancellor Schuschnigg had just signed an agreement with Hitler whereby the German threat to Austrian autonomy was removed; Austria would be Austria still.

They stayed at one of the fine hotels within walking distance of the old city and nearer still to the fashionable shops. Their accommodations were the nicest thus far: a bedroom each and a parlor-writing room where among the awesome furniture, gilded and brocaded chairs, a carved desk and an ivory inlaid card table, was a piano, a piano which was in tune. Standing, her left hand still gloved, Elizabeth played a few bars of a Schubert etude with her right. Martha had been looking out on the park she could see beyond the corner of the Museum, and turned from the window in time to see her mother close the lid upon the keys. Martha went up and opened it, saying, quite authoritatively, "No."

Her mother said, "No?" and, trailing her fingernail up the keys, she described a question in sound. Then with the knuckles of her left hand she struck three black keys at once at the bottom of the bass. Smiling, she took off her other glove.

At that moment they both discovered the flowers, a vaseful of red and white roses. "That's being rather explicit about us, isn't it? Red roses and white roses. I hadn't thought the Austrians so neat."

"Sometimes you say the strangest things, mother."

"Not dull, I trust."

"No. Amusing, really."

"I've often thought the world lost a great bawd in me."

"It isn't too late, is it, mother?" Martha said, in mock naïveté.

Her mother, glancing up sharply, caught the mischief in Martha's eyes and was amused. She paused, opening the envelope which accompanied the flowers. "I hope you will have the chance to go among Parisian society this winter, Martha. I shall do what I can before I leave. But in the end, it depends on yourself, on the friends you make. For heaven's sake, don't make any attachments out of pity. It's a waste of everybody's time, especially among the young." She opened the note, scanned it and exclaimed, "How nice!" She read aloud: " 'I shall be honored if you will be my guests for dinner. May I call for you at seven? Respectfully yours, Nathan Reiss.' That's through Marcus's father's friend, isn't it?"

Martha was enormously pleased. Then she said, "How do you answer it?"

Elizabeth picked up a telephone which vaguely reminded one of the scales of justice by the delicacy of its balance. She inquired of the concierge the proper procedure. But a servant was waiting downstairs for her answer when convenient, he told her.

"Really?" Martha said. "But then I suppose there's a great deal of unemployment, and it's better than doing nothing."

Her mother, composing an answer in her mind, did not answer for a moment. She sat down at the desk. "I understand the Austrian Jews and the Hapsburgs have a—rapprochement." She wrote the note of acceptance and sent for the messenger. "Martha, you must tell me all you can about Marcus's friend—Doctor Mueller, is it?"

Nothing could have less adequately prepared anyone for Nathan Reiss than a description of Erich Mueller. Reiss was not a tall man, five foot ten probably, slender, and strikingly handsome. What neither of them had expected was that he was young, under forty it might be supposed. His eyes were very black, his mouth almost feminine, sensuous, in the full redness of the lips. He drew himself even more erect when they stepped from the lift, and then came to them, his hands extended, and took one of theirs in each of his. "Doctor Mueller did not tell me so much," he said. "But then Mueller is a scientist, not an artist." He lifted Elizabeth's gloved hand first to his lips, then Martha's bare hand, for she had turned back her glove at the wrist.

It might very well have been a natural gesture with him, but Martha got the distinct feeling of being given the treatment saved for unescorted American ladies. The whole blessed staff of the hotel was standing at attention, benevolent to the last smiling face of them. Her mother had assumed her regal air: it made her seem a little above everything that was going on about her. Martha was tempted to laugh.

"I understand you play the piano," Dr. Reiss said to Elizabeth. "It is too bad the season is not musical."

Elizabeth said, smiling, "You are at a great advantage over us, Dr. Reiss, we know so little about you."

"A tremendous advantage," Reiss said. "My automobile is outside." To Martha he said, "And you are the very dear friend of Doctor Hogan who is the son . . . of the friend of Doctor Mueller!"

"We've come a long way to avail ourselves of your kindness, doctor," Mrs. Fitzgerald said.

"Who knows? The way things are today, I may have to do the same thing—only a little faster, perhaps. Who knows?"

Martha could not escape, as the evening wore on, making comparisons between Dr. Reiss and Marcus. It was foolish—they were continents apart in many ways. Reiss was successful, she supposed, wealthy surely; but he simply did not seem like a doctor to her at all. They drove circuitously to a height beyond the city to dine, Dr. Reiss pointing out monuments and palaces, parks and museums on the way, where someone died, where someone else was crowned king. Martha had always been weak in history. They seemed not to pass a hospital.

"Vienna," he said, "is a city—like a beautiful woman—you want to stand back sometimes and admire. I love to show her off to people coming for the first time."

"Then you are a native-born, doctor?" Elizabeth said.

"No, no. Perhaps that is why I am patriotic. I was a poor boy from a small village, and I had a patron who was very good to me—a patron and patroness—is that what you call them?"

"Your English is excellent, doctor."

"Thank you."

"I did not mean to interrupt," Mrs. Fitzgerald said.

He shrugged. "I am very fortunate. It is a fairy tale—if you believe in them. I do."

"I expect you're being modest."

"No, I am not. Oh, I am a very good surgeon. Make no mistake about that."

"That's what Doctor Mueller said," Martha put in.

"How is my friend? All those children. He is a fat man—I have a theory about it. Are you interested in the Olympic events?"

They never did get to hear about his theory. Nor did he seem especially interested in his friend Mueller. He was very keen on sports, and much regretted not being able to go to Berlin himself.

"Because of the Nazis, doctor?" Martha ventured.

"No, no, no. I have another obligation. That is very much exaggerated in my opinion. But I am wrong, they say. I am not political, you see. But we are always being told about the Nazis, you see, because in this country—unlike France—the Socialists and the Communists are being kept where they will not make trouble. But they try. Always the agitation. The Nazis are coming. Hitler wants Austria. But, as I say, I am not political. There is a story I heard today. May I tell you?"

Both women nodded.

"I do not think Austria is going to send any great athletes to Berlin. But one classification where we may excel—the Austrians are great weight-lifters, and here is the story: Who is the greatest weight-lifter of them all? That is the question, and the answer: Doctor Von Schuschnigg, who has just lifted Germany off Austria's back."

He had leaned forward to tell the story and now sat back and accepted the wine list. They were sitting on the restaurant terrace and far below them, beyond a forest of tree tops, a ribbon of water, they could see jewels of light come up in the city as the twilight faded. Wisps of cloud trailed round the highest church steeples. Dr. Reiss pointed out St. Stephen's. Within the restaurant a string orchestra played the waltzes Martha had expected.

"You like to dance, Miss Martha, I can see," Dr. Reiss said. He had strong, even teeth, especially white in contrast to his sunburned face.

"So does mother."

Reiss smiled and ordered the wine.

"May I recommend the *pâté*, Mrs. Fitzgerald? It goes very nicely with the wine I have chosen. But perhaps you do not like *pâté*? Some Americans do not."

The *pâté* was ordered.

"I am told that when the present King of England visited Vienna, they sent for this same *pâté* for him. His namesake uncle was a connoisseur and someone remembered. That is very like Vienna. Always they remember. I don't suppose you have ever met the American friend, Mrs. Simpson?"

"I'm afraid not," Elizabeth said gravely, and without looking at Martha.

"She is an attractive woman, I will tell you. But most American women are. It is all very sad about them so much in love—and more important than some things. But I don't suppose, being Americans, you think so?"

"I'm afraid not," Elizabeth said again.

"Oh," Reiss said, smiling so that there was a little self-mockery in his words: "You are *so* political! May I ask your daughter to dance with me?"

Elizabeth watched them and she would continue to watch them if they were to be very much together. She found herself wondering if Nathan Reiss was a good surgeon, or if he was simply a good lover, an oddly satisfying speculation for her. So many things seemed long ago. Distance was much better than time, and there was a great deal more of distance than of time at one's disposal when she had reached the age of forty-four.

It was after midnight when they returned to the hotel. Dr. Reiss inquired if he might call them in the morning. "I want to send something that will not burden you to Doctor Mueller."

"Of course," Elizabeth said. "Perhaps you could come to us for tea or a drink?"

"Alas, I cannot. But I have an idea—would you like to see the arrival of the Olympic torch in Vienna? About sunset, I think! I shall arrange it."

And he left them with a very gay *"Auf wiedersehen."*

Upstairs, looking at her mother in the dressing table mirror, Martha said, "Do you like him, mother?"

Elizabeth looked up. "I should be ashamed of myself to admit it—but I do. Your father—and most American men—are so earnest. I know Marcus has a marvelous sense of humor—you've said it many times—but even he can't have that audacious frivolity women insist on thinking gallant."

Martha said, "He's going to be in Paris at Christmas time. I wonder if I shall see him."

"No doubt," Elizabeth said dryly. This was something that had not been in her calculations quite, although she had known he spent time in Paris. She wondered if it were accidental that mention of it had come up when they were dancing, not when they were at the table.

"Do you really think so? And just tonight you were wishing I'd have the chance to go among Parisian society. Remember? I'm sure he's very well received. Don't you think?"

"Very."

Martha braided her hair in silence for a moment. "You don't trust Doctor Reiss, do you, mother?"

Elizabeth looked at her frankly. "I trust you, Martha. That's the important thing, isn't it?"

"I must write to Marcus. I wonder if he'll be jealous—a little? I shall have to tell him about Doctor Reiss—so that he can tell Doctor Mueller. I suppose not, since you were there all the time."

"I was just thinking about what I should write your father. I hate to send him another menu. And I doubt he'd find Doctor Reiss amusing. He would probably cable us to get right back on the tour."

"He's much more your type than mine, really," Martha said.

"Doctor Reiss?"

Martha nodded.

"What on earth makes you say that?"

"Oh, he's . . ." Martha hesitated and the color rose in her face. "He's sophisticated," she finished, not having meant to say that at all.

"But he's not sophisticated, Martha, not in our sense of the word. Worldly, perhaps. I suspect he's a very shallow man, and I don't doubt, very spoiled all his life by older women." Elizabeth looked around sharply. "Is that what you meant?"

Martha's cheeks were a sudden and lovely pink.

"Oh, you vixen!" Elizabeth cried, and laughed aloud. After a moment she said, "Actually, that was perceptive of you, Martha. He will be an interesting man to observe—especially if it turns out that he is a good doctor."

Their hotel was a short distance from the Heldenplatz and a crowd was already gathering when Dr. Reiss met them. He had reserved a place for them for dinner afterwards at the most famous restaurant in Austria—within walking distance. It was a clear blue evening, with ever so little mist hanging above the Danube and gradually sifting over the city. The excitement of the hurrying people set Martha tingling. Dr. Reiss was like a small boy himself, eager, excited, even now and then standing on tiptoe the better to see over and about men taller and broader than himself. He behaved as though all the good places would be gone if they did not make haste.

"I am a very fine swimmer, you know," he said with engaging immodesty.

"Heldenplatz," Martha said, "that means hero's place, doesn't it? I like the sound of it."

"It gives one a thrill—eh?" Reiss said. He took her arm because someone brushed against her—not rudely, inevitably, because the park was filling up as though people were tumbling into it from all directions. "I did not think there would be so many people. Not in all Vienna." Again he stood on tiptoe, scanning the far reaches of the park. Martha and Elizabeth looked also. People everywhere, laughing, hurrying in toward them, past them, surrounding them. "Perhaps we should have stayed on the boulevard. We could not have seen very much, but there will be loudspeakers. Ach, but you do not know the language."

"It doesn't matter really," Elizabeth said.

"You are not frightened?"

This he said to Martha, and she had not been until the moment he said it. She said that she was not.

"Let us try and get back a distance, doctor," Elizabeth said, for now they were being gradually carried forward and not of their own wills. "At this rate, we shall be among the speakers soon."

"That would not be so bad," Reiss said, and tried to hold back and open a way for them to move out. He kept excusing himself to the people, who only laughed at him—or with him. They were very gay. He could make no more vent in the wall than if the forward line of humanity had linked arms to bar him. He prodded toward the side, but to no avail, Martha and her mother at his back with each probe. Elizabeth herself tried to open a way in the other direction. It was impossible. But everyone was smiling. No one seemed distressed or fearful. At any little opening the crowd surged in, slowly heaving forward like a great mound of dough. People no longer brushed, but rubbed against them, laughing still, and with every sway of the crowd, the women gurgled in rich mirth; some squealed with pleasure. There was the smell of wine and beer on their breaths, of bread, onions; there were perfumes made pungent by the warmth of the body, and there was the smell of sweat. Dr. Reiss smiled at Martha and, twisting his head to see around her, he said, "I am sorry, Mrs. Fitzgerald. Who could know this would happen?"

"A very athletic people," Elizabeth said tartly.

A murmur ran through the crowd, part whisper as though with questioning in it. Everyone stretched and strained for sight of something outside the core he was part of. The torch-bearer might be arriving, for he was due at dusk, Reiss suggested. Officials were on the platform, the loudspeakers being tested. Then came the sound of a beat, a one-two rhythm, as from the furthest edge of the throng, a sparse, thin sound of distant chanting slowly becoming louder and finally articulate, as the crowd was momentarily hushed. Then voices within the crowd picked it up, men and women at their backs, and soon the very night was rocking with it:

"*Sieg Heil! Sieg Heil! Sieg Heil! Sieg Heil!* . . ."

Martha, looking at Dr. Reiss, saw him at the instant of comprehension: he was stunned, hurt, disappointed beyond speech.

Elizabeth felt the sickening grow within her from the first hushed rhythm which she understood until she was nearly retching at the high cries thick in the lusty throats of the men and boys nearby her. Her first association held: the rhythm was that of sexual overture, becoming more and more imperative, the pound, the drive, the thrust, the strike, all whirling into an orgastic spiral . . . She could feel the splash of spittle on her cheek with every "*Sieg*" of the man behind her. "Let us go, for God's sake," she said.

"Please be patient for my sake," Reiss said, understanding, although neither of them could hear the other's words, and he reached a hand across to her that was cold with fear.

The chant broke suddenly, another cry bursting boldly through and almost instantly predominant:

"*Heil Hitler! Heil Hitler! Heil Hitler* . . ."

An official on the platform was waving his arms; he gestured vainly for silence and then, at last, in sheer frustration, shook his fists at the sky. The words came over the loudspeakers: "*Polizei! Polizei! Weiter gehen!*"

Wherever the police were, they were apparently at ease. Here and there within the crowd, a woman shrieked out as if in ecstasy, and the high, shrill voices of the females began chorusing even louder than the men:

"*Heil Hitler! Heil Hitler!* . . ."

But this is Austria, not Germany, and these are Austrians, not Germans.

Martha felt her mother's arm around her, hard and firm, protective. "I'm not afraid, mother," she shouted.

Elizabeth said into her ear, "I am, and so is Doctor Reiss."

In the fast-fading twilight, Martha glimpsed his face. He made no sound, but his lips were parted, and the play of his tongue told that silently he was repeating the words as the crowd prescribed them.

The torch-bearer came from the south then at last, bearing the torch high. Though the flame was fitful and small, it was nonetheless sufficient to start a roar from the crowd that mercifully drowned out the *Heil Hitler's*. Music then blasted over the loudspeakers; Dr. Reiss put his hand to his breast instinctively. It was the Austrian National Anthem.

But through the crowd the singing rose to a clashing contrast: *Deutschland Über Alles*. Slowly, surreptitiously, as though he had searched something that itched his body, Dr. Reiss removed his hand. The loud, bold voices finished their singing well after the anthem was done, and the speaker, the chief sports leader, was trying to address his welcome to the torch bearer.

The crowd took up a new song . . .

> *"Die Fahne hoch!*
> *Die Reihen fest geschlossen!*
> *SA marschiert mit ruhig festem Schritt!"*

Starhemberg, the speaker, said, *"Die Polizei wird der Lage Herr sein . . ."* And he ordered that the crowd be dispersed. There were shouts of derision: *"Pfui! Pfui Starhemberg!"* Yet the police signals could be heard. The singing continued, but slowly, as the police moved among them, the crowd was turned outward and slowly seeped out of the park, their voices dwindling, and no longer in unison. The Fitzgeralds and Dr. Reiss shuffled in the wake of the people before them. As the crowd opened out, Reiss moistened his lips and said,

"Well, that was exciting, wasn't it?"

The ground was littered with handbills. Martha stopped to pick one up.

"Don't!" Reiss cried, and then more gently, "Communist agitation. Always, everywhere."

Elizabeth said, "Doctor Reiss, which way is our hotel?"

"Herr Doktor?"

Reiss stopped. They were beneath one of the floodlights. A man with an open-collared shirt detained him and spoke to him in German. Reiss' face seemed green, but all color was distorted in the cruel light. Reiss made a noise in his throat as though he were demonstrating hoarseness, and the man laughed and derisively repeated the noise, looking toward three other men who had joined them. Two of these, curiously, Martha thought, were wearing white stockings. It was much later she learned this to be their agreed-upon Storm Trooper emblem.

"Hör mal, Jud!" the man said into Reiss' face.

Dr. Reiss stood very erect, clicked his heels and pulled in his chin, military fashion. *"Ich bin kein Jüde."*

"Nein?" Again the man laughed.

Reiss turned slowly to Elizabeth. "This is my sister," he said in German, "an American, Mrs. Fitzgerald, and my niece."

The man stood a moment, looking from Reiss to Elizabeth and back. He was a head taller than Reiss, blond, and by no means brutish-looking. He clicked his heels and bowed to the women. He turned to Reiss and thrust out his hand in the Nazi salute. *"Heil Hitler!"*

"Heil Hitler," Reiss said, but he scarcely raised his hand.

The young men gave the Nazi salute and then laughingly ordered Reiss to go.

Elizabeth said, "We shall go back to the hotel and have our dinner there. We can have it sent up to us."

Reiss did not say anything until they were out of the park. "The fools," he said then, his voice scarcely louder than a hoarse whisper. "The stupid fools, all of them!" In their sitting room a few minutes later he repeated the words.

"I don't know what they are," Elizabeth said. "I doubt that it is that, but it is something more terrible. I want to leave in the morning, Martha. We can rejoin the tour later if you wish."

"So soon," Reiss said. He was still quite pale beneath the tan. "I am ashamed," he said. "I behaved badly in your eyes."

"Do not feel badly—not on our account, doctor. There is a time for bravery, a time when it means something. It is not anything you can put on, like a dress shirt, in order to entertain your guests."

"You are very kind. But you must understand, Mrs. Fitzgerald, I could not afford to be searched tonight. Otherwise, I might have managed a certain . . . bravura. For your good impression. You see, I was carrying this communication for Doctor Mueller." He drew a letter-sized envelope from his inside pocket. "If things get very bad here, Doctor Mueller has relatives, you see. I have only friends."

He was not backward, Elizabeth thought, but few Austrians were. "I am to give that to Doctor Mueller?" she said.

"If you will be so kind. You may assume it is a letter to him."

Elizabeth took the open envelope from him and sealed it in his presence.

"Thank you very much, dear friend."

She put it in her leather writing box. Very soon he was quite gay again and begged her to play the piano for him until their supper was served.

·17

ELIZABETH returned to Traders City at the end of September. She had misgivings about leaving Martha in Europe, although their visit after Austria to England, Ireland and Paris had been reassuring. And there was among the nuns whom Martha would attend a fine imperturbability that suggested the rock of Peter himself. Indeed, if she had had the courage of her own preference, she also would have stayed on in Europe. Not on the continent, but in the Ireland of her childhood, which seemed to have changed very little since she had been sent from it without a by-her-own-leave. Her brother made it plain, though the word was not spoken, that if ever she chose, McMahon Manor was hers to mistress. The word was his, but by its association she was turned homeward the more determinedly.

She came back leaden-hearted, if anything a little more contemptuous of Walter Fitzgerald than she had been on leaving. That he accepted her return to the Sacraments as making something of a connubial demand upon himself would have been farcical, did it not carry one so close to the edge of madness. Two people trying to oblige the forms of love without passion—one, presumably, without understanding and the other without desire—was obscene. Immoral, surely. It was little wonder the French priest had asked if she would be able to receive her husband. She had thought so then, a continent away from him. Walter's demands had from the beginning been modest.

No one likely would ever know how much Walter Fitzgerald understood, not even he. It was one of the consolations of his philosophy that there were many things man was not meant to understand. For example, to understand a murderer he would have thought very nearly criminous in itself. Willing as he was to judge, he was as ready to admit the imperfectability of man. Otherwise, as he saw it, there would be no reason for law, divine or temporal.

One of the reasons he held Alexander Winthrop in such high esteem was Winthrop's regard also for the forms. He was a man who might have been a wastrel and worked; he was not well educated, but he was a trustee of the University; he did not practice medicine, but he could administer—and had done so—others' practice of it; he had never held elective office, but he was going to be mayor. Of that Walter Fitzgerald was absolutely certain. He believed every placard in the city that said so, every radio broadcast. He saw nothing incongruous in his having himself raised the money to buy the air time on which it was said—or that Michael Shea was financing identical statements on behalf of the Democratic candidate as were the Republicans for theirs.

It was, he kept telling Elizabeth, the cleanest campaign in the history of Traders City, for which, along with George Bergner, he took a fair share of the credit.

"I understand Marcus is getting along very well," Elizabeth said on one of his mentions of the name Bergner. "It was perspicacious of you, Walter, to have helped him."

They were finishing luncheon on the terrace, for the day was warm with the autumn sun. He wiped his lips and put his napkin in the ring. "It was also perspicacious of me not to have expected gratitude from them."

"That is always wise," she said, "no matter of whom."

"Clergymen of three faiths have spoken out—a dozen professors have stumped—yes, stumped, for Alex. But not a word on his behalf from Jonathan Hogan."

"I met him at luncheon, you know, Walter—him and Doctor Mueller for whom I brought a letter."

"I know. You told me."

As it turned out, the envelope Reiss had given her contained more than a letter. Unknowing, herself, she had carried out of the country for him a draft on the Bank of Austria for a great deal of money; but this she had not told Walter.

"He does not look at all well—Marcus's father. Perhaps that's why he hasn't helped you."

"He hasn't looked well in years. That's not the reason. He manages all right for these Communist fronts."

"I understand he withdrew his name from some anti-Fascist group —I forget which."

"You still take the opposite side, Elizabeth. When I say white, you say black. There is only one thing I ask out of Martha's sojourn in Europe: I pray to God she will forget Marcus Hogan."

"I wonder if you would feel that way, Walter, if you realized the alternatives."

"I think I would. Anthony Fields, for example. He's in love with her. He came to see me while you were gone."

"How nice. They say *his* sister is a Communist."

"You're repeating filthy rumor, Elizabeth. Sylvia Fields has been working heart and soul for Alex's election."

"My only point was—I don't think Marcus has any politics. But you identify him with his father's."

"They're very close, those two—closer than I have ever got to my daughter." He frowned and then suddenly looked up. "Do you think there's any chance ever of Martha's becoming a nun?"

"It never entered my mind. At least, it hasn't for years." Sometimes, when Martha had been in high school, and she had watched the girl go off to church with her father so often, she had thought about that possibility.

"Would it trouble you a great deal if she did, Elizabeth?" The question was by no means casual. Nor was it sarcastic. He was, she realized, testing the sincerity of her own return to religious practice.

"I have been thinking lately," she said, out of God knows what wild subconscious, "of setting such an example myself."

"How interesting, how very interesting," he said in a tone of sudden and complete understanding, and he smiled.

"Christ have mercy," she said scarcely above her breath, and more in exclamation than in prayer. She gathered the luncheon things onto a tray and took them indoors.

·18

On the third of October, just a month before elections, Dr. Winthrop received a phone call from Mike Shea. It was their first communication since the day after the primaries. Winthrop felt a little sick when he took the phone and no better on hearing the smile in Mike's voice. He could see the cold blue eyes as clearly as if he were face to face with Mike himself.

"Oh, a fine campaign, Alex. You're to be congratulated, win, lose or draw."

"A clean one anyway, Mike."

"Clean as a whistle. I was just saying to the mayor a few minutes ago, a man like Winthrop—what a shame it is to tear down the gorgeous picture he's created of himself for the people of Traders City." So it had come at last, Winthrop thought, and he supposed he had known all along that it would come. "And do you know what the mayor said to me, Alex? He said, 'Mike, do we really have to do it?' And I said, 'Well, I tell you what we can do—we can put it up to Alex himself.' And as the mayor and I said then, we have a moral duty here to put it up to him before it goes to the people. It's like reading, you know: it isn't so much what gets into print that's bad; it's what comes into people's minds reading it."

"I don't know what you're talking about, Mike."

"Don't you now? I was hoping if I made a parable out of it, I wouldn't have to be more explicit. Or do you want me to be?"

"That's up to you, Mike."

"Ah, Alex . . . I don't even like to say the word 'cuckold.' It's a dirty, old-fashioned word, isn't it?" He paused. "Are you there, Alex?"

"I am."

"And a man's best friend . . . Mind now, I wouldn't be the one to gainsay temptation of the flesh. The world and all its palaces are as nothing to them . . ."

Very gently Winthrop hung up the phone. Shea could be no worse an enemy angry than benevolent, and to be righteous himself, he could no more listen to what Mike had to say than he could acknowledge there was a grain of truth in it. He called Walter Fitzgerald and told him that he would be at the house within the hour to speak to him and Elizabeth. Arriving there, he discovered that Elizabeth had a guest.

Fitzgerald said, "She has our protégé to tea."

"Hogan?"

Fitzgerald nodded. "He won't be staying long—such a busy man these days."

Winthrop was amused despite the grimness of his own mission. All summer long Fitzgerald's resentment of the Hogans had been building. As his loneliness had increased, he had increasingly focused the blame for his wife and daughter's absence on them. "You don't forget easily, do you, Walter?"

"Ingratitude is one of the basest things I know."

"You'll know of something baser before you're much older," Winthrop said. "Where are they?"

He went into the dining room himself where Elizabeth was pouring tea at a small table overlooking the garden. "Alexander!" she said, "What a lovely surprise." She did not look at him, not directly ever now, merely glancing toward him to acknowledge his presence.

Marcus stood up and extended his hand, a confident man, unashamed of his past, sure of his future. Winthrop had probably never envied anyone before in his life. He said, "I'm very proud of you, Hogan."

"Thank you, Doctor Winthrop," Marcus said. "It means a great deal to me that you are."

Their hands met in a firm clasp and they looked for an instant directly at one another. It was a better moment for him, Winthrop thought, than he deserved, and there was honor in it as there was not in the thing he was about to do. "I'm sorry to interrupt your tea, but it is absolutely necessary that I talk with Elizabeth and Walter immediately."

Curiously, the last time Marcus had gone to tea with Elizabeth Fitzgerald—at her studio then—he had not got to finish it either. She too remembered it. "Our teas are ill-fated, Marcus. We must try for dinner some time soon. I shall call you." She got up. "Please finish and don't hurry. Annie made the cake especially for you. I shall come back as soon as I can."

Marcus did not mean to watch them, but he glanced over his shoulder, thinking one of them had spoken to him, and saw Winthrop slowly nod his head, perhaps affirming a questioning look. As soon as they were gone, he left the house himself, going out by way of the terrace, and carrying with him a piece of cake which he ate in the car.

Elizabeth had never liked her husband's study: the leather chairs were cold and odorous, the prints of the wild geese forlorn. A hunter's horn and a rifle hung over the fireplace although Walter himself had a distinct aversion to the sport. She had once thought, looking in, it was so much a man's room it did not need a man in it. It was entirely apt that what must now be acted out be done here.

Winthrop stood, his hands behind his back, his shoulders hunched, his head down. "I don't know how to say this to you. I can begin by apologizing—particularly to Elizabeth. I got a call from Mike Shea this afternoon, Walter. He's threatening to link Elizabeth's and my name in scandal if I don't withdraw from the race."

Fitzgerald sat for a moment, his forefingers pointed together, the fingernails touching his teeth. "We had to assume he'd use such tactics when he got desperate."

"I'm genuinely sorry, Elizabeth," Winthrop said.

She roused herself and said flatly, "So am I." She had rather expected, returning to the church, and in the way of the prodigal, to have been spared retribution.

"Are you surprised?" Fitzgerald said to his wife. "I'd always thought you were made of more worldly stuff than that." Of Winthrop he asked, "Just what is he proposing to say?"

"I don't know exactly. I hung up on him, but it's along the lines that Elizabeth and I were having an affair behind your back."

"Not to my face?" Fitzgerald said. The remark disclosed a self-flagellation that turned Elizabeth cold. "If you can get him to repeat whatever it is publicly," Fitzgerald went on, "you can sue him for slander, can't you?"

"Of course. But the harm will have been done to you and your family, Walter."

Fitzgerald looked at his wife. "Isn't it fortunate you persuaded me to allow Martha this year abroad, Elizabeth?"

She simply could not look at him. "It will reach her there, too, I'm afraid. But it is better."

Fitzgerald laid his head on the back of the chair and studied the ceiling. "I suppose he must have something that seems like evidence on which to base such charges. Have you any idea what it could be?" He gave a dry laugh. "I've never thought you two got on together at all."

Winthrop said, "I've always been very fond of Elizabeth, Walter. I've considered you a lucky man."

Fitzgerald nodded and made a noise of agreement. "I suppose maybe that's what he's got hold of."

"I'm not sure I know what you mean, Walter."

"I've sometimes wondered if your friendship for me hadn't something in it of covetousness of my wife. And it has given me an odd kind of satisfaction." He sat up in his chair and spoke out harshly.

"She could take in any man, any man at all. I've seen her do it time and again. And I've profited by it, I'm well aware, in the patronage of men more successful than myself. I've profited by their lusting eyes, and watching, I've thought to myself, you poor benighted fools. What woman is what she pretends to be? Not my wife. My wife has the body of Venus—forgive me, Elizabeth—and the soul of Famine. And what none of you knew, Alex, what none of you knew . . ." His voice sank almost to a whisper ". . . I could not have lived with her otherwise." He hunched forward and buried his face in his hands.

Elizabeth thought she was going to faint; her mouth was dry, her lips almost numb and the taste in her throat was sickening.

Winthrop felt as though something was crawling up his back. It was not easy to watch a man, even a fool, make a spectacle of himself. And the odd idea occurred to him that even if he and Elizabeth were to confess their affair to Walter right now, he would not believe them. And this, of course, was the situation that was going to make it possible for him to spit in the blue, blue eye of Mike Shea.

"I could withdraw from the race," he said. "Reasons of health. I am sure there are a few doctors around town who would be willing to certify to it."

Fitzgerald slowly drew his face out from the cover of his hands. "No."

Winthrop said, "Elizabeth, say the word. It's your good name at stake here."

"I think I am going to be sick," she said, and managed somehow to get out of the room before it happened.

Fitzgerald said, "Alex, we shall fight them to the last scrap of courage. Let them dump their garbage where they will."

Mike Shea's charges, handed to the evening papers, created a furor in the city: they were going to be good for many a headline. Yet they did Shea's candidate very little good. In fact, it was not long before Mike could begin to calculate the harm it was doing him. Shameful as might be the charges against Winthrop, if true, the people felt it was even more shameful of the mayor to bring them up at this time. It was a desperate move, and nobody wanted to vote for a desperate candidate.

Mike Shea could count this, everybody said, a major blunder. Then Winthrop himself made one. Against George Bergner's advice to do nothing about Shea's libel—beyond making a public denial—until the campaign was over, Winthrop had no choice but to play it righteous all the way. Fitzgerald insisted on it and Winthrop filed suit. Shea filed counter-suit, and made the affidavits he had collected a matter of public records. Three employees of the International Building gave testimony, including a window washer whose very occupation, when published, suggested the most damning evidence of all. A state trooper testified to Winthrop's occasional visits to a cabin in the dunes in the company of a woman.

But through it all, Walter Fitzgerald was steadfast. He might not even have read the papers. The only thing which humiliated him, he told each of his classes, was that the University was once more in the newspapers, and he had never, never thought it would be on his account. Purposefully now he spent a little while every day in the men's faculty lounge: he was available for any question, any scrutiny. And it was there that Jonathan Hogan spoke to him.

"I don't know whether it will help his cause—or sink it, but I've undertaken to make a few speeches for Winthrop."

"It's a little late, isn't it, Hogan?"

"Yes."

"Do you mind my asking what prompted you to change your mind?"

The little twitching at Hogan's eye became more intense, his head nodding. "I've had my own days of persecution at the hands of the newspapers."

"Then you propose, by association, to prove Alexander Winthrop also innocent?" Fitzgerald said in bitter sarcasm.

"I do not have an opinion in the matter. I do not judge."

"I do," Fitzgerald snapped.

Hogan nodded his head. "I know that well enough, professor."

It would not make a great difference, but a few votes came along with Jonathan Hogan into Winthrop's camp. And they were not likely to be necessary. His supporters seemed to be holding fast. It was the die-hard Democrats who were defecting from Mike Shea—to, of all things, the Republican candidate, saying in effect to Winthrop and to the mayor, a plague on both your houses.

But Elizabeth found her first pleasure in many days in the rallying of the Hogans to their side. It was largely a gesture of loyalty, for she knew that nothing really had changed and that Marcus must now see confirmed what he earlier suspected. Perhaps it was Jonathan Hogan's reasoning that he was rallying to one more lost cause. She, too, and on the briefest of acquaintanceship, had been won to the man as had her daughter. He had the kindest face of any man she knew.

"Loyalty?" Fitzgerald said. "The man doesn't know the meaning of the word—not to country, nor to school, nor to any man."

"What does it mean then—his coming out for Alexander?"

"I don't know," he said, and then added vehemently, "but I am ashamed for Alexander that he accepted him."

"Ashamed? You are ashamed for that, Walter, and for nothing else?"

"Do not defend him to me, Elizabeth. I have seen the president of a university compromise his integrity on that man's behalf, and it is one of the greatest regrets in my life that I allowed myself to compromise also. I can see the pattern of corruption. I can feel its presence! In my own house, I can feel it closing in to destroy me. I shall do no more work for Alex now. If I could, I would undo what I've done for him."

He sat, tired and gray and full of hatred, and for the first time in so very long, Elizabeth was moved to pity. He saw what he had to see, and knew far more than he was aware of knowing. How arrogant of her to have supposed she could read him as though he were a child's primer.

She went to him and put a hand upon his shoulder. "Must you hate, Walter?"

It was some seconds before he said anything, then just the word "love," as though he were contemplating it.

They had an early dinner that night so that Annie could wash up and be off for the weekend with her relatives. She was bitter company in the house, these days of scandal. Professor Fitzgerald went into his study and closed the door; it was his old habit which he had fallen out of during the election campaign. Elizabeth went upstairs early and read late into the night. Now and then she heard a sound in the house. She did not hear him come upstairs, but dozing off, she might have missed him. The bathroom divided their bedrooms. But on the first instant of waking in the morning, she sensed herself to be alone in the house.

His bed had not been slept in. His study was empty, but his top-coat was in the closet. She called down into the basement and then went down. It was neat, and he was not there. Dressing, she went outdoors. She found him where he had hung himself in the tool shed, by the light of a now flickering, fading flashlight which was propped up on the potting bench. It was, to her knowledge, the first time he had even been in the building. His body was cold and stiff, but she cut him down and held him in her arms for a little while before going to call for help.

· 19

THE Mother Superior told Martha of her father's death. He was found to have taken his own life while temporarily insane, for he was not a man to have done it otherwise. A devout man really, Martha herself qualified. The nun nodded and said, "But of course! He is being given Christian burial." A requiem high Mass was sung for him in the school chapel on the day of his funeral.

Martha could not say that she grieved. She mourned her father, putting on the black which the nuns advised. Perhaps if she had knelt before the body, if she had attended the wake, seen Annie's tear-reddened eyes—for it was Annie who could grieve in the Irish way—there might have been a greater reality for her to his death. What she felt was melancholy, not sorrow. Then her mother wrote her briefly, but frankly, of the scandal. "They say Alexander and I have been lovers . . ." Martha was never to forget the shock of reading those words. The room seemed to tip sidewise so that she had to hold onto the chair in order not to lose her balance. But after it was straight again, the words were still there. They were there even after she no longer felt anything, reading them.

The two months which followed were to Martha time without definition, a clock without hands. She could not seem to relate to anything, to anybody. She studied and took her examinations. That she passed them mildly surprised her but did not especially please her. She wrote affectionate, comforting letters to her mother and to Marcus as though to console them because they did not feel that they could console her. She wrote the letters; they were in her handwriting, but she sensed no emotion, writing them. This was, she supposed, hypocrisy. But she could not find anything true within herself.

The nuns were understanding. They were French, after all, and however explosive a combination politics and cuckoldry, they all too often went together in French history. The good nuns were, however, at a loss to understand the girl's aloofness at such a time. She was expected, indeed she was encouraged, to confide, to weep, to beat her fists; in other words, to take full advantage of the chance to dramatize herself and thus to spend her travail in a natural and profitable manner.

How could she explain that she felt no travail?

Another American student who seemed in some unremembered way associated with the trauma was Genevieve Revere who had that autumn made herself quite despicable to Martha. In art class and before the lay instructor she had told how she had teased poor Sister Mathilde. Martha discovered then that she had not been the only girl to whom Mathilde had confided her crush on Revere. The poor unbalanced nun had told it to anyone she thought would carry it back to Genevieve.

"And finally," Revere had said, telling her tale in the art class, "finally she destroyed my painting."

"She did not," Martha had said. "I destroyed it."

"You did! Why? It was a joke, Martha."

"Then it was a filthy joke."

"Do you mean filthy—dirty?"

"Yes. That, too."

And that, Martha had discovered, perversely won her the unwanted devotion of Genevieve Revere. The girl renewed an old invitation to share an apartment in the Latin Quarter of Paris instead of going home. Revere had Parisian friends who gathered all the American papers for her and she became the most informed person on the Winthrop-Fitzgerald scandal on that side of the Atlantic. She got it all to Martha as though it were the duty of a friend, and as though it ought to win her friendship in return. So Martha came to know, whether or not she wanted to, that Dr. Winthrop was denounced by Judge Phipps in a front page editorial in the *Dispatch* on election eve, that he was defeated and a Republican victorious in Traders City, and she knew that before Christmas Dr. Winthrop withdrew his libel suit against Michael Shea.

When Genevieve said in feigned innocence, "Why would he do that?" Martha said coldly, "Because it costs a great deal of money." But she knew very well that was not the reason. She could not be shocked again, however. Her mother's plain telling of the charges in the first place had been to her admission of their truth. What did happen to Martha now, however, was a sudden desire for change, to leave the convent school for freedom, for—as she wrote to Marcus because there was no one else to whom she could write or say it— "a house without eyes, a place among strangers."

Although she did not realize it, she had voiced her first personal protest, her first consciousness of being, perhaps, herself a victim of the tragedy.

And then one day she was called to the visitor's parlor where Dr. Nathan Reiss was waiting. He took both her hands in his, thanked the portress loudly, and winked at Martha when he saw the old nun take her place just outside the open door.

"This is a beautiful chateau," he said, and he touched his fingers to the draperies. "Gold damask. There is a poor school attached? There always is."

"To the elementary school," Martha said. "I don't think they've ever thought of a college for the poor."

"The poor it does not take so long to finish, eh? Unless they are stubborn like me."

Martha smiled and sat down opposite a chair she thought he might find comfortable. "Please, doctor," she said.

He sat down, crossed his knees, and smiled. "Would you find it very difficult to call me Nathan?"

"I probably should . . . here," she said, and then blushed because it sounded as though she were looking for an invitation.

"I understand. But I do not have a beard so that they will not believe I am a doctor in any case." He indicated the nun with a nod of his head. "I have been wondering—if you do not have other arrangements—would you care to be the New Year's week guest of a very dear friend of mine, the Baroness Schwarzbach? She will write to you herself, of course, and to the sisters if that is proper. But I thought I should prepare the way first. She is very nice and gay, and she entertains people from all over the world."

"You are very kind, Doctor Reiss."

He glanced in the nun's direction, so that what he said seemed merely mischievous, not improper. "And you are very beautiful. I may then arrange it?"

"Thank you."

It was a holiday such as Martha had never known. She truly found her place among strangers, except that no one treated her like a

stranger; no one treated anyone like a stranger. She discovered people, men and women, whom she would have said were casually acquainted, engaged in the most intimate discussions.

The Baroness herself, a plump but delicately cared for woman,
came into Martha's room the first morning of her visit. "Nathan tells
me there is such a tragedy, poor child. Tell me." She seated herself
in a chair at the side of Martha's bed, and arranged something in
her lap which Martha realized was a small gray poodle with glistening bright eyes, red-rimmed, and a black nose that also glistened.
"You must tell me now, my dear. Do not mind Pépé." She spoke
sometimes in English, sometimes in French to Martha. Yet her accent was not French.

Slowly, with great diffidence, Martha told the story. It was the
first time she had told it to anyone, and there was some gratification
in the telling. Her hostess kept making clicking noises of sympathy
at which sound the dog would look up into her face and then to
Martha, for all the world as though he, too, felt sympathy.

"Tell me, my dear, is your mother French?"

"Irish."

"Of one thing I was certain—not German or English." And presently she said, "You will not wear black tonight, my dear: a touch
of red for gallantry. Oh, yes! It takes great courage to commit suicide.
One has to care very much about what happens because he dies by
his own hand. It is the ultimate weapon, death. Is it not? Some men
turn it on themselves, some upon the other. There is no mercy in
killing oneself. To kill the other—one hopes for vindication, for
mercy."

But, Martha thought, how could a madman so reason? Did then
the Church's finding of temporary insanity restore her father to
grace by depriving him of reason?

"Why men die," the Baroness said, "it is very interesting." She
picked up a crumb from Martha's breakfast tray and fed it to the
dog, and another and another while she talked. "My first husband
was killed in a diamond mine—a cave in because he went too fast.
I've always thought it interesting that he, the master, was killed.
Usually it is the natives, the slaves who are killed, and the accident
has no meaning. Significance, but no meaning. My second husband
was clawed to death by a wounded tiger—I have often thought because he could not bring himself to shoot straight the first time.
That was Baron Schwarzbach. Poor boy. He was raised to the hunt,

but he preferred Mozart." Again the dog was presented a crumb which he licked from the tip of her finger. "That is sad, isn't it? But the thing that is terrible—to be raised to Mozart and to crave the hunt. I understand you were disappointed in Vienna? We behaved very badly for you."

"You are Austrian, Baroness?"

"But, of course. My title is French, however. The Austrians are not so generous to Schwarzbachs. Paris is my second home, or perhaps my third. I love also Naples. The most romantic part of me will live there forever . . . Pépé, you are going to get fat! But why not? You are a Frenchman." She got up and tucked the little dog under her arm life a muff, and picking up the nub of the flaky roll which was left, she dipped it into the last curl of butter and gave it to him. "Such a darling beast, what can I do?" she said, and shrugged so that just for the instant Martha saw the several lines drawn tightly beneath her chin all the way to her ear.

"We must talk longer together, you and I—but another day. I will send my maid to you within the hour, child. But do not wear black to the fete tonight."

"May I wear my white brocade? I don't have so much choice, Baroness."

The Baroness thought about it. "White with red roses. That will be very nice. Pépé, red roses. We must remember red roses."

At luncheon Nathan Reiss proposed that he take Martha shopping that afternoon since they must both buy New Year's gifts. They need buy only for the other house guests and their hostess, but since there were eight other house guests it was a considerable undertaking. The excursion was gay. As Dr. Reiss said, a doctor's holiday is like no other man's, he has so few of them. Martha was pleased to hear him say that, for she had never quite got over the notion that he was not really a doctor.

"Do you practice in Paris, doctor?"

"Yes."

"In a hospital?"

"But, of course, only in a hospital. I am a surgeon."

"I know. Doctor Mueller told me."

"Would you like to see the hospital?"

"Very much."

"But why?"

"I could tell Marcus about it. He also is a surgeon."

"May I tell you something? There is no place in all Paris he will care less to hear about in a letter from you."

Martha laughed.

They had bought small gifts on the Rue de Rivoli, knit gloves and ties, and stopped at the Ritz for an apéritif. At a shop on the Avenue de l'Opéra, they bought linen handkerchiefs, the lace trim of which, Reiss said, would raise a blister on the nose of a gargoyle.

"Even on Pépé's," Martha said.

"You noticed, too? That dog is obscene—red eyes and a running nose, and a belly like a tea kettle." He shuddered, having shaped his hand as he might to hold the dog in it. "Perhaps we can go to the opera one evening before Epiphany. Would you like that?"

"Very much, doctor."

"No, only if you call me Nathan. I will not have people say I am escorting a child who calls me doctor."

"Do you think I am a child?"

"An adorable one," he said, and gently pressed her hand.

"Nathan, how old would you suppose the Baroness is?"

He stood apart from her and laughed aloud. "I have known her twenty years and she is no older now. My dear, she is ageless. But if you were to look up in the social register or whatever they call it, it would tell you she was born fifty and some years ago."

"No!"

"And you were going to write your fiancé about the hospital!"

Martha smiled and took his arm to cross the street. "He's not really my fiancé, I suppose."

"You aren't going to be married?"

"Oh, yes, but . . ."

When she hesitated, he added, "But he doesn't know it yet." He threw up his hand, gesturing for a taxi. "We have two hours. Where would you like to go?"

"Montmartre, if it's possible. I have a letter to friends—of a friend."

"An artist?"

"Actually, friends of Doctor Mueller's wife."

"It is a very expensive time to visit artists, let me tell you. Come, we shall make an unforgettable impression."

As it happened, Julia Mueller's friends had gone to the south of France for the holiday, not to the Riviera, but to Arles. They had left behind a number of very sociable acquaintances, however.

"Now there is where I wish I could take you to find them," Reiss said.

"Mother and I were there," Martha said.

"I think I could make you forget that." He made a face of mock chagrin at what he had said, and Martha laughed. He bought a great many artists a number of cognacs, who, for the most part, drank death to war, and life to the heart.

When they were leaving a veritable colony waved them down the steps of Sacré Coeur.

"They are pacifists," Martha said on the way down.

"Communists," Nathan said, "or possibly Nazis. They are the greatest pacifists of all among the French."

"Are there French Nazis?"

"Mmmmm. Some. In very high places and by some other names. You may very well meet some tonight, but you will not know it . . . until they start talking peace. That is when I can tell."

"Nathan, isn't the Baroness Schwarzbach Jewish?"

"Yes," he said, his tone philosophic if his answer was equivocal. "I want to buy you something, my dear. Nothing intimate, but something you would like." He signaled a taxi.

"A book?" Martha suggested. "That's what I got you, you know. A book about America."

He turned in the cab and smiled broadly, his teeth gleaming in the winter twilight.

"I shouldn't have told you," Martha said. "It should have been a surprise."

"I am surprised and I am delighted, but now *you* shall not know. You must sit in the taxi and wait for me."

He stopped the cab at the monument at Place Vendôme, left it and walked to beyond where Martha could see him. When he returned, he said, "In my right pocket is the Baroness. In my left, you."

Martha said, "It must be very difficult to select a gift for the Baroness."

"Not as difficult as it is for her to select for herself."

Martha did not see him very much that evening. He sat at the Baroness' right at dinner, and he danced first with her at midnight. Martha's dinner partner was the son of an Italian diplomat who could talk of very little except skiing, or at least very little which Martha could understand. But she was reminded of Tony Fields, and he danced beautifully, and she was not really very happy; but gay she was, or thought she was, which matched the mood of everyone. People said even the most serious things lightly, as did the Italian diplomat to a Frenchman—a newspaper publisher—as it seemed practically all important Frenchmen were. The Italian said, "But to sign a pact with the Soviets. You have made even Belgium an enemy." The Frenchman shrugged. "She is better that than a friend, for us." Martha drank quite a lot of champagne. And when at last he came up to her, Nathan seemed to have drunk a great deal too. The lids were a little heavy upon his eyes, and his mouth, delicate, sensuous, seemed just a little pouty now—or wistful; that was a better word.

"I have had to wait so long tonight for this moment," he said. "But it is a waltz." He turned to the Italian boy, saying, "You will excuse us?" not even waiting for an answer. Dancing, he drew her close to him for a moment: "It is not our first waltz, if you remember. But it was from then I began to plan this one. Did you know that?"

"No. Or maybe I did," Martha said, being strictly honest.

"I have your present in my pocket. I want to give it to you now."

"But we are to give them all together," Martha said.

"I will give you something else all together," Reiss said, and then sensing uneasiness, "Do not be alarmed. It will not compromise you."

Martha said nothing.

There were many avenues of privacy in the Baroness' home, alcoves shadowed by great potted palms, and it was into one of these they danced. The walls were exquisitely papered with plump, gamboling children, lighted by wall-sconced candles.

"They're like Boucher," Martha said. "Or are they Boucher?"

Reiss did not answer, taking from his pocket the small box from which he drew a narrow gold bracelet delicately etched so that it caught the light. "You see, it has no hidden meanings, only my pleasure in making you a gift."

"It is lovely," Martha said.

"You will wear it and sometimes think of me?"

"Oh, yes," she said, and put it on.

"The book you are giving me about America—may I suppose that is because you hope I shall come there?"

"That would be very nice," Martha said.

"You are very cautious—and yet provocative. You have a devil, young lady."

Martha smiled and showed the bracelet. She asked, looking up suddenly, "But is it proper? It *is* jewelry."

"Not the dangerous kind," he said. "A Happy New Year, Martha."

"Happy New Year, Nathan."

She had known he would kiss her, and she had wanted it, and she was—quite definitely, she told herself at the instant their lips met— her mother's daughter. He kissed her gently at first, then suddenly in a manner strange and terrible. It roused in her nonetheless the desire to feel his body against hers as she now did, intimately, for they were almost of a height.

But this was the flesh, the flesh without love. Only self-love. She broke the hold of his arms and moved from him. "Nathan, I do not love you."

"You are lonely. Let me love you. It will be enough for tonight. And tomorrow—if you wish—you will forget."

"But I love Marcus. Don't you understand?"

"Yes—but you are not affianced, so you said."

"I should not have said it then. I consider myself to be."

"A woman in love—needs love. And I need it—I am as far from love as you. Much farther. No one will ever know."

She shook her head and turned away from him. Behind her, he put his arms about her, his hands lingering a moment at her breasts, then folding around her waist. "Please?" He put his mouth to her ear with the word, and then touched the lobe of her ear with his tongue.

She averted her head sharply.

He drew a deep breath and released her. "You must not be angry. So be it! But when I come to America, I want to meet this great man Marcus—for whom you are holding such treasure."

Martha tried to conceal the depth of her own need for breath. "Thank you, Nathan . . . for everything," she said, facing him guardedly.

"I wish you were thanking me for more," he said, his eyes still limpid beneath the half-closed lids.

But he kissed her lightly on either cheek, without touching his hands to her, and then taking her arm, led her out from among the sheltering palms and into the dance once more.

From where she sat at the end of the ballroom, her head tilted

back as though she were listening to the man who had her ear, a
jeweled hand supporting her chin, the Baroness watched them return
to the dance. She touched her hand to her companion's knee.

"Excuse me, my friend, what time is it now?"

"My God, it is but three minutes since you asked." But he looked
at his watch. "Four minutes, Baroness. It is half past one."

She nodded in satisfaction. "You were saying?"

The night was interminable, Martha thought, and she must wait
up until after the ball and the giving of gifts among the household.
One had to be born to this; Americans might play at it, but they
could never understand it. The only people in Paris she could truly
understand were now propped up by the elbows at the Ritz or some
other bar, singing "Back Home in Indiana" or "The Sidewalks of
New York."

At five o'clock in the morning, the gifts distributed and hot coffee
passed, the Baroness called for attention.

"A Happy New Year to our friends across the sea!" A footman
had turned in the short wave radio and now turned it up. "A Happy
New Year from Times Square, Broadway and Forty-second Street,
United States of America." And among the cheers weaving up and
down on the waves of sound came the thin strain of "Auld Lang
Syne," to which everyone present joined his voice in the accent and
words of his own tongue.

Martha wept openly, and gave her cheek to a kiss from the Baroness, thanked her, and went up to her room.

Later in the morning, New Year's, she was awakened by the arrival
of a cablegram:

HAVE PLACE FOR YOU NOT AMONG STRANGERS. COME
HOME AND MARRY ME NOW. EDUCATION WILL
FOLLOW. CABLE YES AND MOTHER WILL CABLE
SCHOOL. I LOVE YOU WITH ALL MY HEART. MARCUS.

Within the week Martha sailed for home, and on January 31, 1937,
she and Marcus were married in the parish house of the church in
which she had been baptized almost twenty years before.

PART
TWO

1941

• 1

ALEXANDER WINTHROP was not a man likely to long remain idle in any case, but the circumstances of his defeat in the mayoralty campaign of 1936 were such that instead of his being frustrated, he was sped to new ambitions, his energies in full flood, no longer dissipated in that most enervating of human experiences, a misalliance. And in one of the sweet uses of adversity, he became better known nationally from that time on than might have been his lot as mayor of Traders City.

One of the first things he did, defeated, was call personally on the Presidential Cabinet Secretary in whose Washington office George Bergner had been working. His purpose was to save George, insofar as he could, from the acrimonious aftermath of the defeat. His visit was the beginning of a strong friendship between him and the Secretary. He came very near to taking an administrative post in Washington himself. He was forestalled, however, by the deathbed decision of old Alicia Fields to set up a foundation in the family name for medical research. She asked him to be its first administrator.

She did not put conditions, but he supposed he knew what was at the back of her mind: it had been in her mind, back and front, for many years. It had graced his own more than once while Sylvia was working so earnestly for his election. He had always had a comradely sort of feeling for Sylvia; she was passionate about a number of things, an attitude he admired although he thought his own candidacy her first sensible cause. As for feminine attractions, he would once have said the old lady had more for him than had her daughter. His feelings had somewhat altered. He did not commit himself except on the Fields Foundation, but the old lady died happy, secure in the conviction that her wish would prevail. She had always said he was a man of conscience.

He had been so long a man of conscience, he reveled in becoming a man of expedition. After Martha's marriage Elizabeth went to live in Ireland, but by then she might as well have stayed in Traders City for all her presence would have affected him: nothing severs an attachment so fast as the rebuff of a correspondent at the moment of mutually wrought disaster. He no longer measured himself by what

155

he had long supposed her scale; nor did he hark back to his father and his own ill-bought inheritance. What he was, he was. He liked to think that he was now able to see realities, and it was in this period that he acquired a habit which stayed with him the rest of his life: he would sound a table with his knuckles, a wall, a piece of brass or stone, and was likely to say, if the sound pleased him, "That's the real thing."

The Fields Foundation, endowed from the outset with sixty million dollars, was certainly "the real thing." Its first large grant, to a project already going forth jointly in Great Britain and the United States and, incidentally, recommended to Winthrop's attention by the Cabinet Secretary, received notice in all the national magazines. It also provided Judge Phipps with the editorial grist his mill ground best.

The publisher prided himself on having brought Winthrop down in 1936, and there was no doubt he had helped. But no one ever credited the *Dispatch* with the influence Phipps claimed for it—no one could. But a number of people kept trying to discredit it: the fogy sheet, the bogy sheet, the newspaper on a crusade to nowhere. Phipps encouraged the notion of a personal feud between himself and Winthrop. Having long since abandoned hope of gaining distinguished friends for the *Dispatch,* the judge cherished its enemies. He managed to get enough facts about the grant to compound with his prejudice into a story of international intrigue, Washington betrayal, and Winthrop's disbursement of a proud American fortune: a fortune gleaned from the plains of the Middle West to be squandered on imperial English soil. It made great local copy at the time, but no impression whatever on the trustees of the foundation or on politics, national or international. History was beginning to outrun the judge.

Mike Shea, through these years, watched both men cagily. He spent his four years after 1936 shoring up the dikes, knowing the tide was against him, but looking always to the day it would turn. He even supported the governor in 1938, for in his Irish heart he loved lost causes, albeit he could rarely afford to champion them. The governor went down inevitably. As Mike said dryly, he could have done it without his help: almost every village and city in the state that year, including Traders City, went Republican; the popularity of the national administration was ebbing fast. But in 1940 there was war in Europe, Roosevelt won over Willkie, and in Traders City, hanging on for dear life to the President's coattails, Mike Shea and his Democratic candidate for mayor rode back into office. Winthrop, on an impulse, sent Mike a telegram of congratulations.

Mike called him up. "Alex, that was a grand gesture." And after a while: "Alex, I don't suppose you'd consider going back as Health Commissioner for this administration?"

Winthrop laughed heartily. "No, Mike, thanks, I had nothing like that in mind."

"Ah, you're too big for it now, of course," Mike said. "And to tell you the truth, I'm damn glad of that. I don't know where we're going to get the jobs to go round this time. But let me know if there's anything I can do for you now, won't you?"

It left a bad taste in Winthrop's mouth, the realization that the same old pork barrel was rolling into the city again. But back of the impulse on which he had congratulated Mike was advice from Washington. For over a year now, every time he and the Secretary got together, they had explored—very informally and in mutual confidence—the need for a new morning newspaper in Traders City. Winthrop had begun to take it seriously, for the Fields Foundation by then required only part of his time. The Secretary, apparently, was also serious. He called Winthrop one night in February of '41 and told him he was sending George Bergner out to see him.

Winthrop, therefore, was not surprised when George arrived at his office the following afternoon with some rather fully developed plans. What did surprise and then amuse him was that Bergner spoke as though the whole idea was his, as though he had no notion the matter had been gone over for months by the Secretary and Winthrop. Perhaps he did not know it, and just possibly it had been his idea in the first place. But Winthrop could not help feeling that George was going at it in the way of a promoter selling a product already half-sold, ignoring the previous salesmanship lest he have to share the commission. That Bergner was a promoter, he knew; how much more he was, he wondered. George was speaking rather too fervently just now to be his superior's emissary.

Winthrop went to the window and stood, his back to George, the better to think while he listened. George was saying how enthusiastic the President was over the idea. Winthrop was staring down at the new bridge which the President himself had come to Traders City to dedicate the year before. He had had the good sense not to praise

its engineering: somebody had stretched an extra mile of construction contract out of the approaches with two otherwise inexplicable
hairpin curves. He could see, out of the corner of his eye, Bergner's
polished shoe describing impatient circles.

Winthrop said, "Does the President want to see me himself—if
he's all that enthusiastic?"

"I'm sure an appointment could be set up, Alex."

"I'm sure it could, too. That was not what I asked."

"He did not specifically say so—to my knowledge. As a matter of
fact, it's the Secretary who is carrying the ball to the White House."

Winthrop returned to his desk. "As a matter of fact, George—
just between ourselves—wasn't it the Secretary's idea in the first
place?"

Bergner's face flushed. It was getting a bit puffy under the eyes.
He had been eager and young and saved, diving into the arms of
the New Deal out of college. He, too, was needing artificial stimu-
lants now. He said with considerable dignity, "All ideas coming
out of our office are the Secretary's."

"You wouldn't be willing to give up your job—for something here,
would you?" Winthrop tested.

"I'd be a damned fool if I wouldn't," George said bluntly.

Something in the exchange played a trick on Winthrop's memory: it was like a twice played scene. Then he remembered the association, his asking Marcus Hogan if he saw himself head of the
new sanatorium he proposed during their first interview. He wondered, in passing, if Hogan's answer would be the same today as
then.

Strangely, George's mind had also turned to a Hogan. He said,
"I remember old Jonathan Hogan saying why he had to get out of
Washington: he couldn't understand how so much that was decent
got done by men so indecent in their competition to do it."

"It's that bad," Winthrop said. Bergner was not a man to prosper
on competition. It was to his credit now that he could admit it.

"Either you go up, or you ought to get out."

"What's your job down there?" Winthrop asked.

"The manufacture of titles for people about to be kicked upstairs."

Winthrop laughed. It was surprising that George had survived
this long with the Secretary: there was surely no more competitive

man in the administration, and probably no more competent. "Is the Secretary as much an autocrat as they say?"

"Let me put it this way, Alex: he's the best offensive man on the team."

Winthrop leaned back in his chair. "Why the hell don't you teach school somewhere and get out of politics, George? Or hang up your shingle again. You're a lawyer."

"There ought to be a pretty good place for a lawyer like me in the office of a liberal newspaper," George said doggedly.

"What do you mean by a liberal newspaper? A war sheet, that's what your boss wants, isn't it? Something to stack up against Phipps's isolationism. Isn't that it?"

"That's it only in part, Alex . . ."

Winthrop interrupted. "And what the devil do you fellows think —that we're still in the days of James Gordon Bennett? Three million dollars to put the first edition on the streets—without a plant, that is—and that's a careful estimate."

"The Secretary figures it closer to four."

"That's because he's a liberal," Winthrop said. "Why doesn't he come home and start it himself?"

"He's an old man, Alex."

"These are times when the old men thrive. The young ones 'll be going to war soon. Where does he think this four million dollars is coming from?"

"I have the names with me of several men interested in the investment." George said the words blandly, reached down to the floor for his briefcase and opened it there.

"And the staff—where are you going to get them?"

"There are some good men who'll come over to us. There aren't many liberal newspapers in this country."

"If they're not damn fools they'll stick to their conservative jobs. They'll be in business longer."

George did not attempt to interrupt. He brought up a folder and separated one page from several, putting it before Winthrop. Winthrop glimpsed the names without looking directly at it: he wanted only the notion of who they were. Texas money, he observed, and New York. He mused aloud: "I wonder how Mike Shea would feel about this."

Without hesitation and unsmiling, Bergner said, "The city will need two hundred thousand dollars' worth of space during the first year."

Winthrop leaned back in his chair and laughed: Mike Shea would soon be paying off on a telegram. He said, scarcely touching the piece of paper in front of him, "You can put that away, George."

"Don't you want to see who the potential investors are?"

"No. I do not. If it's to be my newspaper, I'll choose my own investors." He got out an address and phone book from his desk drawer. "Where do you think you'd like to put your desk, George?" He spoke half-jokingly.

"In management. I'm not a newspaper man," George said.

"What makes you think you're a manager?"

"I think *you* are, Alex, and wherever I put my desk, I have no doubts about who's going to be sitting at it most of the time."

Winthrop grinned, and it passed through his mind that if George was as good with the hatchet on others as he was on himself, he could become a very nearly indispensable man. He called Washington and got through directly to the Secretary, using his private number.

The only other man daring to do that, Bergner thought, was the President of the United States.

That evening, its being Thursday, Winthrop attended the Traders City Symphony concert. He sat with Sylvia and thought, as he always did on musical occasions, of Elizabeth Fitzgerald. It was odd that a man as unmusical as himself should be attracted to women to whom music meant so much. He glanced at Sylvia, alert, her severe chin poised, and having something in common he felt with the conductor's baton. He admired her intensity, the way she had of going heart and soul into everything in which she was at all involved. At the moment it was Mendelssohn. No pose, no guile, really. Straight. And she had probably exhausted any man who had ever had the guts to take up with her. He could not number many such possibilities over their long acquaintanceship. She had been a school girl when he acquired Tamarack. He had bought it for its size and isolation, with vague ideas of Elizabeth as its mistress, and under the mistaken notion that there was privacy in Lakewood. From the first, Alicia Fields had taken him over: in the beginning perversely as though to mock him—she had advised him on his art collection, and what nobody to this day was aware that he knew, the old witch had loaded him with expensive duds: she had, simultaneous to building his collection, improved her own on the advice of dealers, for which he was sure he had paid. He never went into his own gallery—or his library. They had been his tribute to the gods he worshiped, expecting by it to gain their heaven. But in the end Alicia had come round: she had been the real thing, the old aristocrat, and she had had her own test of a man's mettle.

He stirred in his seat and Sylvia put her hand on his as she might on a restless child's. He caught it and was tempted to lift it to his lips, but the lights never went that low in Orchestra Hall. He squeezed it and they glanced at one another with very little turning of their heads. He saw the color suffuse her long neck, and disappear beneath the iron grey curls. And to this he responded within himself . . . and was grateful that it happened to him. A man of conscience truly.

· 2

THE house on Oak Street, deeded by Elizabeth to Martha and her husband, became soon after they moved into it, a convenient meeting place for many people. Rather too many, Martha sometimes thought, but the envy of her childhood and youth had been the houses of her friends which seemed to have no locks upon the doors. The Muellers came; Sylvia Fields and Martha had become close friends, the closest Martha had ever had, in fact; Tony Fields was in the habit of bringing his girl to dinner every month or so, and almost invariably a new one who, he would assure Martha in a stolen moment's confidence, was truly the only one for him. And Jonathan kept a pair of pajamas and a change of linens in his temporary quarters, Martha's own old room, which was destined, when the time came, to be the nursery. But in four years Martha had suffered two miscarriages, one of them after six months.

The Hogan house served among its numerous offices in those days as headquarters for the University branch of "Bundles for Britain." Annie said the place looked more like the laundry of International House or Treadwell Street (the famous Sunday morning market in the Jewish section). But, however she described it, she always added to Martha, "Mind now, I'm not complaining."

Annie would not for the world have complained at this point in her life: she had seen this house grow cold with hate, crooked with deception, still with death and warm again with love . . . All this she had seen, she told her friends, unbeknownst to herself. But whatever she had known or felt, her wild red hair had turned a rusty gray. She had gone back to Ireland with Elizabeth Fitzgerald in the cold of February—and had returned forever to America the same spring.

"Mind, I'm not complaining," she said to Martha, starting up the stairs when the front doorbell rang. But her mind was on a lovely gray sweater in that day's lot which she would have liked to have for one of her nieces in Ireland, who, God knew, needed it almost as much as the British, poor things. It was a charity that warmed her heart, parceling out bundles for Britain, but her occasional honest thievery on behalf of the impoverished Irish salved her conscience for having denounced the land of her birth when Martha invited her to come back and keep house for her and the doctor. It was a case, by Annie's logic, of a wrong and a right making a right and a wrong.

She opened the front door to Sylvia Fields. A cold rain was pelting down.

"I should have gone round by the basement," Sylvia said, "but I didn't think of it till I'd rung the bell." She took off her coat and hat and shook her head like a colt.

"It's all right, Miss," Annie said, and watched her then unwrap an enormous package. It was a raccoon coat. "Lord, I haven't seen one of them in years."

"Do you think it's too ostentatious—I mean to give to the British?"

"Indeed not. It'll be better at night than a sleeping bag."

Sylvia wondered if Annie had been reading *For Whom the Bell Tolls*. Not very likely.

"Look what I've brought," she called out to Martha on the stairs. She put the coat on herself and wore it going down.

"You look pregnant," Martha said, and felt very strange when Sylvia blushed.

Sylvia took off the coat and put it alongside several others hung from the water pipe near the ceiling. "I don't suppose Marcus is coming home early? Annie says she'll call down when tea's ready, by the way."

"If your luck is good," Martha said. "I've decided it's all a matter of luck when I get him home, having absolutely nothing to do with clocks."

Sylvia looked at her scrutinously. "You're looking stunning."

Martha smiled in her sudden way. "I feel stunning—when I don't feel nauseated."

"I thought so!" Sylvia cried, meaning she had suspected Martha to be pregnant again. "You've got that look in your eye."

"This time for keeps, please God." Martha clasped her hands together in determination. "It's still raining, isn't it?"

Sylvia broke away from the sudden digression of her own thoughts. "Torrents." She looked around. "My God, people wear extraordinary things, don't they?" She picked up an inner garment gingerly.

"That is a corset cover, according to Annie."

"I'd hate to tell you what I thought it was," Sylvia said. "Martha . . ."

Martha waited out the hesitation.

"Never mind, I'll tell you at tea. Annie invited me. She said to tell you she'd call down when it's ready. I just said that, didn't I?"

"It's something tremendous, isn't it? You can't even look at me in the face," Martha prodded.

"For heaven's sake, don't start guessing." She laid her hand on Martha's and gave it a quick, nervous squeeze. "I'm going to be married."

It was indeed startling news to Martha. "I think that's just marvelous, Syl. Look at me." She gave her friend a shake. "You certainly managed to keep things to yourself."

"For years and years," Sylvia said. "I'm going to marry Alexander . . . some time this spring."

Martha's hands fell away; she needed them to steady herself against the wash tub at her back. She failed to control the little shudder of revulsion that ran through her at the whole chain of association.

Neither of them spoke for a long moment, but Sylvia had seen what happened. "I didn't think you were going to feel that way about it."

Martha said, "I didn't have time . . . to think about it at all. I'm surprised. That's all."

"Thanks," Sylvia said.

Martha could not amend her reaction. Nor could she wax enthusiastic when her heart was simply not in it. "I'm sorry."

"For what?" Sylvia flared. "That I'm marrying him? I've loved him long enough and well enough to wait all the days your mother had him at her discretion. Think of it, Martha. From your high perch, look down a minute and think what it would be like if you hadn't got Marcus when you wanted him, if he'd gone off to someone else. And always there was the chance it would break up. After all, who knows better than you that it should have broken up? Would you have been cured in my position?"

"No," Martha said quietly. "Nothing would ever have cured me of Marcus. Nothing will."

"Then wish me Godspeed, at least."

Sylvia's eyes were filling. Martha pulled her into her arms and hugged her. "Forgive me, Sylvia. Please. Do forgive me."

Sylvia responded to her affection awkwardly, and then drew back. "You've got to forgive Alexander, Martha. I don't suppose I can make you like him, but that's where you've got to start. You must. It wasn't all his fault, you know."

"It's never the man's," Martha said, repeating a line of Annie's she had heard so often it came out without her summoning it. "That's what Annie will say. She's going to be very happy about this. She *is*." Martha thought further about it. "She has a marvelous sense of the fitness of things. It will put Doctor Winthrop right back up on the pedestal where she had him for years."

"I'm very fond of Annie, but I'm not marrying Alexander to put her scales in balance."

Martha said, looking at her and seeing her in a new way, really, "I want you to be very happy, Syl. I want it for both of you."

Sylvia moved away and back again, restless, excited. "When I was your age, I could have fallen in love too if I'd got the chance at somebody decent. I managed to live for a while in New York's Greenwich Village. I used to stand for hours outside where Edna St. Vincent Millay lived—hoping she'd ask me what time it was—or drop something on my head. An old lover, maybe, she was throwing out. I even gave away all my furniture because I heard that everyone sat around on cushions in her place. I let an artist paint murals on my walls. Deep purple. My mother was absolutely horrified. She said, and I remember it quite clearly, 'Sylvia, I am going to make you a final offer. Come home with me, and I shall buy you any painter of your choice. Stay, and you must earn your own bread.' I've often won-

dered what she would have done if I'd asked for a live painter."
Martha laughed. Sylvia smiled, but sighed at the same time.

Presently Martha asked, "Where will you live—you and Alexander?" She supposed it was the first time she had ever spoken of him by his given name.

Nor was it lost on Sylvia. "I think Tony must have our house in Lakewood. Mother's will didn't specify. She could be deliberately vague on some things. As for that Italian grotesque of Alexander's. . . ."

Martha laughed aloud.

"You must not repeat that, friend Martha. Something will happen to it one of these days. Alex can't really afford it, unless he becomes a tax-free institution . . . The inheritance tax on mother's estate was over seven million dollars, by the way."

"*Pauvre, pauvre,*" Martha said.

Sylvia laughed at herself. "We have a farm just north of Lakewood with a house about this size. I have an idea that's where . . ." She interrupted herself. She was much too apt to plan for everybody. "But you and Marcus have got to come this spring to Alex's soiree. You've got to, and I shall see that some of our people are there: the Muellers, sans children, and Jonathan. I don't know which of Tony's females should be invited. All of them, I suppose. My God, Mother will turn over in her grave. She considered an excess of females at any party positively gauche."

"I expect we'd better get started packing these things," Martha said. "The truck will be here at five."

They worked a few moments in silence. Then at the sound of footsteps overhead, Martha stopped. "Marcus is home," she said.

She said it as though her very heart was on tiptoe, Sylvia thought. But for once, as Marcus came down the stairs, she was able to watch them, to see the meeting of their eyes, and not to be ashamed for her own embarrassment.

"Beautiful people, move over," Sylvia said. "I'm coming to the party."

· 3

IN ORDER for Marcus to attend the Winthrop affair at all he needed to so arrange his schedule that he could combine the party with his weekly visit to Dr. Bergner. The old gentleman had not been going into the city for over a year, but he insisted on Marcus's consultation, and when necessary they used the facilities of Lakewood Hospital, for example, to look at X rays. Dr. Bergner had been a trustee and an honorary member of the Lakewood staff for many years. It was a small hospital, well endowed and well staffed, at least technologically: the doctors of the community were mainly general practitioners, most of whom still took a turn in surgery, some good, some adequate and some very nearly dangerous.

"We've got to break that," the old man said, sitting in the car with Marcus outside the hospital. "Old-fashioned vanity, that's all it is. I have an idea how we shall do it, too. There's no reason, with our facilities, we can't be a teaching hospital. Accredited. You see, Marc, you see?" He gave Marcus a poke with his glasses. "Then all these— these tailors in white coats will have to go round again, pass a board of surgeons before they do any more cutting up here. Eh? Why not? We shall be going to war. We'll need more doctors. Why not a school here? Patients galore. There is an army of them to the south and a navy of them to the north." (He spoke of the two nearby government installations.) "How would you like to teach here, Marc?"

Marcus laughed aloud at the abruptness of the question. "I don't think so, Doctor Albert. For one thing, I shouldn't think the first outsiders on the staff would be very popular."

"What does that matter? You're not a salesman or a politician."

"I'm not a teacher either," Marcus said, which was an evasion of the point.

"You're too busy," Bergner said with some sarcasm.

"No, I'm not, and that's part of it, Doctor Albert."

"I see, I see," the old man said. "A popularity contest after all, eh?"

"I'm beginning to win," Marcus said, "but it hasn't been easy without you."

"What do you mean, without me?"

166

"Well, since you're not there—it's like being teacher's pet as a kid. God help you when the teacher goes out of the room."

"Isn't it enough that I recommend you, that I stand behind you?"

"It's enough for me," Marcus said, "and that's what's deeply important, isn't it? But you can't impose your confidence in me on others any more than you could transfer your skill. I've got to win it without you. I am winning. There are men who'll take me now when they can't get somebody else. It used to be they'd only take me when they couldn't get *any*body else. And you see that's what you really made possible, Dr. Albert: I'm now worth having on a case."

"You were worth having the day I took you."

"You thought so. Nobody else was that sure—including myself."

"What?"

"Nobody but you and I thought so," Marcus amended, "and my father."

Bergner grunted his satisfaction with the answer.

Marcus drove him home, declining to stop for a drink when the old gentleman asked him.

"I don't blame you. Madness. Children all over the place. I'm going to put our two into boarding school myself, I'll tell you that." Louise and George had moved back from Washington and were temporarily living with Dr. Bergner.

Marcus went around the car to help him out and up to the steps. The old man delayed him at the car door. "Do you know why George Allan came home?"

"I understand he's working for Winthrop."

"I mean to live, to live. He's afraid I might do something like Alicia did." He gave his dry spate of laughter. "And I just might. Remember how the University got its telescope? Three months to build a planetarium. They got it up, didn't they? Think about Lakewood. It doesn't matter whether you think you can teach or not. Men who want to learn, learn. You know that. Was I a teacher? Pah! And it will give you that thing they call . . . prestige. You know what that is, eh, Marc? That's the extra zero you can put on your statement at the first of the month." He took Marcus's arm and they moved up the step slowly. "As for George Allan, every man's son has a right to earn his own living, I say."

"He hasn't done badly, Doctor Albert, considering the start you gave him," Marcus said dryly.

The old man looked up at him from under the thunderous brow

of which Marcus had never really been afraid. Marcus smiled almost impudently, and they went on. His hand on the door knocker, Dr. Bergner said, "Bring your bride to see me next time, eh? There's nothing wrong with my eyes—just my hands."

Marcus dressed at the Fields' for the evening, Martha having waited there for him while he visited Dr. Bergner, and before leaving for Winthrop's they had a leisurely drink with Tony and a lovely Chinese girl whom he was taking to the party. Martha knew her slightly from the University; she was in one of Jonathan's classes. Sylvia left early, having what she called a proprietary interest these days in how things were done at Tamarack. Marcus observed the maturity Tony was reaching, but afterwards when Martha commented on it, he teased her for becoming matronly.

Already a little late, they decided to be yet a little later and drove in the twilight to the bluff overlooking the lake. After sitting a moment in the car, they got out and stood listening to the early murmur of spring. Creeks were bursting in the first long thaw and the birds were not quite settled for the night. A sudden fanfare of chirping made them both smile, for there was the distinct sound of disgruntlement in it as though one bird had said to the other: for heaven's sake, can't I get any sleep in this nest? The green of maturing pussy willows flecked the tawny bushes at the crest of the ravine, the forsythia was popping open its numerous yellow mouths.

The sky, merging coral with pink with mother-of-pearl, was strung with small, golden-bellied clouds which reflected the setting sun, and were themselves hazily mirrored in the dark, rumpled waters of the lake. When the golds and reds were faded, the watchers returned silently to the car.

Martha was aware, arriving at Tamarack, of a deep, almost mesmeric contentment which she felt no one could intrude upon. Winthrop came up to greet them, both his hands extended.

"My tardy congratulations, Doctor Winthrop," Martha said. "I hope you and Sylvia will be very happy."

"Thank you. I'm glad you've come," he said.

For the moment Martha came very nearly liking him. She knew that Marcus did. And now she must somehow.

"Your father's here," Winthrop said to Marcus, "and those other friends of yours and Sylvia's. You shouldn't miss the violinist, by the way." He nodded toward the great closed doors. "He's our new concert master."

Martha realized how little she really knew about him. Sylvia, she knew, was a patron of the Traders City Symphony. As she and Marcus went into the drawing room she regretted having dragged her heels to have arrived so late. They heard but the final number of the musicale. As the musicians put away their instruments, the guests broke up into small groups, immediately convivial among themselves. Martha caught sight of the Muellers with Sylvia at the far end of the room, but lost them a moment later with the commingling of people in her line of vision. It was all so different from Martha's memory of her last party here: the room was not so large, more crowded, the guests not so aloof although, to be sure, none fell upon her and Marcus in welcome.

Jonathan intercepted them as they moved toward their friends. He had driven out with the Muellers, and Martha thought he looked notably handsome in dinner dress, his gray hair brushed into a neat crest. He seemed in no way ill at ease. Nor would he be in any gathering, whether it be here or in Peking, Buenos Aires or Kankakee. A scholar, yet a gregarious man, he enjoyed talking with tinsmith or tycoon. He always listened with interest, even to her, Martha thought. He was naturally curious about almost everything and not at all hesitant about exposing his own ignorances, minute or monumental. Of the latter, despite his protests, she thought there must be exceedingly few.

Martha counted it one of the truly important things to have happened in her life, friendship with Jonathan. They talked of many things together, often of religion, but neither of them to the purpose of converting the other. Martha had never quite forgotten the Christian burial given her father, the Church in its magnanimity depriving him forever of dignity of purpose, as she saw it. Jonathan had never said one word that might have been construed as deprecation of her father, although she knew how profoundly he must have disagreed with him. He was even sometimes able to explain certain of Fitzgerald's prejudices. Martha was devout and faithful to the Church still, but she gained through Jonathan her first understanding of why that was uncritically so, and why people of other conviction or faithless, as was Jonathan, might also be as faithful as herself. One could not help it, accepting the creed in which one was reared as the measure of logic as well as ethic. It was almost impossible to criticize the doctrines one *felt* were true: about as difficult, Jonathan said, as pulling oneself up by the bootstraps. There was gravity of mind as well as of body.

With Jonathan she and Marcus finally reached the Muellers who, too, had the faculty of fitting in even, Martha decided, where they stuck out. Julia was possessed of what Marcus called the joy of the earth. She was a handsome, laughing woman, well built and corseted, her white bosom brimming the snug, black velvet gown she wore that night; her cheeks were flushed and her black eyes dancing with frank pleasure. She did not have to talk to enjoy herself. Her presence, Marcus observed, had caused a number of gentlemen to join their group. He felt smug, taking a kiss by old prerogative.

"Ah, Martha," Erich cried, "do you know who has come. . ?"

But Martha did not hear more for at that instant she saw, standing half-face from them a few feet away and talking animatedly to quite a large group of people, Nathan Reiss. He seemed not a stranger at all . . . and very little changed. The slightest of fleshiness beneath his chin when he smiled was the only suggestion of middle age.

"You know the gentleman, I see," Jonathan said, his smile somewhat sardonic.

"I met him in Europe," Martha said. "He's Doctor Mueller's friend."

"I know. I had the pleasure of his company driving out from the city."

"I should speak to him," Martha said.

"Why?" The question was mischievous.

"He was very kind to me at a difficult time."

"But he, obviously, is not having a difficult time," Jonathan said. His tone was half-humorous, but Martha, knowing his moods, his levities at moments of least patience, suspected that Nathan Reiss had rubbed him the wrong way.

"He is a snob, isn't he?" she said.

"That, too?" said Jonathan, again a little mockingly. But he took her arm and together they moved to the edge of Reiss' audience.

Nathan Reiss had arrived in Traders City only the day before. He told of a harrowing escape from the Nazis, first at the Swiss border, then through France, and finally of a long and nerve-wracking wait in Spain for the necessary papers by which he could and did gain entry to America. The question in any intelligent man's mind was: why had he waited so long to leave? It was a question Jonathan had asked bluntly on the drive from the city, and with something less, their mutual friend Mueller calculated, than his usual tact.

"I had obligations," was Reiss' explanation, and of course, Jonathan thought, one does not press a gentleman on his obligations.

Erich had got him aside briefly on their arrival at Winthrop's and explained that there was a woman involved. This Jonathan had not doubted.

There were at the moment several women involved as well as men, attending Reiss' discourse on the European situation. He was accounting in some detail the political intrigue behind the fall of France:

". . . One could not say he was not an honorable man. Some would say stubborn. And believe me, the Countess would agree! It was told of him, he was the only man entering her house saying, 'No,' and leaving it also saying, 'No.' Daladier, on the other hand, was flattered by the attention, the patronage of the Marquise. He is, after all, a peasant, you might say—the baker's son. It was an extraordinary thing, let me tell you, to watch these two remarkable women playing with men like puppets in the game for France. What they were able to do, they never did. For them the only thing worth doing was the impossible. Therefore . . ." (He gave a shrug of despair.) ". . . The Moslems, they have something, you know? They cover the faces of the women." He looked to the women nearest him. "But I would not want to be a Moslem myself . . ."

He had a way, Jonathan thought, as the refugee was pressed for more of his intimate journal, of giving a boudoir atmosphere to matters of grave import.

Martha, it should be said, cherished an uncritical belief, not necessarily in the truth of what Reiss told, but in the appropriateness of his knowing it. She had remarked during her visit at the Baroness' the intimacy among her guests, and the casualness with which they discussed the most portentous of national affairs.

"It is," Reiss was saying, "the great pity, of course, that the Russians could not have been persuaded to neutrality." (The Soviet-German Pact was in operation at this time.) "But perhaps it is better: this way we know all our enemies at once."

"Does Hitler know his friends? That's what I'd like to know," a man prompted.

Reiss cocked his head. "I do not understand. Please?"

Jonathan squeezed Martha's elbow and whispered, "I wonder if Herr Doktor knows his."

The explaining gentleman opened with an astounding phrase: "If I were in Hitler's shoes, I'd be damned sure I deployed half my armies to the east. The Russians are going to turn on him, you'll see.

All that nonsense about their inefficiency, bad equipment—sheer propaganda. It's my idea they went into Finland in the first place just to pull the wool over our eyes. A red herring, how's that? They haven't shown anything like their real strength yet. Nobody knows what they've got. When the bear gets the bit between his teeth, God help us all, including Hitler."

Jonathan spoke to the man next to him, who was standing, glass in hand. "Excuse me. Who is the gentleman?"

"Edgar Murray."

Jonathan murmured his thanks. Murray was a manufacturer of transport equipment.

"He's in a pretty good spot to know what he's talking about. The Murrays have a lodge in Germany. Hitler's taken it over for his own use, I understand."

"Lend-lease," Jonathan said dryly.

His neighbor laughed. "I don't believe we've met. I'm Charlie Forsberg."

"Jonathan Hogan." The two men shook hands. Jonathan introduced his daughter-in-law. He supposed, as they all turned back to the mainstream of the conversation, Forsberg was trying to place him. He was doing the same of Forsberg, without success.

"It won't be Hitler's first mistake, if Ed's right," someone else joined in. The conversation was on the verge of breaking away from Reiss' domination. "He's gone a little too far with the Jewish business, I think."

There was no great outburst of approval with the observation.

Then Reiss said, smiling, "You would be surprised, let me tell you, how far they will go to . . . collect . . . one Jew."

People were amused.

Someone asked Reiss if he thought the United States would allow itself to be drawn into the war, and Jonathan wondered if the refugee knew he was being tested.

"No. I don't think so," Reiss said carefully. "Perhaps—if what the gentleman proposes—I am sorry, I do not know you by name . . ."

Edgar Murray identified himself to Reiss, who acknowledged by bringing his aristocratic body to attention. "I am honored. If, as you propose, Russia is persuaded to stab Germany in the back, you should then be prepared, I think. I do not truly believe Great Britain can stand up to Russia. You do not know, perhaps, how strong the Communist parties are among the working class people in Great Britain

—and in France. France is the lesson of the world, let me tell you. If it were not for the Hitler-Stalin collaboration, France would still be France. I should still be in Paris myself." He went on, very loosely documenting the effectiveness of Communism at internal subversion, and its part in the fall of France; no one seemed to think it in any way contradictory of his prior account of the fall.

And Jonathan mused on the bitter irony of its truth outside historical context: there was no doubt in his mind that International Communism was now less a Marxist movement than an arm of Soviet foreign policy. The strongest dialectic enemy of Fascism had become its practical abettor. No one here was likely to acknowledge Hitler's progress an outgrowth of the struggle between capital and labor, or to attribute his appeasement to the fearful horror the British and French upper classes had of joining with the Soviet in any cause, including Hitler's containment. There were eulogists here for Mussolini, men who could say of Hitler: "If I were in his shoes . . ." There were, of course, admirers of Churchill, albeit his friendship with Roosevelt was hard for them to stomach. But not a man except himself, not his friend Mueller, a violent anti-Nazi, not his onetime worshiper, Sylvia Fields; no one except himself would realistically credit Stalin with being a practical politician. Sylvia, whom he suspected of once having belonged to the Party, he assumed had left it following the Hitler-Stalin pact, and was these days utterly out of patience with him who had never been in the Party. "Love looks not with the eyes but with mind," Shakespeare said. Then, said Jonathan, hate looks not with the mind but with the eyes.

"Then it is your opinion, Doctor Reiss," a woman said, her words affectedly precise, "that the *real* enemy is Russia?" Americans, particularly Midwesterners, have a passion for precision. The word "real" is the most frequent adjective—or adverb—in their speech.

"But of course!" Reiss cried with superb éclat.

"I'm very glad to hear you say it," the woman remarked and, turning to the man at her side, she added, but loudly enough for everyone to hear, "I must say I felt much better about it all, having Hitler and them on the same side."

Much as Martha admired Jonathan, she could not but admit that deeply within herself she felt the same way about it. Fascists were more explicitly detestable in alliance with the Russians. One needed no longer give them credit for having done some good things—as for example, Mussolini's signing of the Lateran Treaty with the Vatican.

One could now clearly understand that his motives were in no way religious.

The moment Martha's and Nathan Reiss' eyes met, his smile was as quick as her own. She felt the color rise in her cheeks. He excused himself to those nearest him and made his way to her.

"There were times I did not think this moment would ever come," he said, and pressing her hand, lifted it to his lips.

"You already seem at home, Nathan. But I bid you welcome anyway."

"I have had your little book to guide me. Do you remember?"

"Yes." She turned to include him, but Jonathan was gone from her side.

"I suppose my bracelet to you is at the bottom of the sea?"

"It must be at the bottom of somewhere," Martha admitted. "I want you to meet my husband."

"So do I," Reiss said. "A man so fortunate."

She wished he would not say such things. Even in Paris she had scarcely been able to cope with the self-consciousness they caused her. "Is the Baroness well, Nathan?"

"If God is with her, she is well. I was not able to get her out."

"She is in Germany?"

"I should suppose she is in a concentration camp somewhere. I have not been able to find out."

"The Red Cross, perhaps," Martha suggested.

"Perhaps. It is a very tragic story. I will tell you some time. But not tonight." The pursing of his mouth, the full lower lip protruding, gave his mien a quality of sadness, regret. It made a demand on one's sympathy. Martha remembered his having had something of the same expression after the incident at the Heldenplatz. She took his arm by way of guiding him to Marcus, and moved by this frank quest of sympathy, she pressed his arm ever so slightly. Lo! even as on that other occasion, he was immediately gay again. "I have not been in company such as this for a very long time. Lakewood I have heard of, of course, but I did not know. You do not live here?"

"No."

He sighed. "One would need a great deal of money, I suppose."

Marcus was with Tony Fields and Miss Ling, and with them also were George and Louise Bergner. The introductions accomplished, Reiss was soon talking with Tony about sailing. He had a "social instinct," as Martha's mother called good breeding. Yet, Martha thought, there was something about him which would stay her from saying he was well bred. Perhaps, she realized, it was the fact that she knew him to be Jewish. He did sense quickly the interests of those with whom he was talking, and if he was shallow, as Martha suspected, he was so graceful it scarcely mattered. He could, without seeming abrupt, turn from talk of sailing ships to say to Marcus, "I wonder if your wife has told you—I tried to win her away from you in Paris?"

"I'd be insulted if you hadn't," Marcus said.

Everyone laughed.

"He didn't try very hard," Martha said.

Reiss said, "How do they say it in Brooklyn—*now* she tells me that?"

Again laughter.

"Did you like Brooklyn, Doctor Reiss?" Louise Bergner inquired.

"It was difficult for me to tell, Mrs. Bergner. You see, there is the language barrier."

Others were amused, but Louise said, "You speak English beautifully, doctor . . ." Then she added, "Oh, I see what you mean."

It was, Martha thought, much to his credit that as the evening progressed, Nathan gave much of his attention to Louise Bergner. And she had need of it as did no one else of the women who might have gladly accepted. Her husband's contempt of her was ill disguised, a relationship Martha found agonizing to observe. Louise fairly shone in the reflected glory of Lakewood's popular refugee.

Jonathan was persuaded by the man who had introduced himself as Charlie Forsberg to accompany him to the Trophy Room. He was affable with the drink and as he put his arm through Jonathan's, the latter thought of the Charlie Chaplin movie, "City Lights," and the millionaire who, drunk, adored him, and sober, threw him out.

"There are some of us old-fashioned enough," Forsberg explained having ordered a double Scotch, "to want our whisky straight and our champagne with the ladies."

Jonathan took bourbon.

Forsberg, he would have said, was a banker. He lacked the rough cut of most men on the Exchange or in industry. Having made his guess, he would not have then been surprised to learn that his companion was a meat packer. A generation had done wonders of refinement to the heirs of those dynasties.

Forsberg touched his glass with his. "Jonathan Hogan: the name's familiar."

"I teach at Midwestern University."

"Ohhh," Forsberg said, the prolonged sound of understanding. "That one."

"That one," Jonathan said, and sipped his whisky.

Forsberg was a long moment in contemplation of his own glass. Then he looked up, squinting, probably in reaction to Jonathan's tic. "I'm an old radical myself, believe it or not. You wouldn't believe that, would you? Look at my fingernails." He held up a hand, the carefully manicured nails of which had been buffed to a polish. "I've been twenty years growing these nails, twenty years getting the coal dust out from under them. I got my start in life stoking furnaces in the steel mills. How do you like that?"

Jonathan smiled, as much amused in a grim way at himself. Now he knew who Forsberg was: President of the steel company whose local plant Jonathan had proposed to do his bit to help strike before he was "immunized" by the Red charges at the University. The strike had been one of the bloodiest in Traders City history.

"Do you know Clarence Darrow?" the steel man asked.

"I've met him."

"There's a maverick. Like yourself. If it wasn't for my wife, we'd be the best of friends to this day. Not, mind you, that she thinks there's anything wrong with him. It's the people, you see, he takes up the cudgels for." Forsberg ran his finger along the rail of the bar. He called to the bartender for a towel, wiped his finger on it and showed the man the dust. To Jonathan he said, "I'm a fanatic about dust."

With his next drink Forsberg's reminiscences became more confidential. "I started out a Populist. Remember them? Oh, by God, they were right! Those were the days. But let me tell you, the man who opened my eyes—what's his name—Norsten Theblan?"

Jonathan grinned. "Thorstein Veblen."

"That's the one. *Theory of the Leisure Class* . . . A man's instinct for workmanship. I never forgot it. That's what God put us here for, isn't it? Workmanship. And now look at me, a goddamned medicine man. Do you know what I'm talking about?"

"I think so," Jonathan said. He had had occasion to lecture on Veblen himself, but it had been a long time since he had heard a lecture on him, however inchoate.

His companion nodded. "In 1912 I voted for Eugene Debs. He had more guts than the whole New Deal put together. Do you play golf?"

"No."

"What do you do?"

"I'm afraid the only thing I play is chess."

Forsberg prodded him with his finger. "Don't be afraid. I always tell my friends, when you're doing what you want to do, don't be afraid. You believe that, don't you?"

"I have reason to believe it," Jonathan said.

"That's the boy. This is America. Not any of those other places they were talking about down there. They're all alike, you know. One way or another, they're all alike. But I'm not an isolationist. I haven't gone that far. We can't let them go down." He made a slightly drunken gesture with his hand. "We got to keep them afloat. Take Churchill. There's a man for you. I don't mind having him on our side. An American mother, you can tell that. Or is it his wife? You admire him, don't you?"

"I do," Jonathan said.

" 'Blood, sweat and tears.' Oh, by God, there is a man."

" 'Take him for all in all, I shall not look upon his like again,' " Jonathan quoted.

"That's right," Forsberg said thoughtfully, and added, "We've got to keep him afloat."

Dinner was announced, but Forsberg made a gesture of disregard. "Confidentially," he said, "I think we ought to send the Marines over right now. But mind, if you quote me, when we get downstairs, I'll deny it."

"I think there are a number of people here who would agree with you," Jonathan said.

"Don't *you*?" His show of shock was exaggerated by the effects of the whisky.

"I'm afraid not," Jonathan said.

"Don't be afraid," Forsberg said impatiently. "Why?"

"It's a long story. And we might just be missed at dinner if we don't go."

Forsberg gave him an elbow. "So you're a Communist, after all." His manner became more confidentially affable than ever.

"By that logic," Jonathan said, "you could say the same for most of the guests downstairs. They don't want us to get into the war either."

"We know what they are. But what are you? I was kidding about you being a Communist. I know one of them when I see one."

"I am a pacifist."

"That's what the Communists say they are. And you know why?"

"I know," Jonathan said.

"They're no more pacifist than I am."

The bartender was waiting to get a word in. Jonathan deferred to him. "I have to go down and help serve now, Mr. Forsberg," the man said.

Forsberg looked at him a moment. "We won't steal the whisky." Then to Jonathan, "Just tell me why you're a pacifist, and we'll go."

Jonathan drew a long breath. "I don't think killing stops killing. I think wars are seeded in economics, and I see nothing in the alignment of this war that does not promise another to come after it. I do not think Britain and France would have stood up to Hitler if they had not finally seen the economic *status quo* threatened. And if we get into it, I am convinced it will be for the same reason."

Forsberg nodded. "You know something, Hogan? I think you're dead right. I just wish I could get it across to some of my pig-headed friends who can't see it in terms of their own survival. It's our way of life that's at stake, isn't it?"

"Yes," Jonathan said.

"Then how in hell can you be a pacifist?"

Jonathan laughed heartily and not a little because he was relieved at not having been understood.

·4

SYLVIA FIELDS and Alexander Winthrop were married late in April. The ceremony was private, performed in the Fields home, with only the Bergners and Tony present, and Nathan Reiss, who was at the time staying with Tony.

For all its nativism, Lakewood had for many years imported royalty and the friends of royalty with much the same zeal it imported European art, furniture and glass for its mansions, themselves imitative of Old World splendor. By 1941, however, what might have been called the foreign contingent in Lakewood had dispersed, some to their beleaguered homelands or at least to a more useful exile. Some were in the process of becoming American citizens, having taken up residence more becoming their own incomes. Their absence but confirmed the changing of the old order. Many of the Lakewood families realized, as did Sylvia Fields Winthrop, that Lakewood itself would soon vanish as they had known it, yielding to the scythe of taxes, giving ground literally to the newly moneyed for whom an acre or two would be estate enough so long as their neighbors had no more than an acre or two. Estates were soon to mean conformity in, not contrasts of, architecture and landscape. It was, therefore, a society in flux that welcomed Nathan Reiss. His being a refugee, and some might say, symbolically rather than recognizably, a Jew, he obliged the conscience of those who might have otherwise been squeamish. He conducted himself with an elegance of manner, a proper snobbishness, and the self-assurance of a man skilled in a useful profession as well as social grace. He allowed it to be known that he was a surgeon although presently confined from practice by state law, and at the appropriate moments, when, say, a hostess would confide a particular pain to him, he was likely to recall attending So-and-So in Vienna or Paris or on the Riviera for just such a complaint. It would probably entail minor surgery some day, he was likely to say. Once he was asked what he considered major surgery, to which he replied, "With a first-rate surgeon there is no such thing as major surgery." It sounded reassuring. But some doctors felt there was no such thing as minor surgery.

Meanwhile, he sailed with Tony, and helped him close the greater part of the Fields' house after Sylvia moved out of it. And he was in those days a frequent visitor of Louise Bergner.

His attentions to her amused George, and rather flattered him, aware as he was of Reiss' general acceptability in Lakewood. George actually stood up to his father when Reiss' frequent presence in the house became an issue with the old man.

Dr. Bergner had liked Reiss at first. There was no doubt in the old man's mind that Reiss knew his profession; he might be a social fraud, but medically he seemed more sound than most Europeans Bergner had encountered over the years. He considered it a myth that Viennese made the best doctors, that Vienna hospitals were superior to others on the Continent. And, of course, Reiss undertook to confirm this suspicion for him with numerous documentation. But with the old gentleman Reiss committed one of his few blunders. He supposed, when Dr. Bergner was probing him on his origins, that the old man was getting at him again—as he had on previous occasions —for his orientation toward the moneyed class, and Reiss decided to disarm him by admitting that he was an orphan who had made his own way out of the ghetto into the most fashionable salons of Europe.

From that day on the old doctor had no more time for him. He had been proposing in his own mind to add another study to his work on heredity: as well have a eunuch as an orphan! With the cantankerousness of age, he found thereafter that when most he wanted Louise's attentions she was occupied with Reiss. In the midst of his complaints one day, George turned on him and accused him of anti-Semitism.

"Nonsense, nonsense. A Jew would have served me fine; I have several in the book. Need them for the whole picture."

"That goddamned book," George said.

"When you read it, you'll have the right to curse it, George Allan. There's always been anti-Semitism, and I dare say there always will be—or a reasonable facsimile of it, but you didn't learn yours from your father. Send Louise up to me. She understands me better than you do."

As on all similar occasions, George left the room in a rage at his own impotence.

And, as though further to confound him, Dr. Bergner shortly proposed that Nathan Reiss be added to the teaching staff of Lakewood Hospital where he might at the same time take his own internship and prepare for the state examinations.

· 5

THE *Traders City Star* gathered some fine talent, mixing idealism with money. The editor-in-chief had been long associated with a chain of newspapers headquartered in Washington, D. C.; the head of the foreign desk came home from London to take on the job, having been European correspondent to a national magazine for over a decade. A book supplement to the Sunday paper was created under the editorship of a young firebrand; its criticism was sharp and manly. "Books Alive" was its signet, and if all the books reviewed were not that lively, the reviewing of them was. A man of national reputation took on the music desk. Theatre went to an acid Irishman who had abandoned Dublin at about the time Sean O'Casey had, and for much the same reason. The announced purpose of the paper was service to all members of the community, and there was not to be found in its pages anywhere the class and race distinctions in its reporting long a practice of its chief competitor.

There was, to say the least, a rather heady atmosphere in the editorial office in the early days, but from where George Bergner sat, the harsher facts of publishing and circulation had to be dealt with. The *Star,* for the time being, used the plant and printing facilities of one of the afternoon dailies, but a week before publication of its first edition, Winthrop had not been able to obtain a franchise to a major wire service: persuasion had to go forth at a very high level and among a diversity of publishing members who subscribed to the services. The vote to allow the *Star* a franchise to the one service it had to have was terrifyingly close. The same situation prevailed with the so-called "feature" syndicates, as though it weren't going to be hard enough to introduce any new comic or cartoon, much less the rejects of the papers already operating in the city.

A contest for subscriptions was set up for delivery boys, the first prize a year's scholarship to college.

Winthrop himself worked as hard as did George, and not only on the top level of persuasion: he personally contacted more than four hundred news dealers and made it plain that Christmas wasn't half so far away as it seemed. Nor did he hesitate to use his old contacts among the ward politicians of guaranteed persuasiveness in their own neighborhoods. There are at least two definitions to liberalism.

George recruited the drivers for the trucks that had to dispute the streets of Traders City with Judge Phipps's deliverers, a rugged crew that rode herd on city traffic on their ordinary rounds. He signed on ex-cops and ex-rumrunners alike.

Sylvia spent her honeymoon in the *Star* offices, and in truth, neither she nor Winthrop could have found a tour more to their liking. She had never been a woman for passive observance, and nothing in her experience till then had so obliged both her talents and her energies. They shared a camaraderie, the Winthrops, Bergner, and the editorial staff, that all of them would remember; the long days' work, negotiation and manipulation, and then good drinks and supper together afterwards at Cellini's Restaurant or sometimes at Winthrop's flat. Vanities and jealousies had no part in the organization of the *Star*. These waited upon more leisured times. Winthrop himself believed in what he was doing, not in what he hoped to do. What dreamers there were among the staff got to him through Sylvia, the trouble-shooters through George. The three of them had maturity enough—and each in diverse ways, experience enough—to forestall in them any dilettantist meddling. As close as Sylvia came to it was an idea which in time proved both solid and profitable.

A week after the *Star* was successfully on the streets, she persuaded George one day to drive down with her to the Stockyards Tavern. It was a rambling, dust-bound building, tawdry in its best days, still vaguely Spanish like a gypsy who had lost her way in the wasteland of the city. One got the feeling within the building of being in an underground cave with the wide, low-ceilinged passageways. The walls were hung with faded prints of prize steers, of trotting champions and hunters, and with photographs of bearded meat packers. The windows were dirty enough to seem but lighter patches of wall on which someone had been playing ticktacktoe. It was not a place frequented by ladies, even those of more colorful complexion than Sylvia. She felt a certain tribute when two of the drovers standing at the bar removed their hats as she came in. The bartender saluted her.

"There's a certain delicacy in choosing a table," Sylvia explained. "It must be out of range of their conversation, yet within walking distance for Tom, the bartender."

"This is not exactly the place to bring a man on your honeymon," George said, "especially when he's not your husband."

Sylvia took off her gloves. "Alex just wouldn't fit." She looked around, her attitude somewhat proprietary. "I used to be a social worker down here—among other things."

George grinned. "Workers of the world, unite?"

"You've got nothing to lose but your entrails. There's a great little neighborhood back of the Yards." She looked up at the bartender. "How are you, Tom?"

"Fine, miss, thank you." He gave a jerk of his head. "Your friend called up he'll be a mite late. He's misplaced his papers, can't find his hat." Tom, a round-faced man with a warm smile but cold blue eyes, had the strong tune of Gaelic in his voice.

"Is he sober?" Sylvia asked.

Tom shrugged. "We'll know if he comes. What'll you folks have to drink?"

"Harper's for me with a little soda," Sylvia said. "Tom, this is Mr. George Bergner. Tom Jefferson."

George looked up sharply. The two men nodded. Tom said, "It's Jeffries is my name, sir, but you can't change a woman's notion once she's got it in her head. And I could be mistook for worse."

"Harper's is fine," George said. He could not share Sylvia's fellowship here, but he could and did relish the idea of being in her confidence. She was one mare that money had made go, he thought, and he was a lot surer of himself in her company than he was with Winthrop. It might be said in passing he had been very happy to dance at their wedding. When Tom went back to the bar, George asked, "Who's the fellow who's out looking for his hat?"

"Did you ever hear of Billy Kirk?"

"No."

"He's a native-born Southsider, and he's been known to claim—at different times, of course—every nationality in the world. He used to run around with the newspaper crowd in the early twenties, that wild, gorgeous bunch of geniuses. It's said that Billy ghosted some of their best columns on nights when they were drunk enough to let him."

George shrugged, but good-naturedly, and waited. He was scarcely more sanguine of the man, meeting him: he had little faith in "characters," much less in ghosts. Kirk was small and sinewy, wrinkled of face and jacket, his watery eyes veined like geographic globes. He smoked a pipe that hadn't been scraped out since his days of regular employment on the *Drovers' Tattler,* some fifteen years out of print. It was soon evident that Kirk felt as much affinity with George as George felt with Kirk's pipe.

"You know, Miss Fields, none of the respectable spectacles of publishing will hire me. Not that they wouldn't like to. It's their lawyers who stand in the way. There's nothing more squeamish than a lawyer before the fact—or less after it."

"Mr. Bergner is our lawyer," Sylvia said with mischievous relish.

"Well, I knew the minute I saw him *he* wasn't going to hire me." Kirk threw down his whisky neat.

Sylvia laughed. "It was not my idea to tie you down to regular employment, Billy. Rather, I was hoping to interest our people in leasing two or three pieces from you a week."

Billy gazed mournfully into his empty glass. "I suppose you'd want nothing but hilarity."

"I don't know. I'm fond of some of your sad stories, that one, for example, about the man who shot his horse in the tavern doorway."

"That was a saloon, my dear. The only thing you can shoot in a tavern door is your wife if you're lucky enough to see her first. Ah, but you're right: that is a *sad* story. I'll wager all the same it would make Mr. Berger here laugh."

"Bergner," George corrected. "And I doubt it."

Billy Kirk smiled at him disarmingly, showing a row of strong, yellowed teeth. He brought a dirty Manila envelope up from under his chair, and took out several neatly and freshly typed pages, the condition of which was not what George had expected. He divided the stories between Sylvia and Bergner. "Frogs along the Potomac," he read the title aloud of the top story he gave to George. "That's an idea on how to sustain a filibuster without wear and tear on Senatorial rhetoric. It came to me one night listening to Bertie Rice trying to tell a story at the Rotary banquet. Every few sentences he would suppress a burp and politely excuse himself before going on— and you know, before he finished, I would have given anything to hear just one good belch out of him."

George was amused in spite of himself. The story had bite and grace. He asked Kirk, "Do you write things like this to specifications?"

"If we got the same specifications," Kirk said, almost with a drawl. "I write shaggy dogs and dirty dogs, and yalla dogs. And then, some of them are just plain dogs. It takes a heap of livin' to make a Kirk a house." He circled his lips with the tip of a very red tongue.

Afterwards, when she and George were driving back to the office, Sylvia said, "I also know a writer of children's books. He's awfully good, illustrates them himself—clever, fantastic things, yet real. The kind of creatures children talk to in gardens when they're alone."

"Uh-huh," George said.

"I guess I've said that badly, but I have an idea he could do a really good comic strip. What I should like to see one day, George, a *Star* Syndicate. Let's give them back something for the trash they've given us. Why not?"

George glanced at her. "As your brother always says when he wants something done: 'Siccum, Sylvia.' "

·6

It was an evening in late June when Louise Bergner called, a time easily remembered afterwards because when the phone rang, Marcus and Martha were listening to the news of Germany's invasion of Russia. Louise sounded distraught or possibly drunk, but when she said at the end, "Marcus, please don't let on I called you," he sensed the urgency behind her vague message. Martha rode out to Lakewood with him.

The house, when they approached it, was lighted from attic to cellar, a sign Marcus thought as ominous as total darkness. In the best of times, George and his father living under one roof was not an easy arrangement, and now that the old man was ailing and difficult—as Marcus well knew from his weekly visits—there was almost constant friction. What Dr. Albert wanted of his son, Marcus did not know any more than he thought George himself knew. George was more successful at the moment as general manager of the *Star* than most men's sons at his age. Marcus did not like him, but decency compelled him to defend the son to the father, the more for knowing that Dr. Bergner made no secret of his preference for Marcus to his own flesh and blood.

Martha waited in the car.

Going up the walk Marcus saw George at the window, shading his eyes, trying to see who had driven in. Behind him in the room, Louise was squeezing her nose in a limp handkerchief. Marcus glimpsed a quick gesture of impatience on George's part, a brusque admonition to his wife. It was easy to imagine him trying on his father's disposition where he could get away with it. Marcus gave the bell knob a hard, long turn. Since he had come, he wanted everyone in the house to know it.

George opened the door to him. "Well," he said with scant hospitality, "isn't it late for you to be on the road?"

Marcus said: "Martha's in the car. I thought as long as we were out this way I might save myself a trip tomorrow."

"He's asleep. Old men keep better hours than we do."

Louise came up and offered Marcus her moist hand. The sweet

185

scent of it lingered on his own afterwards. "He's awful low tonight, Marcus. I'm glad you've come."

"High, low, jack and a spade," George said impatiently. "He's what he wants to be."

And at that moment from the room upstairs came the violent ringing of a hand bell. George turned and started up the steps two at a time.

Louise, her voice on the edge of hysteria, cried, "Don't aggravate him any more, George. He'll die tonight. I know it. Doctor Reiss said he might."

George stopped abruptly and came down the steps again. "Why don't you go up to him, Louise? You understand him so much better than I do. Your Doctor Reiss said that too, didn't he?"

"I should never have told you," Louise said.

Marcus said: "Do you have any objection to my going up, George?"

"His own doctor said he's not to be disturbed," George said.

Marcus moved by him on the stairs, saying: "I'll try not to."

George followed at his heels.

Propped up on the pillows, Dr. Bergner looked to have shrunk since Marcus had last seen him. His eyes were sunken and the once ferocious mien looked merely choleric. There was an unhealthy ruddiness to his cheeks.

"Marc?" The old gentleman squinted, straining to see without his glasses. His mouth hung open slightly. He grunted a couple of times before he was able to speak again. Then his speech was slurred. "Out of town, eh? I didn't think it likely."

"He's here. That's the important thing, isn't it, father?" George said.

The old man made a dry, almost crackling sound with his tongue and lips as though trying to coax saliva into his mouth. Marcus felt his pulse: too fast, and he knew his blood pressure to be up. He helped him to drink a little water.

The elder Bergner said, "You think so, George Allan? Did he call you, Marc? Did he?"

"Martha and I were in Lakewood," Marcus lied. "Lean back and take it easy. You've got a long way to go yet."

"Pah! Hear my breathing? How far will I go on that?" He lay quiet for a few seconds. "Why don't I have my grandchildren standing round—waiting to catch their first glimpse of death? I remember the death of *my* grandfather. He was so shriveled up they could have buried him in a shoe box." Dr. Bergner gave several wheezes of attempted laughter.

George gazed down on him, his distaste undisguised.

"Nowadays if there is anything important, they send the children away."

"It was you wanted them in camp," George said.

His father ignored him, or rather his remark. He might not have heard it. "Look at George Allan—look at him. Never had a better time in his life than tonight. He was a colonel in the Mexican War. What do you think of that?" Marcus realized that he was again talking about the grandfather. "That was a war, let me tell you: the war to make Mexico safe for democracy." George started to walk away. "You don't like my history either, eh, my son? But I will teach it all the same. The country that makes itself guardian of another country is a tyrant. Guarantee a man his freedom and you make a slave." His speech became inarticulate and Marcus observed a little sagging at one corner of his mouth. It was like a hole beneath one side of the dark, drooping mustaches.

Marcus pressed his hand. "Rest, Doctor Albert."

The old man's penetrating eyes focused on his son while he groped at his own neck. Marcus, assuming he was looking for his glasses, took them from the bedside table and offered them to him. He pushed them away. "I want to talk to Marc, George Allan. Go down and console Louise. She will miss me."

George stood for a moment, truculent, and then yielded to his father's command. "Call me if you want anything," he said, and went out.

The old man's eyes followed him until the door closed. "An admirable sort, my son, eh?"

Marcus said: "Whatever it is between you, you're letting it kill you. You know that."

"Oh no. *You* did that, Marcus Hogan. How long ago? The day I gave over to you, that was my end." He began again to grope at his throat and Marcus helping him found the cord beneath the collar of his pajamas. There was a key on it. The key had turned green with the sweat of his body as had the skin where the key had lain against it. "I want you to get something and take it with you tonight." He lowered his voice. "We must not let George Allan interfere. Go into my study. Through there." He indicated the door to an adjoining room. "The binders—in the bottom drawer of the filing cabinet. Bring them."

Marcus knew then that he was speaking of his work on genetics. In the five years of their association, he had said every now and then that he must show it to Marcus. Marcus was reasonably sure that no one had seen it in its entirety except its author. It was a work that would never be finished so long as the man was alive. He was himself unsure of it, forever pulling out a section to research it further, for all that he talked constantly of it and offered parts of it for publication.

Marcus discovered the door between the two rooms locked.

Bergner became agitated. "Go round through the hall then. Go quickly."

Marcus found George Bergner in the study sitting at his father's desk. George said imperturbably: "I thought I ought to stay close by in case you needed me. Our wives have each other down there."

Marcus said nothing. He went directly to the filing cabinet.

"Martha looks fine," George said chattily. "Pregnancy becomes her. I remember Louise used to puff up all over—cheeks, bust and belly. She used to cry all the time. She likes to cry. Some women do."

He fell silent, watching Marcus lift out one after another, five binders. "Magnus opus," he said. He leaped to his feet when Marcus closed the file drawer. "What are you going to do with it?"

"Whatever he wants me to," Marcus said.

George hastened to the door between the study and the bedroom and unlocked it while Marcus waited. "Let me take it in to him, will you?"

"I'd better do it," Marcus said, "since he asked me to."

Without a word George crossed the room and left him, going downstairs. Marcus regretted his own intransigence in following the old man's dictum. He knew that the socio-political views, presumably reflected in the papers he carried, had long been an issue between father and son. George called them Fascistic. But what harm in letting him carry the book to the bedside? There might even have come of it a moment's rapprochement. It would have suited Marcus better to serve as mediator than the role he now took up.

Dr. Bergner was muttering to himself. Marcus made out the words: "No ballast . . ."

"No ballast to what, Doctor Albert?"

"A ship without ballast . . . menace on a stormy sea."

Marcus agreed cajolingly. "I have the book here, Doctor Albert."

"Put on my glasses for me, will you, boy?" He caught hold of Marcus's hand. "We haven't had a good laugh in a long time, Marc. All those puns. I can't remember a one. I've been lying here all day trying to remember. Not a one." He released Marcus's hand and, the glasses on, he immediately shook them off. "Pah! I can't see with them and I can't see without them. No ballast . . . I wish you would put something under the feet of this damned bed. I keep sliding off." Marcus realized he had lurched to the side again. It had happened several times. The bed itself was perfectly straight.

Marcus bunched the pillows a bit more tightly beneath him. He wanted now to know the opinion of the doctor attending Bergner that evening. There was no doubt the old man had had a partial stroke. Dr. Bergner put his unsteady hand on the folders which Marcus had set on the edge of the bed.

"I want these published . . . if . . . ." There was a long pause and then what Marcus was sure was a complete *non sequitur:* "You're a good boy." He could tell by the change in the eyes, the old man's mind had spun off somewhere else.

Marcus felt his pulse. "Easy, easy, Doctor Albert. Rest awhile. Then we can talk."

The old man merely stared, but not quite at him.

George opened the door. He hesitated only a second on the threshold. "Marcus, will you come here a moment? I think you ought to go down and take a look at Martha. I don't like her color at all."

Marcus was out of the room and downstairs more quickly than he knew himself. He was a moment or two discovering where the women were. He found them in the conservatory. Both of them turned, startled, when he appeared.

Louise got up, her eyes wide. "He's dead!"

Marcus knew instantly that George had created the ruse to get him out of the bedroom, had in fact set it up in his father's study, soft-talking about Martha's condition. Martha was quite as she had been when he had last seen her. Without a word he ran back upstairs. Dr. Bergner was alone, a perplexed but unwrathful look upon his face. His fury was spent forever. Nor was he likely to speak again. It was doubtful that he now knew him from George or had known George from him in those last few moments, but George and the binders were gone from the room.

Marcus went to the door and called downstairs to Louise that she had better come. He returned to the bedside and lowered the dying man so that he could not tumble from the bed. The breathing was heavier and Marcus thought then as he had many times before that there was truly a rattle to death. And soon there would be the smell of it also in the room, for proud men who die in bed go as ignominiously as cowards on the field of battle. If we have not spirits it is no great privilege to have been born human.

Louise came, weeping softly, and sat at the side of the bed, gazing at the old man. Marcus looked in the study: somewhere in the house he could imagine George leafing through the pages, uncritically critical.

Martha reached the top of the stairs, climbing slowly to protect her own.

"Stay with Louise till I come," Marcus said. "I'm going to call the Winthrops and Doctor Albert's physician. And I've got to find George."

Marcus phoned from the hall. Then he went from room to room calling out George's name. The only response was the reverberation of his own voice. That George was deliberately concealing himself or had left the house sped Marcus the quicker through it. The basement door was locked when he reached it, the key on the inside. Marcus pounded and rattled the knob. He could see light shining from beneath the door. He cursed George aloud as though that might summon him. Then bracing himself against the wall, he kicked the door free of the lock. But the basement also was empty. There, however, George, coming in from outdoors, found him. He carried the empty binders in one hand, a fuel can in the other, and as Marcus moved past him he could smell the reek of kerosene. Marcus went up the outside steps only as far as ground level. In a wire incinerator, the kerosene-soaked manuscript was shooting up flames far past extinction. Even as he observed it, the blaze passed its height, the flaking ashes scattering like snow in the wind.

Marcus went indoors and upstairs again. George had already returned to the sickroom, adding the stench of kerosene to that of the dying. He was standing behind his wife, his face now serene as was no other in the room. Martha was at the window, her mouth close to the frame where she could draw in a little fresh air to her lungs and keep herself from being ill. Dr. Albert lay as Marcus had left him except that the lids had drooped, half-closing the perplexed eyes.

The labored breathing sawed across the stillness. Louise wept silently. Marcus took Martha from the room and bade her wait in the car until he came. He waited only for Dr. Albert's physician to arrive.

George came downstairs just before Marcus left. "I did something that had to be done. You see that, don't you?"

Marcus was a few seconds answering him. "No, but you did something that's fashionable these days, anyway."

Martha had the car radio on: the Germans had already penetrated two hundred miles into Russia.

·7

THE summer of 1941 was a troubled time for many Americans of conscience and for none more than Jonathan Hogan. He had the feeling of being pushed into the sea. "Thou'dst shun a bear, but if thy flight lay toward the raging sea thou'dst meet the bear i' the mouth." And still he could not bring himself to it. He could find no praise for war, however gallant the allies, however just their cause. His was an incredible position in most eyes, a bitter one in his own. His persistent cries for peace, for arms embargo, made him tolerable only among the men whom he loathed the most: Americans of the extreme right. They could justify him even as they could ignore Hitler. Even his friend Mueller was no longer comfortable in his company. He almost invariably found a reason not to see Jonathan.

Martha watched what she could only feel was Jonathan's physical decline. She knew his solitariness a torture, for when he stayed overnight she could hear him moving about his room at any hour she chanced to listen. She could not help him, but neither would she let him go. Nor did she intend to make it easy for Erich to do it either. She called Julie oftener by far than Julie called her, and at considerable pain to everyone concerned forced her to make excuses, or to accept an invitation only to call back and say that Erich would not be able to get away from work that night. She did not tell Marcus how dogged she was about this: his father's politics had become something he and Jonathan did not speak about either.

It was in late August that she chanced one afternoon to get Erich himself on the phone, and promptly asked him to come to dinner.

"Tonight? But we cannot, Martha," Erich said. "We have Nathan with us, and not often do we see him now."

"Why don't you bring him, Erich? May I speak to him?" And so, violating her every inclination, she persisted and prevailed.

She had not known, of course, the depth of Jonathan's antipathy to Reiss. His intention in praising Reiss' American progress had always been ironic. He could not allow himself to be more overt: the privileges of pacifism at such a time were few. But it was a curious Jew, he felt, for whom Fascism held so little horror. There was a time when he might himself have been amused by such a man. But in 1941 Reiss was an anachronism and a dangerous one: he blinded the already purblind to the plight of millions of Jews. Society might accept him as their exception, but if ever there was an axiomatic nonsense it was that an exception proved a rule. Yet, who was Jonathan to speak of an anachronism?

The evening did not go well. People spoke at once or not at all. And bent by the strain to carelessness, Jonathan decided to challenge his old friend. "Erich, remember the meetings I used to drag you to to hear me speak? Come with me tomorrow night. It may be my valedictory."

"Ah, I am sorry, old friend. But I have a meeting at the laboratory. Don't I, Julie?"

If he had not turned to his wife for confirmation, Jonathan would not have been so outraged.

Nathan Reiss asked, "What kind of a speech, professor? Is everyone welcome?"

"It is a public rally of the Anti-Fascist Conference," Hogan said.

Reiss arched his neat, dark brows. "That is the Communist organization, is it not?"

"It is an organization of anti-Fascists, some of whom no doubt are Communists," Jonathan said coldly.

Reiss puckered his lips, the kiss of regret, the kiss of death. Jonathan was ashamed of himself, but he could not tolerate this polished interloper.

Martha, pouring coffee, working and sitting sideways in that lopsided way of women in the late months of pregnancy, said, "I should like to go, Jonathan—if you will have time for me. It's Marcus's night at the Clinic." Marcus went frequently to the Brandon Clinic: the pledge of an endowment from the Fields Foundation was going to make possible a special wing for diseases of the chest.

Marcus said, "I'm not at all sure you should go among crowds of that size just now, Martha."

Reiss said, "What a shame, I have to study. Imagine—at my age and in a foreign language. It is humiliating. I shall fail the examinations."

Marcus said dryly, "I doubt it."

Reiss smiled at Martha. "But if I could go with you, I could make it up to you for the Heldenplatz embarrassment. I always remember, you see."

"I have forgotten it, Nathan, believe me."

"Such fools. With all this fighting, everyone will need doctors, no?"

"I have no doubt you could join the American Army and be there soon enough, doctor," Jonathan said in a mixture of bitterness and malice.

"No, I have had quite enough of war already."

"Have you?"

Reiss turned to him, smiling still. "Sometimes, professor, the hardest thing a man does is to run away. Is it not so?"

Jonathan, with his tic, grimaced in his attempt to smile. The point had been well scored.

In the cab on the way to the Stadium the night of the rally, Jonathan went over his notes. Several times throughout the day he had been tempted to destroy them. Several times in the last weeks he had been on the verge of withdrawing from the conference rally. Yet he knew that to be the coward's way. Nor was his work done. His message, he felt, was more important now than at any moment heretofore. Had he been a religious man, he would have prayed during that brief journey. Instead, having pocketed his notes, he sat back in the corner of the cab from where he could glance sidewise at Martha. Seeing her sit serene behind her burden, he took comfort from her and from all that pregnancy is symbol of in times of man's destruction of himself.

Martha had never been in the Stadium, which served most of the time as a sports arena, and she was reminded, looking up at it while Jonathan paid the driver, of the Castel d'Angelo in Rome. No angel, however, sat atop it. But around it like a moat hung the vaporous heat. Men in shirt sleeves and women in sleeveless dresses passed through the entrances, moving among numerous police. She and Jonathan moved inside and up the ramp, Jonathan protecting her like an old gallant from an occasional surge of the crowd.

The Stadium was cavernous despite the trooping people. Huge buntings seemed no more than ribbons draped at either end, and a haze hung between the remote ceiling lights and the gathering audience. At the moment the loudspeakers were tested Martha was thrust back in memory to where she wanted least to go: the Heldenplatz. These were Americans, she told herself, for all that some of them might be Communists. She and Jonathan took seats at the end of a row near the speaker's platform at the heart of the oval structure.

Many people, passing to and fro, stopped to speak to Jonathan or pat him on the back. "Remember, Professor Hogan, if ever we needed you, we need you now."

Martha wondered if you could tell the Communists by their use of the word "comrade," and naïvely asked Jonathan.

He laughed and said, "There are other ways. For one, when everyone else is gone from here tonight, they'll still be here."

Martha did not understand, but it was the least of her ignorances. While the Stadium filled, an organist started playing and very soon people started to sing. Then everyone was singing: work songs, folk songs, spirituals, the tunes to most of which she knew although the words were sometimes unfamiliar. There was a prevalence of martial music; one song that Martha liked especially was the Red Army Cavalry Song.

During a lull, Jonathan said, " 'Will you love me in December as you did in May?' How does that go?" The question was rhetorical. He added, "Franklin doesn't want war. Neither does Eleanor." He smiled then at Martha. "The majority of these people were pacifists last spring. How do you think they feel tonight?"

Martha said, "Things have changed." She meant that the war had spread. Russia was now with the Allies.

"And the more they are the same," Jonathan said.

The gray light of day faded at the small, high windows deepset in concrete, and when the darkness fell outside, spotlights came up on the speakers' platform, encircling the rostrum and a half-dozen chairs. Then a roving spot picked up one after another behind the platform the flags of many nations. Everyone stood up and cheered. Martha put her hand on her father-in-law's arm. He patted it gently.

"We are nothing if not dramatic. I shall have to go up in a minute. I'll come back here for you afterwards."

The speaker at the rostrum leaned into the microphone and announced "Our National Anthem." The playing and singing of it brought the crowd to order. He called the speakers to the platform one by one. There were names among them Martha recognized: a clergyman, a labor leader, a well-known sociologist. Jonathan Hogan, she thought, received the warmest welcome of all.

The keynote speaker sounded the rallying cry of the evening: American preparation for war. He called it a just war, a war that was inevitable, a war of liberation, and he was frequently interrupted by applause. He called for increased arms production, for no-strike pledges from the unions; for legislation to prohibit profiteering, for American pressure on the Allies to open a second front.

Martha could not keep her attention focused. So much in what the speakers said was repetitious. She observed that there often recurred the reference to "the brave Russian people," "the heroic Russian people," and she longed for someone to get up and pay tribute to the British. From her mother she knew their plight: Elizabeth had turned McMahon Manor in Northern Ireland into a home for the orphaned refugees from the London blitz. She was surprised at how little enthusiasm greeted mention of the Atlantic Charter and decided it must be too mild a document for this crowd. How emotional they were, these stiff-necked, high-headed people, working men and women, most of them, with a sprinkling of intellectuals. She could not escape the feeling of their foreignness. She did not know very many working people, she realized. Sylvia would have been much more at home here than she was; Sylvia, she supposed, was a much more complete human being. She came to think—bored with the speeches and given to the speculative sort of reflection one may sometimes enjoy in a church not of one's own creed—that if intelligence discovered the error in false creeds, their best combatant, nonetheless, was a mass ignorance. It was not his meaning at all, but Martha thought of the words of a learned monsignor who could make theology romantic: two kinds of people find God, he said, the very wise and the very simple.

Jonathan sat, his head bowed, his hands in his lap, until his name was called. He stood then in the glaring light, acknowledging with the barest of nods in one direction and then the other, the applause; in it Martha joined heartily.

"I have ever believed myself among friends here," he began, his voice quite different on the microphone, deeper and resonant. "And I know that in this I exalt myself . . . We have together long cried peace. But there is no peace . . . and I have come to the agonizing conclusion that there can be no peace while men like Hitler stalk the earth."

The crowd gave a virtual whoop of cheer. Jonathan held up his hand to restrain them and shook his head the while. He went on: "But I will not, for I cannot, sound the trumpet of war. In my deep heart's core, I feel that we in the United States, and men anywhere fortunate enough to be free, can best serve mankind preparing, not for war—as has been so eloquently petitioned here among us pacifists —but for the peace . . ."

A confused murmur ran through the audience, a mixture of laugh-ter and protest.

"Hear me, as I have heard you—each the other over many years now . . . We shall not conquer our enemies by imitating them. If war is thrust upon us, we shall need defend ourselves and our friends. But let us not now or later confuse our purpose with our allies' ambi-tions. Let us not defend colonialism . . ."

The cheers returned mingled with cries of "No! No!"

"Let us not justify exploitation . . ."

"No, no, NO, *NO!*" The response was chanted as though to a familiar pattern set long ago between Jonathan and his audience.

"Let us not wink at expansionism . . ."

"No, no, NO, *NO!*"

". . . whether it is that of the so-called empires . . . or that of the Soviet Union."

There was a stunned silence of at least a few seconds' duration. Then a flutter of applause broke upon it.

"In all conscience I must tell you," Jonathan went on slowly, de-terminedly, "I am no more influenced to enthusiasm for the war by Germany's march into Russia than I was dissuaded of the true meaning of anti-Fascism by Stalin's march into Finland. I am only less sanguine of peace.

"Dictators breed dictators, war breeds war . . ."

From that instant on Jonathan's words could not be heard for the sudden booing and hissing of the crowd, the stomping of their feet, the chanting then of a rhythmic, even "No, No, No, No . . . Go home, Jonathan . . . Go home, Jonathan . . ."

Jonathan stood, yielding the microphone to the chairman who

was powerless to impose silence. He spread his hands in despair. It seemed to Martha that Jonathan stood there forever. Yet everything happened with incredible speed. She seemed herself numb, immovable, weighted like stone. With austere mockery, Jonathan bowed from the waist and left the platform.

A sector of the crowd had struck up a tune to set their words to. They sang, "Go home, Jonathan—Go home, Jonathan. It's time to leave you now." The whole auditorium seemed to rock with it.

Jonathan went directly up the ramp nearest the platform. Only when he disappeared from her sight was Martha able to gather motion into her body and hasten after him. The discord of the organ pumping out martial music against the persistent singing voices heightened the wild madness of sound and motion. Everything seemed zigzag, the ascending ramps and rails, the buttresses beneath the tiers, and the only light for guidance the red and white eye-like bulbs, guide lights of the exits.

Martha was a moment before she saw him, his head against one of the steel girders. While she watched, on her way to him, he began to pound his head against the girder, harder and harder, as though he would knock himself senseless. She took hold of him and, failing to pull him away from the post, pried one hand loose of it. He swung at her with the hand, in no way an injurious blow, but only then did he seem to come to his senses. He let go of the girder and stood before her, limp, his face all awry. Martha got him outside as quickly as she could to where a little air was stirring.

"I've got to vomit," he said. "I should not have had supper."

It was the worst possible moment for a newspaper man to appear, but a *Star* reporter identified himself. "Hey, professor! Are you disillusioned with the Commies now?"

"Couldn't you see? They were disillusioned with me."

"Aw, come on, professor. Let's make a story out of it. It's the *Star* you're talking to. We'll give you a break. How about it, lady? Are you his daughter? What did it feel like—having that crowd turn on the old man?"

"I have nothing to say," Martha said.

Jonathan was trying to move away, to reach the shadow of the building; the reporter started after him.

"Leave him alone! He's sick," Martha said.

"I'll say he is." The reporter stood by and watched Jonathan throw up. While Hogan wiped his face with his handkerchief, the reporter insisted, "What made you sick, professor? Come on. They're a bunch of muckers, aren't they, to turn on an old guy like you— the best friend they got in America? Christ, haven't you got any guts?"

Martha was trying to get the attention of a policeman.

"I'm not going to say anything tonight for publication," Jonathan said.

Martha had attracted attention, but that of other members of the press, including a photographer.

"And who the hell will publish it, do you think, when you get around to it? Professor, you aren't going to be news after tonight. Better have a last fling at the headlines."

Hogan said nothing.

A policeman was finally coming.

" 'Professor Hogan walks out on Reds.' That's the truth, isn't it? Make the most of it. Or do you want me to file this way: 'The Reds kick Hogan out'?"

"Officer, will you please help us get a taxi? My father is ill."

"Come on, Jerry, get us a picture and let's get out of here," the reporter said.

"Shame on you!" Martha cried, and at the moment the flash bulbs went off. Her arm was crooked in Jonathan's.

The policeman guided them through a small crowd of street gawkers, the ever available but nameless and silent witnesses to any incident on the city streets.

"The worst of it is—I knew," Jonathan said within the cab. "I knew it was going to happen."

Martha said nothing, for the first time hating Traders City because she did not know where else to focus her revulsion. She insisted that Jonathan stay the night on Oak Street.

He was past arguing. He was past a great many things which until now had kept in working condition his sparse and infirm body. Marcus was shocked at the change in him. There were bruised lacerations on his father's forehead. These he could and did patch up instantly. The other condition made him furious. And he would have liked to make his father furious.

"You know you had it coming to you, don't you, dad?"

"Yes, I know."

This was not what Marcus wanted at all. Nor was he prepared for Martha's turning on him.

"You weren't there, Marcus. You've got no right to judge. He was magnificent!"

"I've had a pretty fair sampling of his opinions in my lifetime," Marcus said, "and there comes a time when the best of fashions go out of date."

"Meaning?" Jonathan said.

"That it's too late for your doctrine of passive resistance. Could you go to that window, look out, and see one man clubbing hell out of another, and do nothing about it?"

"No. I would have to go out—get help if need be—and take the club from him. And then I should have to see forever that he did not get another club. But, Marc—what would it avail me to club him to death, even with his own club? What man dares trust himself with the power of destruction? Not I. Killing kills."

"I'm sorry, dad. But I do not believe there is any way to deal with force except with force. There is a time we have to kill."

Jonathan said, "If you feel that way, Marc, you must." The silence in the room became as heavy as the atmosphere. All three of them knew something more had to be said, a final word. There is always that last bit of self-justification which puts the matter neatly out of reach, perhaps not forever, but at least for a time, a sort of deliberate alienation, meant not so much to score against the other person, as to clear a ground for oneself in which to rest and sort out the truths from the over-truths, principle from posture. "I don't disown you," Jonathan added, spreading his hands, "but I'm not sure I know you."

They sat, all of them disconsolate. The hall clock struck midnight. Marcus proposed they light a citronella candle and go out on the terrace. Martha said it ought to rain soon. At that moment the telephone rang.

Martha said, "I'll take it, Marcus." Wherever she could she tried to intercept late calls for him.

But that night Marcus said, "No, you've had enough for one night."

He took the call in the library. It was George Bergner. Marcus had not seen him since the night of his father's death, their only communication an exchange of letters on matters relating to the estate. The work on genetics might never have been done for all the worth of the fragments Marcus had been able to gather from Dr. Bergner's secretary.

"I've just been talking to the city editor at the *Star*, Marcus,"
Bergner said. "That was an ugly business tonight at the Stadium."

"Would you like to speak to my father, George?"

"No, no. I wouldn't disturb him. You can tell he was upset. The
reason I've called you—one of our boys got a picture, one of those
heart-breaking, human interest shots that come along maybe once
in a photographer's life? You know what I mean, Marcus?"

Marcus did not answer, but he suspected what was coming.

"A pregnant girl supporting a broken old man. The cruelty of
life, as my father used to say—but it would be a little thick, wouldn't
it, me quoting him to you? The thing is, Marcus . . . well, I thought
I ought to tell you before it appears in the morning. You get the *Star*,
don't you?" A sound like muffled, nervous laughter ran through the
last sentence.

"Sometimes."

Bergner said: "Well, I just thought I'd tell you before it's locked
up . . . you knowing the publisher and all."

Marcus realized he had been given an invitation to call Winthrop.
George did not care whom he asked to destroy the picture, so long
as he asked it. Marcus was caught: there is no position so vulnerable
as the high ground of righteousness.

"Thank you very much, George," Marcus said and hung up.

It was some moments before he returned to the living room. By
then Martha and his father had moved out to the terrace. The damp,
slightly putrid smell of late summer hung in the unstirring air.

"You don't have to go out, do you, Marcus?"

"It was George Bergner. The *Star* photographer seems to have got
a picture of you two."

"Oh," was all Martha said.

"I'm sorry, Marc," Jonathan said after a moment. "It isn't every
son has a bad boy for a father."

"For God's sake, get off that line. If I were going to be embarrassed by you it would have happened a long time ago. Was it your
pride that got hurt tonight or your principles?"

"That's a very good question," Jonathan said. "Mostly my pride."

To Martha, Marcus said gently: "Why don't you go up to bed?
I shall be along soon."

Martha asked: "Are you going to call Doctor Winthrop?"

"I was thinking of it."

"To ask him not to allow the picture?"

Marcus did not say anything.

"Please don't, Marcus. Jonathan has had his picture in the paper before, and I am not ashamed to be seen with him. As you said, his principles weren't compromised tonight. I wish it all hadn't happened, but it did. A picture in the newspaper isn't going to change anything much, is it?"

Marcus shook a cigaret out of a damp package, gave it to his father and took one for himself. He lit them both. "Not much." He brushed Martha's cheek with the back of his hand.

Much later and when they had talked of many other things, Jonathan remarked: "Something I have observed—I wonder if either of you has: when two people in love live a number of years together, they tend not only to reconcile their differences. They are quite likely to change positions with one another. Have you noticed it?"

He turned round to Martha, but she had fallen asleep in the chair.

·8

NOTHING was more illustrative of Lakewood's estimate of a man's position than the attitude of the commuters on the eight o'clock train to Traders City. No one had ever made a point of snubbing Alexander Winthrop, and no one now made a point of including him, yet a change had occurred and he could feel it. It was in the inflection of a one-word greeting, in the way Hurd Abington for example would say "Winthrop," without, so far as Winthrop had been able to observe, having lifted his eyes from the *Journal of Commerce*. A few of the men who carried more than one newspaper took the *Star*, although Winthrop was sure they opened it almost as gingerly as they would a Hearst sheet. With Hearst they agreed in principle but preferred to disassociate from his exploitation. Winthrop suspected they mistook the *Star's* principles for exploitation and perversely honored its publisher for a successful stratagem. Then too, his marriage to Sylvia Fields, presumably on his own terms, further bound him within the community. It was considered sage and apt of him to have waited until the old lady died. Winthrop understood how much the rich can admire abstemiousness.

He supposed it was an affectation, but he could not bring himself to read his own newspaper on the train. Thus it was not until George Bergner came back from the smoking car and, as was their custom, sat with him the last fifteen minutes of the journey, that he learned of Martha's and Jonathan Hogan's picture on the front page.

The first sight of it turned his stomach: Hogan gaunt and withered, Martha as undisguisedly pregnant as a she-goat in the same condition, and as belligerent-looking, the police holding back what appeared to be a baiting mob. (It was not: merely the curious bystanders trying to get a better view; Hogan's baiters were within the Stadium. But all the symbolism was there.)

"Our man, Jerry Adams, will get the Pulitzer Prize for that picture," George said, "I'll lay you odds on it."

Winthrop found himself unable to speak. He read the caption: EXIT OF A HERO.

"We had to use it. You can see that, Alex," George said. "It's a shame—I mean their being who they are—to you and me. But in the end, it's going to do old Hogan more good than harm."

"I don't see how," Winthrop said. "And I don't see why I wasn't consulted on its use. You manage to consult me on damn near everything else."

"I think we'd better wait till we get to the office," George said.

"Yes—since you waited this long."

Winthrop meanwhile read the story: its ending everyone could have expected except Hogan, by the signs. It made Winthrop grateful that he was not himself a man given to causes, to religion. It caused him for the first time in many months to think of Walter Fitzgerald. Walter's daughter and Red Jonathan. The dead had little protest. But he doubted Walter would have had more influence, alive. Martha would cleave her own way. Her loyalties might not be sensible, but they were steadfast. He was in a position to know. She had made one gesture toward him for Sylvia's sake, but after that the drift had been away.

The *Star* switchboard reported having to put on an extra girl to handle the calls coming in about the Stadium story—and the picture, roughly a hundred to one congratulatory.

"I'll bet the *Workers' Guardian* flays our hides," George said, and rubbed his hands together. "That's why we had to do it, Alex."

Winthrop drew a line the width of his finger tip through the dust on his desk. "Have you been answering the phone, too, Miss Kelly?" he said to his secretary.

"Yes, sir." She ignored the sarcasm and handed him a fistful of messages.

Winthrop said, "Now, George, tell me why we had to do it."

"In the first place, Alex, because we're a newspaper. You made fun of me once for thinking myself a newspaper man. I'm going to make you eat those words. But it's all a matter of survival for the *Star*. You know as well as I do, whenever the big boys want to grind us out they'll run up the red flag over us. This sort of thing is the best answer we've got: 'You can't do business with Stalin: ask Jonathan Hogan.' You'll find that on the editorial page."

"I suppose I wrote it," Winthrop said dryly.

"And that was what I meant when I said it would do Hogan more good than harm. They won't be able to tag him a Communist either after this."

Winthrop flicked through his messages.

"Can't you guess the reason I didn't consult you?" George said. "You can't very well be expected to be on top of everything, can you?"

Winthrop looked at him. It was so neat, he could not help but wonder how much personal satisfaction George had got out of this newspaper coup. That he was satisfied with himself was obvious. Was it because he had brought it off leaving Winthrop himself clean, or did the satisfaction go back to his hostility toward Marcus Hogan? The old gentleman, Dr. Bergner, had left nothing in money to Marcus. Most of the estate outside the house in Lakewood—which George was now hard put to keep up himself—had been put in trust for George's two children. In a way it had been more of a slap at George than to have been disinherited. Winthrop had heard Dr. Albert talk at one time and another about his theory of the one good seed in every family line. Too obviously he had skipped George looking for it in his own.

Winthrop said, "Ignorance comes a little too natural to me, George, for me to enjoy pleading it. I'll take the responsibility. After all, I'm responsible for you, amn't I?"

"You could fire me," George said.

"And lose a good newspaper man?" Winthrop had meant it in sarcasm, but a sudden pink suffused George's bald pate and Winthrop conceded that he had no grounds for sarcasm. George was doing a fine job for him. If he were to personally abandon the paper tomorrow, it would go on under George's management quite as though Winthrop himself were there. He said, "Give my congratulations to the photographer. Tell him that picture's the real thing."

But throughout the day, thinking now and then of the paper's sound launching, and the steady pull it must now be on someone's part to increase its circulation and keep up its advertising, he was aware of the stir of restlessness again within himself. In the afternoon he had occasion to write his cabinet friend in Washington. Toward the end of the letter he wrote: "Who knows? A year or two and I may be looking for another enterprise."

That morning Martha received a call from Sylvia, and later in the day, a visit. By then she had got used to the fact that her picture had been in the morning news. The embarrassed sting of it was gone; indeed the picture was no longer in the house, Jonathan having taken the paper to clip for his scrapbook, so he said. He had no scrapbook and supposed now he knew the wisdom of not having kept one. He and Martha both understood: without ceremony he dropped it in the first public trash container.

When Sylvia came the two women met with an awkwardness merely compounded by the incident; they had not seen each other since Sylvia's marriage. Martha knew it would have been proper that she invite the Winthrops to dinner soon thereafter, but she had let it go too long and Marcus understood. They had sent a telegram of congratulations on the day of the wedding and there it had had to stand. She was too honest to do more and she had suffered as those who oblige the forms without qualm cannot suffer. She did not make friends easily and despite some twenty years' difference in their ages, she and Sylvia had become very close. They shared many tastes if few confidences. As Sylvia had once said of Martha to her brother, Tony: "You're always afraid she'll see the truth in something too soon." It had been a futile wish, but from the night she met Martha, she would have liked to see Tony marry her.

When they were sitting opposite one another that afternoon, a hard rain threshing against the terrace doors, Sylvia said, "I haven't changed very much—have you?"

"Not as much as I'd have liked to," Martha said.

They both laughed to deprecate the moment's portent.

"What's happening these days with our B's for B?" Sylvia referred to Bundles for Britain.

"They're piling up again. Marcus calls the basement 'Moth Haven.' I dare say when school starts I shall have some help."

"We're starting on the Russians now in Lakewood, God help them. It's going to be very fashionable. There's a rumor circulating that after *this* war is over, there's going to be another Russian revolution, and the Whites will take over again. 'Ha!' you say, but don't. I could raise ten million dollars for such a cause in one night."

"For the brave Russian people," Martha mused.

"That will be the day."

They glanced at each other and smiled. The time had come. "Alex won't admit it, but he didn't know about the picture, Martha. We are both deeply sorry."

Martha laughed, a small sound of self-derision. "It was colorful though, wasn't it?"

"I'm sure it hurt you very much."

"Not as much as other things last night, Sylvia, and Jonathan took the paper out with him this morning like a dead fish, and we could laugh."

"He must be very wretched, poor man."

"They might have left him his dignity, even if he was wrong," Martha said. "That's the worst of it, he's beginning to feel he may be wrong—and if he is wrong, what is right is utterly abhorrent to him."

" 'Thou shalt not kill.' That's all he's saying, isn't it?"

"I am not a pacifist," Martha said. "Marcus says there are killings every day in hospitals by doctors who are criminally inept. There are accidents: men crushed in machines, or children burned horribly and to no purpose except that we must die, all of us. My father thought he was dying for something, at least. A soldier dies for something. I don't know that living is always so important, is it?"

"I don't know either, but I want to live. Don't you?"

"Yes. Terribly."

Sylvia asked, "Are you afraid, Martha?"

She lifted her chin. "I am, a little. I shouldn't want Marcus to know it, though. It's having got this far, I suppose, when twice before I didn't. Sometimes I feel that if I manage to bear a child—a child that breathes and lives—I must pay forfeit for it."

"What morbid Irish nonsense!" Sylvia cried, and herself began to move about the room. There were times she could no more sit still than could her husband.

"I know," Martha said.

"And feeling that way, you went to that rally last night?"

"I had a feeling about that, too," she said, and then smiled in her sudden reassuring way and tilted her head back. "I shall be hung for a witch in the end, if I'm not careful, shan't I?"

·9

THE boy who was to be named Thaddeus Marcus Hogan, Jr., was born on October 31, 1941, in every way well equipped, it seemed, to cope with living. Assured that her son was a fine healthy baby, Martha asked Marcus who or what he looked like. Marcus said, "Let me put it this way: If anyone were to nickname him Tadpole at this moment, it would be sheer flattery."

When the baby was brought to her, Martha said, "I think he looks like you, Marcus."

To which he answered, "Thank you, dear."

From his office he called Jonathan who was attending a conference in the East.

At home, he and Annie drank a toast. "It's a sign, doctor, surely, to be born on Allhallows' Eve. Maybe he'll grow up to be a priest." And she gave Marcus a nudge with her red knuckles. "Would you mind that?"

"You know, Annie, it's something that never occurred to me. I shouldn't want to say until I've talked it over with him."

Annie breathed a great sigh. "Ah, sure, it's given me a new leash on life."

Marcus grinned and realized by the ache in his jaw muscles that he must have given them a great deal of exercise throughout the day. Nonetheless, alone in the house except for Annie, he felt himself on the verge of depression as the October darkness fell. Looking down from the terrace, he could see beyond the hedge the little ghosts and grotesques of Hallowe'en pass by in search of mischief. Their jack-o-lanterns bobbed like will-o'-the-wisps. The smell of burning leaves hung in the dry, sharp air. Was it a good time to be born? "Too young for this war": he had heard the phrase more than once in Maternity. He had himself been born in 1908. A better time? He had been born too young for *that* war . . . but not for this one if the country was to be involved as it must surely be. There were not many doctors in a better position to serve, and he a surgeon. But to excise disease was one thing, to probe young flesh for lead another; to open cleanly and exactly was what he strove to make his genius. The wounds of war, he knew, were ghastly imprecise. He went indoors and made a note: he needed to remember that Martha asked him to have the handy man check the sacking around the rose bushes.

How desolate the house without Martha in it; how desolate the house for Martha without him in it. But now there was Thaddeus Marcus Hogan, Jr.—Tad. He said the name aloud, getting used to the idea of there being an actual person to go with it. And there was Jonathan who could not bear his house alone either, but who kept it, Marcus knew although it had not been said, for Mrs. Turley's sake. It would fall to him, he supposed, to do something about that tie. A modest pension could be arranged, and she would have to—and very well could—accommodate herself to the notion than Jonathan Hogan could survive without her care, assuming he could survive with it.

Marcus was very grateful when Alexander Winthrop called up to congratulate him and then asked if he could, by any chance, join him and Sylvia at the Union League Club for dinner. They were in town for theater that night.

The occasion being festive, Sylvia chose the menu and Winthrop the wine: fish and a *filet mignon,* champagne before they went to the table, and for dinner Vouvray and a Côte du Rhône, '24.

"This is a great compliment to you, Marcus," Sylvia said when he closed his eyes with pleasure at the Rhône. "The steward has just three bottles more for Alex of this vintage."

"A good wine is the next best thing to a good friend," Winthrop said, "and a good friend to have in that case is the wine steward. I'm going to arrange to have a dozen bottles of the next great year sent you, Marcus, to put away for the boy's twenty-first birthday."

"That's very kind of you, Alex. I didn't realize you had such confidence in my forebearance."

Winthrop laughed.

"Nineteen sixty-two, oh, my God!" Sylvia said.

"We've got a lot of living to do between now and then." Winthrop looked at his wife with an amused affection, which made Marcus think it was going along fine, their marriage, obliging both with what each needed. Pride had never been a stumbling block for either of them.

"We sure as hell better," Sylvia said in the broad way she sometimes had, reminding Winthrop of her mother. "We won't be doing much of it after that."

It was while they were having brandy, and having checked his watch that Winthrop remarked with a casualness Marcus suspected to be deliberate, "Have you given any thought to having someone with you since Doctor Albert died?"

"Not much." But that very evening it had crossed his mind when he was thinking of the war.

"Reiss is doing fine at Lakewood . . . and he started with something of a handicap."

"His religion?" Marcus said after a moment. Winthrop nodded. "It doesn't seem ever to have been much of a handicap."

"And why should it?" Sylvia said with a quickness that made Marcus suppose she might be behind Winthrop's awareness of the man.

"I was not suggesting that it should. But it does seem to have been confining to a number of his people in our times, doesn't it?"

"He's a good doctor," Winthrop said. "Doctor Albert's whim paid off nicely. You ought to watch him, Marcus. You may need someone. You can't tell these days." The chain of association was crudely obvious.

Marcus lit a cigaret. "Do you think he's the real thing, Alex?" He was using Winthrop's own phrase.

"What do you mean?"

"Is he sincere? Does he give a damn about medicine or only money?"

"He's ambitious as they come, but his knife is clean."

Marcus smoked in silence.

Sylvia said, "Whether he's genuine or not, he always does the right thing, Marcus. It almost comes natural to him."

Almost, Marcus noticed. He grinned. "A dozen roses came for Martha this afternoon. I didn't send them. Did you?"

"No. It sounds like Nathan," she said.

"Or George," Winthrop said. "That's where I found out you were a father. He's got a lot of *savoir faire* these days, our George."

Marcus held his tongue, but Sylvia caught the flash in his eyes. She said, "I'm sure it was Reiss. Wasn't there a card?"

"I didn't look," Marcus said. "At the time of childbirth a man feels he has to suffer in any way he can." He knew he was being flippant, but he did not—on this occasion at any rate—want to say the things coming into his mind. He had not told anyone of George's destruction of his father's manuscript. Too many people, judging the old man on personality, his lectures—into which he had been known to introduce gratuitously his theories on the scientific breeding of men—might well have applauded George. Midwestern University had at one time quietly suggested that Dr. Bergner stick to the manual.

When the time came he walked the Winthrops to the theater, and while there bought tickets for Martha and himself for a month hence: *Watch on the Rhine*. He bought the best seats in the house, since he proposed them as a present to Martha. He assumed she would like them better than a dozen roses. He went from the theater to a phone booth in the nearest drugstore. He called his answering service first and then Erich Mueller. It was Mueller himself who answered the phone.

"Erich? This is Marcus Hogan. I've got a pocketful of cigars and an eight-pound son. May I come and see you for an hour?"

"What a question!"

Mueller kissed him on both cheeks, needing to stand on tiptoe to reach him. "So! Now you are a father! If you do not first succeed, try, try again. See?" He called up the stairs, "Julie, come! Here is the new papa."

Julie kissed him and made a noisy fuss over him as only the French can. Marcus saw that she was pregnant.

Mueller said: "A boy, just like that!" and snapped his fingers.

Marcus said: "If you do not first succeed . . ."

"*Oui!*" Julie cried and patted her distended belly while all of them laughed.

They had the good dark coffee that would keep his nerves marching up and down all night, Marcus thought, coffee in tall, narrow cups with the whipped cream in the upper half, and Mueller asked about Jonathan. He was the more solicitous of him for being out of patience with him and his cause.

Afterwards, while Julie was putting away the coffee things, Marcus asked Mueller how much he really knew about Nathan Reiss.

"How much do I need to know about a man? He is a good doctor. They will tell you that up where he is doing this dreadful thing they require in this state, a new internship—a year out of a man's life. Just because he is educated elsewhere, he is stupid? I do not think so."

"He would not have had to do that in some states, as I understand it," Marcus said. "New York, for example."

"Because he is a Jew, you think he should have stopped in New York?"

"That's not worthy of you, Erich." Marcus was the more irritated because it was the second time that night something of the sort had happened to him.

"I don't think it's worthy of you to have said it, Marc. If I misunderstand you, forgive me."

"You do misunderstand me. There is a man in New York—a refugee whose history I know. He has done heart surgery and I have been thinking of going out there to observe him."

"Ach, then you must forgive me, Marc, what I said. It is how Nathan himself says: Many people ask him why he did not stay there. He is very sensitive."

"Not any more than the rest of us," Marcus said.

"Why do you not like him?"

"I'm not sure that I don't. I've not seen very much of him." Marcus gave a short laugh. "But I begin to get the feeling that somewhere back in the years, he was tied into my life, my destiny—to give it a fancy word: Winthrop to Bergner to me to Reiss to Winthrop to me."

"But of course! That's how it is, Marc, we are all waiting someone to complement. We are nothing alone."

"I should like to have some say in it, that's all."

"Now it is *quid pro quo*. Is that what you mean?"

"Exactly."

"But that is marvelous, Marc! I knew Doctor Winthrop would like him. They are both so—vital. We are all linked to one another, Marc, believe me."

"Like sausages," Marcus said irreverently.

Mueller made a noise of mock disapproval.

"Erich, why was he so long in getting out of Europe? Wasn't it risky?"

"But of course. I will tell you, Marc, but I ask you to keep it in confidence. You will understand why he wants it that way. He was out already and went back. The Baroness . . . Look, Marc, we are men. She was for many years his mistress. She did everything for him. In the beginning he was an orphan boy of eighteen she wanted to sleep with, I suppose. I don't know. I've been told there are women like that. He was a beautiful boy, I am sure. But she is a very foolish woman. She thinks money can buy everything . . ." Mueller paused in the story as his wife came into the room. He said to her, "You go upstairs now, Julie, *tout de suite*," and he gave her a brief slap on the backside as he might a child.

When she was gone he continued: "She thought money could even buy off the Nazis. And it did for a time. Then one day she could look down from her window and see the Jews scrubbing the streets of Vienna on their knees. Then she knew it was very late. She telephoned Nathan in Switzerland and he said one word to her: the name of her villa in the Austrian Alps. She got to it all right and she knew—the international lake, you see. And he came for her at night in a boat and waited. And when finally she did not come he went up to look for her and he saw the Nazis taking her away. They were armed, he was not. He is very much ashamed, but he did not try to rescue her. He saved himself only."

Marcus studied the end of the cigar he was smoking. "What happened to her?"

Mueller shrugged. "Who can tell? There is no word. I should think a concentration camp. It is not a story you can blame a man if he does not tell about himself, is it?"

Marcus got up from the round dining room table and brushed an ash from the lace cloth. He should have blown it off not to have left a smudge. "No, I don't blame him . . . for anything. Not even for being so damned footloose and fancy free."

"It is a pose, Marc. All a pose. That man has known trouble and fear. And let me tell you, when you have known real fear you are never again fancy free, as you call it. Yes, I tell you it is a pose. You can believe me: Nathan Reiss will make you a fine partner."

At the door they shook hands. "You must give all the Hogans our love, Marc. A son . . . just like that." He stood grinning and shaking his head while Marcus went down the steps.

Ah, but it was a glorius month for all the Hogans, that November. Jonathan began to act like a grandfather. His other son, Trent, in the Far East, had two children, but Jonathan had never seen them. When Martha came home with the child, he would often sit with her and tell her stories of Trent's and Marcus's boyhood, and it was foreseeable that Tad would grow up asking to hear the stories again and again. Martha could remember the stories she loved of Ireland, her mother's and Annie's, both. He would not be at a loss for entertainment, this child.

The date for his baptism was set for the first Sunday afternoon in December. Jonathan said, "If he's to have a name it might as well be fastened on him proper." And he went to church with them. "I don't mind the atmosphere of churches. I think it would be very nice if atheists like myself had churches of our own in which to sit and think."

Martha always demurred when he called himself an atheist.

"But I am, all the same. We'll leave that in-between business to Marcus. He's very good at it."

When they came out of the church that Sunday afternoon, December 7, 1941, the word was abroad upon the street of the Japanese attack on Pearl Harbor.

· 10

IT WAS one of the things he was simply going to have to get used to in the man, Marcus decided of Reiss' self-assurance. It bordered on arrogance, but he had observed something of the same haughtiness in other Austrians who were also charming, the mixture of nails and velvet. Reiss, at the point where Marcus suggested sharing his downtown office with him, responded as though it were he who was doing Marcus a favor. And perhaps he was, Marcus thought. What amused him of himself was that he had given a great deal of thought on how to approach the matter without seeming to condescend to Reiss. Perhaps in the days Mueller had known him in Paris, when he was young and still in awe of medicine he had been sensitive, but the role of a rich woman's lover had seared the tender heart; the truly remarkable thing was that he was a good surgeon. To his everlasting credit, one would have to say that for him. The temptation to dilettantism must have been very great. But the scalpel in hand, Reiss was coldly, brilliantly professional.

All in all, Marcus enjoyed the association. If Reiss was supremely confident in himself, the patients were also confident in him, particularly the women, and this was no small part of preparation and recovery.

Because Marcus knew that he would be called up for military service when he was needed and that he did not intend to seek an exemption, he was, he supposed, just biding time. He watched the changes in the child, the first laugh, the first tooth, the first illness, the first step, and he watched Martha grow in motherhood. They were at once the happiest and the saddest of days, with parting imminent and the not quite repressible aura of the heroic about him.

Everywhere was change. By the end of 1942 Lakewood, so far as owners of the great estates were concerned, had been virtually abandoned. Gasoline was rationed, taxes compounded. The army had leased a number of houses, breaking them up into multiple dwellings. The Winthrops closed their house and moved into town. Tony sold the Fields estate at auction and joined the Air Force. The Bergners stayed on: their house was not so large and was within walking distance of the railway station. George could not find it in his heart, he said, to separate Louise from the house she adored. And then, he found it convenient to stay in town alone some nights. Louise, blithe soul, became one of those people tradesmen were constantly asking, "Don't you know there's a war on?"

As it turned out, however, the first—except for Tony—among them to make a move directly the result of the war was Alexander Winthrop. Because of his administrative experience and medical background, he was one of the people Washington called upon in anticipation of the occupation period. He was to be given a direct army commission and training preparatory to service overseas. As the time approached for him to leave, Martha knew the time had also come to make another attempt at reconciliation. She proposed to give a small party for the Winthrops before Alexander left.

"The vegetable plate special?" Marcus said.

"Grandpa Jon and I are very proud of that garden," Martha said. "I do much better in vegetables than flowers."

Martha consulted Sylvia on whom to invite.

"Just ourselves," Sylvia said, and then as Martha seemed hesitant she quickly added, "and Nathan and Jonathan. How's that?"

"That will be fine," Martha said, and she was on the verge of adding that just themselves would be all right, too. But she didn't say it, feeling that Nathan's amiable—or even his malicious—small talk might well be what the evening needed. It seemed at the time like a very small decision.

Everyone dressed for dinner. Martha had got a fine plump bird, shopping for it herself as she preferred to do, having now the dubious assistance of Tad. (He walked early, but he steadfastly refused to talk. He was, his father said, a listener, thank God. Jonathan said he was a philosopher, that he would say something when he thought of something worth saying. Martha allowed that it would be the day on which he missed his first meal.) Cocktails and dinner went off well. Jonathan even laughed at an experience of Nathan's. It concerned a man who married late and for company, not for progeny. His wife, nonetheless, conceived. But it was diagnosed as a tumor by her own physician. P.eiss examined her and agreed to break the good news to her husband. "This will surprise you, my friend—your wife's tumor is a pregnancy." "God in heaven, doctor! That's what her father died of!"

Martha, meeting Winthrop as Sylvia's husband, wondered how she had been so long so foolish. The intimate relationships of one being to another were to be felt only by the people involved: it was the basis of marriage, of courtship in all nature. She could not imagine herself lying down at the side of any man save Marcus. She tried, by way of further self-illumination to picture herself in so intimate a situation with Nathan—as he had once proposed. A shudder of revulsion ran through her. But removed to the distance he was across the room from her, he seemed particularly handsome. Her inability to accept Dr. Winthrop until now came, she realized, not out of any sense of righteousness—she had never in her life felt holier than anyone—but out of her inability to put herself in her mother's position.

Dr. Winthrop was less restive than she remembered him. She could see now that he had always been an ambitious man who must have been greatly frustrated during his relationship with her mother. It was a curious experience to begin to see things from his point of view. Then she was hurtled back, hearing him talk about George Bergner, to the day at dinner when he had ridiculed her father and coaxed him into participating in his own humiliation. A little of the old ache returned. Martha found herself speculating on what moments Tad would find to suffer for her or Marcus. They might even be moments of which they themselves were oblivious. The need to suffer was bred deeply in man, more deeply, one might pray, than the need to inflict suffering. She thought almost constantly of the war. There were times she could not look at Marcus lest her eyes show tears. That he would soon go she knew. Every farewell seemed the beginning of their own.

"The thing I've discovered about George," Winthrop was saying, "is that he thrives on a little praise. He needs to be depended on. Why, that's the reason he married a simple, trusting soul like Louise. He'd kill himself married to a woman like Sylvia here."

"I'd be the first to help him, dear," Sylvia said.

Marcus laughed.

"I'm going to leave him in full charge of the paper while I'm gone. Wait and see if the responsibility doesn't make a man of him."

"It's about time something did," Marcus said impatiently.

"You'll see. You don't know what it's like to have a father who'd rather do a stranger a good turn that he would you. I had one. He couldn't get over having made a fortune and he was so damned sure I wasn't worth leaving it to, he had me jumping through hoops for him till the day he died."

He could not see, Martha thought, that that was what he expected people to do for him: he was always manipulating them—true, to their own benefit as in Marcus's case, and Nathan's. Power—he loved power. Once he had it, he was benevolent. But she was never going to find Alexander Winthrop admirable, much less lovable.

"I have been treated with many kindnesses all my life," Marcus said. "By my father and by other men. There is not a man alive more blessed than I have been." He cocked his head and grinned wryly at having come so close to sentimentality. "You're right, Alex. It should make me very tolerant."

Why Nathan chose that moment to speak, who could say? Perhaps he was self-confronting with his own benefactors. Perhaps he was embarrassed by so frank a confession on Marcus's part. Or he might have been, as Jonathan supposed, striking a loud note in his own behalf at the most judicious moment. To everyone it seemed tactless of him.

"I went today and proposed myself for military service," Reiss said. "You see, Sylvia, Alexander—I was going to try to steal the thunder from your farewell party. We are two men, Marcus and I, strong, good surgeons. It is too much—in one family, you might say —and Marcus has the wife and child."

"Yes," Marcus said, reaching for a cigaret, "they are mine, aren't they?"

"Beg pardon?" Reiss said, his dark eyes full of sudden submissiveness in case he had said something wrong.

Jonathan said, "When do you leave, Doctor Reiss?"

Nathan shot out his lower lip. "Alas! When they have nobody else they will take me. I have a disability—I have a heart leakage."

Jonathan laughed aloud. "Oh, Christ," he said rudely, and got up and left the room.

"It is very remarkable—what that man finds amusing about me," Reiss said.

Martha, understanding very well how Jonathan felt, said nonetheless: "It must have been a great shock to you to learn of it, Nathan."

He did not lie, but no one pressed him for the explicit truth of when he had discovered the ailment. He said: "I did not tell it tonight because I wanted sympathy," and shrugged his shoulders as though at a loss to understand the rudeness. He lapsed into a sort of self-pitying silence.

Someone in a gayer crowd or where the women were not Sylvia and herself, Martha thought—if Louise were there—he would now have his wounded feelings succored. He was truly so shallow. She could imagine his response to such coddling, his mock recovery meant only to ingratiate him with his cajoler.

"Jonathan is tired, Marcus," Sylvia said. "The world is too much with him."

"That's it," Marcus said.

"No, I think it's the other way around," Martha said. "He isn't with it at all. And always before he was."

"Patriotism embarrasses him," Marcus said. "I dare say it is a primitive emotion."

"Or the last refuge of scoundrels," Sylvia said.

Reiss looked at her. "That is a most extraordinary remark."

"It's not original," Sylvia said, an amused gleam in her eye.

Everyone knew Nathan Reiss had the makings of a great patriot. When the Winthrops, the last to leave, were going toward midnight, Winthrop lingered to speak to Martha after Sylvia had gone outdoors. "I'll remember tonight," he said. "You have a way like your mother's, kindness that isn't charity."

She allowed him to kiss her cheek.

A moment later with the sound of the door latch loudly clicking, she turned at the foot of the stairs where she had been about to go up and check on the baby, and Marcus paused on his way to put out the downstairs lights. Instead, they moved with utter urgency into one another's arms.

PART
THREE

1943

MARCUS was a long distance from Traders City when he learned of his son's first words. He was sitting in the lounge of the Officers Club in Bizerte, North Africa, and laughed aloud, reading them: "I want a dog like that one." He looked up self-consciously and would have shared the phenomenon of a two-year-old's articulacy had there been anyone at hand likely to give him more than polite attention. The French-Tunisian bartender would have been likely to give him a lecture on Western sentimentalism as opposed to Arab realism. The four officers playing bridge were as unprepossessing prospects. The Englishman among them would say, "Fine show, old chap," or some such Britishism. No one was as British as a British Army man. The three Americans, senior officers, looked like regular Army, and were likely to be far more at home in an officers' club in Bizerte than in, say, the Elks' Club in Beloit. Marcus returned to the letter.

"I should have preferred to tell you he asked, 'Where's papa?' " Martha wrote. "And where I am to find a dog like that one, heaven knows. I don't think its own parents, having it to do over again, could manage . . ."

Marcus read the letter twice, finished his brandy, and went to a writing desk to answer it. If he did not write at once, he would find it difficult, perhaps to the point of impossibility.

In his first weeks overseas writing had been easier, but his letters, Martha wrote, were heavily censored. He knew the reason. He had written about the men and what they thought the war was all about: he could not have taken his own cause from a concensus of theirs, and he had come to the conclusion that no American made a good the Italian mainland with a Fifth Army battalion as soon as the beachhead had been secured. Mud and blood: the position was always fluid. Again and again during the hours of invasion, the sides of the hospital tent had billowed out with the percussion of their own big guns. The littered wounded at such a time came to him almost as on a conveyor belt: there was never a question of whether or not to operate; he saw only the men for whom there was no alternative. The injured who could be evacuated, were. There were times he had operated in twelve-hour shifts, his only relief a change of positions with the anesthetist who was also a surgeon. He had never marveled at his own endurance, only afterwards at the statistics of lives saved.

But neither was this the stuff of which one wrote, putting up the scalpel for the pen.

There had been a day of lull in the Sicilian operation when he had walked out among the ruins—those of time and those of war—and he had come upon a sculptured marble arm, exquisitely delicate, a woman's, among the rubble, and bending down he had put his hand to it, and found himself moved to tears for the first time by any desolation of the war. Later that day, in the company of some G. I.'s who had found a veritable cache of temple statuary, he had thought marvelously funny the remark of one of them: "Gee, look at all the Venuses. D'you suppose we did that to 'em?"

But writing home, he could not find the right words for that story either. And too many of his anecdotes concerned latrines. The censor, he suspected, was the only constipated man in the whole damned army.

Nor could he write of love: he felt inhibited by his own sensuality. He who loathed to dance, danced every night of his leave, every dance he could obtain, with any of the *colon* girls, and as intimately as she allowed. It had nothing to do with Martha, he told himself, only with war and blood and genitals.

He sat and wrote a letter flat as sand and dry as desert. Crazy things kept popping into his head, like: Get him a fat hound dog in case meat rationing gets any tighter—which he did not write. "A hound dog might be best," he wrote. "They are supposed to be the gentlest." He said that he was glad his father had got leave from the University for whatever wartime assignment he was on. He did not even mention Dr. Winthrop whom he supposed to be in Italy since he was on the staff of the Allied Control Commission. He finished the letter: "I'm rested now and feeling fit, ready for reassignment, so that if you don't hear for a while, you will know I am back in the land of beginning again. That's what it is for most of these boys when we get through with them. We're saving more lives this time . . ." More lives than what? Writing "I love you" with a relief that shamed him, he scrawled his name, dispatched the letter, and went quickly to the bar for another brandy.

· 2

THE pilot banked the plane as they approached Naples, and the chief of the mission tapped Jonathan on the arm. "There she is!" he shouted.

Jonathan looked down with some reluctance at the great, gray jagged mountain, Vesuvius, streaked with scars that shone like lightnings through the mist. "I'm glad you didn't say 'there she blows.' "

The plane, in a sudden air pocket, dropped and lurched and then soared upward. The chief laughed aloud, as gay as a youngster on a loop-the-loop. The other civilians smiled rather weakly. Jonathan concentrated on the back of the head of the man in front of him and thought of a line from an Odets play: "Who do you know up there, eagles?" Distinctly, he did not like flying. But assuming they got down safely, the interesting question then would be: whom did he know down there?

Jonathan had over his long years of association with Midwestern University taken many leaves of absence to teach or study abroad. He was as well known at London University, for example, as any foreign lecturer. As one of the best informed anti-Fascists and one with connections abroad, he was highly valued during this period

There were several people with whom Jonathan hoped to make contact. But the first acknowledgment of his presence was from a source he had not expected: a message from Alexander Winthrop awaited him at the mission's headquarters: "If I can be of any assistance, please do not hesitate to call on me. I hope you will find it convenient to have dinner with me during your time in Naples." Winthrop headed a unit with the Allied Control Commission whose work was the restoration of public health facilities. He would probably be a good man to know—if you were an Italian.

The first day in Naples was an agony for Jonathan. Touring the district he saw for himself the war's devastation. He thought he could understand—as certain members of the mission seemed unable to—the people's indifference to their liberation. They were living on a bare subsistence level and the reality was that all the recommendations of missions and commissions were going to bring very little relief until the war was won everywhere. The problem was transport. It was not sufficient even to military necessity. The food was waiting to be delivered to them, but on the other side of the sea. It was something not easily explained to civilians of whom you were inquiring their needs for rehabilitation.

But at the day's end Jonathan was waited on by an old friend, Marcello Ruggeo, the poet and novelist who had returned from his American exile to his native Naples when the city was liberated. With Ruggeo, he sat down that night at a meeting of the Italian Committee of Liberation. He was not long in discovering why they welcomed him: they were looking for an American sympathetic to the anti-Monarchist cause. The Occupation authorities, American and particularly British, had no intention of encouraging an Italian revolution. "Mussolini, no. Badoglio and the King, okay." Thusly an Italian put it in basic American.

Jonathan, of course, did not comment. He merely listened, Ruggeo translating much that went on for him. If he did not understand the language, Jonathan understood the men—well enough at least to speculate on their personal ambitions, their commitments to a political philosophy and their patriotism. Under discussion was the institutional question of the King, the circumstances under which the various anti-Fascist parties would enter a cabinet under Badoglio or under a regency so that an Italian government could be said to represent a majority of the people. A half dozen parties were represented in the room—the paneled dining room of an old villa, half of which had been shorn away by shell fire so that the room, once within the interior of the building, could be entered directly from outdoors; in the marble fireplace a part of the building's own timber was burning noisily—Christian and Social Democrats were there, a publisher and a professor of history; Ruggeo represented the Actionists, himself a curious exception to his family who almost to a name were Monarchists; and a Communist who expressed the mildest views of the meeting. Jonathan wondered if he could not pursue the line in its course: Russia was an ally; the Allies were not going to tolerate a revolution behind their lines; therefore any government was suitable for the present.

Afterwards, walking through the cold, dark streets with Ruggeo to his rooms over a leather shop, Jonathan asked Ruggeo if he did not think this were so.

Ruggeo, his gray hair close-cropped so that it added to his look of explosiveness, said: "Of course, it is so. They will join the King's government, if we all do."

"And pull out when it suits them to bring it down."

"Which of us will not?" Ruggeo said. He lit the one light in his room. It hung over a desk and threw a pale glow on the bed, the bookcases that seemed to hold only newspapers, and on the photograph of a pretty dark woman and two blond children. Ruggeo himself was fair. "I have some inferior wine but it is not as inferior as my coffee.

"My friend," he said, "I do not represent a majority of the people. If any one party does, it is the Communists. I am not afraid of them, not now. They are the strength behind the partisans in the north, underground in Rome it is they. With their help we may have an Actionist premier: then we shall have the land reform without which returns Fascism—or comes communism."

"Exactly," Jonathan said. "Is it realistic to expect them to participate in their own containment?"

Ruggeo pulled the cork from the bottle. "What are those lines from Shakespeare? I remember you quoting them to me once—about meeting the bear in the mouth."

" 'Thou'dst shun a bear, but if thy flight lay toward the sea, thou'dst meet the bear i' the mouth.' "

"I've had ..."

"That'll be the day," Jonathan said.

They talked long into the night for Ruggeo was leaving in the morning to go to Brindisi, the seat of the provisional government, and Jonathan promised to stop in New York if he could manage it to see Ruggeo's family.

"Tell them how beautiful is Naples. Even now. They will have forgotten as I almost had myself. Tell them I shall have a fine home for them after the war, with a garden and a view. Always I have promised my wife a view, and always it has been of someone else's back window."

By the time Jonathan saw Winthrop, he had acquired great respect for the reconstruction work the Allied Control Commission was doing and with little equipment and only salvaged materials. "Wheelbarrows and pulleys," Winthrop said. "Donkeys and small boys." But Jonathan was much less enthusiastic about the Commission's attitude toward the Italians. The top men were at best paternalistic. Most of them were career army men, impatient with civilian ways, especially the ways of Italian civilians. They were looking always for those Italians they "could do business with." And efficiency was still the prevailing myth about Fascism. Jonathan was not so partisan in his thinking however as not to appreciate the British view that Italy, under whatever government, had been an enemy with whom they had been at war for three years. They could scarcely be blamed for caring less about its rehabilitation than winning the war and rehabilitating Britain.

But Italy, in a few weeks' time, was on the way to becoming Jonathan's "cause." He had never been able to live without one, and having found one now, he proposed to enter upon it with all the caution learned of numerous defeats.

He saw in Winthrop the typical *laissez-faire* Occupation officer. It was Winthrop's view that what was good for the Allies was good for the Italians: a transition government of technicians under the King until the war was over. He was little moved by Jonathan's remark that he had found small affection for the King among the people. "I haven't heard anybody say they loved Mussolini either," Winthrop said, "but he was pretty much their boss for twenty years."

"Exactly," Jonathan said, but having got exactly nowhere. As close as he came to moving Winthrop was in his mischievous but true suggestion that Winthrop, speaking as he did, was coming close to the official British opinion. There was enough of the Midwesterner in the man to rile at the association. But there Jonathan let it stand. His assignment was to report to Washington, and it was the only place at the moment, he could properly press his opinion.

And the evening he spent with Winthrop in Naples chanced to be Christmas Eve. They talked more of home than either of them was likely to on another occasion. Winthrop occupied a gloomy, ornate apartment, a bedroom and a sitting room in a *pensione* taken over by the officers of his commission. He displayed a foot-high imitation Christmas tree, dye-green and tinseled, a part of the wartime gadgetry manufactured in the U.S.A. to be sent to the American soldier overseas. Set atop the mantelplace, it cast a shadow stronger than itself across an ancient print of the Pompeii ruins. The room was hung with faded velvet drapes from the high ceiling to the marble floor. The furniture, a mixture of gilt and mahogany, was in an advanced state of decay. Things either decayed or collapsed in Italy, Winthrop said. Either they lasted for centuries or they broke down within a week of manufacture.

"Not the land for installment buying," Jonathan said.

Winthrop opened a bottle of Scotch whisky and while they drank Jonathan took off his shoes and warmed his feet at the gas heater set up on the rim of the fireplace. He could not remember his feet having been warm since he left the States. Just seeing him thus relaxed and grinning gave Winthrop a pleasure associable with home. He arranged the service of their dinner with "the signora" and then after their drinks, the two men walked out in the raw twilight.

The pink-tinted clouds and the ancient yellowing buildings that huddled one in the shelter of another were all reflected in the damp glare of the streets. Looking ahead they might be seeing canals, Jonathan thought. It was a solemn festival, Christmas in Italy, not a time for gifts except to the Christ Child. Every home, however stricken, seemed to have managed a crèche and candles. People hurried along the narrow circuitous streets, pausing now and then to take a hasty poke at a rubble heap. If you watched very closely, Jonathan discovered, you could catch the quick gesture of concealment on the part of the successful scavenger. The cats of the city were no more cunning. What Jonathan did enjoy was a visit to the fish market in S. Brigida, a babble of bargaining, abuse and blessings poignancy of their outstretched hands on that particular night of the year. But the sight of them seared the soul as did no other pathos of the war: great sunken eyes sometimes festered, rickety limbs, rags and shaggy heads; the maimed among them too numerous almost for distinction made infirmity itself a crutch. Jonathan thought of Ruggeo and his message to his family: "Tell them how beautiful Naples is."

"I wish Sylvia was here," Winthrop remarked. "She'd be able to do something for these youngsters. Somebody's got to. Soon."

He spoke loudly for the drone of approaching planes grew steadily louder. They came from the South, Allied planes, and high beyond sight. When they had passed, Winthrop said: "They'll be softening up some place tonight with that load."

And maiming more children, Jonathan thought, but he said nothing. He could be grateful that Marcus's child if not Marcus was a far distance from the Italian shores.

Jonathan's appraisal of the Italian situation was generally shared by his chief and the other members of the mission. Their broad recommendation was that agriculture and certain civilian industry be quickly rehabilitated so that the emphasis might be shifted from relief to self-help. They reported finding little respect for the King and Badoglio among the people, but by the time of their report, the forces at work in Italy to promote the coalition government had already moved in that direction. It was also becoming evident that without partisan help, the war in Italy was not going to be quickly won. The Anzio beachhead was established during the winter at heavy cost in Allied lives. Certain of the high officers were more amenable thereafter to an Italian government in which the Republican forces were represented.

Jonathan was not able to see Ruggeo's family, or for that matter his own family. He did however see Sylvia Winthrop who was in Washington in connection with the newspaper promotion of a War Bond drive. Over lunch, he told her of his evening with Winthrop. Sylvia was restless, impatient with the work a volunteer could do at home and Jonathan suspected that she resented war's being primarily a man's business. Then he told her about the children of Naples and what her husband had said.

She looked at him closely, as though disbelieving. "Is that what he said—that he wished I were there?"

Jonathan nodded.

Sylvia turned her water glass round and round. "It's funny the things that go through your mind. I'd sometimes come to think that that was what he didn't want, that he was taking this in stride as sort of a sabbatical from me."

"War doesn't make much of a sabbatical," Jonathan said.

"I've never seen *you* look better."

"I've got work to do that excites me."

"I'd have almost thought it was a woman."

Jonathan laughed. "My dear, I almost feel as though it were."

Sylvia reached across the table and gave his hand an impulsive squeeze. "We're of a kind in some ways, aren't we, Jonathan?"

"Ah yes."

"My God," she said, "that was humble of me!" She began tidying up the table. A bread crumbler, she now gathered the crumbs into a neat mound. "Tell me exactly what Alex said."

Jonathan set the scene, the dank streets, glistening with frost, the sound of the bombers overhead, and the children scurrying out from their holes to beg and in again, the lame, the diseased and the hungry. And while he talked he watched her eyes, brooding at first, and then lighting up. You did not tell Sylvia anything if you did not want it attended to. At once. During a dessert she scarcely touched, she took her notebook from her purse and began writing names, men she could get to in medicine, in government, in philanthropy. She was on her way, Jonathan thought. She moved like a prairie fire, testing, probing, catching on, and once she had caught on it would be virtually impossible to stop her. The children of Naples had a benefactress.

While they waited for the check, Sylvia asked: "And you, Jonathan, what now?"

"I understand there's a plan afoot to send me to England—on the Italian business. That seems to be my desk now."

"Will you be in Italy again, do you think?"

"I hope so . . . but I shouldn't want to give odds that you won't be there before me."

· 3

AFTER Anzio, Marcus's unit was again withdrawn from the advance
combat zone. The unit was cited for extraordinary service and
awarded the Fifth Army Plaque. Back once more in North Africa,
Marcus was promoted to the rank of major, detached and reassigned
to England. In the moment of vanity in which he indulged himself,
examining his new insignia and decoration in a mirror, he suddenly
looked at his face to see the whole of it for the first time in many
months, not merely the part which needed shaving. He was looking
at someone quite different than he remembered, himself, for the eyes
stared back at him, but not entirely himself either. He had once been
fairly good looking, but he would not say it of the pallid, stark face
that smiled unnaturally at his prompting. And his hair was white at
the temples.

His leave began the moment he set foot on British soil.

He had always believed, having no reason to doubt, that Ireland
was green, but when the plane banked and he saw the earth dappled
with the shapes of clouds like a great emerald quilt asway in the
wind, he felt the green. Like a balm it was to his blood-wearied eyes,
like the cooling of nightfall upon the blaze of day, and the curious
thought struck him that this must be how the dead felt, utterly possessed of and by the enduring green of earth.

He was put down outside of Belfast, a concession, for the big plane
rose at once into the sky again, paradoxically seeming more encum-
bered by its emptiness than it would have been full-laden. It was well
nicknamed the Flying Boxcar. Even as it disappeared in the west, a
formation of its like soared high overhead, steady and fully weighted,
bound for England. In Italy the men were doubting still that there
was ever to come an invasion from the north, but the moment he had
left the hospital plane in England, he knew one was at last imminent.
For him Italy then had been but prologue, and realizing that, he had
not wanted to take his leave at all. To come and go and come again
to the field hospital was worse than never leaving it. There was a
rhythm to war a man could lose himself in, the tempo set by the great
guns booming and the screaming descent of planes, the squeal and

growl of mud-bound trucks, the purr of the hospital generator. He had not wanted this leave, but given it, he had wired Elizabeth and come to Ireland with no more conscious deliberation than a doctor gives to a prescription when he knows the patient as well as he knows the disease.

"Where to, Major?" A craggy-faced old man tugged at the greasy brim of his rumpled cap. There was a stoppage to his R's similar to a Scotsman's.

Marcus named the village in the north. "I have to go by train to Larne, I understand."

"You will, sir, unless we can get you aboard a lorry. They're convoying and conveying night and day." He took Marcus's bag. "I remember the Coast Road when you would not see two vehicles on it at once unless it be the circus coming down this time of year."

Marcus telephoned and then took the train by choice. He saw that there had been a recent raid on Belfast. The smoke still rose from out of the skeletonous rubble along the wharves, but compared to London, the city itself looked solid and whole, ugly, prosperous and middle class, ever so faintly reminiscent in its grayness of Traders City. He did not regret not lingering to see more of it until disquieted by the thought that when next he had the chance to look, there might not be a city left. The train was jammed with travelers who, as the saying went among them, "had people" in the country. They were moving with their blankets, their bolsters, their tinkermended pots and pans, which showed how much of Belfast he had seen: these people were not prosperous. There were dogs and cats aboard, and doubtless other creatures invited and uninvited. It fell to Marcus and his companions to share their compartment with a goose. Its owner set it on the floor while she removed her hat and pinned it to the headrest between her face and that of the man next to her, an elegant plume just clearing the man's nose. The goose meanwhile began to chip at his ankles. The woman took the bird into her lap, and every now and then throughout the journey, it would crank its neck around and nibble gently at the jewel in its mistress' ear, a jewel no more coldly bright, Marcus thought, than the bird's own eye.

He was met and sorted out from the soldiery and the evacuees at the Larne station by two boys in knee pants whose ages he would have put at eleven or twelve. They stood as at attention before him. "Major Hogan, sir, we're sent by the mistress for you."

Marcus nodded gravely. One had the plump, ruddy face of the country lad, and the other the red-spotted cheeks he had observed all too often during the Depression in the city tubercular. "How did you know me?"

"You're American," the spokesman said. It was one of the greatest distinctions a man could claim in Ireland, Marcus soon discovered.

The English boy—for Marcus sized him up as one of Elizabeth's war refugees—took his bag, and Marcus allowed him to boast his strength by it.

They drove out the coast road in a cart at the rump of a donkey. To the west rose the pale green hills of Antrim, spotted yellow with gorse and daffodils, and to the east was water bluer than ever he had seen the Mediterranean. One could look down and see the stones shining on the bottom as smoothly rounded as eggs. Scarcely aware that he spoke, much less that he delved back almost to his own childhood for the words, Marcus quoted: " 'And Noah he ate an ostrich egg from an egg cup big as a pail.' " The boys giggled and made him say it again. After that he found himself laughing with them. Unfortunately, the only other line he could remember from the poem was: " 'I don't care where the water goes if it doesn't get in the wine.' "

The Irish boy laid a frequent whip across the donkey's haunches to which the beast merely tossed his head and wiggled his ears. When Marcus finally bade him put up the whip, the boy said, "If he didn't like it, he'd go faster, sure," a particularly Irish logic which put Marcus in mind of his patients at the Brandon Clinic and of Annie at home.

In time they left the coast road, climbing a gentle upward slope, each turning in the road providing a longer vista: of sheep grazing fat-bellied with lambs and unshorn, occasional cottages of clay and timber, some whitewashed and some not, stone-hedged yards that grew ever noisier with the clamor of chickens and ducks and geese as the cart approached. They stopped at a crossroads pump and drank clear water from a tin cup while the donkey got his from a wooden bucket. As they resumed their journey and the animal relieved himself, his driver remarked, "Now isn't that gratitude for you?"

As they started downhill on the other side of the first long ridge above the sea, Marcus observed in the distance a house of great and solid build. It stood in a grove of trees beyond a long meadow in which he could see numerous workers. As they drew nearer he saw that the workers were children, and that their work did not so thor-

oughly occupy them that they could not stand and stare until the cart
had passed. Marcus asked what they were doing.

"Picking up stones. I'm ploughing the meadow myself in the morning, putting it to 'taties. You can watch me if you like."

"I'll remember," Marcus said.

Suddenly, as they approached the manor house, the English boy
said, "I lives in there." He jerked his head toward the big house.

"Do you?" Marcus said.

"They all do, but not me," the Irish boy said. "My da's overseer of
McMahon Manor."

Elizabeth hastened around the side of the house when the cart entered the grove. She and Marcus lifted their hands in a tentative
salute as the distance between them dwindled, she the while rolling
down the sleeves of her sweater, having left off some bare-armed
chore.

It had been seven years since last he had seen her, the occasion his
marriage to her daughter. He had always held Elizabeth in a sort of
reverential awe and a faint guilt clung to the moments he felt most
warmly toward her. Nothing he had ever done was reason for it so
that it could only be his awareness of her or of her scandal—her love
affair outside marriage, the sudden public knowledge of which had
wrought so furious a climax to many lives, including his own. He was
disturbed at the fleck of guilt he saw upon himself: the Puritan
streak ran more deeply in him than he knew.

Yet, seeing her run to meet him, he felt a thrust of pure joy quicker
by far than conscience or the stagnant lust of war which had op-
pressed his coming. He leaped down from the cart and caught the
hands outstretched to him, and they stood for a second or two, face to
face, measuring the differences in one another from when they last
had met.

She must be nearing fifty, but her hair was dark still as a raven, and
the lines in her face which he remembered were crossed with new
and the lighter ones of laughter. Nothing had marred her high-born
beauty: the spacious forehead, dominant cheek bones, the strong,
sensuous mouth, features unblunted, delicate still as a young
woman's. She had seemed, leaving America, to be going into exile,
but he knew from the sight of her now she had instead come home.

She drew him close and kissed both cheeks. A mixture of fra-
grances clung to her, a faint perfume and cinnamon so that he supposed she had come running from the kitchen.

The two boys were gawking down at them from the cart. Elizabeth said, "Take the doctor's luggage to my cottage, John. Then you and Herbert may go to cook. She has saved your tea for you." To Marcus she said, "You will have the cottage to yourself which I daresay you won't mind. I'm told the army is no place for privacy."

Marcus said, with something of his old wryness, "The army is no place. It's a condition."

But Elizabeth suspected very soon that her guest was in his way as much a victim of the war as any of her numerous brood of English children. It was not that he said so little—he would sit a long while blinking his eyes rapidly, a trait that reminded her of his father's tic, thus of his father, of Alexander and the wife he had married, and summoned up so many associations that the silences obliged her, too; and if their eyes chanced to meet he would smile self-consciously like an old man who had been unable to hold the thread of conversation —but that when he did speak his words seemed an abrupt and delib- erate diversion lest she say something intimate, lest she mention his family.

She would not say again she thought that tragedy befell only the unhappy marriage. If ever a marriage had been made in love it was her daughter's and Marcus's. She could remember him the night she was sure they had fallen in love. At Alexander's ball. Martha had brought him to her and introduced him, her voice high and trem- bling on his name. Proper as the nuns who trained her she was, and Marcus diffident but wise, a young man in a dress suit which did not fit him, but which somehow made him look the better for the wear- ing of it. She had thought then that here was an incorruptible man, and she had been very proud of Martha whose adored father, for all his piety and exactitude in material things, was corrupt of spirit. Now Martha waited for word. To her Marcus's silence must be in- explicable because she knew he was not dead. There were so many things in her life Martha had had to endure without understanding, pity the child of a loveless marriage. Ah, but she had a child of her own, conceived in love under God's Own Eye! Elizabeth was at very tongue-tip of mentioning the pictures of Tad she had received but a few days before when Marcus, seeming to anticipate, said,

"That English child looks tuberculous."

"A number of them do, but I'm supposed to have gotten them in time. I'm hoping you'll go over them for me, Marcus. There's a man comes down from Belfast when he can, but he's harassed as a shrew's husband, poor man, and not a very good doctor even at leisure."

Marcus smiled. "Down from Belfast. I'd have said 'up'."

"That's our contrariness. We're all far-downers up here."

Marcus got up from the tea table and went to the window where he stood a moment. Elizabeth made neat the things on the tray and scraped the bit of butter he had left back into the jar. Returning, he glanced up at the dark portrait hung over the mantel. It was only in the late afternoon light it was distinguishable as the picture of a man.

"Who is it?"

"My great-grandfather, Lord Peter McMahon. He built McMahon Manor—dark and windy as himself from what I've read of him. I dare say it's true from what I know of his descendants—and mine." She had but one—two, counting the child, Tad. But Marcus did not rise to the bait.

"Is there a Lord McMahon now?"

"No. My father gave up the title. He was more a Gael than a nobleman."

"That was when you went to America, at that time, wasn't it?"

"You might say I was exported then."

"You belong here, Elizabeth," he said, willing enough to talk of her if not of himself and his.

"One belongs where one can love," she said.

"Yes!" He agreed with such fervor she was distressed at having probed the wound without yet knowing its nature.

She joined him at the window. "Look at them out there," she said, retreating further within her own experience. "Hungry little beggars, every one. The need for love is the child's need. Some of us never outgrow it, but the time comes for most of us when it's surpassed by the need to give love; whatever we do in response to that need is the best we can do, I am convinced."

Marcus nodded, blinking, studying the end of his cigaret until it began to burn him. He rubbed it out on a brass scuttle and threw it into the grate. "When do you want me to look them over?"

She suppressed a sigh. "Morning would be best, I think, so they won't have nightmares. You'll have to convert some of them, you know."

"To what?"

"Well, now that you ask it, I'm not sure," she said, more ready than he was to end their first interlude, "especially since I've brought them round to soap and water myself. Ah, but they were dear, dirty things when I got them."

"I remembered your voice," he said, "the music in it."

"I never sang," she said.

"And I remember how you played."

She lifted her head. "Yes, I played." For herself only so much of the time, and when she would have given her soul for it to have been otherwise. Her husband had always liked something with a tune in it, God forgive her contempt of the dead, and Alexander was about as musical as a clothespin. She returned to the table for the tea tray and carried it to the ledge of the half-door to the pantry. "I'll take you down now, Marcus. A cottage here is a hut. No electricity, a short walk to the convenience, and a boy will bring you shaving water in the morning." She explained the routine of the farm and the house as they walked a graveled path along which the wild roses were beginning to bud: dinner at noon, supper at seven in the common room. Once it had been called the ballroom although she could not remember a ball in it, only the meetings of the Gaelic League there in her youth. "When Philip is home . . ." Philip was her brother . . . "he and I sup alone sometimes at the cottage, but I like to supervise the children myself. I hope you'll join us, but you don't need to."

"I'd like to," Marcus said.

"I'm glad of that. They're devils, but they do love to have a man to lord it over them."

The cottage lay before them, its roof top deep golden in the afternoon sun.

"A thatched roof, is it?" Marcus said.

"It's a strange economy. The barns are also thatched. One of our tenants is a thatcher, you see, an old man, and it's the only sensible way to take the rent of him."

"Aren't they practical?" He meant the roofs.

"Marcus, nothing in all Ireland is practical—except the British landlords."

He laughed for the first time with her and stopped in the path. "Elizabeth, I can go on from here alone if you don't mind."

"I don't mind at all." But she laid her hand on his arm. "Marcus, you will put things as you want them—for your own comfort." She was thinking of the pictures with which one of the walls was hung, the sight of which, she could only suppose, he would want to avoid until his own good time.

"I'll find my way," he said whether or not he understood her.

Somewhere nearby cattle were lowing and as Marcus reached the cottage he heard a voice that cracked between youth and manhood calling out to them. He surmised it to be milking time. "All things come home at eventide . . .": he had not thought of the song for years. There was a heroic middle section to it he had used to bawl at the top of his lungs when his own voice was not long changed. It occurred to him that patriotism was in the universal character of youth. In old age it was stronger among those who had never properly grown up.

It was not quite necessary, but he stooped to enter the doorway. The room, insofar as a cottage allowed severity, was severe: books in order along the walls, and a piano, but nothing of the clutter and knicknackery he remembered about Elizabeth's studio in Traders City. A small bedroom opened to the side. He had never seen a monk's cell but this would serve a monk he thought, not ungrateful. He saw the row of pictures toward the eaves and instantly put off looking at them until it was time to light a candle. He went outdoors again, and tilting a chair against the side of the house he settled in it and watched the setting of the sun. There was a slight haze and a smell in the air he supposed to be the smoke of peat since it made him think of Irish whisky. Almost constant was the bleating of sheep, sometimes near, sometimes distant as an echo, and the forlorn cry of the curlew. He could hear children's voices, the jerk and halt of a pump handle and the splash of water as it began to draw, but nowhere in the blessed twilight was there smoke or blast of guns.

Sitting at the supper table that night with twenty children lined, boys down one side, girls up the other, he might have been both doctor and major—either of which title was to them, Elizabeth said, as good as a knighthood—but the God's truth was he felt more like a priest, exalted and indulged, given the first cut of meat and the last drop of gravy.

Herbie, his English companion of the cart, treated him with a respectful familiarity. The boy himself was marvelously cured of shyness among his own. "Major-doctor, 'ave 'e looked up the poem yet, eh?"

"Not yet, but I shall, Herbie."

"Say the bit, will 'e?"

"And Noah he ate an ostrich egg in an egg cup big as a pail," Marcus thought he said it with feeling, though he had begun to suspect the line was not quite as written.

But Herbie said it after him with style.

Marcus murmured to Elizabeth, "He sounds like Gracie Fields."

"Wait till Saturday night. We have a regular music hall revue."

After supper when the children had taken out their plates and utensils, each washing his own, and the tables were taken apart being no more than planks on sawhorses, in the midst of games a minor misfortune occurred: one of the boys jammed his head against an iron sconce and laid open an inch of scalp.

Marcus, taking a look at the gash, said, "You wanted to find out if I'm really a doctor, didn't you? Come along."

Elizabeth led the way up a drafty stairway to the infirmary. "I'm afraid it's rather primitive."

Marcus agreed silently when he saw the stock of remedies and antiseptics. He looked again at the wound. "I think we can get it to close up without stitches."

"I'm not a bloody chicken," the boy said, seeing himself compared to a trussed bird at the mention of stitches.

Elizabeth said, "You're a wee fighting cock." Which praise gave him pleasure almost commensurate to his pain. He let out but one howl as Marcus cauterized the wound.

"Brave fellow," Marcus said, and finished things off with a large handsome patch.

"Can I go back now, Major-doctor?"

"Yes, but I think you need a day or two of rest."

"If they makes me a sergeant-major, could I play?"

When the boy was gone, Marcus said, "Are they all war orphans?"

"They've lost at least one parent each in the blitz."

"And still they play at war." He was going over her store of medicines in an abstracted sort of way, rearranging, tossing some into the waste box much to her amusement, without a by-your-leave or explanation. He stopped suddenly, glanced at her, and then into space beyond the medicine table. "I have a funny dream, Elizabeth. When I was a child I used to dream of rising off the earth—many children do—but now it's come back and it's changed. I'm able to see myself from up there, wherever it is. I look down and the hospital tent is removed, and I'm working, operating. One after another, faceless, nameless, numbered soldiers, and the litterers take them away as I'm through. But the stranger thing yet: they litter them back to the front, and I can see these—grotesques rise up and take guns. Even they don't have hands, in my dream they can manage guns without them. I suppose it's all over in a minute, as they say dreams are, but seems endless. And you know, I've never actually seen combat. We're four or five miles back from the front generally. I've been closer. And I've seen reinforcements come up the beach to meet a counter-attack . . . I guess I have seen combat. But I sometimes wonder if a man knows the satisfaction of killing until he's done it hand-to-hand. Doesn't it seem futile to you—rushing men in to kill and be killed, then rushing them out the minute they've fallen—decimated, de-humanized—as though they were the most precious treasure on earth? How can you kill and save at once?"

He waited and only looked at her sidewise, the blinking started again.

"They are precious at that moment, I suppose," she said, "because any one of them might have been you or me—or whoever's alive to carry them out."

"And what we're doing is showing our gratitude?"

"Do they complain of it?"

"No," he said. "Very little. That's the truth. Only the able-bodied men complain."

"And do they want to die?"

"Some who know, do—and some who don't know. Not many. No, not many." He gave a short, self-deprecatory laugh. "How I loathe myself after those dreams."

"Why?"

He shrugged. "I don't know. For being there, I suppose. I don't know."

She went back to something he had said before. "I don't know why men must kill, but I don't think it's for satisfaction. Perhaps because they're afraid."

"Was Hitler afraid? Is he afraid?"

"Possibly."

"No." Marcus shook his head. "I know a surgeon at home—I sup-pose you know him, too. Yes, of course, you do. I swear to you, Eliza-beth, that man enjoys using the knife. I think it's merest chance that he's a surgeon and not a butcher. Mind, everyone would say he does good work. He does. He can remove a tumor as neatly as a speck from your eye."

"Marcus, is it possible that he's attending all the people you are not attending?"

"Yes," he said, glancing at her and then away. "I guess it's partly that." But she could tell he did not really think so.

"Mind, let it not be said I spoke too loudly in praise of Nathan Reiss."

Marcus laughed. "Most women do, you know."

"Not over here any more, I shouldn't think. America is the right place for him. Do you mind my asking, Marcus, why you took him in with you?"

"Reciprocity, I suppose. Doctor Winthrop suggested it—and it had to be someone."

"Alexander? I wonder why . . . But I know, of course. Whenever it is a matter of taste, Alexander has none. He relies entirely on someone else's judgment. And I suppose his wife to be politically sentimental. Am I right?"

"On the nail."

"I'm glad it wasn't Martha pushed him," Elizabeth said. How much there was of deliberate mischief in the words, she could not have measured, herself. It was a woman's wile, but surely the cause was just. Love might exist without jealousy, but where jealousy kindled there must be love.

Marcus took a cigaret from his pocket but did not light it. "I think I shall be able to get a few things for you from the Army Medical Depot. For God's sake, let us save the children if we can. Perhaps they'll be wiser. They could scarcely be less."

"Marcus, Marcus," she said and went to the door, not seeing the way in which he looked after her as though he would call her back. He followed and she switched off the infirmary light. The three unoccupied white-covered beds shone bleakly in the afterglow. "What was it Goethe said: 'Nothing is more terrible than active ignorance'?"

"There was a time I would have said passive intelligence is worse. I'm not so sure now." He lit his cigaret.

Elizabeth said, "We must go down. It's time for music to soothe my little savages."

"Do you play for them?"

"I beat out rhythms on the piano for them to sing by."

He touched his hand to her elbow to detain her. "Will you play for me while I'm here?"

"I will. But you must not be too appreciative. I mightn't be up to that." She glanced up at him and smiled, trying to make light of her words as soon as they were out.

"You are a most beautiful woman, Elizabeth."

She met his eyes with frankness, honesty, and fortunate it was she thought afterwards that the landing light was no more than a candle's worth. "I always have thought you the only beautiful man I knew."

She fled down the stairs and gathered in the children as they flocked about her. Then all of them swarmed in one sweep together to the piano. Marcus sat for a long while on the drafty stairway, smoking and listening. He left quietly while they sang the hymn that was to end the day.

He lay in bed afterwards, and when a flicker of the candlelight started a whisper of motion across the wall he saw again the row of pictures. He knew of whom they were and felt himself stiffen into an almost rigid concentration as he tried to draw them before him in his mind. He started up, having almost broken through, and then fell back, empty. He turned and blew out the candle and lay in the darkness listening to the loud stillness until he heard, or imagined that he heard, the rhythmic wash of the sea. Deliberately he sank himself into it and then he slept.

"However did we manage without you?" Elizabeth remarked at tea a few days later.

"I'm beginning to wonder, myself," Marcus said. He had by now examined not merely the children, but half the cottagers and farmers for miles around. Word spread quickly that an American doctor was staying at the manor and ills that would never have got beyond the chemist's shop were put into his confidence. In addition he refereed badly, not sure of the rules, the Saturday afternoon cricket match between the village boys and the manor boys, but the sum of his errors was impartial. It fell to his charge on Sunday morning to take the Protestant children to the Established Church, while Elizabeth went with her handful to the Roman Catholic, and he promised afterwards to come to tea with the vicar whose church mouse he suspected to be richer. But the country poor, except in the case of famine, have at least their dignity. It was a good tea in a threadbare house: fresh-made bread, sweet butter and gooseberry jam. The vicar's proudest luxury was his pipe tobacco brought him from London by Philip McMahon which he stored in a crock in the well alongside the butter. Marcus enjoyed a pipe with him, while he heard tales of the manor in the old days and of its present owner whom he was not to meet. McMahon was member of Parliament from the district and now in London.

What Marcus came to remark most in Ireland was the sufficiency of the people to themselves: their lives were spent more in mending and making than in getting. Not that the majority wouldn't have traded all for a one-way ticket to America; he knew that. And if he had not known it, Elizabeth reminded him.

"It will change, Marcus. It must. But I'm glad it may not happen in my lifetime. Work is better for man than leisure—if it's work he can see the shape of and take pride in. To be sure, too much of either will kill him, one the body, the other the spirit."

"And you are content here?"

"To the deep heart's core."

"You don't miss company of your own sort?" He was remembering her at Winthrop's ball on the night he had met her, exquisitely groomed and gowned, the center of interest among the people of Traders City to whom music was almost as important as Society. She was said to have been a fine teacher.

"I'm glad you've come, Marcus. It is enough."

"Perhaps you'll return for a visit some day?"

"No, no. Not ever. You see I'm the greatest snob of them all."

He understood.

"But I want you and Martha and the child to come to me."

"Do you?" He probed more deeply than she dared probe him.

"I do, as God is my witness. But you are right about . . . till now. I was never loved as I wanted. I would have found it cruel to watch you. I might even have been cruel—as I managed often enough to my unfortunate husband. I would have loved a man like you until the death even as will my daughter. There, I've said it, Marcus. But there is nothing in us deeper than the need to love, Martha and me . . ."

"I know . . ." he said, trailing out the word as though it pained him. He stood as in a daze, intent, his face a grimace, piteous as a beggar who has abandoned shame. Except that charity could not help him.

It crossed her mind to try to break him down completely then. She thought she could do it. But she dared not say it would be best, not she, the father of whose child had hung himself in the garden.

And this was but an instant's trembling. Marcus drew a long breath and was again the master of his own presence. He took out a cigaret. His hand was almost steady as he lit it.

"You ought to apply for your discharge, Marcus," she said. "You've had enough. You ought not to have to go back."

"But I want to more than anything else," he said, although he avoided her eyes, saying it.

The music she played for him was Chopin and Schumann and then the darker sonatas of Beethoven. She had put on a velvet gown that evening and wore gold pendulous earrings that shone in the lamp light. The light also shimmered through the jewels of the Spanish combs she wore in her crown of black hair. Her long neck and bare throat reminded him of the marble fragment he had wept over in the Salerno ruins.

He got up and crossed the room and, bending down, kissed the back of her neck. She continued playing so that he went to the door where it was open, and leaned against the frame, looking out. A crest of white mist hung behind the ridges of the hills. Presently she finished and came and stood beside him.

"We shall have the long twilights soon now," she said. "Almost till midnight it will linger day. And I'll remember, standing here alone."

He did not say anything. Nor did he move.

"Marcus."

He turned his head. He was only a little taller than she so that she reached up her hands and took his face in them and kissed him on the mouth. "Good night, my dear one," she said, still holding his face in her hands, "my dearly loved one." She left him, and taking her shawl, went up the path.

He stood some moments watching the way she had gone. Then, feeling the wind with a mist in it, he went inside and closed the door. Taking the lamp to the table, he sat down and commenced a letter home.

"My dear," he wrote. "I know my silence puts a heavy burden on you. My presence when the time comes may put even a heavier one. You may have to come and get me—which is a manner of speaking, you understand. Not literal. But you must remember I have said this or I may not be able to say it again. Tonight I am alive. Alive. I know because I love . . ." He paused and thought for a moment and decided to end the sentence there: "I know because I love."

·4

DURING the later war years Martha spent a part of almost every day at the South Side USO Canteen. It was difficult for her at first, slow as she was to find rapport with strangers, but the shyness of so many of the boys quickened her sympathy and hence her tongue, and the boldness of some of her anger and hence, also, her tongue. She would have much preferred, after Jonathan left, to keep Tad with her all his waking hours and to spend her leisure painting again, solitary, but not altogether lonely: there was not an hour of the day she did not think of Marcus. For a while it did not alter her communion with him that he wrote so rarely. There was in the mystical aspect of her religious life the power of conjuring a presence.

But she suspected some time before receiving the letter he wrote her from the North of Ireland that Marcus had lost the intimate sense of her, and from that letter on her own conjuring began to fail her. And as well, she decided. They would not return to one another unchanged. "You may even have to come and get me," he had written, meaning, she supposed, that they should have to fall in love all over again, and perhaps she be the wooer. Gladly, gladly. But imagination cannot conjure without the heart's certainty. In the end she waited and accepted memory and tried not to seek the future in it, lest the memory itself diffuse and she be left with nothing of him.

She had not known until the letter from Ireland that Marcus had been in Italy, and while she conjectured from the new APO number that he was next in France or Holland, she did not know it for certain. When her mother wrote, following his visit, Martha resented her ardent praise of him. As though she needed to be told of Marcus's virtues. Could she love him more for her mother's praise of him? If he weren't Marcus she might love him the less for it. She wondered sometimes if she were not jealous of her mother and that ten-day interlude: she was hard put to take unselfish pleasure in it.

After breakfast every morning Tad played in the library where he could watch for the mailman's coming. He and the mailman always shook hands after a fashion: Tad would run to the front door when he saw him and stick his fingers out through the mail slot. The mailman would take hold of them and give them a shake of sorts. Then when Tad withdrew his hand the letters would cascade in upon the floor. At the age of three, he could recognize a letter from "Grandma n'Ireland" although he could not pronounce the R in Ireland. Any other overseas mail he came to attribute to his Grandpa Jon. He was going to need to be a wise child to recognize his father, Martha thought. And there was bitterness for the silence: she could not entirely suppress it.

Tad was keeping his regular vigil for the postman when, through the first snow of December, a Western Union messenger turned up the walk. The child cried out in his excitement, seeing the uniform, and both Annie and his mother came running. They flung open the door even as the man put his finger to the bell, and stopped all, in deadly apprehension of the message that must pass from his hand to theirs. Then Martha took the telegram and signed for it, and before the door closed them unto themselves, Annie began to pray aloud.

Martha could not pray. Stonily, remote from child and friend both, she tore open the envelope. Marcus had been taken prisoner of war by the Germans.

Throughout the day she grew more and more accustomed to the idea. It was not death; from such anticipation, she felt only relief at the other. Many people called, for the name was published with the latest local casualties: even strangers phoned among whose own close relatives were prisoners of war from whom they had heard through the Red Cross. To them she was very grateful. It was supposed from comparison of APO numbers that Marcus had been taken at the breakthrough in Belgium. It soon became uneasy consolation, however, that for him the war was over; there now existed too much documentation of Nazi cruelty, and if she allowed her imagination any play at all it suggested that a doctor would be to them a prize capture. And as so many people said, the pity of all this was its happening at The Bulge, when we had been led to feel that victory was all but won.

In the afternoon Nathan came. She had not seen him for a month although regularly a check came from the office to her. He looked vigorous and strong, and as always, on the verge of saying something rather too intimate. It was his manner only, but she never failed to be on the defensive with him.

"You look well, Nathan."

"It is a handicap—would you believe me? Such an upsided world."

Martha smiled.

"Oh, no. I see old ladies looking at me as much as to say . . . but you know what they would say. It is not so bad, Martha, what happened to Marcus. He is an officer, you must remember that. And he is Aryan. He will be treated well. You will see."

"It is so terrible," Martha said, "to know a little and know nothing, to sit and drink tea and know that someone whose right it is to be sitting with you—is sunk in God knows what desolation." She looked within her cup. "And yet the tea is tea, not gall, not vinegar."

Nathan leaned forward in his chair, his hands clasped between his knees. "You are so beautiful when you are tragic."

"I am not tragic," she said. "I am only helpless. Nathan, I swear to you, if I were near and saw anyone hurt Marcus, I should physically attack them. Like a beast with claws. It is not right that war is there and we are here. However shall we face them coming back to us?"

He threw up his hands. "Make heroes of them. That is all. What is it but a spin of the wheel—who shall be heroes and who cowards. Once I was ashamed. Twice. But no more. Nothing you will say, nothing anybody says. I do what I can do. What is shame? It is a perfume, no, a disinfectant. That's what it is. We shake it over ourselves so people will think we are clean."

"I did not reproach you, Nathan."

"Your eyes did. But I am no longer going to hide from them."

"There is no need," she said, but without looking at him.

He left his chair and, standing in front of her, he touched his long cool fingers to beneath her chin. "I would rather you looked at me no matter what I see in your eyes." He caught her face and held it until she looked up at him. "Poor little unhappy one. How you suffer. May I tell you some news about myself?" He waited for her to answer. But she drew away from the touch of his hand. He returned to his chair. "I have been nominated to the Board of the County Medical Association."

"How very nice, Nathan. I am sure you deserve it."

"Thank you."

"Marcus will be very pleased."

There was an instant of dissonance in his aplomb—or she might have imagined it. "You are too kind," he murmured. She suspected he meant quite the opposite, having taken her words for patronizing. "But you understand, nomination is not election. I wish your husband were here."

"So do I."

"Of course you do. That is why I am hoping you will do what he would do. I want you to write some letters for me, Martha. Only one or two. They are to very important men in the profession."

"Do I know them?" she asked after a moment.

"Marcus knows them. They were friends, associates, of Doctor Bergner. You will say you are writing on behalf of your husband to recommend personally his colleague. If you are generous, you will say you met me when I was a distinguished Jewish surgeon on the Continent." Observing the unguarded reservation in her eyes, he spread his hands. "I am at your mercy, you see. But sometime you were at mine, weren't you?" The color flared up in her cheeks and he added quickly, "But, my dear, I did not mean our moment . . . of intimacy at all! What I meant, we are all sometimes at one another's mercy, the most irreproachable of us. It is so. And if you were to tell of me what you observed in Vienna, it would not create a very distinguished impression, especially with these gentlemen. My friend, Mueller, by the way, is writing such a letter as I am asking of you. And if it is too difficult for you, but, of course, I will understand."

Martha lifted her chin. "You were a distinguished surgeon. I have no reason to doubt it."

"And a Jew." His eyes also challenged her to remember the worst of him, his denial of it.

"I think it would be out of place for me to say that, Nathan."

"Perhaps you are right. But you will write the letters?"

Having got so far beyond the mere matter of a letter of recommendation, she could not hesitate.

"To whom am I to write the letters, Nathan?"

He wrote out the names and addresses of two prominent Traders City physicians. Martha knew them by reputation only, and she knew that they were Jewish.

"I must go this way now because I did not go directly among them at first—for reasons unheroic. One does not boast survival when someone for whom he feels responsible does not survive."

"The Baroness is dead?"

"Surely I should have heard by now if she were not. After all, she was not an ordinary Jewess."

"She was not an ordinary woman," Martha said.

"You are right. An ordinary woman I could have saved. But because of what happened, I had to go—not to my own people. It is not my fault I live in such times."

There was the question. But whose fault was it? Whose fault that

Marcus stood now, perhaps, in some compound, half-starved among the starving, he who had never had a gun in his hands? Whose fault Hitler?

"You are remarkably well assimilated, Nathan." If she had thought more deeply of the words, she might not have said them, for all that she believed them to be true. She could not help but suspect his sudden nostalgia for "his own people" to have a cause not yet revealed to her.

"I do not wish to be assimilated," he said finally. "You cannot say I denied once in this country what I am."

"I do not know what you are, Nathan, beyond what you say you are. I do not even know that I care, but I am sorry if I offended you." She put her cup and saucer on the tray. She got up, a sign that it was time for him to go. "I shall write the letters in the morning."

"I am too sensitive," he said, and rising, held out both his hands as though hopeful that she might take them.

"Are you?" She went to the door and waited there, then going from the library before him. When he had put on his overcoat, she offered her hand. "I am sure you will be elected to the County Board, Nathan. Some day, I should think, you will be president of the American Medical Association."

"And do you think Marcus will be pleased then too?"

Thus he succeeded in putting her on the defensive again. She should not think of him as a weak man, she knew, for he very well compelled her to his way. The cowardice of conscience? She could not say.

·5

How much can a doctor do without medications, without soap and with only a splash of water? What he could do, Marcus did. The war was almost over, everyone knew, but to be won, some in Marcus's camp thought bitterly—they had almost all been taken at the Ardennes—by the Russians. The camp received over a thousand additional Allied prisoners in April of 1945 force-marched five hundred miles from where they had been interned in Poland: this upon the

Russian break-through. Gangrene and dysentery came with them and even more diseases of malnutrition than Marcus had already learned of. And with them came the first eye-witness accounts of the extermination camps, the crematoria. Who could but say then Godspeed the Russians?

Night after night the skies were aglow over Hamburg and Berlin, and the all-night roar of the Allied bombers was the sweetest spoiler of sleep. Some men thought they heard artillery fire in the day; the German guards said it was machinery at the factory on the edge of town. And then one morning, when Marcus was out at dawn whittling splints out of a broom handle he had stolen during the night, a solitary figure came running across the compound from the barracks of the enlisted men.

"Doc," he cried out, "doc, they're gone! Look for yourself! There isn't a God damned Nazi bastard in the whole stinking compound!" The soldier was half-laughing, half-crying, the spittle running out of his mouth. Marcus slowly looked from one watch post to another. He had long since trained himself to concentrate on what he was doing, not to look, the less to spend himself in loathing. He felt his head nodding and the rising in him of a sickening kind of joy. The youngster opened his mouth and let out a great, wild cry: "Halloooo-oo!" Soon everyone was running, men half-dressed, some barefoot, and above their shouts and jubilation, the distant thumping of guns could soon be heard to the north.

Marcus ran with the rest through the open gates, down the hill to the heart of the village where all the blinds and shutters were drawn. Prisoners from other camps were there and more yet coming; French, British, Canadians converged with the Americans, all abandoned by their guards. They broke into stores and warehouses, private homes, the villagers scuttling out in all directions, and no one bade them stay. The looters came out with milk and bread, with wine, with towels in which they rubbed their unwashed faces. Marcus watched the pillage with unmitigated joy.

Within the hour advance units of the American Ninth Army moved into the town. Marcus, in search of the medics, was on hand for an early exchange of information: the French P.O.W.s' intelligence of a women's concentration camp at the northeast end of town. He rode out in a jeep with the first platoons assigned its liberation. On the way he smoked his first cigaret in five months. It was the only pleasure he was to have for several hours.

Seeing the sight in the distance, Marcus was put first in mind of animal kennels, the creatures within leaping against the fences. But they were women, all, clinging, writhing at the wires, emaciated to where their faces were but frames for eyes, teeth and hair. They set up a din of screaming horror, those unable to reach the fence, tearing at the backs of those in front. The smell of them on the fresh spring air was as terrible as the sight and sound. Several German guards stood outside the compound gates, their hands in the air. The first American soldiers took command of them and marched them down the hill, eager themselves to forego the glory of the actual liberation. The remaining soldiers stood staring, obviously terrified of the women. Marcus went with the sergeant into the gatehouse where the latter turned off the electricity. As soon as they came out the women knew what they had done. With utter abandon they charged the gate and brought it down themselves while the petrified soldiers watched. Marcus cupped his hands over his mouth and shouted to the men, "Just let them go! Let them run out!"

They would not run far, he thought; God help them, they would not run far. Gaunt with starvation, crazed with joy, having freedom they were instantly bewildered by it. A few of them hugged those of the soldiers with the courage to accept their embraces, but most of them hobbled around, bleeding, oozing with sores, sobbing, remote, especially from one another, wretched with self-loathing and loathing of their other selves as all were, each to one another.

The medics came, and a canteen truck with soup. The unfortunates fought one another in the line the soldiers tried to keep them in, while a translator begged them in several languages not to destroy themselves, that they were saved.

Marcus went down the hill and waited. In comparison, the prisoners among whom he had been interned were blooming healthy. He reported himself to command headquarters.

Marcus stayed on in the town for several days after the other military internees had been evacuated. He lived in the burgomaster's house and slept in a feather bed, and worked all his waking hours among the survivors of the labor camp. Most of the women were Eastern European Jews with a handful of Western political prisoners among them. That they had been young enough to work in twelve-hour shifts at the munitions factory was the reason they were alive. Many of the Jewish girls had come out of Auschwitz: their arms were indelibly numbered, their eyes soulless. They were got into clean quarters—the former barracks of the German officers—washed, given medication, and fed such foods as their starved bodies could accommodate.

Building by building, the foul barracks were burned to the ground. Some of the former inmates stood outside the fence watching, raising a howl of lamentation—or of joy; who could say? They would wander off, many of them, vague and lost, and sometimes if a hand were put out to guide them, they would shy away from it or scream defiance. But the worst pose of all to see them in, Marcus thought, was that of wheedling beggary, which must nonetheless have been one way of survival. There were not many ways. Enough food to keep twenty-five of them alive had been daily apportioned to every hundred internees. Nor was there anything now one could give the survivors except to ease their bodies. What they needed was beyond man's giving: they needed to be born again.

"Doctor, when comes the train from Paris, do you say?"

Both the woman and Marcus were watching the engineers repair the railroad tracks. Marcus had already observed her: in her prime she must have been a proud, fine-looking girl. Now she was a rack of sinew and bone. She had in hand a Red Cross satchel which he supposed contained a toothbrush, a towel, soap and a nightgown, possibly a change of underwear.

"Soon," Marcus said. "Maybe today." He was himself expecting supplies on the first train through.

"Maybe yesterday, maybe today. Tomorrow surely, eh?" The Frenchwoman spoke English well, or better by far than he could speak French. "I am glad it is not today," she said resignedly.

Marcus nodded, knowing what she meant. "I wonder if those are cherry trees," he said, indicating a clump of gnarled blossoming trees. "I suppose not. It's late for them."

"The chestnuts will be out in Paris. Have you been here long, doctor?"

"Since Christmas. I've been out of the States for two and a half years."

"Ha! Since 1940 I have not been home. I am in the Underground, but I am betrayed." She shrugged. "I am alive. You would not believe it was better to be a Communist than a Jew. Do you have a family, doctor?"

"I have a wife and son."

"And a house?"

"Yes."

"And a doctor can find work easily, no?"

Marcus nodded, smiling.

She spread her hands. "Then why do you not go home?"

He laughed. "Soon. Very soon."

"For me they say there is a plaque, a memorial—you know? On a street where there was shooting where I used to live. Now it is spring and people will put flowers there. I will go and look at it, and I will weep because I am not dead and everybody thinks so. What will I say if somebody asks me who I am?"

"You will have to tell them. We may all have to tell who we are when we get home. Or try."

"But you they will not ask. You will only have to tell them if you want to," she said with French exactness.

"You are quite right," Marcus said. "It is not the same."

"I have no money," the woman said, "and they say Paris is expensive. I do not even know if my husband is alive or dead. And I tell you, I do not know which is better, he is alive or dead. I feel in my heart he was a collaborator. Is it better I know or I don't know?" She looked up at him with sudden cunning. "Your wife is faithful, do you think, doctor?"

Marcus smiled. "What makes you ask that?"

She shrugged. "It is the same thing. Do you have any American dollars you could give me, doctor? On the black market in Paris I could get a great many francs for them."

Marcus did have ten dollars. He had got it from an American medical officer on his personal I.O.U. He would have liked to keep it for an emergency until he could draw his own back pay. But he gave it now to the Frenchwoman. Before his eyes and the eyes of a platoon of army engineers, she lifted her skirt and tucked the money beneath a garment next to her skin and fastened it there with a safety pin. Some of the soldiers whistled. Her face became vivid with a smile.

"How did you get a safety pin?" Marcus asked, amused.

She gave a throaty laugh and for just an instant he could see her as she must have been before the war: pretty, earnest, but sometimes full of mischief. "But I asked for it, too, that is all."

She left him and walked back through the town, swinging her satchel at her thigh. He had thought her over forty when first they spoke. Now he realized she was still in her early twenties. And whether or not there was a word of truth in her story, he would never know.

Marcus flew home aboard a hospital plane, the patients in his charge bound, almost to a man, to a lifetime of invalidism. They would not die of their wounds; that was about the only thing any of them was sure of. And at that, it was more than the men still fighting in the Pacific could be sure of.

"How does it feel to be going home, doc?" one of the boys asked. His maimed hands were hung up in improvised traction for the flight.

"Great," Marcus said.

"Me, too," the youngster said, and Marcus was ashamed because there was no irony in the boy's words.

He called Martha as soon as possible on landing, and from the moment of hearing her voice, his need for her brooked neither barrier nor delay. Let the dead bury the dead; time and again the words ran through his mind on the last of his homeward flight. Truly, he felt he had done little, but he did not see how he could have done more. Looking at his watch as the plane circled the Traders City airport, the thought occurred to him that no matter where one was coming from or by what mode of transportation, he always seemed to arrive at Traders City in the morning. That the sky was blotched with dirty-looking clouds by the time he got on the ground only served to make him feel more sure that he had indeed come home.

Martha, watching from the garden where from dawn she had been walking up and down, saw the cab drawn up in front of the house. She thought she had felt its turn into Oak Street. She ran to the edge of the terrace and then called out his name, her voice seeming to shut off in her throat. But he heard it and came directly to the terrace. She waited at the far end. Marcus, too, stopped. Tad came out through French doors and looked from one of them to the other. They all ran at once then, but when the child put his arms around Marcus's legs and hugged him, Marcus broke down completely and did not try to hide his tears.

· 6

"ONCE I can get down inside things . . . Do you know what I mean?" Marcus sometimes tried to explain the peculiar peripheral sensation, not entirely unlike his wartime nightmare of watching himself at work.

"It's going to have to wear off," Martha said, "like a scab on a sore and it's not going to help to keep picking at it."

"That's very good," Marcus said, but it wasn't really. One felt a sore, picking at it. He did not seem to be able to feel anything, only an aloof distaste for the city and the work once so dearly familiar.

The truth was, and perhaps deep within his own subconscious Marcus knew it—indeed it might account for his inability to submerge as it were—very little he saw outside his own home pleased him. The whole of Traders City seemed flat, dirty and insular. Only the lake front and The Avenue were in any way beautiful. That a city untouched by war since the Indian raids should be so squalid and ramshackle irritated him. It went no deeper: just irritation.

Nor did his first visit to Mount Clement Hospital enable him to break across the moat of disassociation. The hospital path was littered with cigaret butts, the shrubbery clogged with debris, candy wrappers, cigaret packages the brand names of which he had never heard before: Lucky Strike green had gone to war. The brass fixtures on the doors were tarnished, the windows smudgy, the painted walls a coffee yellow. At the admissions window—the visitors' reception desk had been removed, he noticed—he waited his turn to speak to the girl on duty. Observing the name T. M. Hogan on the staff roster he gave an instant's wonder as to whether there were another Dr. T. M. Hogan in the city. The attendant, a new girl since his time, had got herself a bad case of sunburn. Otherwise there was nothing sunny about her. Few places of business—and what hospitals weren't that? Cash and carry, you might say—tolerated such rudeness to the customers. Or maybe they did now that there was a war on. Inevitably he thought of England where good manners were a part of national survival.

He was startled by the abruptness with which the girl gave him her attention: a twist of the head and a "Yes?"

254

"I wonder—is Redmond or MacQueen on duty?" One was the head nurse, the other in charge of surgery.

"Who is your doctor, please?"

She very nearly intimidated him, assuming, he supposed, that he was about to launch a complaint. He might even look to her like a lawyer, not like a doctor obviously.

"Doctor Hogan," Marcus said with a self-conscious grin entirely lost on her.

"I suggest you talk to Doctor Reiss who's taking his patients. If you will please step around the corner to the switchboard, the operator will give you his office address."

"What about Hogan?" Marcus could not resist asking.

The girl sighed, having already turned away from him. "He's in service. There's still a war on, you know."

"Doctor Hogan is out of service, for your information, miss." Marcus left, immediately feeling foolish. Out of service. He probably was at that.

But because something had got to him a little deeper than mere irritation, he went along that same day to see Reiss in the office. He knew Reiss had taken new offices for them in the same building, and he had vaguely thought it a good idea. Bergner's old office which Marcus had inherited was out-of-date and small. But riding up in the elevator to the twenty-sixth floor he suffered a new discomfiture, something very nearly claustrophobic. The whine of the mechanism made him nauseous: the sound was like that of a plane going into a dive. The nausea passed as soon as he got out of the elevator. But he could feel the cold sweat and the traces of strain must have shown in his face.

Reiss took him by the arm and forced him into a chair.

"I got a bit nauseous in the elevator," Marcus said.

Reiss brought a flask of brandy from the desk drawer and poured him a shot of it. Marcus drank it down.

"I know the feeling," Reiss said. "It's the rush—all at once."

Marcus nodded.

"You must not hurry to come back. It is better to do it gradually. Perhaps only consultation at first. I do not mind if our arrangement stands as it is for a time longer."

"You've been very generous." Marcus roused himself and looked about the new offices: a lot of glass and air, thank God.

"No more than you were to me." Reiss smiled, his white teeth glowing. He was as tanned as an Italian fisherman. "I have looked forward to this day, Marcus. I have been greedy to show you how far I could go from a small beginning. When a man starts over at my age—well, you will find out. It is like that, isn't it, starting over?"

Marcus felt himself on the verge of floating off into space. He took hold of the arms of the chair. "Yes, it's like that."

Reiss, assuming that he was about to get up, proposed to show him the offices. Marcus followed him submissively. Reiss had taken the top floor suite that spring at a cost Marcus was sure considerably exceeded their old rental. Instinctively he felt there was a higher tone to the patients now, too. And Miss Sorenson, the secretary Marcus had inherited from Dr. Bergner, was retired. True, she had reached a fine age for it. Miss Kohler, her successor, looked efficient, sensuous, and not particularly anxious to meet him.

"You are not afraid of heights?" Reiss inquired. He was opening the casement doors off the waiting room onto a small, cement-railed outdoor balcony.

"Not even of depths," Marcus said.

Reiss looked at him reproachfully. "There are no debts. I would not do that without your consent. The X-ray equipment, that will be something else, perhaps . . ."

"Depths, I said, not debts, Nathan. Heights and depths."

"Ah. I misunderstood. Come and see the view."

Marcus stepped outside. From the balcony one could look down over the graceful spread of green park, the sweep of the drives and the hairpin curves approaching the bridge. Beyond was the lake, the horizon unbroken. One remembered that horizon, having forgotten many things about Traders City.

Reiss took him by the arm. "From here you can signal me in an emergency," he said, his tone jocular, "with a red handkerchief. That is it: with a red handkerchief. I have a boat down there." He pointed to the basin. There were not many pleasure craft in the water except sailboats.

"A sailboat?"

"What other kind? Mechanical devices—they are not boats. I hate to think what it will be like after gasoline rationing ends. They will foul the water. Like beetles."

Reiss leaned over the balcony rail and looked down at Lake Front Avenue. "It is like a child's game, the buses and the cars and the people."

Marcus had no wish to look down. "How are the Muellers, Nathan?"

The two men moved back into the office, the breeze that was almost constant off the lake following them indoors.

"I have not seen them for months. Julie is a doll, but getting so fat. Too many children. And Erich, you will be surprised: an old man, a grouch, doubled up like a toad."

"I am beginning to feel like a grouch myself," Marcus said. The word 'doll' hung in his mind, an irritant.

Reiss used it again a little later speaking of Martha.

Marcus said, "I wish you wouldn't use that word 'doll'. I don't like it." He thought then how unlikely he would have been to comment to anyone else on his selection of words. "I've still got nerves. I suppose that's what it is. Forgive my bad manners." He lit a cigaret.

Reiss looked at him sympathetically, his heavily lidded eyes limpid. Marcus was even more uncomfortable. He would have preferred Reiss to show him less patience.

"It takes time to come home, let me tell you." Reiss spoke as though he, too, had come home. He stepped to the door of the inner office where the secretary was working. "Will you please set up the Morgan X rays, Miss Kohler?" He returned to Marcus. "I want to know what you see in these pictures. There is a peculiar progress of malignancy." He looked at his watch. "Then I must go."

Marcus knew the consultation was a gesture but he went along with it. Afterwards he said, "What did you do with the old office equipment?"

"I sold it. There is a great demand for equipment because of the war." He laid his hand upon the arm of the X-ray machine and fondled it sensuously. "Beautiful is it not? You are a priority, you know."

"Me?" Marcus said.

Reiss nodded. He put the folder of X rays into his case and instructed Miss Kohler on his schedule.

"Hooray for me," Marcus murmured, and through his mind began to run the words: hooray for me, to hell with you, hooray for me, to hell with you. It took a severe effort of will to shut them off.

Reiss said, "Why don't you come with me to the hospital? Put on the mask and gown. You don't have to do anything."

"That's a fine idea—but not today, Nathan." He did, however, sit for a few moments in the office that was now his. Reiss had given him the better of the two.

The desk drawers were empty except for the *Manual of Operative Surgery*. Marcus took it out and opened it. His name was on the flyleaf in his own handwriting, "Rodgers University, School of Medicine."

Reiss came to the door. "I must go now, Marcus."

Marcus picked up the book, rising. "I think I'll take this along with me."

"If you wish, of course," Reiss said, "but I sometimes refer to it."

Marcus put the book back in the drawer. Reiss, he knew, was using it as a therapeutic symbol. He would have something more recent of his own.

They went down in the elevator together. Marcus's distress did not recur. Reiss and he shook hands when they reached the street.

"It is up to you to say when you are coming back, Marcus. I am in no hurry to change our arrangement though I should like a short holiday if you agree. You will know I have done well in your absence. I have made important contacts. You understand they are yours also. I shall recommend you if you do not know them. But you must see people yourself. They forget. Let me tell you, how they forget. They must be made to know they are not without obligation to you. It was you who went to war, not they, not I." Almost as an afterthought he added: "Perhaps you will come sailing with me Sunday morning, you and Tad? The boy can swim. Have you seen? He loves the water."

Marcus had not seen.

"Like a puppy dog," Reiss said. He was about to go on his way. He turned back and asked, "Why did you ask about the old equipment, Marcus?"

Marcus shrugged. He did not quite know himself.

Reiss shook hands again and settled an expensive Panama on his head. "*Au revoir, mon confrère.*"

Marcus stood a long moment on Lake Front Avenue looking after him. Then he wondered what had ever happened to the dog Tad had asked for with his first words. He could not remember mention of it again in Martha's letters. The whole thing was a fable, he decided, intended to charm a displaced parent. Standing on the Avenue, the long blocks of elegant shops stretching as far as his eyesight carried, haberdasheries, perfumeries, the showrooms of the future in automobiles, housewares, all to be had—just come in and get it as soon as there wasn't a war on. He thought how much akin his present feeling of futility was to what he had known during the Depression. He had not been able to get inside anything then either. He looked at his hands, the fingers yellowed with nicotine, and he remembered the night Dr. Bergner had steadied his own palsied hands in front of that very confident young man, Thaddeus Marcus Hogan, M.D.

But instead of taking command of himself, Marcus found it more and more of an effort to leave the house unless he took Tad with him. From day to day he put off such things as visiting the Brandon Clinic. The Clinic, he told himself, would not have changed. It was built on a firm foundation of charity and dedicated to the proposition that the poor we shall always have with us. That it might not have changed became, in his present condition, even more of a deterrent to him. He and Tad roamed every block of the University campus. He pointed out the windows of the room in the social science building where Jonathan had taught for many years, and standing in the shadows of Anders Hall, he remembered the night of his encounter with the students and the policeman. Now he too was one of the veterans, entitled to the patriot's sinecure. Reiss had said it: Let them not forget. And remembering still further back—to his own boyhood— he could hear Jonathan's invocational reading to him of Siegfried Sassoon's anti-war poems . . . "Have you forgotten yet? . . . Look down, and swear by the slain of the War that you'll never forget." Now that was curious: "Look *down*." Dreams were founded on funny things. He looked up the poem and reread it several times. The line he liked far better now: "Look up and swear by the green of the Spring that you'll never forget!"

There was not a museum in the city he and Tad did not visit, not a lagoon on which they did not cast bread and watch for fish. The roses faded and the gladioli bloomed. The snowberries turned brown on the bushes but refused to fall. People were impatient, resentful, many of them that the war had not ended with Hitler. As Marcus overheard a woman in the streetcar say: "Sure, the war would be over long before the duration if it wasn't for the politicians in Washington."

Martha wondered if she were jealous of his and Tad's comradeship. She had tried during Marcus's absence not to allow the child to become too dependent on her. Plainly she had succeeded. But her

own days were full and without its having any specific peaks, she
was enjoying what might be called her ascendance in the family.
She knew Marcus admired her garden although, like her father, he
made no gesture to help in it. She and Annie put up strawberry,
raspberry and gooseberry jam, red currant jelly, string beans and
tomatoes. And she had learned to cook—to make vegetables taste
almost as good as meat. They opened a bottle of wine every night,
she and Marcus, and talked around many issues without ever getting to the heart of them. She did not ask direct questions. As a
child she had been taught not to by her mother: people would tell
what they wanted to tell. Only in fragments did she learn anything
of his visit to her mother—as on the night he got down a poetry
anthology and read her G. K. Chesterton's poem *Wine and Water*.
"I knew I had that wrong," he said.

> " 'Old Noah he had an ostrich farm and fowls on the largest
>   scale,
> He ate his eggs with a ladle in an egg cup big as a pail.' "

And he told her about Herbie and the overseer's son.

But it was in the depth of night as she listened to his heavy, un-
interrupted breathing that anxiety came upon her. She had never
really known financial worry. Her father's estate yielded a modest
income, and Marcus had done very well after Dr. Bergner's death,
and he had come home with an accumulation of army pay. But prop-
erty taxes now made the house and garden a luxury. She supposed
the way she felt about Nathan's check each month to be false pride
. . . and Marcus's business.

But suddenly one night she shook Marcus awake out of a deep
slumber and begged him to tell her the truth: had he taken drugs
to make him sleep so soundly?

"No, of course not. But I wonder if maybe we shouldn't get you
something."

"I'm all right as long as I know," she said. She had an almost religious aversion to the sedative drugs—and to psychiatry, a subject
turning up rather frequently in their random conversations. She
was, she knew, in many ways her father's daughter.

One August afternoon, Marcus and Tad were crossing the park
at the back of Anders Hall about to go into the University Museum

of Science when Marcus stopped to look more closely at a man coming down the museum steps. He suspected it was Mueller, but he
was a long moment being sure. He saw what Reiss had meant about
the resemblance to a toad. Mueller's shoulders were hunched, his
head pulled in, which made him look even more squat than was his
natural posture, and he wore a frightful scowl. Marcus was very
near to turning aside, but this time pity stayed him. In the August
days of 1945, Erich Mueller's name was among those suddenly in
the news, the atomic scientists. Hiroshima and Nagasaki had been
bombed; Japan was about to surrender. But Mueller looked like a
man defeated; the glory of the day had passed him by.

A shudder ran through Marcus. He was remembering his father
and Mueller, his father always the older man of them. He leaned
down and put his hand on Tad's shoulder, causing the boy to wait
—and himself with him. And he said when the boy looked up at
him, "I'll tell you a story later if you remind me, a Chinese story."

Mueller came on and would have passed without even looking
up at them. Marcus said, "Excuse me, sir—about that dowry—my
son and I are ready to discuss it with you."

Mueller cocked his head round and up, his whole expression
slowly changing, his mouth open an instant before he cried out as
though the world should hear him, "Ma-arc!"

The two men embraced embarrassedly, comically (because of
their contrast in sizes) but with great joy, and for the moment at
least on the public thoroughfare Mueller became his old bouncing,
exuberant self.

They made their way to a nearby park bench, Mueller looking now
and then at Tad, and exclaiming over and over, "So! Tad, is it?"
Then, "Yes. A fine match for my youngest. We can make the arrangement." He pulled out his handkerchief and blew his nose
noisily.

Marcus was ashamed that he had not known till then even the
sex of Mueller's youngest child. "All girls?"

Mueller plopped down with a sigh. "Yes, I am a defeated man!"

Tad was looking at him solemnly. Finally he said, "Are you a
Chinaman?"

Mueller shook his head, his heavy jowl quivering. "No," he said
good-humoredly, and winked at Marcus. "It is enough I am a Jew."

"Chinese," Marcus said gently to the boy, "not Chinaman."

"Annie says 'Chinaman.'"

Marcus hesitated only a second. "Annie also says 'terr*ass*'—'will I serve the tea on the terr*ass?*' But you and I know the word is terrace, don't we?"

"Sometimes she says terrace," Tad said.

"Sometimes. So if you remind her, sometimes she will say 'Chinese.' "

Mueller clapped Marcus on the shoulder. "There you have it, Marc. Ha! I can remember your father saying that," and he shook his finger in imitation of Jonathan Hogan. " 'There you have it, Erich. There you have it.' And you know something, Marc? He was right about more things than you or I ever were. Never mind. Where is Jonathan? He was in Italy, England now, is it? How I have missed him."

"I too," Marcus said.

"You have been a long way, the two of you."

"A long way. Where do we go from here, Erich?"

Mueller flung out his hand. "Much further. We go to the moon, Marc. And shoot it up also. But right now . . ." he touched Tad's nose with the tip of his finger, "we are going to my house, to see Julie and all my girls." He got up and took Tad's hand. "First we are going to buy a bagful of hotdogs. Always you can buy hotdogs. Sometimes I wonder what they put inside them. Better we don't know, eh? You do like hotdogs, Tad?"

The child nodded.

"So! Then we will call your mama and she will come also. The most beautiful Martha, yes?"

"The most," Marcus said and grinned.

Mueller gave him a hug. "Ah, Marc, it is good, good. Let me see now. Where did I leave the car? I have a C-ration book, you know? I am a very important person." He steered them toward the parking lot at the back of the museum. "A very important person."

Mueller went through a veritable ceremony to get the car started, prompting Marcus to ask: "What kind of a car is it?"

"A Frankenstein." And twisting his head so that he could look at Marcus, he said: "That's a joke, son. Ah, Marc, Marc. I listen to the radio all the time: the comedians. What do you do?"

Marcus gave a short laugh. "I sleep."

But that afternoon, sitting on the Mueller front porch, Marcus spoke openly in a way he had not been able to until then. He told something of what Ireland had meant to him, the stillnesses, the day to day importance of drawing sustenance from the soil, out of the sea, of coaxing heat from a peat fire, of talk that was like poetry, and poetry as simple as talk.

"But we cannot be primitives again, you and I," Mueller said, "and you know, it is sinful for us to want to be. We are responsible for our own times."

"I know, I know. I'll tell you something, Erich, I didn't come home to operate on women for imaginary diseases."

Why he had said that he did not know and instantly admitted it. There were only the four adults present, the children romping through the house: but it was a strange thing to have said. Martha looked at him quizzically, trying to know what he had really meant to say if it were not that.

"Ah-ha," Mueller said. "I know. I am no psychiatrist, but I think I know. Europe is sick. Maybe so is America, but she does not know it. She is a mixture of crankiness and fat. You saw the concentration camps, eh, Marc?"

"One of them. And not the worst."

"Tell me—can they happen here?"

Marcus sat a moment. "I suppose you're right, they couldn't happen here."

Mueller leaped to his feet. "Shame on you! You do not understand anything to shrug your shoulders and say that. You say they cannot happen here. What makes you say it? Because you are lazy, it can't happen?"

Mueller was, Marcus realized, himself taken aback by it, in a very real fury. Julie merely sat, hugging her plump body as she rocked faintly back and forth in the swing. It was a family sort of gesture, protective of what she could protect while her husband was profligate with his energies.

"You are a sentimental fool, Marc," Mueller started again. "An ignorant giant is no better than a vicious dwarf. Look what we have done with our miracle! You cannot know what nuclear power is."

"Morally, I will take Hiroshima over Dachau any day, Erich."

Mueller flew into a new rage. "What has that got to do with it? We are responsible for Hiroshima. Dachau does not justify us. The death march of Bataan, all the cruel, barbaric atrocities do not justify us. What justice is there for the monstrous crime? Only the ironic. Punishment equal to crime degrades the society which administers it. When all men kill, who will stanch the wounds, eh? What happens when there is only justice—no charity?"

"That's all, Erich. When there are no more good Samaritans, that's the end of us. I have no quarrel with you there."

Mueller stood glowering down on him, his small, dark eyes aglow within their puffy lids. His voice changed. "No? Then I will quarrel with myself. There will be no more war. I, Erich Mueller, says so. The politician-scientist. Where your father left off, I am starting. The people must know." He held his hands apart, each cupped as though a balance to the other. "Dachau and Hiroshima. Either one could happen here, but they will not. They must not. Not here or anywhere in the world again. War does not right wrong. The people must know it."

"The people," Marcus repeated.

Mueller thumped his chest. "I am the people."

Time and again through the afternoon, both Marcus and Martha glimpsed the violence the war had done Mueller who was as close to a pure man, Marcus thought, as any he had ever known. Very few Americans, including Martha and himself, thought of the atomic bomb as anything more than a very large bomb, and the number of lives its use saved, American and, it was easily assumed, Japanese, by the earlier termination of hostilities seemed moral justification enough. And Marcus knew, too, perhaps better than did Mueller, how imprecise virtually all bombing was. But something of the magnitude of this man-wrought miracle, this capture of the sun's own power, came through to them from Mueller. He was alternately humble and furious. "It is like a bear whom you have trained to do prodigious things . . . and fools, irresponsibles, have come on a stormy night and taken off his shackles. Now I must be vigilant they do not put the shackles on me."

Marcus said, "Erich, isn't it possible that it would have been better never to have shackled the bear in the first place?"

"No, Marc! No. No. No." And Mueller caught him by the lapels and shook him like a small boy.

At bedtime that night Tad reminded his father of the Chinese story he had promised to tell him.

"Well, it's not a very long story," Marcus said. "Once there was a man standing at the foot of a mountain, and away off, he saw something move. He thought at first it was—a bear—yes, a bear. But then it came closer, and he saw that it was a man. And pretty soon, when the man came closer still, he saw that it was his brother."

Nathan Reiss often called at the house in those days, or telephoned. He was the more solicitous, Martha supposed, for his own conscience' sake, Marcus having suffered where he had not. But there was also, she suspected, the matter of the financial arrangement although it was never mentioned. She had thought for a time that Marcus might be able to take hold after his reunion with Mueller. But he fell more and more into unshared contemplation. Day after day passed and nothing changed except for the worse. The deeper the attachment grew between Marcus and his son, the less either of them seemed to need her.

Always Nathan would say, "Tell me what I can do?"

What she needed was someone to tell her what she could do. But she was the last person to ask it of anyone. She found herself thinking often of her mother and grew in understanding of a marriage that was not altogether marriage. But she loved Marcus as she was sure her mother had never loved her father. Yet her love was not enough, obviously. Marcus told her often, painfully often, that he loved her. She understood, but she was helpless, and to be made helpless by the helpless was too terrible.

So that there came the morning when Martha rose and bathed, and hearing Tad at breakfast in the kitchen with Annie, returned to the bedroom and sat down on Marcus's side of the bed. He was awake, smiling tentatively.

"Where's Tad?" he asked.

"Marcus, is it Nathan?"

He was hesitant in answering. "Do you mean am I jealous of him?"

"I wish you were," she said. "I don't mean that at all, and I should think you know it. Why don't you break the arrangement with him, Marcus? It might be better for both of you."

He sat up and leaned on his elbow. "Has Nathan suggested that?"

"Is that what you're waiting for—for him to suggest it?" Martha said, on the verge of anger because she seemed about to be put in the position of defending Reiss.

"I asked you, Martha—did he suggest it?"

"Not ever," Martha said. "I'm not thinking of him at all."

"I have a responsibility. I shall be able to take it on soon. The trouble is, with this kind of responsibility, a man ought to care a great deal more about people than I've been able to since I've been home."

"A responsibility to Nathan?"

Marcus leaned back on his pillow, not relaxed, but away from her direct scrutiny. "No. For him in a way." He laughed shortly. "To assume that kind of responsibility takes the martyr's arrogance, doesn't it? Or do you think martyrs are humble?"

She ignored the gibe, feeling it was that and unlike Marcus so that she supposed he was diverting her from some other meaning on which he did not wish to elaborate.

"I remember our talking about something like this a long time ago. Do you remember my telling you about Sister Mathilde?"

He did not remember.

"Are you thinking about the people who were killed—in the concentration camps?"

"In a way. But I'm thinking more about those who weren't, those who have no idea of what happened over there. A doctor can't do much for the dead. It ought to be enough for me to be a surgeon. But I don't seem to be able to make that arrangement with myself. What about Sister Mathilde?"

"I'm not sure now it's relevant. I was only thinking that we cannot persecute ourselves for not having been called upon to die in such a manner."

"We can't blame Nathan for being alive and healthy, is that it? I quite agree with you." Then he added, "Especially since Nathan doesn't blame Nathan."

"I think he does—in his fashion."

Marcus laughed. "You, too."

"Marcus, I don't give the slightest damn for Nathan. It's you I love and want, and sometimes feel I've lost entirely since you came home. I live in this family, too, you know. I'm not just its guardian angel, or its matriarch."

Marcus reached out and pulled her down, resisting, atop him.

"You said I would have to come and get you. But I can't, Marcus, if you won't let me. Don't you understand? I've got to feel your hand upon me, not just your words, your tolerance, your patronage. I'm hungry for the love of you, and aching with loneliness. I cannot say it all. I cannot touch you and feel that dreadful faraway-ness you have now."

His mouth was at her ear. "Don't say any more. Please, dear."

"I am trying to turn myself inside out for you. You have always said I am so introverted. Then if you don't want my love, I must understand it."

He managed to catch her head in his hands. Holding her face above him, he kissed her mouth, long and tenderly, so that she submitted and put her head on the pillow after it and wept quietly, while he stroked her hair.

"I'm home," he whispered, and over again, and within himself determining that it be so, began to feel it so: there was a kind of exaltation in his release, and, in that euphoric state, his senses were suddenly assaulted by the silken softness and the fragrance of Martha's streaming hair, in which he then burrowed his face.

· 7

SYLVIA, at home and particularly abroad, much preferred to give an intimate party to the grand affairs such as those for which Winthrop was famous in Lakewood. But in the autumn of 1945 when the pressures for early industrial and business transition were very great in Italy, Winthrop felt that such a party might be expeditious. No American of his rank was in as good a position as he to do it. He could afford it financially, his wife was with him, their house was adequate to such an affair, and they were sufficiently acquainted with Neapolitan society by then to carry it off with a degree of grace. There was nothing Neapolitans admired more than concealed purpose—and what else was grace?

Sylvia agreed to give the party, but she had never felt less sure of herself in such an undertaking. It was a feeling she did not enjoy. She knew that she was not liked in the upper circles, and for her own sake, cared little. The society of Naples found her too direct for a woman, brassy, and of course an American. She had too intimate a rapport with the lower clergy, for it was with their help she had gotten under way her project of rehabilitating the war-maimed children. Having no need for prelates was in itself an offense to prelacy. But it was the ceremony, not the sacrifice, in which too many of them would have wished to join: so Sylvia felt, and she was ever impatient with ceremony. It was only after an incident during one of her early ventures with Winthrop into local society that she had realized herself to have been the object of a covert jest. The Marchesa of somewhere she had since forgotten, remarked across her to their hostess, and in English: "It is a South wind blows tonight. It is scented with Fra Giacomo." Fra Giacomo was a mendicant who begged of the wealthy on behalf of the children. Sylvia thought it as well she had not got the point. But the truth was she often did smell of her associates, and nothing stank quite so dramatically as an aged cassock.

She was hard put to overcome her misgivings about the party. If she had herself been invited to such an affair as she and Winthrop were arranging, she would have found an excuse to escape it: the population of Naples and much of Italy was living in dire poverty, the harvest was the worst in years, rumors of a harsh peace came out of the foreign ministers' conference in London, and the country, particularly the North, was on the verge of political turmoil. She was not at all sure, although she could not elicit such an admission from her husband, that Winthrop was not persuaded to give the grand affair by precisely that consideration: their party was bound to be taken as a not too oblique gesture on behalf of the old ruling class.

"Poets and peasants," Sylvia said, sitting down with her secretary to compose the guest list, "why in hell couldn't I have been born one of them?"

Maria smiled brightly. It was not the first of her employer's remarks she had not understood, although she served as interpreter, purchasing agent and household mediator. Maria had applied for the position supposing it from Sylvia's advertisement to be that of a governess. She was delighted at her status, and she was hopeful of returning to America with the family. Her father had been a caterer before the war and she had been educated in one of the better convent schools. She had had some business school training afterwards at her father's insistence, for he had no son to inherit from him. But her father was dead, the business gone, and at twenty-six, Maria became the perfect assistant to Sylvia. In the matter of the guest list she was able to give the backgrounds of most of Naples' aristocracy, and to drill Sylvia in their titles.

Now and then Sylvia would ask of certain of them: "He wasn't a Fascist, was he?"

"Never. A Monarchist." Maria's answer was invariable.

The King's own presence was all she needed, Sylvia thought, to hold court. There was a name on the list that gave her pause: Johanna Maria Rachel, the Baroness Schwarzbach. She had not to her knowledge met the woman, but something in the name rang familiarly. Or perhaps it stood out in her mind because it was not Italian.

Maria said, in answer to her question: "It is a name familiar in banking. I believe the Baroness has been living in Ischia during the war."

There was a number of names on her list familiar in banking, Sylvia thought, and dispatched the invitation with the others. To satisfy her own sense of proportion, Sylvia included persons eminent in theater, music, and the arts, including the writer, Marcello Ruggeo, whom she knew to be a friend of Jonathan Hogan's. The moment she added that name, Sylvia began to feel better about the whole affair.

The Winthrop house in Naples, above the park on the Via Curcciola, commanded a spectacular view of the Bay from the grand salon. The mansion itself reminded her of Tamarack which had been, after all, transplanted Italian. She would not have chosen a place anywhere near so pretentious, but Winthrop said his choice had been that or a share-the-bath *pensione*. Its owner had spent the war in Brazil. A partisan in nuts, Sylvia suggested. Winthrop was amused, but for all that he had once run for mayor of Traders City, a town gauchely but proudly scornful of royalty, he was still much in awe of titles.

On the morning Marcello Ruggeo received his invitation to the Winthrop dinner, his mail arrived at the same time as his newspapers. He paid a gamin of the neighborhood twenty lire to bring his papers to him every day, and that morning, having just received a package from his wife in New York, he gave the boy a chocolate bar as well. He had rather counted on the pleasure of seeing him eat it. But the youngster buried it in his coat lining and set off at a deliberate pace. He could sell it on the black market for two hundred lire, Ruggeo supposed. A cunning arab, he would piously take the twenty lire home and spend the two hundred—God knows on what —something he could further trade on the black market.

Ruggeo left the windows open. The air was ripe with the smell of fish, its pungency a great deal more pleasant than that of the green leather in the process of home tanning on the floor beneath him.

He glanced at his mail, and seeing nothing he wanted to open at once, read the papers first. Their reading gave him no satisfaction. The word from London bode ill for Italy at the peace table. Jonathan had prophesied better than he knew. Or fate had played it his way. Roosevelt was dead. Jonathan had been more sanguine of Italy's chances when the Labor Government replaced Churchill. Bevin himself had said: "We must not continue to treat Italy as if Mussolini were still in power." But it was hard to see a difference in Britain's attitude. And Stalin had a long arm at the end of which was an iron fist.

Ruggeo's man, Parri, the Actionist, was now premier of a delicately balanced coalition government: his new economic policy was outlined in that day's *L'Italia Libera*.

In the north at the time of the liberation, the partisans had taken over control of the factories, displacing such managers as had Fascist histories; Parri, on becoming premier, had pledged the financial purge of those who had become rich through Fascism. Now his economic plan called for allocation of raw materials to favor small firms over the trusts entrenched during Mussolini's rule. It was a brave program—with small chance under Allied occupation. In the name of efficiency—of getting Italy back on its feet, a favorite American expression, the Allies preferred the old management system. They admitted the faults, but resisted the reforms. Parri was seeking general elections, a popular mandate for his program. The right was stalling. The Allies, officially aloof, unofficially favored delay. The rumor of it was abroad; so was rumor of dissension among the Left. And again as Hogan had prophesied, the Communists while ostensibly backing Parri, were maneuvering at his expense, trying to make a deal with the Christian Democrats.

Ruggeo paged through the paper and then turned to one he read for news, not for opinion. An item at the bottom of page one made him laugh aloud, a sound that might as well have been a howl of pain. The American financier, Gemini, had arrived in Rome to explore the possibilities for private American bank loans to acceptable Italian industry. *Acceptable.*

Ruggeo crumpled the newspaper and flung it across the room.

"The Resistance is dead," he said aloud. "Write the word into history. The harvest of Fascism is Fascism. What folly to sow grain in a field unpurged of mustard seed." He lit a cigaret and repeated the words and then sat down to write them.

It was noontime, his fever of despair broken by the writing, and while he drank a cup of instant coffee and ate a heel of yesterday's bread that he opened the invitation from Colonel and Mrs. Alexander Winthrop.

He read it and sat a long time thinking about it, looking now and then from it to the twelve pages he had just finished writing. He looked around the room and contemplated each object separately, his necessities of life: the iron gas burner on the ledge of the gray marble sink, the swan-necked faucet which either leaked or drew no water at all; the half-made bed against the sweating yellow plaster wall; the bookcase stacked with manuscript, propaganda all; the uncurtained windows opening upon his neighbor's laundry; the rug worn thin by the tread of his own feet, the fly-specked pictures of his wife and children who were waiting a welcome home to a country which the children by now had forgotten.

"I am a novelist," he said. "Not a statesman, not even a politician, not a propagandist." And staring yet at the pictures, but not seeing them any longer, he thought about a cottage in some quiet valley where he could smell the earth and the smoke of a wood fire, and write of love and loneliness and a vintage of bitter wine.

After a time he typed the article and prepared it for mailing. But before he went out with it, he wrote a letter to Jonathan who was in London, an American adviser on how to save Italy! He wrote in part: "My friend, you said in your last letter you proposed a trip to Italy during your first recess. I hope it can be arranged to coincide with the date of an affair to which I have this morning received an invitation. I am sure you will be as welcome among that company as myself . . ."

The guests began arriving promptly at nine o'clock. The Marchese of Bordagne, for one, who trained his chauffeur as he might an athlete in timing the distance between his villa and the few houses he chose to visit in the city. Since he was making an exception of the "American affair", he was so delighted to arrive on the instant that his high booming laughter rang out when he and the chauffeur checked the latter's watch as soon as the Marchese stepped from the car. It was a reassuring sound, that laughter, when he emitted another peal of it having urged the Marchesa to make haste getting out lest they be late through no fault of his or Paolo's, reassuring to those within the house that guests were indeed coming, and to those in the next automobile who did not wish to arrive before someone more important than themselves. Thereafter the guests drew up in a constant, slow-moving procession, and emerged by twos and fours from limousines of ancient but enduring elegance. Jeweled tiaras sparkled. The gloss of shimmering furs, too, was caught in the soft light of the lamps set out along the walk. The great outer gates of iron grill work stood open, the crest of the DiNatale family freshly gilded shone above the entry. The hall within was a pearl-like suffusion of candle and muted electric bulbs. The walls betwixt mirrors and doors were an oyster white, and gave off the faintest odor of fresh paint which only occasionally penetrated the more prevailing fragrance of flowers. Two great urns of carnations, red and white, stood on either side of the entry to the grand salon.

Sylvia received with as little ceremony as possible, making no effort to commend her guests to a company they knew far better than did she. She wore a close-fitting gown of pale gold lamé, her only jewelry black pendulous earrings of onyx. Maria, with almost mystical inconspicuousness, was never beyond her reach. Sylvia herself could not even judge the prestige of her party by her guests' selection among their jewels for the occasion as she could have done at Lakewood. From the assortment of sashes and medallions worn by the gentlemen, however, she suspected they were doing all right. And Winthrop, in his one aside to her of the evening, said: "By God! This is the real thing."

It would be a shame if it weren't, Sylvia thought, considering how much it had cost.

Drinks and hors d'oeuvres were served in the middle salon as Sylvia understood to have been the custom of the house. The room was particularly felicitous, at once spacious and intimate. The ceiling beams divided scenes from Virgil and Ovid done in warm mosaic. The walls were rose-colored silk damask and were hung with portraits of the DiNatale family which showed the Spanish strain— not so much in the family, although the Spanish blood was strong in it as in numerous Neapolitan families of the class—but in the artist who had painted them. At either end of the room were smaller salons providing refuge for those wishing more intimate conversation, or in the case of the "piccolo salon", for gentlemen wishing to smoke cigars and talk of politics.

A woman, however handicapped by the language barrier—and gossip employs the subtlest shadings of language—can nonetheless sense its presence. A special shaping of mouths accompanies it, an ascent of the eyebrows, a little quiver of nostrils, for the most refined of human huntresses reverts at the moment to the instinct of scent, and a welling within the eyes of some untold suspicion which is at once sniggled out by the quickened observer. Of such manifestations was Sylvia aware among a coterie of guests surrounding the Countess Bardoni. That Sylvia herself was drawn into their midst by a compliment from the Countess, an austere, dark woman noted among her kind for an aspen tongue, and held there by a series of inquiries about a charity she knew they resented, led Sylvia to suppose the object of their gossip had not yet arrived. She awaited a clue among the delicate ploys.

"Americans are impatient of nature's healing," Madame de Lignon said, referring to Sylvia's rehabilitation center.

Sylvia said: "True. We cultivate impatience as though it were a virtue."

"Direct, direct," the Countess said, speaking in French. "Precision in everything except government. Is that not so?"

"We delude ourselves about being precise there, too," Sylvia said, intending a small witticism.

There was a flurry of assents as though to please her.

The moment Sylvia allowed her eyes to stray to the door provided Madame de Lignon the subtle association by which she could at last broach the subject of her curiosity.

"We are to be honored tonight, I have heard rumor, by the company of the Baroness Schwarzbach."

"She accepted," Sylvia said, and since Maria had reported most of the guests to have arrived, she added: "I've been wondering if she's in the habit of making an entrance."

She was pressed for the meaning of her words and in trying to explain, Sylvia used the Italian phrase, *bella figura*. It brought her companions to the brim of mirth. She had scored a splendid *mot* with them unintentionally, and going over in her mind the meaning of the colloquialism she had used, she realized it had the sense of "putting up a good front." She had asked, in effect, if the Baroness Schwarzbach was putting up a good front. Observing thereafter a quite unsubtle warming in the atmosphere, Sylvia thought: Oh, God. Now I'm one of the girls.

On the arrival then of other guests, she escaped them with a mixture of gratitude and regret. Her own curiosity had been aroused.

Sylvia caught sight of Jonathan from the salon door and abandoned decorum in her joy to see him. Her haste was constrained only by the snugness of her gown. "Jonathan! How marvelous you are here! And you must stay some time with us. As long as you like." She kissed him on both cheeks, holding fast his cold, dry hands. He looked tired, the tic pronounced, but to her by far the handsomest man present. She would never understand how it was possible for anyone not to love him. Just to look at him, the kind eyes, quizzical, humorous, the shy smile, gave her pleasure. From her youth she had idolized him, and she felt deeply privileged in the right to show her love of him.

Ruggeo watched them, amused, but his fair brow was drawn nonetheless. His very stance, feet slightly spread, bespoke belligerency. He well knew he had come to camp with his enemies. But much, he thought, was to be observed under a flag of truce.

Winthrop shook his hand warmly and drew both men toward the salon door. There however he had to leave them, for at that moment the Baroness Schwarzbach arrived, and with her Alberto Gemini, the American banker.

Ruggeo said, quoting a Jonathan phrase to Jonathan: "There you have it, my boy. There you have it. In the trusts we trust. I may get drunk tonight. I should have warned you."

"Who is she?" Jonathan said. Who Gemini was he knew.

"It would be far easier for me to tell you what she is," Ruggeo said under his breath.

The name Schwarzbach occurred frequently in the financial history of Europe, but Jonathan did not know it in any contemporary reference.

The two men drew aside not to impede the entrance of so estimable a couple to the waiting company. Gemini was a bald, sturdy man in his sixties. He might have been a wrestler in his youth, Jonathan thought, for it was easy to surmise a supple, muscled body beneath the well-tailored clothes. But the Baroness: who could tell the face of a woman beneath its facsimile? Not Jonathan. She was plump, gowned in black sequin above which she burgeoned, a vast exposure of shoulder and bosom. She wore her hair a reddish tint beyond the reach of nature. Her eyes, he could not be sure, but he thought were dusted round with sparkle. Not diamond dust, surely!

Bold she was and a little vulgar, a quality Jonathan did not find unattractive when set against the austere repression locked within the eyes of a majority of the women present. He sensed rather than actually saw the electric response of the men to the pair's entrance, and he did not suppose the cupidity which Gemini might arouse to be quite that voluble. Did none of them have mistresses, he wondered.

"For heaven's sake, tell me something about the woman," Jonathan said.

"She's an Austrian Jew. She could and did get out in 1940."

"There were others," Jonathan said. He thought at the moment of Nathan Reiss, little realizing the connection.

"She must have come close to outstaying her welcome," Ruggeo went on. "It was probably a scandal in the Third Reich. Afterwards, she lived out the war in a special kind of retirement in Ischia."

"So she bought her way out," Jonathan said when his friend again hesitated. "It happened."

Ruggeo threw back his head and bared his teeth although he was not smiling. "It's a loathsome story. Are you sure you want to hear it?"

Jonathan was watching, fascinated at the moment, a curious pattern of social activity that struck him as being very nearly ritualistic: the women, each apparently after a signal from her own husband, were disengaging themselves from the group to which they were attached at the time of Gemini and the Baroness' entrance, and then joining their husbands and approaching the Baroness and her escort. The movement was not quite that pronounced—and certain individuals hung back, also observing—but Ruggeo was aware of it too, Jonathan saw. His mouth set in a hard, sardonic grin.

"Yes, I want to hear it," Jonathan said.

"She crossed into Swiss waters with the Gestapo officer charged with her arrest." Ruggeo's words became clipped. "I never saw him. Handsome, I've heard. Virile, we may be sure. Theirs must have been an idyllic life for five secluded years. What rumors came out of those remote hills, I don't know. She was not herself unknown to the islanders. The estate has been in the Schwarzbach family for generations, from the days Ischia was more stylish than Capri. As I say, what rumors escaped, I don't know. But when the partisans rose in the North last spring, a certain group arrived in Ischia also. They surrounded, captured and hung the Nordic stud at the villa gate."

Jonathan said nothing.

"Decadence and barbarism, the full circle of man," Ruggeo said, his lips pale as he again drew them tightly across his teeth.

Jonathan put his hand to the man's elbow. "Let's have a drink."

They moved toward the long buffet, abandoned at the moment by all except the servants and a few people whom Ruggeo could call his kind, the painter, Cavelli, the Rome correspondent for the *London Record* whom Jonathan also knew, a composer and a scenic designer who lived together on Capri, others. British and Americans, high in the Allied Commission, were also apart, observing while making desultory conversation.

Jonathan indicated the group surrounding the Baroness and Gemini. "Do they know the story?"

Ruggeo shrugged. "I know it. It was never printed in the public press, if that's what you mean. The conservative press has a strong instinct for self-preservation where a matter is likely to affect their own class. And the liberals among us, Jonathan, have a conscience. It stings us every time we hear the word, Jew."

"If we are truly liberals," Jonathan said, "that should not happen."

"Be honest, old friend. Doesn't it happen to you? Could you read such a story, and in the context of its time not say that it should not have been written?"

"It happened in the context of its time," Jonathan said. "Forgive me, Marcello, but you have spoken with such hatred, I should like to hear her version of the story. I doubt that I ever shall. I am not attracted to such society any more than it is attracted to me. I can only say there are Jews who did not die in Buchenwald or Auschwitz and who do not live as does the Baroness. You and I have no premium on conscience. I will not judge."

Ruggeo mocked him: "The true liberal. He will not judge. Not even the war criminals. Not even Hitler."

"He is judged," Jonathan said quietly. "I'm not sure he didn't judge himself."

"Rubbish!" Ruggeo cried. "Godalmighty rubbish!" In one long tilt of his head he emptied the glass of gin and bitters. He gave a sweep of his arm, a gesture that encompassed the titled and the elite of the evening. "Why don't you join them? They say the same thing. Hitler made a mistake. He went a little too far. A few less Jews and a few more Communists, and such a party as this might have been given in his honor." Ruggeo thrust his empty glass into the hand of the attendant to be refilled. His voice purred at Jonathan with sarcasm. "But you can say this for him: he died like a gentleman, took his own life. Not like our ragamuffin screaming for the rabble's mercy at the end. I've heard it, Jonathan! Their only regret in having supported Mussolini was not that he became a tyrant, but that he proved a coward." He took the refilled glass from the server's hand.

Jonathan did not protest. He had not said anything quite like that, but Ruggeo was gathering an audience. Aware of it himself he addressed only Jonathan and more quietly. "Tell me the truth, my friend: what part of my story offended you the most—the lechery or the lynching?"

"The lynching," Jonathan said without hesitation.

Ruggeo laughed. And having started, he did not seem to be able to stop laughing, not loudly, but gasping out the repetitious sounds. Suddenly he stopped. "And so with me! A revolutionary!" his voice was thick with self-derision. "Christ! Christ, liberate us from the inhibitions of your Christianity!"

Jonathan sipped his own drink, and taking Ruggeo's arm persuaded him away from the buffet. "We are in danger of distracting attention from the main event," he said. "Introduce me to your friends."

Sylvia, just before dinner was announced, did a dangerous thing: she slipped into the dining hall and made an alteration in the seating arrangement. She had with scrupulous care decided on tables of twelve, distributing important personages at each of them, thereby avoiding in an order of precedence she had no hope of understanding. The change she made brought the Baroness Schwarzbach to her own table. She did it, not because of the attention paid the Baroness on arrival, but because of the attitude of the grand dames when they had involved her in a moment of intimacy. She was by no means certain her solicitude wasn't that of a lamb shielding a tigress. But in the end, Sylvia could only be Sylvia obliging her strong if not very feminine sense of fair play. She left Gemini where she had placed him in the first place, near her husband.

The Baroness at table had great charm. She spoke three languages fluently, Italian, French and English, finding the particular nuance she wished in one language for her conversation in the other. She deferred often to the other women at the table, rarely to the men, ingratiating herself the more with both for it. In a less articulate person, her curiosity, her moments of almost naïve wonder at incidents, opinions ventured, would have seemed coy, Sylvia thought.

But in her they seemed genuine, and afterwards she would exclaim: "Ah-ha, ah-ha!" as though having arrived at belated understanding. And two or three times during the evening she explained to Sylvia, "I have been removed from so much that has happened."

Sylvia wished to God she knew more about her and wondered if Maria had deliberately failed her in this particular biography. She was not a girl for gossip, Maria, especially about her own people to an American.

Out of her experience Sylvia could not have asked more of the way dinner went. The wines drew nods of satisfaction: Soave Bertani with the fish, Haut Brion with the fowl, the Pommery champagne with dessert. Only once during dinner did she catch the eye of Jonathan. He seemed earnestly occupied with the wife of a British admiral whom she had seated between him and his friend, Ruggeo. When it was time to leave the tables, a group of musicians began to play in the grand salon.

The Baroness spoke briefly to her hostess: "You have arranged marvelously. I should not have thought it could be done."

Sylvia felt herself, of all silly things, to be blushing. "Thank you very much," she murmured.

The Baroness added: "It might have been presumptuous of me to say so. I am glad that it was not."

"I'm not so sure of myself," Sylvia said.

The Baroness looked up at her, and for the first time Sylvia realized she was very nearly an old woman. "If I ask you to have luncheon with me, will you do it?"

"I should be honored," Sylvia said.

Alberto Gemini intercepted them. The Baroness said: "In America, I understand, you are not acquainted with each other, Madame Winthrop?"

Gemini said: "I've just found out you're a Fields, Mrs. Winthrop. I knew your mother. A fine lady—and no flies on her either." His small blue eyes blinked at the Baroness. "Like you, Johanna. To the point."

"Alberto, I do not like to be compared with anybody's mother, even the delightful Madame Winthrop's."

Sylvia laughed. Gemini said: *"Touché,"* in an unmistakable American accent. Sylvia was remembering his history: A Brooklyn boy, the son of an Italian silversmith, he had laid the foundation of his fortune during World War I.

Before leaving them to join the men for cigars and brandy, Gemini said: "I'm going to have to leave soon. If I don't see you, Johanna, I'll be in touch with you. I'll see what can be done."

"You are most kind," the Baroness said, and gave him both her hands. Her smile up into his face embarrassed Sylvia. Surely he must see the falseness of its mock adulation. And of course he did! and was as pleased with it as with the real thing. He was a man who would relish saying to himself and even more to others: she hates my guts, but . . .

With stolid awkwardness he lifted the Baroness' hand to his lips. He took leave of Sylvia with better grace, a hand shake much more his style. He had no humor in his eyes, she thought, and from the back, his red neck bulging above the stiff white collar, he looked more Prussian than either American or Italian. He made his way through people with the aplomb of a bulldozer. He had only one thing to recommend him: money.

In his wake, the Baroness' eyes clouded over with a cold cynicism that she immediately batted out of them, turning to her hostess. Nonetheless, Sylvia felt herself an innocent abroad.

Withrop's feeling toward Gemini had progressed through the evening from resentment to a hostility it was difficult for him to conceal. He had added the banker's name to Sylvia's guest list tardily, learning after the other invitations were out that he would be in Italy. But from the moment of his entrance, Gemini acted as though the occasion had been planned in his honor. For that matter, every Italian present whose business was business acted as if he assumed it also. Winthrop had not supposed these people were interested in UNRRA, but neither did he choose to have his house used for the convening of an international banking cabal, and that was what he saw happening before his eyes. He could not prevent it, but determined not to join it, he sought out Jonathan Hogan.

Gemini was at the moment the center of a group of attentive gentlemen, giving a fluid account of his view on the prospects of Italy's financial recovery. Count Fabroni acted as translator, for Gemini spoke a very plain English. Gemini had spent two weeks touring Italy and had come by facts and figures, the accuracy of which no one would question, such was his command of them. Having responsibility to no government, and obviously contemptuous of the peace negotiations, the preparations for which were now going on, he was outspoken and ruthless. Various of his points brought color to the faces of his listeners. Not a man took issue with him.

"I can tell you what will come out of the peace conference," the banker answered the weakest of protests. "In twenty years Germany will be the most prosperous country in Europe. They won't resist occupation like your left-wing coalitions. They'll make the most of it: American money and German know-how. Mark my words, gentlemen, there will be more foreign investment in Germany by the end of next year than there was before the war."

To Jonathan, Winthrop said: "I got something I didn't bargain for, inviting him."

Jonathan was watching, listening, a tight smile on his lips. Ruggeo, next to him, was rocking back and forth on his heels, his bright eyes boring straight ahead. He had the look of a man about to explode. Winthrop's annoyance with the banker was suddenly mingled with alarm. He had just seen Ruggeo's face. He said: "Hogan, if I get their attention, will you say a few words about the prime ministers' conference and get this fellow offstage?"

Jonathan shook his head. "I'm not at liberty to do it. And if I were, it would be bad form—for you. I'm a mere adviser, not even a negotiator." He indicated the group. "I'm not in their league, Colonel."

"I'll put my cards on the table," Gemini was saying. "I've got a press conference in Rome tomorrow, and I'll tell you what I'm going to say . . ."

"An outspoken chap, isn't he?" Ruggeo said, his eyes snapping.

Even Gemini was momentarily distracted for Ruggeo had spoken loudly. He looked around with the others for the speaker. But seeing who it was, they shook their heads and urged the banker to go on.

Winthrop moved toward the cabal. "May I intrude for a moment, gentlemen? The ladies are waiting to dance."

"I thought I was among friends," Gemini said.

"You are." Winthrop smiled at him.

Others of the group were quick to reassure him.

Gemini made a slow exploration of their faces. Like a gangster in a movie, Jonathan thought. Gemini said: "As I was saying . . ." He made an off-hand gesture of dismissal toward Winthrop. "This won't take long, Colonel . . ."

"There's a representative of the *London Record* in the room, sir," Winthrop said.

"Good. He'll have a scoop."

Winthrop was caught. To intrude further was to alienate the very people he had gathered for the purpose of ingratiating. He withdrew as gracefully as he could.

Jonathan offered him a cigaret. He accepted it although he rarely smoked. Jonathan said: "Hang your clothes on the hickory limb, but don't go near the water. Remember the old song?"

He was in no mood to be reprimanded, whatever the source. "Shall we go into the grand ball room?"

"Wait," Ruggeo said, as Jonathan started to move off. "I want to hear this."

Having been invited to do so, the London correspondent took a notebook and pencil from his pocket.

Gemini was well aware that he was giving a statement:

"I'll go as far as to say that as long as the partisans are in control of the factories, there won't be any loans—not from the men I represent. Get rid of the Parri government, put a sound man in office, somebody strong enough to pull the country together, and then we can talk business."

"There you have it," Jonathan said quietly. "There you have it." He could feel defeat like a stone between his shoulders.

"Are you coming?" Winthrop said.

Ruggeo was standing, his fists clenched. "The son of a bitch," he said. "The filthy, arrogant Fascist son of a bitch."

"That's enough," Winthrop said.

"Far, far more than enough," Ruggeo said. His whole body was quivering with rage, and with the terror of the future he had mortgaged to an empty victory.

Jonathan put out his cigaret. "Goodnight, Alex. Tell Sylvia I shall call her," and taking Ruggeo by the arm, he persuaded him from the room.

Within the month, the Parri government had fallen. De Gasperi, the Social Democrat became premier. On the same day Marcello Ruggeo's article—that written on the morning he had received his invitation to the Winthrop party—was published. "The resistance is dead. Write the word into history . . ." It was his last political writing. The following summer his wife and children joined him in Switzerland. By then he had almost finished a novel commenced before the war.

Jonathan, returning to England from his brief, unhappy holiday in Italy, was soon faced with a decision in his own life. He had gained recognition during his wartime service as something of an expert on Italian affairs, and he was asked to stay on in his advisory post by the State Department preparatory to the drafting of the peace treaty.

But the cause he had championed in Italy was lost. And in truth, a government such as De Gasperi's was likely to do better at the peace conference than, say, Parri's. It was stronger, having the might of the Right. The coming struggle for world influence between the United States and the Soviet Union was plainly evident. Italy could be expected in time to become part of an alliance with Britain, France, and the United States if America did not revert to isolationism. The Soviet Union's inflexibility on Italian reparations showed plainly that she considered Italy outside her sphere of domination.

Jonathan's frank evaluation of his own position was that his usefulness to his government was at an end. Henceforth, a good statistician could do the job better. The exigencies of balancing power would dictate this, like all other peaces: men of good will would write its rationalization.

That nothing changed, he would not say. He believed with William James in that one per cent of change which made the difference called progress. All the same, his mind went constantly back to the days following World War I, to Woodrow Wilson's heartbreak, to the Palmer raids and the bonus marchers. Loyalists and conformists: he was not their kind of patriot. Yet at this point in his life, Jonathan wished himself removed from where his conscience would compel his tongue. His message had been tried and found wanting: just possibly it also belonged on the ninety-nine per cent side of history's ledger. In a very few years he would be an old man; some would say he already was. He wanted to shoot with the quill for a change and not with his tongue, to write and to study. A post at London University, where from time to time in the past he had happily taught and studied, had been somewhat casually proposed to him during his recent sojourn in England. He resigned his government job and went after it. Securing it, he went home to permanently sever his association with Midwestern and to spend Christmas with his family.

Meanwhile, Sylvia went to luncheon with the Baroness.

·8

THE Baroness called for Sylvia in her chauffeured car. She wore black and a simple make-up Sylvia found far more becoming than her gaudy evening splendor. "I have arranged our luncheon at a country inn. You will not mind to drive a few kilometers?"

Sylvia said that she would like it. The day was clear and sharp, and as often happened on late autumn days, Sylvia was homesick. She longed for the browns and the acrid smell of smoke so reminiscent of Lakewood at that time of year. Lake Michigan was not to be compared with the Mediterranean, nor the prairies of home with the Campagna, but she knew where her own choice lay.

"I shall be going home soon," Sylvia said as the car climbed above the city. The Bay stretched far and gloriously blue beneath them.

"And you are anxious?"

Sylvia nodded.

"Home," the Baroness said. She repressed a sigh. "I shall be going somewhere myself soon. But where I do not know. I must wait. Always the refugee must wait."

Sylvia smiled. The Baroness did not in any way conform to her notion of a refugee. Fleetingly she thought of the story Jonathan had told her in their one afternoon together before his return to London. She could not credence the story. She had probed Maria for it without success and without herself repeating it. She did not think the gossip of Neapolitan society concerned it. Gossip and horror she did not suppose could be reconciled in any society. What she had elicited from Maria was a tale of the Baroness' lovers. She had never been known in the old days to appear without one, even while married to the Baron, a man long since dead. And during the war years? Sylvia had prompted. Maria had shrugged. "During the war years she did not appear at all." Sylvia had remarked then: "My God! Alberto Gemini?" Maria had burst out laughing. "No, no, no. That was why, you see, they did not hesitate to accept her at your party. The matter of a lover is—very delicate on such occasions." Whatever could be said of Gemini the word delicate in no way became him.

283

"Perhaps I shall come to America," the Baroness said. "I have not been there in a long time."

"But you have friends," Sylvia said.

The Baroness looked at her sharply as though in search of a hidden meaning. She sat back, satisfied that there was none. "Friends. Home. Americans are very sentimental."

Sylvia was annoyed. These people were always making generalizations about Americans. And to Americans: that was what irked her, as though they were children to be told all about themselves. She pointed to the ruins of a stone wall near which a washing of shirts and undergarments were hung on a line. Before them at the side of the road a boy was tending two goats. "There are people living in the shelter of the wall," she said.

"So there are," the Baroness said. "It is better perhaps than in the caves. For many years people in this region have lived in caves. It is a very poor country—for most people. If I were Italian, I should be ashamed."

As they passed the goatherd who stared at them impassively, Sylvia lifted her hand and waved. The boy scrambled for a stone and threw it after the car. The Baroness, catching sight of his motion, turned to observe its fulfillment. "That I have not seen before." She sighed and settled back. "Tell me about your children. You call it a rehabilitation house? What will happen to them when you go home?"

"I have arranged to take two of them with me," Sylvia said. "For medical care in America. Others will come later, a few at a time. For artificial limbs, surgery, and a period of recuperation. I'm planning to build a hospital at home for that purpose."

The Baroness nodded. "You have no children of your own?"

"No. I married late."

Again the Baroness inclined her head slowly. The line showed from the corner of her mouth clear to beneath her chin and in a taut pattern seemed to proceed from there to just below the ear. Her face had been lifted, Sylvia realized.

"And of course," the Baroness said, "in America you have superior doctors."

There was something in the way she said it: at that instant Sylvia made the association of the woman at her side with Nathan Reiss. She knew then where she had heard the name: the doctor's European patroness. The two women looked at each other. The Baroness puckered her lips in a smile that was at once mocking and wistful. "Do you know a child by the name of Martha Fitzgerald?"

"Martha Hogan now," Sylvia said. "She is a very dear friend."

"The world is no larger than the head of a pin," the Baroness said. "I thought and thought about the name Winthrop, and at first I wondered if you were her mother. But you have no children."

Sylvia, for the life of her, could not say anything.

The Baroness went on: "I was thinking of her a few moments ago when you said you were going home. It was from my home in Paris she went like a young doe when the cablegram came from her fiancé that he wished immediately to marry her. I cannot forget the moment, her face, like God's own child. It was a privileged moment. From nothing in my own experience could I have conjured such a moment. Do you understand me, my dear?"

Sylvia nodded. She was ridiculously close to tears.

The Baroness stretched her gloved hand to Sylvia's and patted it gently, reassuringly. She looked out the car window for a time. "Look, we are coming to a village. There is a lovely bell in the monastery. We shall pass it on the other side. When I was here— it is a long time ago—I used to come here with someone. We would bring our luncheon. There is a ledge on a cliff where we would sit and look out over the tops of the vineyards and the orchards to the sea. And sometimes we would hide in a little cave if anyone was passing too close to us, and we would tell the time only by the chiming of the monastery bell . . ."

Was she speaking of Nathan Reiss, Sylvia wondered. Instinct told her that she was. With the next words she was sure of it.

"He was a racing genius." She shook her head. "I spoiled him."

Sylvia met her eyes.

The Baroness asked: "He is in your city, Dr. Nathan Reiss?"

"Yes."

"He would not have told of me, I suppose. But Martha I should have expected to ask about me."

"He has spoken very highly of you—it was only the name I did not know." Sylvia chose her words with care. "He told what he thought had happened to you. He didn't tell it to me, but I do know that he was deeply chagrined at not having been able to help you."

The slightest arch appeared in the Baroness' lightly penciled eyebrows.

"He tried, you know," Sylvia said. "I don't suppose I have the story right. I didn't want to hear the story—from him, I mean. I'm nobody to confess failures to, I've got enough of my own." She laughed uneasily. Having started to talk about Reiss she could not seem to bring the matter to a head. It was unlike her, priding herself as she did on her directness.

"My dear, you should not have discomfited yourself. Nathan could always beat his breast in public with the utmost ease. I thought it to be part of his charm. I was always forgiving him for something."

"I suppose most women do find it that," Sylvia said flatly.

The Baroness sat in a silence Sylvia was glad to respect. The road through the village was rough, rutted from the fall rains. The driver used his horn to persuade men and mules out of his way.

"Tell me," the Baroness said, "what does Nathan suppose happened to me?"

"The concentration camp was what he feared."

The Baroness lifted her head. "And now that we know what took place in the concentration camps, do you suppose when you go home, he will be grieving his great loss?" Her voice was like velvet: "You must relieve his melancholy."

Sylvia did not answer.

"Do you know what did happen to me, Madame Winthrop?"

Sylvia was slow to reply: "I did hear a story."

"Of a crucifixion?" Sylvia nodded. "It is true. And if you will tell the story to Nathan, I am sure it will ease his conscience."

Sylvia finally glanced at her, knowing the woman to be waiting to meet her eyes. The Baroness' own eyes were glittery, like polished stone, and she exploded a smile on Sylvia that reminded her instantly of that with which she had looked archly up into the face of Alberto Gemini. For all her affectionate words about Martha, the Baroness was using Sylvia to carry back to Traders City a far from tender message. She did not know her very well.

How she was to get through luncheon Sylvia didn't know. The nerves at the back of her head were as taut as iron bands. Indeed her whole head felt as though clasped within a rigid mask.

Suddenly the Baroness observed that they had passed through the village. She leaned forward and tapped on the glass partition. The chauffeur opened it.

"Turn around and go back to the village," she said in Italian. "We wish to see the monastery."

The chauffeur shook his head and answered, also in Italian: "It is gone. It was bombed out at the time of Anzio. Not even the shell is left. They have made a new school in the village of the old stone. Do you wish to see it?"

"On the way back," she said, and then: "No, no. I do not want to see anything on the way back. Drive ahead!"

·9

SYLVIA came home to stay in the spring of 1946, Winthrop moving to the Commission headquarters in Rome. He expected to return himself within the year.

Martha watched from the terminal window as the big plane landed. She saw the ramp and steps adjusted and the door opened, the hostess stepping out. She recognized Sylvia instantly: so characteristic the directness with which she emerged, looked up to the sky and then took over the management of her own affairs. Two children came down the ramp with her, one a boy on crutches. Behind them was a woman obviously in their party, strong and dark complexioned, who Martha surmised was a nurse. Sylvia was Sylvia still, lean, silver-haired, her curls close-cut around the small, plain hat. She would always look well-groomed, expensively dressed, but never chic.

"Oh, my God, you look good," she cried, gathering Martha into a hug.

"So do you. You even smell good." The perfume was also expensive.

"Which is more than can be said . . ." Sylvia left the sentence unfinished. She introduced the children: "This is Angelina." She was a girl of eight perhaps with a vicious red and purple scar that sliced her cheek like an apple that had been cut into and was going bad. "And this is Francesco." Francesco was the boy on crutches. He had but one leg. "Angie and Frankie. This is Mrs. Hogan. And this is Maria, who has been all Italy to me. Martha, we are going to do such things, all of us. We stopped in New York for consultation. But soon New York will come to Traders City, the hospital we shall have here." She looked around. "Did George send the limousine?

Good. We'll fill that up with the luggage, and we can ride with you. Where's Tad?"

"In nursery school."

"My God!"

They drove first to the Winthrop flat where temporary rooms had been prepared for the children and Maria. Not far from the Washington Park Zoo, Sylvia explained to them. "I always speak to them in English," she said to Martha, "primarily because I don't want them to learn my bad Italian. Their own is bad enough, God knows. You cannot believe what they have been through. And how many there are like them. All over Europe, Martha."

"All over the world," Martha amended.

"It gets bigger as it gets smaller, doesn't it?"

In the late morning Martha and Sylvia drove out to Lakewood, and Sylvia spoke at length of her plan for making a children's rehabilitation center out of the farm north of Lakewood. "It's going to take a lot of doing, the State Department and all, even temporary visas. But I've promised Alex I shan't get into any fights. He's being wonderful about it. I go into things heart, soul and headlong. I keep thinking: if only they could see the children, these to-the-letter-of-the-law bureaucrats."

"That might make it harder—their seeing the children," Martha said.

"Yes, I see what you mean. People don't like to look at them, do they? But they're going to, Martha. Before and after, they're going to see them. I want Marcus, you know. I've never thought of this project without him. And Alex agrees. I hope you'll be on my side—when I put it up to him."

"I don't think you'll need me," Martha said.

At Martha's persuasion Sylvia drove out by the Lake road: she preferred the faster one herself. But she remarked that she was glad they had come that way. The trees were nearing the fullness of their foliage and the road banks were purple and yellow with violets and buttercups and dandelions.

"We saw Tony, you know. The Sorbonne, no less. Our Tony becoming a scholar. He's grown a beard and he actually lives in a garret. My God, how I'd like to have done that at his age."

"Grown a beard, too?"

Sylvia laughed. "I couldn't even get away with Greenwich Village. But it's going to be all right. All you have to do is live long enough."

As they approached the stone gates of Tamarack, Sylvia cried out: "My God, look at that sign!"

An advertisement of billboard proportions announced: TAMA-RACK ESTATES, ONE AND TWO ACRE PLOTS.

Sylvia came close to turning the car around at a right angle sharply changing her direction. "No, we won't even stop. We shall call the farm Tamarack. It's never had a name except the Fields farm. I'm glad Alex isn't here to see this. But then it might not affect him at all. He might even call it progress. Maybe it is." She drove into the village of Lakewod deep in her own thoughts. "Alex has done a touchy job well, Martha. And he involved the people. That's what's good about him: he isn't jealous of his authority. He can stand people up on their own." And after a moment: "Look at George Bergner. He's done better with the *Star*—because Alex had confidence in him —than we'd have done ourselves if we'd been here. We'd have got into all sorts of things. George just holds steady."

"We don't see the Bergners," Martha said.

"And the Muellers?"

"Sometimes. Erich is a very funny man—trying to be a politician. Only it's not funny, his crusade for peace. And he's beginning to make us understand what the atomic bomb really meant."

"They'll be calling him a Communist," Sylvia said.

"I don't think so."

They went to lunch at the Green Tea Pot where Martha had often gone when she was at St. Cecilia's. The waitress recognized them both.

"Isn't it nice to be recognized?" Sylvia said. "You know, I'd always thought it would be Alexander who'd be homesick, he's so American. I miss him very much. I keep feeling as though I'd forgotten to bring something important."

Sylvia forced herself finally to inquire about Nathan Reiss. She supposed that for the rest of her life whenever she met him or spoke of him she would think of the Baroness. It was one of the things she would have liked to blot out of her memory, and of course it was therefore the more vivid: the child's throwing of the stone on the road above Naples, the chauffeur's back, his handsome profile as he told of the vanished monastery; and then the most shocking thing of all to Sylvia: the Baroness' caressing of his hand, leaving the car, careless of whether Sylvia observed it or not. In such capacity had Nathan Reiss also served her, and the crucified Nazi . . .

She had gone back to the children of Naples' streets from that luncheon with the gladness of salvation to be among them. She cherished the very nits in their hair. And she had not been able to tell Winthrop about the woman. Nor—if Reiss were to learn of her survival—was it to be from Sylvia.

"He's been quite wonderful to Marcus," Martha concluded. "I don't know what we should have done without him."

So be it, Sylvia thought. A man was entitled to forget. She would even go so far as to say he was entitled to escape.

Louise Bergner managed to gather a great many of the old Lakewood crowd to celebrate Sylvia's homecoming: almost everyone present still called her Sylvia Fields, and more than once through the evening Martha though that when Alexander Winthrop was mentioned it was rather as though he had been a guest among them at some time. They were much more solicitous about what had happened to the Fields estate than to Tamarack. Someone suddenly did inquire about Winthrop's art collection. "We decided to break it up," Sylvia said. "We've kept a few pieces." To which a gentleman replied, a seeming *non-sequitur* but not really, "A chip off the old block, you are, Sylvia."

It was Marcus's first time in the Bergner house since the old doctor's death. Virtually nothing in it had been changed or rearranged and Louise presided with the fussy concern of a curator who has been given a lifetime benefice. He found himself wondering if she were not acting out a fantasy, given this house to play with, a transportation backward into a South she had known only from books or some grandparent's tale: George would fit nicely, the combination businessman-politician-publisher whose intimate demands were minimal. And George, paunchier of belly than when Marcus had last seen him, and with his bald pate burnished brown, would take easily to the arrangement. He would come home to entertain, but not to be entertained, to oblige the forms by which he assumed society was best governed. It was a curiosity of logic in men like him that they supposed the forms strengthened by their own digressions, even as they thought their digressions a show of strength in themselves, not weakness. He observed, too, how much Nathan was at home here: part of the drawing room *décor*. He was in a way the liaison, the interlocutor between the undeceived and the self-deceived.

Louise gave her hand to Marcus every time they came together as though it were the first time that evening, and she would say, "It's so good to see you again," or "It was so good of you to come," so that Marcus wondered if she had not been put up to this over-extension of grace. And when she said, "You *are* looking well, Marcus," he responded:

"Why shouldn't I, feeling as well as I do?"

"But you did have a difficult time adjusting after the war?" She didn't wait for an answer. "Now, Nathan says, you're doing just beautiful."

"Nathan ought to know," Marcus said dryly.

She took him by the arm. "Come and meet my daughter. She's been dying to meet you and Martha. I want her to talk to Martha. She's a very talented painter, my Eleanor. I wish her father'd let her go to Paris. I'd just love her to meet Tony . . . but what mother wouldn't?" When last Marcus had seen the Bergner children, Eleanor had been a gawky twelve-year-old, her brother a thumbsucker at ten, both of whom their grandfather was about to put in boarding school. Louise presented a girl who was standing tiptoe to womanhood and Marcus was struck with two thoughts almost simultaneously: it was at such a moment in Martha's girlhood he had met her; and Eleanor Bergner now bore a very strong resemblance about the eyes and nose to her paternal grandfather.

"Eleanor," her mother said, "this is our dear Doctor Hogan."

"Not so dear," Marcus remarked slyly. "According to Doctor Reiss, not nearly dear enough." The girl smiled winningly and Marcus said, "Shall I take you to meet my wife?"

But Marcus fell to thinking about the old gentleman who had built this house in the style he had most admired, who had dominated the pale woman in the faded picture at the top of the stairs and who had hoped for a son who would stand up to him. He wondered how much of himself the old man might have seen in this slight but passionate-eyed girl and how it would have fitted into the theory of eugenics he had spent his life documenting. Marcus could remember the smell of kerosene in this house and the taste of ashes: it was like a tragi-comic nightmare, remembering the downstairs-upstairs search. And he wondered now if he had not had some intimation of what would happen to that manuscript before it had been too late. He had, he supposed, lacked something of courage himself that night. He had had in him a core of naïveté or weakness which allowed him to avert his mind lest it perceive evil and he be compelled to confront it. The only gesture he had been able to make in the end was a pious taunt on the comparability of book-burnings —after the fact. One avenges no one but oneself. He had gone forth from that night blaming George for something he could, pressing responsibility, assume not a little blame for himself.

"I know," Sylvia was saying, "there are good arguments for making use of Lakewood Hospital." Everyone favored her plans for a children's rehabilitation center. Nor had she heard once any demur on the grounds that most of the children would be foreign. Lakewood had a conscience commensurate to its pocketbook, and many people were anxious to subscribe. Lakewood Hospital, its facilities enlarged preparatory to and during war, was presently too large for the community. Marcus, however, was opposed to confining the Plan to one hospital, especially one as far out of the way as Lakewood. He agreed that the farm, as a sort of clearing house—for preparation and recovery—was fine. "But," Sylvia went on, "there is an overriding reason—for me—not to use it: Doctor Hogan does not think we should."

Marcus, hearing his name, came to attention. The people with Sylvia looking around and spotting him, seemed to be waiting.

Sylvia said, "Marcus, will you come and help me explain why we don't want to use Lakewood Hospital?"

He would, himself addressing these people, have preferred to put it less directly. But Sylvia was as forthright in speech as she was strong in will, and she was probably right to give no ground in the first place.

"For one thing," Marcus said, observing George's sharp attention (after all, he was a trustee of Lakewood and Nathan was on the staff), "Lakewood is a community hospital." He went on to explain the difficulties he foresaw in mixing the children, particularly those with language and cultural difficulties in addition to their deformities, with local appendectomies and tonsillectomies. A therapy center was one thing, but for the actual treatment, the child should be taken to the doctor, rather than ask the doctor to come to the child. "We shall want the best specialist available to us in each case."

"And you will decide who the best man is, Doctor Hogan?" George addressed him formally for the benefit of the people there who did not know him.

Nathan said instantly: "But who would be in a better position to know, George?"

Marcus got the curious feeling of being knocked down by the one and picked up by the other. He wondered if Reiss were trying to allay any possible suspicion that he, Reiss, might be envious. He doubted that Reiss was in fact. He might temporarily covet the prestige attendant on such a project, but he was too much the virtuoso to bind himself with administrative and consultative routine. That, Marcus thought a little wryly, better became him—since the war. He was not himself ever going to be the master surgeon he had once supposed. "Actually, George, the men will recommend themselves—bone specialists, neurosurgeons, their specializations make them known throughout the profession, don't you see?"

Bergner said: "Yes, I see. But it occurs to me—and there's the whole new wing of the Lakewood so that there wouldn't be such a mixture of breeds as you suggest—that a setup such as there is in some of the veterans' hospitals where a number of good doctors can come together at times—have an exchange of views—might be an advantage. Of course, I speak with the prejudice of having a hospital to sell."

Whatever his prejudice, George spoke with authority. Winthrop, far away and having been besieged by a zealous and idealistic wife, had devised an excellent system of check and balance to her scheme: he had insisted that George administer the finances of the Rehabilitation Plan, the money for which was to come from The Fields Foundation.

Sylvia said, "Marcus, most of these good people here tonight are going to be involved if I can help it. You must speak frankly."

Marcus opened his hands. "I have spoken frankly."

"Tell them why you consented to take on the job—aside from the fact that I wouldn't take no for an answer."

Marcus was embarrassed. He hedged a moment, glancing at Martha whose eyes held fast upon him. "I suppose a hurt child is the best friend one's conscience has . . ." He would have liked to have had those words back as soon as they were out. He rubbed the back of his neck and amended: "At least he's the best messenger you can get to call on somebody else's conscience . . ."

Sylvia took advantage of a murmur of amusement and cut in: "Doctor Hogan agreed to direct the Plan because we all felt that it was absolutely essential that no one use the hospital or its work as a vehicle for personal advancement. My husband—" Sylvia lifted her chin, a gesture of pride and defiance to all of Lakewood— "said that

Marcus Hogan was the only man he knew who would put this job above himself."

Marcus again rubbed the back of his neck and said quietly but audibly, "And God have mercy on his soul."

Those who heard him laughed and whatever tensions there seemed to have been in the room eased off. There had been no public announcement of his appointment or of the Plan itself, for that matter. It was still largely in Sylvia's mind. But the two children she had brought from Italy were introduced that night, and they were already under treatment. Nathan, leaving the party early, offered to drive them and their Italian governess back to Traders City.

Afterwards Martha commented on it. "You don't think Nathan's jealous, do you? He's terribly ambitious, and he loves publicity—he loves to read about himself in the paper . . ." Even as she groped for a way to put her own estimate of him, Martha was testing. She had never been able to quite know Marcus's feeling about Nathan.

"He wouldn't be right for the job and I think he knows it," Marcus said, but committed himself no further. They were about to get into the car. He looked up into the sky. The air was scented with chestnut blossoms and he suddenly remembered the girl from the concentration camp who had talked him out of his ten dollars.

Martha said: "Could we drive down to the lake for a few minutes?"

"Why not?"

On the way Marcus was several times at the point of speaking about Reiss, of trying to speak frankly. There had hung between him and Martha from the beginning a reluctance to talk about him —as they did about, say, Winthrop or Sylvia, George, even Martha's father—and it was because he was Jewish, Marcus thought. If Reiss had been patently a good man like Erich Mueller this would not have happened either. But in a way, their reluctance to talk about him had very little to do with Reiss: it was as though such conversation might discover in one of them something obscene. No, not quite that, but something damaging to the ideal each had of the other, the ideal each wished to be in the other's eyes; something a little comparable to an adolescent sex digression, long since suppressed, untold and untellable, but unforgotten. The time was coming—not for the tearing away of masks: neither of them was dishonest—but for the dropping of veils. And he knew it would be the more difficult for Martha: hers was the background of intolerance on which she still kept vigil—although he doubted she knew he was aware of it. But this in itself was almost as crippling as prejudice—to both of them.

If Reiss were not Jewish, then, it would have been easy to talk about him. But talking of him, would they know him any the better for it? He doubted it. Reiss was a chameleon. He took on the coloration and the virtue of the society he kept—except for one oddness: his distressing habit of making people acknowledge his Jewishness.

They drove down the steep road through the ravine and parked a few yards from the water's edge. Marcus turned off the car motor and lights. Along the crescent shore line to the south, some twenty miles away, the lights of Traders City glittered like a ridge of stars. The water rippled quietly and the white sands shifted, making the sound of a soft and constant sighing.

"I've been so lonely here," Martha said. "And so much in love."

"I've never been here alone and always in love here," Marcus said.

And they remembered the hurried nights out of which they had stolen a little time there before Martha's return to St. Cecilia's.

Presently Martha said: "We're not going to have any more children, are we?"

"It doesn't look like it, does it?"

She buried her face in his shoulder.

But he continued on the same level: "I don't see how we could improve on what we've done, do you?"

"No," she whispered, and straightened up and blew her nose.

On the way home Martha said, "You're happy about the Children's Plan, aren't you?"

"Oh, Lord, yes. I can't begin to tell you what that's done for me— from the moment I saw that child's face. Wait till you see what a good plastic surgeon will do for it."

"Sylvia knew how you'd feel."

"It was a very great moment," Marcus said humbly, and then, thinking aloud, "Something happens, you see. Medicine—surgery— was no longer enough for me after the war. Or maybe too much. There was a time when I thought I would never be able to go into the operating room again . . ."

"I know," Martha said. "I knew that day at the Muellers."

"That was almost the turning point. But I'm not politically capable like my father—or like Erich, God bless him. And God help him. I'm afraid he'll go down my father's road twenty years later. All their arts and sciences and professions won't get the bomb back into the box. But I understand them, I think. A liberal cannot live without faith in man: that's his creed. And the public forum is the only pulpit he's got. But I'm afraid I feel now that all creeds are vain. There is only vigilance—and kindness. Creeds make men blind."

He drove in silence for several miles. It was after midnight and the roads were almost empty.

"I would not say a surgeon doesn't need a heart—but this surgeon anyway needs to know more of his fellow men than their critical insides. As I started to say a while back, something happens. A man makes money and that becomes a measure even to himself. Reputations are built on fees and charities. And a man's reputation is the only guide his colleagues and their patients have to him. Fees and charities." Again he glanced at Martha and smiled. "I'm very grateful to Sylvia. She's given me a new leash on life."

Martha smiled. One thing about Annie: her malapropisms never changed but they were reliable helps in tying up the ends of emotion in the family.

"Of course," Marcus added, "ten years from now, if I live, it may be something else again. But for now, I know where I'm going." He reached across and took Martha's gloved hand and held it between them on the seat. "And I know who's going with me."

· 10

WITHIN a few days of the gathering at the Bergners' Sylvia found herself in a position that at one and the same time angered and bewildered her: the citizens of Lakewood had decided they wanted a Children's Rehabilitation Hospital within the village limits, in fact, to be associated with Lakewood Hospital. They were to a man, at least to a moneyed man, opposed to Marcus Hogan's proposal. In a way, Sylvia had herself to blame for the situation. Her own idea in the first place had been to found such a hospital, and she had confided this in her correspondence home, paving the way for what she had then supposed would be the village's coolness to the project. She had misjudged the psychology of her own people, failing to weigh against their nativism their compulsive charity. Too late, she could say one had only to look at their "Orphans of the Road" where any stray dog could live like a monarch's pug to realize the benefaction of which they were capable.

Their zeal was spontaneous. It could be traced to no other source than Sylvia's own original enthusiasm. The perceptible change to have taken place during her absence was their conscious pride in Lakewood Hospital, and she could assume that Nathan Reiss had something to do with that. He had become its first chief surgeon, and the hospital had achieved top classification from the Medical Association. Sylvia profoundly doubted, however, that he had gained the social stature in Lakewood to appreciably influence such a community.

She decided to visit an old family friend, Hurd Abington, by way of exploring through a source she was sure was not going to be overly sanguine of the immigrant doctor's contribution. Indeed, there were moments during her talk with Abington that she regretted having come to him: his continual reference to Reiss as "our pet Jew" made her flinch inwardly every time he said it. It was the more disconcerting because she had her own prejudicial association to fight where Reiss was concerned.

"But my dear girl," Abington explained of Reiss' progress, "once he was in, there's nothing surprising about it. Don't you see, he makes our local mediocrities look good. I dare say some of them may be all right, but that he is a first-rate surgeon is indisputable. Every man has his price, Sylvia, especially a Jew. His price was the title, chief surgeon. And the vote of the staff was unanimous." Her host chuckled. "Having voted it in their own interests, they are now convinced they did it out of tolerance. We have become a hotbed of tolerance. That, my dear girl, is democracy. For years the crown courts of Europe had their pet Jews as the power behind them. I shouldn't be surprised if history turns up one or two behind Hitler, would you?"

"Six million I believe," Sylvia said, her temper very nearly out of control.

"I think that figure is somewhat exaggerated," Abington murmured.

Sylvia held her tongue. To abandon it at that moment might have been to abandon Lakewood, the Children's Plan, everything. The admission of this fact brought her to the edge of panic—which was itself an antidote to temper. She felt like someone trying to manage both sides of a see-saw. The whole plan was hers, but now with very nearly the same suddenness in which she had conceived it, she could lose its control. The financing of the plan was to come through the

Fields Foundation into which, for taxation purposes, she and Winthrop had been putting their own surplus funds. Sylvia, from the time she had thought of the Children's Plan, had diverted to the Foundation monies she had been advised by her broker to place elsewhere. Except for Winthrop and herself, the trustees of the Fund were now residing in Lakewood. A two-thirds majority of them could overrule her! Sylvia made a bolt from the chair to where the French doors opened on one of the most famous gardens in the country. With the gesture of physical release she was able to turn back to the complacent old gentleman who watched her with an expression both benign and cynical.

"I thought I smelt delphinium," she said inanely.

"No. Not yet. Roses, I should think. I'm having the flower show here this year, did you know?"

"No," Sylvia said, and thought that another barrier was down when the Abington gardens were opened to the public. Abington, a childless widower, had made even more exquisite the famous formal gardens following his wife's death. Her ashes were buried in an urn from which center the floral beds radiated even as rays go out from the sun.

"Year after year, they've asked. I thought it was about time—since your Children's Plan is to be its beneficiary—through the Foundation, of course."

Nor had she known that. He talked a few minutes about the gardens, the incompetence of the younger gardeners. Then he said, almost offhandedly: "This Hogan fellow, he's something of a radical, isn't he?"

"That was his father," Sylvia said, and only a few seconds later did she realize that here might be actual issue in Lakewood. "Doctor Hogan was Albert Bergner's protégé, his successor, really."

"I shouldn't go so far as to say that," Abington said easily. He brushed his fine white hair back from his forehead as though it were a cobweb. "If he has a successor, I should say it was our friend."

"Reiss?"

Abington nodded. "A touch of conscience, I shouldn't wonder. It was old Doctor Albert who put Reiss into Lakewood, you know. I should have thought it would have been the place for . . . your man if he thought so highly of him."

Sylvia came very close to saying that Marcus might not have wanted Lakewood, which she supposed could very well have been the truth. The community was not for him surely. But to have said it at that moment would have further compromised Marcus whom she now suspected to have been rather thoroughly done over already. She harked back to a phrase Abington had used: "A touch of conscience, did you say, Hurd?"

Abington shrugged. "Doctor Albert, as I recall hearing it, had some peculiar notions about a superior race of men. I suppose you're too young to remember the discourses he used to give us at the drop of a hat."

"I remember them. He used to give mother and me first refusal."

Abington laughed. "I'd forgotten how fond he was of Alicia."

"I don't remember anything anti-Semitic in them," Sylvia said. "They were just bloody boring."

"That's how I felt myself. But some of our more sensitive people took exception to them. There was talk, Sylvia, talk. The University made him confine himself to the surgeon's manual—which was remarkable in its way, considering their permissiveness in other cases." This was of course a snide reference to the Jonathan Hogan affair. Abington looked at her almost mournfully. "He was always going to have them published, if you remember. But in the end, he didn't do it, did he? I shouldn't be surprised to learn that young Hogan had some influence there, would you?"

"There's one way to find out," Sylvia said. "I shall ask him."

Abington changed his position in the chair. He might have been changing tack. "It's not a matter of genuine relevance at this point, is it? George seems to feel it was just as well that they weren't published. The old fellow was getting a bit dotty on it, as the English say. Still, it occurred to some of us that in the end, young Hogan might have out-smarted himself." He looked at her. "I understand he has a distinguished war record?"

"Does that surprise you, Hurd?"

"Frankly, yes. But I keep forgetting, the Russians were on our side then."

"Jesus Christ in the morning, Hurd! Marcus Hogan is no more a Communist than you are."

He leaned across the small Chinese lacquer table between them and patted her hand. "If you say so, Sylvia. If you say so."

Sylvia was at a loss to know where to turn next in the matter. She did not suppose George Bergner would dare to oppose her openly.

After all, she was co-publisher of the *Star* on which his fine new prestige was founded. And he did not need to oppose her: the whole of Lakewood was doing the job for him. She talked with Reiss: he had nothing but praise for Marcus although he admitted disappointment that the Rehabilitation Plan was to be taken away from Lakewood Hospital. He sounded sincere.

"Nathan, the Plan has never been *in* the Lakewood Hospital."

"Yes, of course. And I agree with you, Sylvia, its director must have entire freedom in determining its requirements. I have come round myself, by the way, to Marcus's view: I am disappointed, but I agree. It is more practical to take the children to the doctors than to bring the doctors to the children. Much more. After all, there is a limit to what a man can do in his own field even."

"Have you said this in Lakewood, Nathan—that you agree with Marcus and me?"

Reiss smiled ruefully. "My dear Sylvia, when I say it they do not believe me. It is incredible, but they do not believe me. They simply think I am being excessively loyal to my associate."

Sylvia knew enough of the nature of people to realize that the more she probed the opposition, the deeper would grow its roots. She did not want to confide the situation to Marcus: it would hurt him personally, and it might even hurt his effectiveness. Distrust can get at a sensitive man in subtle ways. She settled herself, the two Italian children and Maria in at the farm, giving herself up entirely to that chore. She intended to forestall any precipitate action, which she knew very well to be her tendency.

In the end, weighing as much as she knew, Sylvia concluded that George Bergner had at very least contributed to the undermining of Marcus. She doubted that the majority of Lakewood knew his animosity to be underlying their own altruistic fervor on behalf of Lakewood Hospital. She had not thought George capable of going underground.

Sylvia rode horseback with characteristic abandon in the days of dilemma that followed, but both she and the horses were older. Nor was her mind made any more supple for the cruel stiffness in her body. Yet she rode again and again, and rode out the soreness. She also succeeded in bringing a horse that had not been properly exercised into condition, and the morning she realized what had happened to her and her mount, she decided to take somewhat the same course in the matter of the Children's Rehabilitation Plan. She made up her mind to go full tilt ahead as though there were no opposition and thus to force it into the open.

She arranged a meeting for the following afternoon among George Bergner, Marcus and herself. It was Marcus's suggestion that they meet in his office. It seemed to Sylvia as good a place as any: she wanted Marcus to have what advantage might come of being on home grounds as it were. The day was a Friday and Fridays, ordinarily, Reiss spent at Lakewood. In a way Sylvia would have liked to have had him present so that if matters did come to a showdown, he would have to make his own position clear. She had every intention of quoting him to George in his agreement with Marcus. As it turned out, the question of his being present was all but taken out of her hands. Reiss was in his office when she arrived, and George remarked with perhaps studied casualness: "I've asked Nathan to sit in on the meeting. I assume it's all right with you?"

Both she and Marcus agreed without so much as an exchange of glances.

George added: "I've had the benefit of his advice on the Foundation affairs since Alex has been away." Bergner was Winthrop's proxy on the Foundation Board. "I'm only one vote out of twelve, but at that it's probably a better informed vote than most of them."

Sylvia could think of nothing to say that would not smack of sarcasm, but she knew now that Bergner was going to force the issue of the Foundation: it was among its trustees that he had done his mischief, and thoroughly enough to give him self-confidence. So be it. She looked about the office and commented on its *décor*. Very modern. This was her first visit since the move to the top floor.

"Nothing modern about the service," George complained. "I had to wait ten minutes for an elevator."

Reiss brought a bottle of Scotch, a siphon bottle and some ice.

Outside the wind blew forlornly at the windows. It was a sound Sylvia supposed one grew used to. They were sitting in the waiting room, their chairs drawn in a circle, but it occurred to her that such a mournful sound as the wind made here must be distressing to a patient waiting consultation with a surgeon. One could see only sky through the windows. She watched the thunderheads gathering over the lake. Nearer My God to Thee: that's what they needed up here, an organ playing "Nearer My God to Thee." She laughed at herself.

302

Marcus said: "So?"

"You'd be surprised," she said.

Miss Kohler came to the door. "I'll stay late if you'd like me to take notes of the meeting," she said.

Reiss looked to Sylvia. "I don't think it's necessary, thank you."

"Then good night, all."

"Better put the phone on service so we won't be disturbed," Marcus said.

"I've already done that, doctor," Miss Kohler said a little reproachfully.

When she was gone, Sylvia said: "She must be appallingly efficient."

"Like a second lieutenant," Marcus said.

Sylvia took a cigaret from her purse and tapped it. Marcus lighted it for her and then lit one of his own. Reiss passed the drinks.

George lifted his glass: "Well, to what we're here for," he said by way of a toast and sipped the whisky. Then he said: "I wonder if we shouldn't have asked the Director of the Foundation to come this afternoon? I'd meant to mention it, but I've been so busy it slipped my mind."

"It will be time enough," Sylvia said, "when we have our plan ready to put before them."

"They like to be in on the beginning of things. Sometimes it makes it easier later on."

Sylvia looked at him as directly as it was possible. As soon as their eyes met, his slipped away. "I don't expect to have trouble with the Foundation, George. I have put almost a million dollars into it myself in the last two years."

George looked pained. The discussion of money always offended him, like the mention of an infirmity. He said: "You should the more readily agree then in the Foundation's first principle: resistance to undue influence on the part of its benefactors."

Sylvia was speechless.

"Let's talk for a moment about the children, may we?" Marcus said, seeking to divert what he supposed was merely a wrangle over titles of authority: he knew how much they meant to Bergner, and for his own part, he did not mind catering to the man in that regard if it facilitated getting the Plan under way. If Winthrop wanted George to administer its finances, he should be given a title and told to go to work. He thought Sylvia was being unduly stiff-necked.

"Before settling on the director's salary?" George said.

Marcus smiled and put out his cigaret. "Good Lord, yes. The last person people think of paying is the doctor, especially those who can afford to. I've had a talk with Zacharis—the plastic man, you know? He's easily the best in this part of the country, wouldn't you say, Nathan?"

"Very fine."

"He's seen Angelina twice now—ran a series of pictures. It will take a year at least, but he's confident her face can be brought completely into balance."

George, studying the ice cubes within his glass, said nothing. He might not even have heard him. Sylvia and Reiss both commented.

Marcus went on, trying the while to fathom George's indifference. "He's an interesting man, Zacharis. He's about to take off for a week in Japan. He wants to see some of the Hiroshima victims. There's divergent opinion on whether surgery will help—whether it will work in cases of radium burns. But he wants to see for himself."

George lifted his eyes from the glass. "A friend of Mueller's?"

Marcus was a moment making the association. Sylvia made it at once: Mueller's crusade against further development of the atomic bomb.

"I never thought to ask him," Marcus said, an intended irony.

"It may prove to have been a relevant question," George said.

It was Sylvia who digressed this time. She would have liked to take issue but not just then. "Marcus, I've decided we must have a national board of advisers for The Plan, a few men like Zacharis, and Jerome Feinberg, perhaps." She named the latter, president of the Medical Association, because it was the name coming into her mind at the moment, her subconscious counter-balance to Bergner's reaction to Zacharis. She knew nothing herself about Zacharis; nor had she intention of presuming to evaluate men in medicine. But having said what she had, she exposed her position to both Marcus and Bergner.

A little smile was playing at the corners of George's mouth.

Marcus said: "I see." He lit another cigaret. His opinion of Feinberg, Sylvia knew, was not high. "Sylvia, to whom are we being made acceptable, may I ask?"

Sylvia got up and crushed out the cigaret which had burned down to her fingers. "No one, Marcus. As of right now: no one. My mind is made up. If the Fields Foundation will not support the Children's

Rehabilitation Plan as we—you, Marcus Hogan, and I,—conceive its functioning, we shall go it alone."

Marcus sat blinking his eyes rapidly, trying to fathom the opposition.

George said: "Don't you think Alex ought to be consulted?"

Sylvia ignored him. "And if we have to do it, I shall go into the courts and seek to break the trust fund by which the Foundation was set up."

George smiled. "Sylvia, you are a barnburner. You are, you know."

Sylvia's fury was beyond the curb of logic. "God damn you, George, don't patronize me. Let's dig the rat out of the barn and have a look at it."

"All right," George said. "Let's do that." He carefully pushed aside a stack of magazines and put his glass down on the table. "Your mother set up the Fields Foundation in the interests of medical research . . ."

Sylvia interrupted him: "The Fields Foundation is not really at issue here, and do not presume to tell me its function."

Marcus said: "Sylvia, what is at issue? Me?"

Reiss said with deliberate calm: "Perhaps because I am not concerned I may presume to explain? May I try, Sylvia?" She said nothing and he went on: "You see, Marcus, a great number of people in Lakewood do want the Children's Plan as Sylvia herself originally proposed it, an actual hospital, you know? I have put myself on record as favoring your plan so I am above or perhaps below the battle. I do not matter. That is all I am trying to say . . ."

"Forgive me, Nathan," Sylvia said, "but you, too, are talking about what has come to the top, not what's at the bottom of it."

Reiss shrugged, and George spread his hands. He said: "I must say I'm at a loss myself to see what you're getting at, Sylvia."

"Are you telling me, George, that you are unaware of what I can only call a smear campaign in Lakewood against Marcus?" It had to come, she thought. Marcus himself would have forced it if she had not.

George said: "That's a good old Communist phrase, smear campaign, isn't it?"

"If it's a Communist phrase, which I doubt, it is also a Fascist technique."

The color rose to George's face and Sylvia knew she had touched something vulnerable. It did a great deal to restore her own equa bility. She was able to contemplate point by point her conversation with Hurd Abington.

"Marcus," she said, "do you remember Doctor Albert's papers that he was always working on—his doctorate or whatever you'd call it—on a superior line of human beings?"

"I remember it," Marcus said evenly. "I was in it. He did a search of my mother's family."

"Did you collaborate with him?"

"I don't think he wanted a collaborator. He wanted an audience." Marcus looked at George.

"Did you persuade him not to publish it?" Sylvia said, following Abington's train of remarks.

"I was not given that prerogative," Marcus said quietly.

There followed a few seconds of silence and George gazed up at Sylvia where she stood looking from one to the other of them. He said: "I suppose you're wondering what became of father's papers? Tell her, Marcus."

Marcus hesitated but an instant. "I don't see that it matters now."

But George said: "Marcus burned them the night of my father's death, I presume at Father's request."

Marcus turned very pale and his hand trembled so violently as he tried to set his glass on the table that the glass upset and tumbled to the floor. He caught hold of the arms of the chair and pushed himself up. "I'm not going to be able to work with this man, Sylvia. I'm sorry, but I'm not." He had been clenching and unclenching his fists. He looked at his hands, the palms of them, and then rubbed them together. He was quite overwrought. "I don't even seem to be able to stay in the same room with him," he said, and made his way to the door, bumping first into a chair, and then a typewriter table which he pushed violently, blindly out of his way. He went the length of the office without stopping, and out.

Reiss leaped up from where he had sat, all but mesmerized. All of them had become momentarily paralyzed. Reiss said, "Excuse me," and ran after Marcus, calling out his name.

"Well, George," Sylvia said, "I feel the way Marcus does."

"For God's sake, Sylvia, can't you see that the man's unstable? He should be in a rehabilitation hospital himself."

"That, too," Sylvia said with bitter calm.

"I don't know what you're accusing me of, but I think Alex ought

to be apprised of the whole situation. I work for him, you know.
don't want a damn thing out of your Children's Plan . . ."

George stopped. There was a noise or a shout from the hall beyon
the office. Sylvia started running, and Bergner lumbered after her
She reached the office door to hear Reiss shout again and again fo
help. He and Marcus seemed to be scuffling at the elevator gate
Marcus half in, half out. Other people were running down the hal
from other offices. Reiss thrust his hand through the wire cage, tryin
to reach the mechanism. But Sylvia saw Marcus teeter backwards a
the doors began to close. The elevator within plunged down. Reis
screamed, his hand caught in the gate. The gate, its mechanism in
terrupted, snapped open, releasing his hand. But Marcus, with muc
the pendulum-like motion of a drunk man, lurched forward and hur
tled silently down the shaft, twenty-one floors to his death.

Reiss was doubled up, holding his hand between his arm and hi
breast, the blood from it streaming down all the way to the tops o
white shoes. He lay down on the floor and writhed with the pain.

PART
FOUR

Interlude

· 1

THE rain beat noisily upon the roof. It was the harsh rain of September after which the birds go south and nothing in the garden grows any more. Because it allowed no other sound to reach her ears it was to Martha the best of sounds. She would not hear the chiming of the tower clock, the cars that passed without stopping, or stopping when she would have sped them on; she would not hear the clatter Annie made in the kitchen by the sudden crescendos in which she would know her to be venting in her own loud way her Irish grief. In such deluged silence one could stand before the easel making a mirror of one's mind on canvas. One could put a bold dark stroke in space—and see it there forever.

She put down brush and palette and went to the window, wiping her hands in a rag. On a day like this Tad, with Sylvia in the country, would be having a story before the fire or playing Chinese checkers. Looking down at the garden she thought that some of the green tomatoes should be brought indoors to ripen. It was a good thing to think about: green tomatoes ripening, and grapes that needed to be picked before the first frost. The grapes grew well planted along an arbor where the tool shed once had stood. Something always grew even in the soil of graves: that much she could believe. The rain coursed down the roof, bubbling over the drainpipe at the joint beneath the eaves where the shoot was blocked by bits and pieces which might once have been a bird's nest. "My heart is like a singing bird whose nest is in a watered shoot . . ." She closed out the poem from her mind knowing instantly where the lines would take her. But even as she turned back to the easel another line slipped into her consciousness to take her thence anyway: "I don't care where the water goes if it doesn't get in the wine."

One must paint and paint and paint and think of oneself as one, thus making two of one, company for each other and in that way neither of them cries. When next she went to the window, she saw the black umbrella bobbing along the far side of the hedge. From the gait of its carrier she knew her to be Annie, and this being Saturday afternoon, she would be on her way to confession. Marcus had

309

come to believe that all creeds were vain, and so now did she, un-utterably vain. Which did but speed Annie the more often to tattle into the ear of God.

Secure in being alone in the house, Martha went downstairs to make herself a cup of tea. Tea and toast: a sane and salutary ritual. A note from Annie was propped against the toaster in the center of the kitchen table. "I'll be stopping for tea with your father's cousin," the note said in part. Her father's cousin was also Annie's cousin, and once or twice less removed, but Annie always spoke of her as "your father's cousin"—whether to give herself station or Martha "a rub" Martha did not know. There were certain defects Annie expected to find in all natures, and if they did not show up outright, Annie assumed they were there all the same.

The kettle was about to boil when the front doorbell rang. It rang twice more before Martha moved from the kitchen. She went because there was in the ringing the suggestion of someone who would not—possibly who could not—go away. It was an impulse of mercy that sent her to a door she often left unanswered.

Nathan Reiss stood on the lower step, the rain falling between them like a scrim. She drew back and held the door open to him: he stepped into the hallway on her wordless invitation.

"I am alone," he said. "Do you mind that I have come?"

She did not know whether she minded or not. The sense of urgency she had supposed in the ringing of the bell did not altogether abate. "I am making tea," she said. "Better bring your coat into the kitchen where it will dry."

He needed to take a silk scarf from his bandaged hand before he could remove his coat. The last time she had seen him he had been wearing a cotton glove so that she supposed he had recently had another operation.

"Is it painful, Nathan?"

"Only when I am impatient—which is most of the time. They have accomplished nothing. In three months you would expect some change, wouldn't you?"

"Three months is a long time," she said. She gave him a fresh towel with which he wiped the rain from his face. She arranged the tea tray on the cart. "We'll have it in the library. Can you manage the fire there? Annie may have already set it."

He smiled, and seeing the smile, she was glad that he had come. "I can do almost anything," he said, "except the thing I want to do most."

"It will take time," she said, and remembered saying the same banal phrase to Marcus of his condition after the war. She searched the pantry for something sweet to serve with the tea. Without Tad home, Annie provided a scant assortment. She returned from the pantry to find him reading Annie's note where it lay on the table.

"Forgive me," he said, looking up. "I did that automatically. I was not thinking about what I was doing."

"Annie's notes are scarcely private. I've been trying to figure out why she always tells me that she's visiting my father's cousin when it's her cousin also, and one I don't think my father ever actually met. Perhaps that's it," Martha answered herself.

Reiss went on into the library and when Martha came with the tea tray, the fire was already glowing.

"Do you have a very strong family feeling?" Reiss inquired.

"About Tad I suppose I do," Martha said.

"I mean about your parents, your own origins."

"No. When I was a child I often thought I must be an orphan. Most children think that sometimes, I understand, but I never really got over it. I came in time to understand it."

"Your mother I remember to be a beautiful woman, but with a beauty different from yours."

"Nonetheless, I am reasonably sure she is my mother," Martha said in sly jest.

But Reiss was serious: "No one could doubt it, comparing wit as well as comeliness."

"That's a nice word, comeliness," Martha said. "One does not hear it often."

"I remember liking the sound of it myself and then I found it in the dictionary." He explained himself with a sort of innocent candor she found beguiling.

Martha tried the tea for strength. As the fire flared up, the sluice of rain occasionally hissed in the chimney. She thought: the harshness of the letter "s" had all but disappeared from Nathan's speech.

"Something brought me here this afternoon," Reiss said. "You have never asked me, but I felt that I must come even if I must ask myself."

"I have asked no one, and I'm not always grateful to those who come anyway. But I am glad to see you, Nathan."

"It is enough. More in my present condition I could not endure. One must not be too kind to the infirm. Which is what you have just said to me, isn't it?"

"In a way, I suppose it is."

"One comes to understand," he said. "I have been terribly spoiled —for an orphan."

She brought his tea to him and set it on the low table before the fire. He was looking at the painting above the mantel. "Is that yours, Martha?"

"Yes."

He said nothing except a murmured thanks for the tea.

"You've seen worse, haven't you?" she said, amused at his silence.

"Much worse," he said quickly. "And the pictures I have liked better were probably much worse also."

Martha laughed. She brought her own tea and sat beside him.

"The Baroness tried very hard to give me a proper education, but always I have had the one-track mind, to be a surgeon."

"What do they say of your hand, Nathan?"

"Maybe. That is the most they will say: maybe." He looked at her. "Which is better than never, isn't it?"

Martha touched her fingers to the plate of confection on the table, moving it a little toward him. "These cookies have Tad to recommend them," she said. "But one's taste must run to raisins to like them."

He caught her hand where it fell on the couch as she leaned back and drew it gently the half-distance between them. "I hurt you, Martha, because I would heal you. Sometimes that is the way."

Martha did not withdraw her hand from his. They sat thusly, mute, for a long time, the tea growing cold on the table before them, and the fire brighter in the grate.

"Oh, Nathan, I am desolate," she said at last. "I often wish for death and I think of my father and try to remind myself that I am his daughter."

"You are also your son's mother."

"Yes. I think of that even more often."

"It is not good to be alone when one is hurt—and useless."

She glanced at him, her eyes soft with sympathy.

"That is even worse," he said, "to see you look at me like that."

Suddenly the tears rose to Martha's eyes—pity for him, for herself, God might know. She did not.

"I have made you cry," he said. "Perhaps I should have tried to make you laugh."

She shook her head.

He lifted her hand and turning it palm upward, put it to his lips. She allowed her fingers to caress his face.

Again their hands rested, folded between them.

"The tea will be cold," she said, but leaned her head back on the sofa and closed her eyes.

"We are alive, Martha," he said, his mouth close to her ear. "Can you feel it?"

"Yes."

"Alive," he whispered and kissed her mouth.

· 2

EVERY night after supper Sylvia and Tad were in the habit of waiting for Martha's phone call. Sylvia tended to worry if it came late. She had tried to persuade her to come more often than she did or to stay on for a time entirely. Tad loved the farm, and it was much better for him than the house on Oak Street, Martha agreed. But she could not bring herself to leave the house. She had not slept a night away from it since Marcus's death. That night when the call had not come by seven-thirty Sylvia called Traders City. It was Annie who answered the phone. She had got home from her cousin's to find a note saying that Martha would be away for the week-end. She had assumed Miss Martha was in the country with them, the very thing she had prayed for that afternoon.

"She'll be wanting to surprise us," Sylvia said. "Let's not spoil it. Thank you, Annie."

She spoke to reassure both Annie and Tad who was within hearing. Hanging up the phone, she said to the child: "Go upstairs to Maria. I'll come up as soon as I hear from your mother."

"Surprise?" Tad said.

"Maybe," Sylvia said, putting on an air of conspiracy.

But alone she began to pace up and down the long, low room, pausing now and then to listen to the sounds from upstairs: Francesco's noisy thump across the floor. He was almost accustomed to his new leg. It no longer pained him to wear it and he had put away his crutches. He would be taking them home soon, a gift to a child who needed them still, but a gift with a legend: he would be the proudest boy on Via del Duomo.

Outdoors the rain had stopped, but the wind was coming up, a sound Sylvia could not abide.

At ten minutes to eight the phone rang. It was Western Union. Sylvia picked up a pencil but she did not write the message. After the first four words she felt a sickness creeping over her that made her very nearly faint.

NATHAN AND I MARRIED AT CROWN PEAK. KISS TAD FOR ME AND TELL HIM WE SHALL COME TOMORROW. WISH US WELL DEAR SYLVIA. MARTHA.

A few minutes later Sylvia went upstairs to where Tad was waiting. He had heard the phone ring, but all the same he waited to be called.

"Your mother is coming tomorrow, Tad—she and your Uncle Nathan."

The boy looked puzzled. To save her soul Sylvia could think of nothing more to say to him. But Tad said: "It's too cold to go swimming, isn't it?"

Swimming: such was his association with Nathan Reiss. She wished to Almighty God hers was as simple.

· 3

SYLVIA and Maria returned the children to Naples in time for Christmas. In another year, Angelina would return to America for further surgery, but her face was much improved. Francesco was home to stay —until he was old enough to emigrate to the United States. Winthrop remarked, when Sylvia told him of the boy's intentions: "He'd better put in now for his quota number."

Winthrop and Sylvia spent the holiday together in Rome. The first snow of winter was falling the day Sylvia arrived, great heavy flakes that sank upon the ground and dissolved immediately into slush. They were glad to stay within the comfort of their hotel suite. Winthrop was winding up his work with the Commission, but, as he finally got round to telling her after probing several ways to the subject unsuccessfully, he had been asked by the State Department to do a short tour of duty in Greece.

"My God," Sylvia said. "It'll be China next."

"I'm afraid it won't be China for any of us for a long time."

"You don't want to come home, do you, Alex?"

"I think I've got a more important job to do over here just now."

"One you don't have to manufacture for yourself?"

Winthrop brushed the hair back from his forehead. "My dear, it's a wonder you ever got a husband at all—much less one like me."

"I've manufactured too many jobs for myself," Sylvia said, "not to know the symptoms. The curse of being rich is too much choice and no necessity."

"It's a pity you weren't born poor," Winthrop teased.

"I've often thought that myself," she said.

They sat in a newly decorated room, furnished in modern style, very un-Romanish, Sylvia said. Even the glasses sent up with the ice for their drinks were grotesquely modern. Sylvia got up and began to rearrange the tinsel on the artificial Christmas tree that stood in the center of the teakwood table.

"I don't know why I got that damned thing," Winthrop said. "I don't like them. Superstitious probably. I've had one every year since I've been over here."

Sylvia turned to him. "Alex, I need your help. I've lost heart in the Children's Plan since Marcus's death. But it's even more imperative now that I go on with it."

"Imperative for whom?"

"You're right," she said. "In human decency Reiss must have the job."

"That was a shocker, wasn't it—their marriage so soon?"

"I've gotten over that," Sylvia said. "Martha had to get out of that house. Maybe it was the only way."

"You don't think she's in love with him?"

"I don't know, Alex. It seemed to me an act of violence on her part, marrying him. But I can't tell. She's making a good show of being normal—whatever that is. I suppose if your will is strong enough you can do anything."

"Why shouldn't Reiss have the job?" he said after a moment.

"The matter of the hospital is still unresolved. I simply cannot, I do not want to cope with George Bergner, Alex." Sylvia poured herself another drink and returned to the chair. When she reached for a cigaret her husband got up and lit it for her.

Winthrop said: "I think we'd better go over the whole affair from the beginning. Whether you know it or not, Sylvia, Doctor Albert was a cruel father. I'm not defending George, but I can understand his resentment of Marcus."

Sylvia threw up her hands. "I don't care what the reason, I don't care if a psychiatrist turns him into St. Francis tomorrow, I will not work with George Bergner."

"And Nathan Reiss?"

"I can manage that, Alex."

"I seem to remember you being all for my recommending Reiss to Marcus—before the war. Remember the night Tad was born?"

"I remember."

"If you have objections to him now, we ought to settle them, Sylvia. It will be difficult later."

"I have none."

"When the best man is dead, my dear, he is no longer the best man."

Sylvia crushed out her cigaret. "Why? Why did it happen?" She bit her lip, grimacing against tears.

"There's no why. Good men die young sometimes. Old age doesn't make a long life either. I think of that myself, more and more. You and I aren't young ourselves. But we've got to make do." He stroked her hand. Sylvia caught his and held it while he went on:

"I've given a good deal of thought to the matter of the hospital myself. I've had quite a correspondence on it . . . from the Foundation people and a few other sources. The University is interested in it, too . . . I understand Reiss has started teaching, by the way."

"He has to earn a living."

"Sylvia, try and think about what I'm going to say—dispassionately. Isn't it possible Marcus was wrong about it? Now think for a moment, dear. Marcus was one of those rare birds who didn't want fame, prestige. I shouldn't be surprised if he was afraid of it, afraid it would get in the way of his being a good doctor. But if he had lived, you would have had to move very slowly with the plan—a few children at a time. The kids you want to help need it now, don't they? The sooner the better, and as many as you can manage? I was in Athens last week, Sylvia. It's worse than Naples. And their souls are bitter. They fought the war against Italy, a war they didn't choose, which Italy did. When I saw those poor wretched kids I thought to myself: Christ in the mountains, what is she waiting for?"

Sylvia thought carefully of all he had said. Finally she asked: "Alex, why haven't you said this to me before?"

"Because for the first time today you said to me: Alex, I need your help."

"I'm a great do-it-yourself type, amn't I?" she said after a moment.

Winthrop smiled. "You have other lovable qualities, however. And I've missed you like the very devil."

"I shall spend some time with you in Greece. If you want me to," she added quickly.

Winthrop drained his glass and got up. "Shall we burn that damned tinsel tree and go out and see if we can find ourselves the real thing? The pines of Rome after all."

"Alex, I'm going to say something sentimental. I don't care, I'm going to say it anyway—you're the real thing." She laughed, embarrassed. "Shall we get drunk? I haven't been drunk in years."

Winthrop said: "I've got a better idea."

·4

SYLVIA double-parked the station wagon outside the apartment building and gave three short beeps with the horn. But Martha was already at the window, having watched for almost an hour. She leaned out and waved. Tad, on the street, shouted up to her. Sylvia got out her side of the car. "How does he look?"

"Marvelous. Put the car in our garage . . ."

"I can't stop," Sylvia said. "Alex's plane is due at six."

She helped Tad upstairs with his luggage. "Here he is, safe, sound and sassy, and at least six inches taller."

"At least," Martha said. He came up to her waist. She gave him a hug and kissed his forehead. There was always an hour of shyness between them when he came home from the farm at the end of summer. He saw Nathan once or twice a week, and Martha several times over the two months, but coming home was not the same as their visiting him.

Annie came pounding down the hall from the kitchen, the floor creaking beneath her. "Where's my boy?" And reaching him, she cried in a great spiraling voice: "Oh, Lord, will you look at the length of him! He's going to be taller than his father. Didn't you feed him at all, Mrs. Winthrop?" She persuaded Tad to the kitchen.

And thus would begin the long winter ceremony of trying to fatten him even as in other days, Annie had devoted herself to putting flesh on one after another of the people she called her own.

Sylvia said: "I must go. Alex will be absolutely beside himself. He's bringing four of the Greek children, and you know how he is about red tape. To say nothing of children. I'm kind of frightened, Martha, his coming home after all this time. I don't want him to be restless. And I know he's going to be. So many things have changed. It's been seven years, do you know that?"

"Stop worrying," Martha said. "With the four children he won't see anything until you've got him home."

"It's home I'm worried about. Can you see Alex living on the farm? Tell me the truth."

"Yes. Part of the time. And you've still got the flat in town."

"I hope so. I mean I hope you're right."

"Dinner here next Saturday," Martha reminded her.

Tell me the truth, Martha thought when Sylvia was gone. Tell the truth and shame the devil: one of Annie's precepts. She went to the living room window and watched Sylvia drive away. She could see her only as far as the curve onto Lake Shore Drive. There would be a lovely sunset, its first traces to be seen reflected in the clouds over the lake. She drew the drapes and lit the lamps over the paintings. She did not very much like Nathan's special lighting effects. But they were dramatic.

By the time he had finished his supper, Tad was at ease with her again. His head was full of things to tell and he needed to be prodded into eating. He was not especially interested in going back to school. At this point he wanted to be a veterinarian which he seemed to think was learned entirely from animals. He came home knowing a great many things about pigs and chickens and cows and horses, that pigs were born with heads nearly as big as their bodies, that cows had two stomachs, tongues like sandpaper and no upper teeth at all. He followed Martha around until bedtime telling her the purposes of such anatomical arrangements. Annie refused to listen to them. She approved fantasy entirely, but physiology not at all.

Martha had to dress for the theater after an early dinner. She and

Nathan were going to a benefit, and since Nathan was one of the sponsors, it was not to be got out of. Nor did she want to. She was determined not to be over-protective of the child who did not want or need an excess of protection. All he really needed, she thought, hurrying along to his room with almost a half-hour before she would have to leave, was an audience.

His eyes were very blue, especially in contrast to the summer tan of his face. More and more he came to resemble Marcus. But his smile was sudden in the way of her own, and his teeth were coming in quite straight.

"Now," Martha said, sitting at the bottom of the bed he had not yet got into, "tell me the most important thing that happened to you this summer."

"The thing I remember best," Tad said instantly, "was the horse falling into the well." He climbed onto the bed and sat, Indian-style, his legs crossed in front of him. "Are you sure you want to hear about it?"

"Of course," Martha said, but she was by no means sure.

"Well, there's this old abandoned well, see, where the barn used to be before it burned down. That was years and years ago. There isn't any water in it any more and it's supposed to be all covered up. But the kids were playing there. They make believe it's a castle dungeon and they got some of the boards loose. Well, the horses get put down in that field to pasture every night, and you see, old Maudie's blind. She could work just as good as King, because when they got the harness on, he could lead her. And she knew the farm better than even Mr. Walker. But Mr. Walker says she must have got mixed up, or maybe a horsefly stung her. Anyway, she must've run that way and she crashed right through the boards and fell way down in. She made a terrible noise then, crying like she was hurt. Mr. Walker ran down and saw what happened and then he got the tractor out and Aunt Sylvia drove her car across the field so the lights would shine, you know? Aunt Sylvia didn't even know I was there. Then the hired man, Al, came. Al was drunk and he couldn't do anything right and Mr. Walker fired him. Only later he let him come back to work. Mrs. Walker ran all the way up to the house to call Doc Bailey, and he wasn't home. So they fixed a great big pulley. And Mr. Walker, you see, was talking down to Maudie all this time, soothing her: 'It's all right, Maudie. I'm going to get you out, Maudie . . .' And Maudie would just go, 'Whaa-aanh.' " He imitated a plaintive whinney.

Martha set her will, her very soul, to hear the story out. Tad, his eyes shining, leaned across suddenly and with his forefinger traced the vein on her forehead from the hairline to where it disappeared at the bridge of her nose. And even as he did it a look of knowing came into his eyes. He had been told that his father had died in an accident and that his Uncle Nathan had tried to save him, that Nathan had hurt the hand on which he now constantly wore a glove. The row of gray gloves hanging on the wash line every week was a constant fascination to him. But what he had known only vaguely, or without understanding, took on meaning at that moment. Martha saw it happening.

He asked, "Mother, how did papa get killed?"

"You know that." Martha tried to keep her voice natural. "In an accident."

"Like Maudie?"

"In a way, I suppose."

For just a few seconds the child thought about it. He asked, "But Uncle Nathan didn't have to shoot him, did he?"

"Of course not!" But Martha's voice cracked. She managed, "Is that what happened to poor Maudie?"

Tad nodded in the affirmative, but plainly his mind had turned to some private contemplation, and when Nathan came a few minutes later, Tad said, "Go away, Nathan."

"*Uncle* Nathan," Reiss corrected. "I shall go away if you wish it. It is almost time for us to leave, Martha. Good night, Tad." He turned and started out of the room, stiffly formal.

Martha said, "That is wicked, Tad."

"Do not make an issue of it," Nathan said, and going out, closed the door.

Martha and the boy faced each other silently, Tad's eyes brooding, his mouth a little puckered as though he were fighting back tears. It occurred to his mother then that he might just be trying to fetch them. She had spent too many years of her own childhood disliking a man for a reason she could not explain, not to sense the danger of this moment, not to know how mercilessly a child uses the emotions of an adult to his own ends. She thought about telling him that he had learned a very adult lesson that summer, how all living things must die. But what a start his imagination could take from that. And what answer could she give to such questions as: why? when?

She laid her hand on his pajamaed knee. "What are you thinking about?"

"Do you love Uncle Nathan?"

Uncle Nathan. The question was not guileless, Martha thought.

"Differently from the way I loved your father—from the way I love you."

He did not press the matter, and after a moment he said, "You better go, mother, or he'll be mean to you."

Martha got up and gave the child a brief but stiff shake which surprised more than hurt him. "Nathan has never been mean to me or to you," she said. "And I don't want to hear you say anything like that again, Tad. It's mischievous."

He sniffed and swallowed, not wanting to cry now, his pride severely injured by the shaking.

"I'll stop in when I come home and wake you for the bathroom," she said gently. "Shall I send Annie in to read you a story?"

He shook his head, then seemed to change his mind. "Does she know *David Copperfield*? That's what Aunt Sylvia was reading to us."

"*Was* she?" Martha said. Tad looked up at her. "Now there *was* a stepfather," she said—with purposeful exaggeration.

Tad laughed, gratefully beyond the crisis. Martha laughed too. She kissed him and hurried out, pausing for a last salute from the door.

It had been a scene neatly ended, much too neatly, she thought, and a situation controlled almost entirely by him.

Annie met her in the hallway. Nathan was waiting at the door, holding her evening cape. Annie said, "Miss Martha, will I take Tad to the eight o'clock Mass with me in the morning? I'll be in bed when you and the doctor gets home."

"I don't think so, Annie, thank you."

The Irishwoman stood her ground, and she was getting solid enough to stand any ground. "I'll be making dinner later in the morning, ma'am. It'll be inconvenient."

"I know. We shan't interfere with your work. Good night, Annie."

Nathan drove. He could use his hand in many ways. He could now articulate two of his fingers and his thumb. In the car he said, "I am glad to see you take a firm stand with her. Now if you will do the same with your son. . . ."

"I am more firm with him than I am with Annie—and he is not as simple."

"He is a child—and he is not his father."

"I have never once pretended that he was, Nathan." Martha's voice rang out, so vehement was her protest.

Nathan took his hand from the wheel for an instant and sought hers. He squeezed hard for want of response. She made no sound.

"Forgive me, my dear," he said. "I love you so much I am jealous of the dead."

Martha said nothing. He used words like instruments. But who didn't? Who in God's name didn't?

· 5

WINTHROP realized within a week of returning to Traders City that he was not ready for retirement at all as he had supposed resigning his post with the European Recovery Plan. The country and the city had changed, and the change was of the sort a man needed to have seen gradually if he were going to have patience with it: all the new houses were alike and built in rows, their only variation, color. And he had not found that much variation in the State Department where everyone suddenly seemed to be thinking neatly and all in a row. A senator named McCarthy had put the fear of dissidence in them.

Winthrop undertook in his first days home to "update" himself, a word George Bergner used with the glibness of having coined it. He went over two years' issues of the *Star* and the *Dispatch* and was more disturbed than he admitted to Sylvia to discover how similar in outlook the two papers had become. And the change was not in old Judge Phipps.

George made a great show of being glad to see him. He took him around the office introducing him as "the boss" to the newcomers, of whom there was quite a number. George himself had got fat and confident. He was not exactly patronizing in his attitude, Winthrop thought, but he had prepared the staff for the boss' return. It was "yes, sir," to him all the way down the line, all in anticipation that he would come and go like an absentee owner . . . which in fact he had been. But something in this not too covert indulgence irritated Winthrop—as much with the staff as with George, their willingness to go along, to keep in line. Uniformity again: teamwork. Not a maverick in the plant. George seemed to have found himself a formula for success. It made Winthrop think again of what Sylvia said had happened in Lakewood when George decided to discredit Marcus Hogan. Winthrop had thought Sylvia to have exaggerated that— as was her nature when anyone tried to obstruct her single-minded determination. He had thought, having the advantage abroad of perspective, albeit the disadvantage of lacking personal observation, that she had managed the whole affair badly. And, of course, Hogan's death in the wake of a quarrel with George had, he had supposed, damned George in Sylvia's eyes out of all proportion to the mischief he had actually done. But an ambitious man, weak-kneed, had to get where he wanted to go on his belly.

Thinking of George, Winthrop saw exactly what was happening to the *Star*. It was traveling happily on its belly.

He resolved not to act precipitously. He needed to know more of what was going on in the country as well as at the newspaper. Bergner seemed to be the unit of strength there, but the more Winthrop observed, the more he felt that George was not actually in power either. The key men on the paper were a closely knit team, men who knew that newspaper publishing was a consolidating business, not an expanding one, men who knew politics and commerce, advertising and their readers' tender hearts, their patriotic souls and their uncritical minds. Winthrop wondered if George, perhaps without knowing it himself, was not simply the front for these men, their liaison with the publisher.

He suggested some of these things to Sylvia.

"It's all so mad," she said. "One no longer owns what he owns. It's become a sort of uncooperative cooperative. One builds when and how the building unions say he can, and when it comes to business there doesn't seem to be anyone to talk to. The president of Fields' Machinery doesn't *do* anything. I'm not even sure he knows anything. He consults."

It was Saturday morning and they were having a second cup of coffee in the small sitting room of the flat, the room he had once called his study. This was the room in which he, George, and Judge Phipps had launched his independent candidacy for mayor of Traders City. He could see the old man yet picking up the phone.

"Judge Phipps must be over eighty now," he said.

He got up and stood at the window. He had often looked downtown from there to the green roof of the International Building where Elizabeth had had her studio. The sky that morning was cloudless, the sunlight putting a harsh glare on the new construction which had interposed between him and the green roof. While he was at the window there passed through the room, through the entire building, a slight tremor that caused a tinkle of glassware in the liquor cabinet.

"Is that the new subway?"

"That is grandfather turning over in his grave," Sylvia said.

Returning from the window, Winthrop bent down and kissed the top of her head, and moved on to blow the dust from the shield of a fifteenth century Tuscan sculpture. "We ought to get a soft brush for these things, something that won't scratch the paint."

"Perhaps a basting brush like cook uses."

"Don't they make feather dusters any more?"

"I don't know. I haven't seen one in years."

"Is Reiss doing a good job for you, Sylvia?"

She stuck the needles into the wool and put her knitting away. "I think so. Not for me. Not for the children's sake either, I shouldn't think. But for Nathan Reiss—from which we all benefit."

"What we didn't want."

"I've come round to accept it. He's an individualist in some ways. I'm sentimental enough for everybody where the children are concerned."

"Funny—you and Elizabeth with the children. I've been wishing lately there was a young Winthrop. I never cared much—for myself or what I came from. But lately . . ." He shrugged, smiling.

Sylvia nodded sympathetically. "You know, after Marcus died and Martha was so desperate, I sometimes was afraid that she might die too, and I used to think that if anything happened we might be able to adopt Tad."

Winthrop said, "It's better this way, isn't it?"

"I'm sure it is. Nathan has to be given a great deal of credit, Alex. You might say he's created a new hand for himself. Operation after operation. I dare say he'll be able to go back to surgery soon."

"And we'll have to find ourselves a new director?"

"No. He won't give that up now. It's become his entree to the important people in medicine. And Nathan likes important people."

"By God, isn't it remarkable the things we can't do, considering that there wouldn't be anything to do if we hadn't started it?"

"Were you thinking of taking over yourself, Alex?" She sounded like a woman who had exactly the project to start a man off on.

"No, no, no," he said to forestall her. "I've got a bit out of touch for that." Alexander Winthrop, M.D.: his mind went back to the days of his column in Judge Phipps' *Dispatch*. Reactionary old coot that the Judge was, he was an individualist.

"No," he went on, "I was thinking of George, actually." He stood, his hands in his pockets, springing a little on his toes as though testing his resilience. "I've made up my mind, Sylvia. Either I do what I think ought to be done with the *Star* or I sell it. I don't like what's happening to this country. I don't much like this man McCarthy. And it isn't himself so much. When I first heard about him I couldn't take it seriously, but I can see what's happening, people taking for cover, getting on the safe side, so that pretty soon there's only going to be one side. You see it more sharply coming home from abroad. But that's how it is with the paper, too. But what to do about George. You couldn't work with him. I wonder if I can."

Sylvia resolved not to interfere. This, she felt, Alex must learn for himself. The issue with George so far as she was concerned had been resolved when Winthrop had transferred his proxy as trustee of the Fields Foundation from George to her. George remained on the board of Lakewood Hospital, of course, having been voted his father's seat after Dr. Albert's death. But in that capacity he dealt with Reiss, not with her.

"He and Nathan get along very well together," she said.

Winthrop merely grunted.

"You know that whatever you do will be all right with me," Sylvia said presently. "In a way, I've run for safety too. In the old days, I'd have been on some committee or other. Something happens. It isn't only money that corrupts—or power. It's a lot of things. I suppose if one had children, they would be the excuse, just as I'm using a parcel of them now. I always think of the Plan. But what has happened to me lately, Alex, I've begun to feel superior to quite a lot of people— to the great mass I used to call comrades in my left wing days. I always wanted what they had and I didn't, and why I liked them: they didn't want what I had. Or so I thought. But money seems to be all anybody wants now. Maybe it's just me that's getting older. But I don't think so. I swear to God, when I was young I'd have loved to change places with a carpenter, a farmer, a shoemaker. I'd have loved to make shoes, and oh my God, but I would have loved to make a picture or a poem . . . I remember being invited into our chauffeur's flat for tea when I was a little girl. I remember every room: scrubbed and neat, and the cat in the window and a great hanging fern all the way to the floor. I used to make believe I lived there, that I was in charge of all the cars in the garage below. He could play their motors like musical instruments, tuning them, you know? He had merry blue eyes and ruddy cheeks . . ." Sylvia broke off abruptly, for talking of the chauffeur, she remembered the Baroness and hers. She shrugged. "I don't know why I'm telling you all this."

"Probably because we need a chauffeur."

"No we don't, Alex."

"I don't like to drive," he said.

"I do."

"I know, but you can't do it for both of us, can you?" he said, a twinkle in his eye.

Sylvia laughed. "Even if I think so, I'm not going to admit it now."

That night they taxied the few blocks north to Martha and Reiss' apartment. There was no joy in Winthrop's anticipation of the reunion. He could only be grateful that it was not the house on Oak Street to which they were going: that was now part of the Midwestern University campus. Reiss opened the door to them, dark from the summer sun and handsomer than ever, the white teeth flashing in his smile. Shaking hands with him, Winthrop felt the scar tissue with the tips of his fingers, and seeing the man flex his fingers afterwards, he supposed the business of shaking hands to be a part of his therapy. The manipulation of his fingers was something Reiss did frequently, not ostentatiously, but in a room with him you grew conscious of it.

Martha came hurrying, half-running down the hall. Winthrop opened his arms and she ran into them and hugged him as never, never had she done before. Then he saw the youngster.

"And this is Tad," Martha said. "Your Uncle Alexander, Tad."

They shook hands and the boy said: "How do you do, sir?" and then: "May I take your hat?"

He was too well mannered for an American: he would need to have a good right punch with those manners. But when an instant later Tad said: "Hi, Syl, put her thar," and the two of them shook hands acrobatically, Winthrop supposed the balance satisfactory in a nine-year old.

Several of Winthrop's observances through the evening pleased him: Martha was mistress of the occasion, Reiss not its master. Always a reserved girl, Martha was now a woman of such poise as he remembered in her mother. Tad stayed a few moments with them in the living room and then went off to do his homework. Annie served dinner, red-faced as ever at a compliment, heavier on her feet. She deferred to Martha even to the point of asking her: "Will the doctor want the red wine now?" And Tad had called Reiss "Nathan." But Reiss was a man who could ride with the punches. He inquired of Winthrop what he thought of the hospital and the farm, and whether he approved the shape the Rehabilitation Plan had taken. Did he think the new spy scare was going to make it more difficult for them to process the foreign children? "Always the Communists. I will tell you the truth: I think the world would be better off to drop a bomb on them and have it over with."

No one said anything for a moment.

Then Sylvia said: "You make it sound like dropping the other shoe."

"Well, perhaps it is. This suspense now—will there be war? Will there not be war? It is holding back the whole country."

"Not that you'd notice it coming home from abroad," Winthrop said. "Do you have a television set?"

He looked at Martha. She smiled and nodded regretfully.

"Personally," Sylvia said, and Winthrop knew the clarion ring to her voice, "I think we should wait until we have a new bomb, this thing Truman's talking about. It's supposed to be much more efficient."

Reiss said: "You are pulling my leg."

"Frankly, Nathan, when you talk like that, I'd like to wring your neck."

Nathan smiled, looking at Winthrop. "Your wife is so charming in pique. I am afraid I often provoke her purposely." He laid his hand on Sylvia's for an instant. "Forgive me."

Sylvia drew her hand away, not abruptly, ostensibly to use her fork, but she said, "I should think that having lost a friend with such pronouncements, you'd think twice before setting them off again."

"Mueller is a fanatic. He is going to get himself into trouble with the government. Scientists do not belong in politics."

"Who do you think does, Nathan?" Winthrop asked.

"Men who make it their business," Reiss said amiably. "It is enough for doctors to be doctors, soldiers soldiers, physicists, physicists."

"It's an interesting theory," Winthrop said, "but it doesn't exactly jibe with the history of this country."

Reiss smiled. "I am afraid I do not know very much about the history of this country, alas—only enough to have got my citizenship papers."

Winthrop said, "But you should know something of German history."

Reiss looked at him quizzically. Then he said, "I see what you mean: Hitler was a politician?"

"Something like that."

Martha asked, "How long is it since you've seen Jonathan, Alexander?"

"It's a long time," Winthrop said. "I intended to stop over in London, but Sylvia took care of that: four children to manage—in Greek."

"Poor Alex," Sylvia said.

"I understand he's got a book under way, a mercantile history . . of something medieval."

Martha smiled in spite of herself. "The Merchant Adventurers."

"You can see, Nathan," Winthrop said dryly, "I'm also an historian." To Martha he said: "The last time I saw Jonathan was at a party we gave, an enormous affair before Sylvia came home from Naples . . ."

"I've told them about it," Sylvia said almost rudely. And she had never mentioned it.

"Yes," Winthrop said. "Well, that's what happens when you and your wife travel separately. Whoever gets there first tells all the stories."

"If I've heard it before," Martha said, and she could not remember having heard it, "I should love to hear it again." Jonathan's letters were sparse and formal since her marriage to Reiss.

"I was in Naples once when I was very young," Reiss said. "It was a most wonderful time of my life. I drove a car in a race—I have never told you, Martha. It was the most daring thing I ever did. Me, a nobody, and all those very important people. It was a society affair."

Sylvia listened, fascinated in spite of the constricted feeling at the pit of her stomach.

Reiss said: "Forgive me, Alex. I have interrupted your story."

"The point seems to have escaped me," Winthrop said.

Martha prompted: "Jonathan."

"Ah, yes. Do you know an Italian writer, Marcello Ruggeo?"

"*Bitter Wine,*" Martha said. "I've just read it—a strange book. Quite beautiful, I thought."

"He's a friend of Jonathan's, you know. He was a partisan, or at least in sympathy with them during the war. It was quite a party we had—I remember Sylvia's saying that all we needed was the king and we could have held court. Well, Sylvia—being Sylvia—invited Ruggeo and Jonathan who was down from London for a few days. And I, much to my own chagrin afterwards, invited Alberto Gemini, the American banker . . ."

Sylvia sat, her nerves taut as the fork she held in her hand.

"I'll never forget," Winthrop went on, "he arrived with the Baroness . . ." He had forgotten the name. "You had lunch with her, Sylvia . . ."

"The Baroness Schwarzbach," Sylvia said without looking at anyone.

Winthrop saw that Reiss had turned a yellowish green beneath his suntan; and the vein was standing out on Martha's forehead. He harkened back then to the story of the patroness he had altogether forgotten in Reiss' background.

Reiss moistened his lips. "She is alive?"

"She was very much alive in 1945," Winthrop said.

Reiss began to get hold of the situation. "But of course you wouldn't know: she was my patroness. I have thought her dead after the Nazis. I saw them taking her away, you know, and I could do nothing."

Sylvia felt him to be waiting, trying to compel her eyes. When she did not look at him he spoke directly to her: "Sylvia, she is all right?"

"It was my understanding that she had spent the war in a villa in Ischia."

"But you saw her. You must have talked. She would know Martha. Why has she not communicated with me?"

Sylvia said carefully: "Perhaps she thought happened to you what you thought happened to her, Nathan."

Reiss smiled tentatively. "It is fantastic. She does not know I am here?"

"She knows."

"Then," he said, all the bravura drained out of him, "she will have thought I betrayed her. Is it so? Is that why you have not spoken to me, Sylvia?"

"She has other interests now," Sylvia said quietly.

"I see." Reiss sat a moment in silence. Then he laughed. "But of course I see. I am a conceited fool." He looked from Winthrop to Sylvia and back to Winthrop. "So. She is in society again. Good." And finally he spoke to his wife: "Dear Martha, do not look so forlorn. It is a great burden lifted from my mind. Shame on you, Sylvia, for not telling me. Did you think I would mind? All that part of my life is ended now. Now it is more happily ended than I ever dared to hope."

An agony of embarrassed silence hung over the Winthrops, primarily for Martha to whom privacy was sacred.

Martha said: "What about Jonathan, Alexander?"

"Oh, it's a part of history now," Winthrop said, rising above his own oppression. "It was awkward at the time, and in a way it came to a head that night. Jonathan was on the side of his friend, Ruggeo. I was caught between the Right and the Left. Not for the first time, by the way . . ."

Sylvia managed to smile, but all the lines in her face showed the effort it cost her. "I think Jonathan was wise to stay in England. He would not like what's happening here today, McCarthy and all."

"He and my Uncle Philip play chess when my uncle is in London," Martha said. "He used to play chess with Erich, but God knows my Uncle Philip is no Erich. He is an Anglo-Irishman who likes to hunt, to listen to a good sermon, to pinch the bottoms of pretty girls, and to sit in Parliament saying 'hear, hear!' at mention of the Empire. Uncle Philip is . . . Establishment. He has managed to restore the McMahon name to very near where his father undid it—when he joined the Gaelic partisans."

Winthrop, for all that he admired Martha in this remarkable—for her—speech, was saddened by it, too. "And your mother?" he said.

Martha smiled. "She's very fond of Jonathan."

They moved into the living room for coffee where Tad came and politely said good night to each of them.

Afterwards Sylvia told her husband the Baroness' story. Winthrop admitted he had also heard the part of it concerning the execution of her Nazi lover.

"When did you hear it?"

"A day or two after the party. Count Bordoni told me. Do you remember him?"

"I remember his wife," Sylvia said.

Winthrop was about to go into his dressing room. Sylvia crushed out a cigaret she had just lighted. "I've smoked too much tonight."

Winthrop said: "Why do you think Reiss married her?"

"Martha?"

He nodded. "Possession or position? Or both?"

"I think he loves her in his fashion," Sylvia said.

"She's living off the top of her head. You know that. All surface."

"It's better," Sylvia said.

"Better than what?"

Sylvia laughed dryly. "I was going to say better than nothing."

"Do you think he married her to make sure he'd get the director-ship of the Children's Plan?"

"Alex, I'll tell you the God's truth: I don't see that it matters. I just don't see that it matters now."

"Perhaps not. But I was thinking—a man who would do that would do almost anything, wouldn't he?"

·6

It was a notable winter, 1950-51, for Nathan Reiss. In January he performed his first major surgery in almost five years. To celebrate he, Tad and Martha went to the Boat Show at the Armory and bought a twenty-foot sloop to be delivered that spring at Fox Lake where they arranged to rent a cottage for the summer. Fox Lake was an hour and a half drive from Traders City and less than a half-hour from Lakewood. Since the war it had become the most fashionable of the resort lakes. In the old days it had been rather more notorious, a hideaway for bootleggers and the cabaret society they entertained there in gaudy splendor. In some of the elegant "cottages" surviving since the twenties, secret panels could still be found where once were concealed caches of contraband whisky.

It was hard to tell whether Nathan or Tad was the more excited about the boat. Outdoors they got along well together, both of them fiercely competitive athletes. Indoors, where they were exposed to each other intellectually, explosions were fairly frequent. "Martha, I cannot understand your son," was Reiss' frequent complaint. Tad had reached the age of answering everything with a shrug. He went to the Baker School which was far more permissive with him than was Martha. He was advanced for his age and knew it, and he was in rather too frequent a habit of bringing home problems to Nathan in science and arithmetic which in the end he could solve better than could his stepfather. The prospect of the boat, however, brought amity indoors as well as out. They drew sketches, studied riggings and heaven knows what, filling Nathan's study with magazines and books on the subject.

Tad was given open sesame to the study even when Nathan was not home, and there one day Martha found him liberally educating himself on matters other than nautical.

"Would you like to be a doctor, Tad?"

"No."

"A sailor," Martha said.

"I get it," Tad said, and took the book on obstetrics back to the shelf where he had found it.

Martha laughed. "No, I didn't mean that, but I should think with that kind of book you ought to ask Nathan to explain it to you."

"I was just looking at the pictures."

"I expect when you get to biology it will be time enough to go into the details," Martha said.

Tad looked into her face in the penetrative way that always made her fear for what he was about to ask. "I want to ask you something . . . some day." At the very last instant he lost courage himself.

"All right," Martha said. "Some day you ask it and I shall try to answer it—some day. Shall we see what Annie has left us for tea?"

But when they were having their tea at the kitchen table, Tad asked: "Was I circumcised when I was a baby?"

"Yes," Martha said. She supposed it a matter already explored in the wash room at school. "Your father believed it to be healthier, cleaner. In fact, I think that's its significance in the Jewish religion, too. I'm not sure. We must ask Nathan."

"He doesn't know," Tad said. "I asked him."

"Then we must look it up," Martha said. It was not Nathan's ignorances that surprised her so much as his lack of curiosity. It would have seemed to her that when Tad asked him, Nathan would have proposed to find out at least.

"He says I ask questions like that on purpose."

"Well, I should think so," Martha said. "On purpose to find out."

"He means to find out he doesn't know."

"That's rather silly, isn't it? As a matter of fact, I remember now—Circumcision is also called the Feast of the Purification. So that is its religious symbolism."

"What's symbolism?"

Compared to some of his questions, symbolism was easily explained.

But Martha herself re-examined another problem in symbolism that winter. She read again *Bitter Wine* by Marcello Ruggeo. It was the story of a poet who left his wife and children for a woman—a marvelous, dreadful woman of beauty, culture and passion, of many affairs—whom he deluded himself into thinking that by his own fidelity he could save from the devil. He wrote her poetry of praise, of exhortation. He kept vigil with and upon her. She was intelligent, wise, gay—and wanton. She ravished him. And when he was spent, body and soul, she left him for another, a banker who wanted only to boast having added her to his possessions. Yet in the end the poet did not blame her. She had been at best only what he pretended her to be.

Nathan arrived home one spring afternoon in a state of high agitation. When Martha followed him into the study, he bade her close the door although Annie was the only one home besides themselves, and she in her room off the kitchen, far down the hall.

"I had visitors this afternoon at the office," Reiss said. He opened and closed one after another of the drawers of his desk, looking for something which after a moment he seemed to forget. "Two investigators from the Federal Bureau of Investigation came to see me."

He spoke with such ominous portent that Martha very nearly laughed with relief when he added: "They were inquiring about Sylvia." He looked at her as though incredulous that she too was not shocked.

Martha said: "What did they want to know?"

"Did she ever try to recruit me into the Communist Party—questions like that. I did not know things like that about her, Martha."

Martha's tendency to mirth passed quickly. "Do you know them now, Nathan?"

"I have sometimes thought," he said, ignoring her question, "but who would believe a woman in her position . . ." He went on for some time, breaking off his sentences in the inarticulateness of his distress. It was as though he had been deliberately compromised, deceived.

Finally Martha said: "Nathan, how does it affect you? I don't understand."

"They will be wanting to know if she is using the Children's Plan for subversion, won't they?"

"Subversion among whom, for heaven's sake? The children?"

"Do not be so sure of yourself, Martha. I know what investigators are like. They probe and hunt and look for pieces. And let me tell you, many pieces can be put into places they were not cut out for. I know." He burst out laughing. The sound was not pleasant. Martha waited. "I have just made a very bad joke on myself. It does not matter."

"I still don't understand," Martha said. "What other questions did they ask?"

"If she talks politics with me . . . oh, and yes: did she post a bond for me when I came into this country. That was their final question." He resumed the search of his desk, this time bringing out his citizenship papers which he glanced through and then put away again.

"Is that what's upset you?"

Again he did not answer directly. "She did not! Erich Mueller . . . and, thank God, the president of the Bankers Trust Company of Traders City."

"Yes, by all means let's thank God for the Bankers Trust Company of Traders City," Martha said mockingly.

"My dear wife," Reiss spoke with exaggerated calmness: "I did not escape the Nazis to be made a dupe of by the Communists."

It was, Martha thought, like arguing religion with a fanatic. Or politics with a Communist. Her inclination was strong to drop the matter there, as she always did with him. But she foresaw in it even further isolation within herself, and at a time she felt able to cope with sensibility as well as her senses. "Dear man, listen to me for a moment. If you believe in what you are doing, isn't that the important thing? Is there politics in straightening a child's back? Was there politics in your mind when you brought your good right hand back to where you can use it?"

"That is precisely what I mean, Martha. I do not want to lose everything again for something I do not care that about." He snapped his fingers. "I am going to withdraw from the Children's Plan. If I do so now it will mean something. Later may be too late."

Martha gazed down at him. She was sitting on the corner of his desk. "It will mean something to whom, Nathan?"

"You are deliberately misunderstanding me."

"I'm not, Nathan. I'm trying to understand you. Does the Children's Plan mean nothing to you any longer?"

"That is not what I am saying. Very well. They asked me a list of associations—did I know Sylvia Fields Winthrop had belonged to them. They are on the Attorney General's list of subversive organizations. Where will I be, its director, an immigrant, when they add the Children's Plan to the list?"

"Nathan, *you* are putting together pieces that don't fit. I've known Sylvia since 1936. In those days I was as politically innocent as you are, as I think you are—and if ignorance is innocence. I'm not sure about that. I don't know if she was actually a Communist or not. It's just possible they wouldn't have her, you know. I think it was Marcus who said that to me once. But after the Hitler-Stalin pact, like a lot of people, she was disillusioned. And really today, Nathan, I think I'm further to the left than Sylvia is."

"Oh, I don't doubt that," he said.

"I don't know why the investigators are asking about Sylvia. I suppose they have to in times like these—they have to go over all the names of people who were once associated with such organizations. I should suppose it's proper and necessary—and this is much to my point: I should suppose that Sylvia, especially for the sake of the Plan, would welcome such an investigation."

Reiss' whole expression changed. Martha repeated: "Especially for the Plan."

"I see," Reiss said. "I see what you mean."

"The Fields Foundation is not on the Attorney General's list, I shouldn't think."

Reiss looked at her and laughed a little. "Hurd Abington—can you imagine?"

"No. But I can't imagine Sylvia belonging there either," Martha said.

Reiss leaned back in his chair, his lower lip protruding, a habit of his that always put her in mind of a repentant child, and said: "If you are right . . ." He glanced up at her, his eyes soft with regret . . . "I hope I have not done her harm."

Martha slid off the desk and went to the window where she could turn her back to him. How revelatory that last remark! She could conjecture from it the whole interview with the interrogators, his anxiety to be cooperative, to ingratiate himself with them, and inevitably she remembered again: "I am not a Jew." Her anger was quick and fierce with him, not for what he was. She knew that, had known it, but for his willingness to expose himself to her in utter indecency, forcing her to look at him at his cowardly worst.

She tried unsuccessfully to control the trembling of her shoulders. "What is it, Martha?"

She shook her head and he repeated his question. She turned and faced him. "You have no shame."

"You are right," he said, satisfied to have wrung from her the accusation. He left the chair and himself half-sat on the desk, his arms folded, and smiled ruefully as he watched her face for the effect upon it of his words. "I have never claimed to be more than worthless. But I have an honorable wife whom I adore. My conscience and my queen. Do not waste your anger on me, Martha. I have given you what I had to give. We both—you and I—give everything . . . and nothing. It is enough for an unimportant man like me. I am sorry if it is not enough for you."

Martha drew a deep, long breath. She had won and lost which was the pattern of their lives. "It is enough," she murmured.

Reiss picked up the phone and dialed Mount Clement Hospital to set up his schedule for the morning. Martha touched his hand, almost as though for luck, passing him to leave the room.

But in a larger scene and with the variation of more people present, Martha went through virtually the same experience a few days later. On a Sunday evening they were returning from Fox Lake and stopped at the farm as was their custom. Sylvia persuaded them to stay to supper. Nathan went on to Lakewood for an hour and then returned. Supper was served on the screened porch.

Winthrop was surprised to discover that he enjoyed his weekends on the farm. The children's dormitory was a half-mile from the house so that he saw them only when he wanted to. He found that crops and a garden for home consumption gave him pleasure in nature that he had never known at the Tamarack estate, a place he now referred to rather ashamedly. He liked to tease Tad, pretending to be more ignorant of the farm than he actually was, just to hear the boy explain with elaborate patience to him the facts of farm life.

"Sylvia's finally got me aboard a horse again," he remarked at supper. "At my age that's a dangerous pastime."

Tad wanted to know which horse he was riding. Being told, he said: "It's not very dangerous."

"I'm glad to hear you say that," Winthrop said. "It relieves my mind if not my backside."

"Do you sail, Uncle Alexander?"

Winthrop said: "I float," and Tad grinned.

"I hope you and Sylvia will come out to the lake soon," Martha said. "I remember you were fond of boats." She was remembering an occasion in her childhood when she, her mother and father had gone sailing with him on Judge Phipps's yacht.

"That would be very nice," Winthrop said, but he was puzzled at what made her think he was fond of boats. Actually he had a strong tendency toward seasickness.

"I remember you put on the pilot's cap and papa took your picture."

"Ah, now I remember," Winthrop said.

Reiss said: "We shall invite the Bergners and make a weekend party of it. What do you say, Sylvia?"

Sylvia did not answer right away. She had been under numerous if more subtle pressures from both her husband and Reiss to restore the Bergners to her social calendar. She glanced at Martha and seeing no reaction to mention of them wondered if living with Nathan Reiss wore down one's sensitivities. But of course the last hour in Marcus's life was not as vivid to Martha as to her: only the loss had been vivid. And as Alexander said, you could accuse George of many things, but you couldn't actually blame him for Marcus's death. Willy nilly hers and George Bergner's paths crossed and recrossed whether or not she accepted him.

She merely said: "I don't like week-end parties."

"Then an afternoon, a picnic perhaps," Reiss persisted.

Tad was looking at her. Sylvia said: "That would be lovely."

"Good," Reiss said. A moment later he took her plate and asked if he might bring her coffee.

"I can get it," she said, starting up.

He persuaded her. "There is something I have been wanting to tell you."

Across the porch, her attention presumably given to Winthrop's account to Tad of the goatherds who lived in caves outside Athens, Martha overheard her husband telling Sylvia of the visit to his office of the F.B.I. investigators. Distinctly she heard him say:

"Martha thought you ought to be told and I had to agree with her."

"I must say I'm not surprised, all things considered," Sylvia said.

Nathan said: "Please?" He could make his curiosity seem very offhand.

"Alex is about to set a new editorial policy with the *Star*. I should think it would stir up a certain amount of . . . uneasiness."

"Ah, I see. Then it has nothing to do with the Children's Plan."

"I should hope that it won't, Nathan."

Reiss glanced at his wife. Martha, aware of his eyes did not meet them however. Reiss took Sylvia's hand for a moment. "I was very noncommital when they asked their questions."

Sylvia laughed. "Thank you, Nathan. But I assure you, my life is an open book. The name Fields was always good for a headline. It was all in the newspapers. But perhaps they don't have time these days for that kind of research."

Martha went outdoors managing to do it without attracting attention and walked the pebbled path to the garden. The evening star shone brightly in the twilight. By way of not thinking, she tried to remember a poem of which both she and Marcus had been very fond. At last she was able to conjure the lines from Yeats by which she had made the association:

". . . how love fled
and paced upon the mountain overhead and hid his face
amid a crowd of stars."

·7

GEORGE BERGNER had been uneasy from the day Winthrop returned to Traders City. He had the feeling of being at the wheel of a machine the steering apparatus of which was about to go out of control: when he acted he got a response, but something did not feel right, something was unsure to his touch. He had prepared the staff for Winthrop's return; he had also let it be known that he expected the boss to be around for a while and then to take off on some new project. But this Winthrop showed no signs of doing. Bergner remained

General Manager of the *Star,* but Winthrop consulted primarily with the editor and neither of them saw fit to fill George in on what was going on. He would have liked by his manner, his aplomb, to seem confident, at least a man in the know, but his own secretary gave him the jitters with her solicitude. It was not long until he was getting sympathy from all sides.

But he stayed at his desk, sifting rumors that came from the front office, reading signs in the requisitions that came to him for approval. For example, he got a day's cheer out of the fact that the foreign editor was authorized to send his own man to Korea: that was not likely to happen if the *Star* was going on the block. He had heard that rumor, too. The country was suddenly in another fighting war in Korea, ill-prepared, most of our troops home, decoyed out of Korea by the Russian withdrawal from their sector. The State Department was under even more severe fire, the charges of disloyalty and security failures exploding like buckshot.

On the day the Korean correspondent was sent out, George was suddenly informed of what had been going on at the top. Winthrop called him in and showed him the copy for a lead editorial. It bore the head: JUST WHO IS JOE McCARTHY?

George kept his eyes on the piece, but he did not read it. He knew then that he had been expecting something of this sort. When he looked up, he said: "You're the boss, Alex. When do you plan to run it?"

"Soon. It's a couple of years late now."

George lit a cigaret. "You shouldn't have left a boy to do a man's work."

"I didn't. I left a man who got old too soon, that's all."

"You've got a newspaper. I'm not sure you'd have had one otherwise."

"Both Sylvia and I would have been willing to take that chance. We're going to take it now."

"Will you grant me this much, Alex: I've brought the *Star* to where it's got enough circulation to make your message count?"

"I'll grant you that—and more, George. Fifteen years ago, left to my own devices I'd have done what you did. I've not forgotten you helped get me out of the basement of City Hall."

George picked up the copy again and this time read a few lines. "You know, Alex, you ought not to run this until you've got a first-rate cartoonist to take up the theme."

Winthrop was quick to agree, and subsequently lavish in paying credit to George when he included him in talks with the editorial staff. Names were suggested. Winthrop said: "Since this is your baby, George, why don't you find us someone?"

"Give me a day or two. There ought to be someone left over from the thirties."

George wondered afterwards, Winthrop shaking hands with him as he left the office, if he had not by that intuitive stroke saved his own job with the *Star*. If he had lost it, he could not have felt Winthrop's treatment of him much shabbier. He presumed Sylvia had got to him.

In the old days he had had the advantage of riding home on the train with Winthrop, a contact which daily reassured him of the mutuality of their enterprise. There was little solace in his own company on these daily journeys, small pleasure in choosing between the contemplation of his own belly or looking out the window at the uniformed construction known as "middle-income housing" strung all the way up the North Shore. He was cursed with both the love and fear of individualism: he knew it and blamed his father. But no more than he blamed himself. He had somehow got mixed up with liberalism in the thirties: he had thought he was hitching his wagon to a star; instead he seemed to have got caught in a chain gang. Mental depression settled on him very easily. He had a job dependent upon another man's whims, a daughter who had not been able to get out of his house soon enough, a son who wouldn't shave his face and a wife who hadn't the guts to encourage a lover.

The latter thought occurred to him when he arrived home—he still walked the near mile from the station—and saw Nathan Reiss' car in the driveway. There had been a time when he thought something was going to happen between them—Louise and Reiss—when the refugee had first arrived on the scene. He had been constantly about the house, flattering and fluttering her, the giddy woman. But Reiss was a man who could always get what he wanted without committing himself, while George, by his own calculation, never got what he wanted and always committed himself. He was the beggar who spat behind the back of his benefactor, loathing himself even while he did it.

He unlocked the front door. Before he had put down his dispatch case Louise called out, "George? We're in the conservatory. Guess who's here, honey."

He looked in the hall-stand mirror and tried to flatten his circle of hair. When it curled up with perspiration it looked like a crepe-paper skirt on a kewpie doll. Once he had been vain about what he considered his good looks.

"Is there a doctor in the house?" he said in answer to Louise as he went in. "How are you, Nathan?"

The two men shook hands.

"I have taken the liberty of mixing martinis—five to one, Louise says. It is barbarous. But you will have one?"

Bergner nodded and kissed Louise lightly on her moist forehead. She smelt of honeysuckle. Always something delicate, fresh at the first whiff, then suddenly too sweet. He took the glass from Nathan's hand.

Reiss said, "Well, to what shall we drink? To the summer? To one another?"

"Let us drink," George said, "to be drunk."

"Oh, dear," Louise said, "I haven't been intoxicated since the night Eleanor left to go to Paris."

"So the Big Man is taking over, eh?" Reiss said.

George glanced at him and said nothing. With Sylvia to inform him, Reiss knew more than he did about what was going on at the *Star*.

"Everything will be all right. It will have to be. We shall find him a new toy, George."

"The Children's Rehabilitation Plan," George said sardonically.

Reiss shrugged. "If that will make him happy, I will give it up to him gladly."

"He already is happy, Nathan. Ecstatically happy."

"So."

George sat down heavily in a white leather chair. Louise had finally done something modern with the conservatory. The leather, however, reminded him of white satin. He kept thinking of a casket-maker's showroom. "We're off on a great crusade. The *Star* is going liberal again."

"But it has always been a liberal newspaper," Louise said.

George looked at her over the rim of his glass. "Perhaps you could convince Alex of that, my dear."

"Maybe I could if I ever had a chance," she said, reacting to his sarcasm.

Reiss said: "As a matter of fact you are all going to be invited to Fox Lake. I have spoken to Sylvia."

"And she's going?" George said. He laughed. "She must be damned sure she's running the show these days."

"What do you think will happen?" Reiss said, "I mean with the newspaper and all?"

"I think he'll run the circulation to hell and sell the newspaper."

Reiss pursed his lips. "It is a great shame," he said then, "that one man can do that to another man's work. It is political, this crusade?"

"I've never known one that wasn't—at bottom," George said.

"So. Is there nothing we can do to persuade him?"

"What would you suggest?"

Reiss shrugged. "I am not political as you know. But if as you say, Sylvia is behind him in this matter, perhaps we should ask how it will affect the Children's Rehabilitation Plan. I have been told she is not exactly invulnerable . . . politically, I mean."

When Reiss groped for his words, George grinned. "Kosher," he said. "She's not quite kosher. Isn't that what you mean?"

"I am not speaking from my own knowledge," Reiss said without humor. "I am merely repeating something I have heard."

"It was never much of a secret," George said. "I don't think anybody took it seriously—except Sylvia."

"I am glad to hear you say that," Reiss said. "I was afraid it might be serious when the government investigators came to see me. I have the European idea of investigators, you see."

"When did they come to see you, Nathan?"

"A couple of weeks ago perhaps."

"Did you tell Sylvia?"

"The other day I did mention it. She was not surprised. But one says that anyway, doesn't one?"

George emptied his glass. "Well, now we'll all be investigated. Have you got anything to hide, Nathan?"

"What man does not have something to hide? All the same, a refugee does not like to be investigated."

"Don't worry, Nathan. As long as you weren't a Communist, nobody's going to bother with you."

George got up and took the mixer from beside Reiss and started to make another batch of martinis. He was trying to figure out precisely what Reiss' concern was. That it was his own hide he was out to protect, George would not doubt for a moment. "There's something we've both got to face up to in this, Nathan: people with as much money as the Winthrops don't scare as easily as the rest of us poor slobs. The fact that Sylvia is under investigation—and knows it—doesn't seem to have made any difference at all as far as the newspaper's concerned. I got my briefing on that today: Damn the torpedoes and full speed ahead. As for the Children's Plan, do you know what can happen? If she thought her name was going to jeopardize it, she would pull out."

Reiss lifted his head and smiled. George knew him well enough to understand the meaning of the smile: when Reiss was hurt he smiled. It was his immediate camouflage. He always hid himself behind that magnificent barricade of teeth. George began to enjoy himself. He elaborated: "She would not want to, of course, but that's the kind of woman she is: sublimated mother love. She would probably turn the whole thing over to the Fields Foundation."

George counted five jiggers of gin into the pitcher.

"Do you think that would seriously affect my position with the Children's Plan?" Reiss asked.

George said: "How do you think you stand with say, Hurd Abington?"

"He was always very pleasant to me," Reiss said with a shrug.

It seemed incredible to George that Reiss would not have been sensitive to the man's rabid anti-Semitism. Reiss was still a conundrum to him: he had what was needed of course to drive to the top and stay there, a refusal to know, much less to care, what some people thought of him.

"There's something you and I have got to remember, Nathan. We're both hired help. Whether we like it or not, that's what we are, hired help." He decided to make a double batch of martinis.

Louise brought her empty glass.

"So," Reiss said, smiling, "we are all in the same boat as they say. Do you like sailing, George?"

It was a few seconds before George realized that he had meant the question literally. "I love it," he said self-mockingly, "as long as it isn't my boat."

"Good. Martha will make the arrangements with Louise and Sylvia."

Louise put her hand through her husband's arm. She was always affectionate after the first drink. After the third, he knew how she really felt. "Shall we go?"

"Don't you want to?"

"Very much. I've been feeling so out of things till now."

"Then accept with pleasure, my dear. Accept with pleasure." And transferring the bottle from one hand to the other, George folded Louise's hand within his, his index finger still doubled from where he had left off counting the jiggers. It became an obscene gesture he had learned in college and had not to his recollection used since. He was much surprised to see his wife blush.

·8

TAD sat on the pier and dangled his feet in the water. Sometimes, with the motion of the lake, the long grass swayed and touched his outstretched toes, and sometimes he could catch a spike of it between his big toe and the one next to it. This was but a passing distraction and he began presently to weep again the tears of the righteous. Righteousness does not last very long with a small boy, however, and he had to stare hard at the receding sailboat with the three men aboard and imagine himself upon it—as it was his right to be—in order to prime the source of his tears. He had the most distinct recollection of his mother's saying that he, Tad, and Nathan sailed the *Lorna Doone* beautifully, and his Uncle Alexander had expected him to be aboard. But at the last moment he had been bumped off, and he knew it was because Mr. Bergner was too fat.

He had behaved badly, he knew, and he did not expect his mother to speak to him until lunch time or until he could go to her and tell her he had apologized to Nathan. He was always having to apologize to Nathan. Not actually. His apologies bored both Nathan and him. All he had to do was tell his mother he had apologized. He discovered he could even get away with the subterfuge if Nathan were present. Afterwards, when they were alone, Nathan would say, "So. You apologized, did you? Where was I at the time?" "Right there," Tad would say, or, "You must've been there." "And what did I say?" Nathan would tease. "You said I was a good boy." "And are you?" Tad would sometimes shrug or sometimes say in a speculative manner, "No, I guess I'm not." And Nathan would laugh and shake his finger and say, "That is one more thing we must not tell your mother. She thinks you are a very good boy." It was a funny game to play, mixing up good with bad, right with wrong. He did not really like Nathan, but that was part of the game, too, pretending that he did. Except on occasions like this morning when Nathan had bumped him off the boat, and he said, "I hate you." Nathan had patted him on the head and said, "How can you say that, mein Tad, when I love you?" "That's a lie!" Tad said, and everyone had been shocked. Thus had he learned what he thought a very important thing about adults: you could say anything was the truth to them, but you couldn't say a lie was a lie.

He did not expect his mother to speak to him, but he had expected his Aunt Sylvia to come out and say, "Oh, there you are!" and suggest that he and she go horseback riding.

The people next door had not come out this weekend, and the caretaker's boy and another youngster from the village were fishing from their pier. They wouldn't catch anything but bullheads, but bullheads were most delicious, skinned and fried outdoors. If he went over and fished with them, or even just watched them, they would invite him to the fishfry, especially if he had fifteen cents for a bag of potato chips. He stood up and started to take the leather strap of the field glasses from around his neck. Nathan had put the glasses in his hands by way of consolation. "You can watch what I do wrong and tell me." To the others he had said, "Tad is a very fine sailor." Tad had felt like throwing the glasses into the lake, and he might have done it had not his Uncle Alexander been there.

He was starting up the steps when he heard the commotion on the water. He turned and saw almost at once that the sailboat was in trouble. The boom looked to be swinging loose. Men in the two fishing boats in its vicinity were trying to start their motors, and one got going, speeding toward the *Lorna Doone*. The boys on the next pier were shouting and pointing. Tad lifted the field glasses and had just got them focused when he heard his mother's voice and Aunt Sylvia's, and then their running footsteps. On the boat he could see Nathan hanging onto one of the other men who seemed to be falling over the side, tilting the *Lorna Doone* terribly. Then he saw Mr. Bergner bracing himself near the stern, not doing anything but sitting, hanging onto either side.

Tad did not hear the questions, exactly, but he said, "It's Uncle Alexander. He's sick. They're going to tip if they don't watch out."

The mainsail described a semi-circle, the boom loose. "Why doesn't Mr. Bergner help?"

His mother took the glasses from him at that moment, but with his naked eyes he saw the *Lorna Doone* go over, the men disappear for the moment.

"It's all right," Martha kept saying. "Nathan has him . . . and the other boats are coming."

"Where's George? Is he in the water?" That was Mrs. Bergner asking a foolish question, Tad thought, since there was no place else he could be after the boat tipped over.

"I see his head," Martha said, then she began to pray: "Sacred Heart of Jesus . . ." Annie prayed, but he had not heard his mother pray since he was very small.

Tad became aware of Sylvia's hands upon his shoulders; they were as hard as the claws of a hammer when he tried to free himself of their grasp. "I wish I was there," Tad said. "I could have saved them."

"I wish you were, too," Sylvia said, but squeezed his shoulders until it was quite painful.

"Maybe I ought to go in and call a doctor," Mrs. Bergner said.

Martha said, "Nathan is a doctor. There now, they're all being hauled aboard that motor boat. It's going to be all right! Thank God—oh, thank God!" Martha thrust the glasses back in Tad's hands and ran up the steps. "I'm going to call for an ambulance anyway."

Sylvia said harshly, "It's not going to be all right. I can tell it in my heart. Go into the house with your mother, Tad." She tried to give him a turn and a shove and then added, but distractedly, "I'll call you if I need you."

"I want to stay with you, Aunt Sylvia."

So the boy stayed and watched the dreadful ceremony of the living trying to stave off the death of one of their own. He watched, fascinated, the deftness of Nathan's hands working at the chest, then the arms of Dr. Winthrop. Then Tad saw with horror what he presumed was Nathan kissing the mouth of Alexander, so that he supposed his uncle dead, but the kiss was so long, and the sound was a sucking sound such as Tad could never bear to hear a poor landed fish make when it gasped for air. Aunt Sylvia's face was gray and stiff as she knelt on the dock beside her husband. Martha brought brandy, and when Nathan said he did not need it, she gave it to

Louise who poured it all over Mr. Bergner's face. Mr. Bergner looked like a balloon, Tad thought, getting more and more puffed up. Tad heard the siren of the ambulance, and a dozen boats were coming where there had not been but two in sight before.

Finally Nathan shook his head, the water dripping from his hair and nose. "It was a coronary in the first place, Sylvia."

"He just d-d-d-doubled up," George said, stuttering with the chill, "and then toppled over."

Sylvia slowly put her head down upon the chest of her husband, whimpering, and everybody else turned away.

Martha picked Tad up in her arms and carried him up to the house. He too was crying because he knew Sylvia was. In the house, Martha sat in the big chair and held him. She smelt like flowers and her breast was soft where he had one fist in it. He would have liked to put his face there, but he was too big, and he had already made himself as small as he could.

· 9

THE strange thing was that in the days after she had heard of Alexander's death, Elizabeth thought oftener of Walter than of him, and sometimes walking down the hill to the Coast Road and along it to the village, she would say aloud to herself, "Alexander's dead," and try to think just what it meant to her. The fact was that Alexander had been dead to her for a long time. A certain wild feeling might flare within her remembering of a moment—as when the door of the cottage among the dunes closed them first alone together—but it passed more quickly than the throb of the heart or a murmur of pain. All the rest of the time, if she thought of him at all, it was in his peculiar relationship to Walter: the man who Walter thought the greatest success in the world. He admired all the unimportant things in Alexander, and dismissed his virtues. Something had got in the way of Walter's understanding very early in life, perhaps in the discipline he tried to put on himself when he thought he could become a priest. He had still been of that mind when he and Elizabeth had met in her aunt's house: a maiden lady's notion of the ideal match, her wild

Elizabeth and the ascetic boy. He had had God in his heart, as the old saying went, but the devil in his britches. When he had given it all up and let the devil out, his condition was soon worse; he must have thought himself spoiled in two ways instead of one, as a priest and as a man.

Love. What had man to give to man but love? What of worth but love's kindness? Yet one remembered one's own cruelties and deceptions. She often thought of the Sunday afternoon when Martha had tried to look deep into her eyes while she asked, "Mother, do you really like Doctor Winthrop?" And she had said as lightly as she could that she did like him. When the girl was gone, hurt, thinking she had lied to her, Elizabeth had thought to herself: I have given up my soul for love of him and now I have given up my child's soul. Which was not so. Martha had found her own way to the goodness and decency there was in Alexander, she had fought for compassion within herself and had found it. It was in her letters, in her reticences as well as in her revelations: she wrote of Alexander and his death remembering Marcus, Elizabeth thought, although Marcus's name never appeared in the letter.

Elizabeth had herself grieved over Marcus's death as no one else could know. The death of a phantom lover she could say now in the half-sentimental, half-cynical self-examination of a woman who knows her passion forever spent. She wondered if anyone except herself could understand Martha's marriage to Nathan Reiss. To embrace a demon fulfilled a lust for death. How near to insanity that could take one, she thought she knew. But day by day, the living hands reached out to pull one back: friends, work, the child, above all the child, and in time the demon could be made to seem respectable, and lies to oneself only lesser truths.

The last of Elizabeth's war refugees had long since returned to England to homes or government schools. A priest had come down from Belfast to try to persuade her to turn McMahon Manor into an orphanage; when she declined, he had broached, with much clearing of his throat, the possibility of making it a home for "waywards." "Father," she had said with an old deviltry, "I didn't know there was prostitution in Ireland."

The priest, with a blandness to match her own, had said, "There isn't, Mrs. Fitzgerald, which is why we have to find a home for the prostitutes."

But to create a charity for its own sake was not Elizabeth's way to self-fulfillment. She had been able and most willing to do a job when there was no one as well situated as herself to do it with the war orphans. She could be charitable for the sake of others, but not for her own sake, a distinction the priest necessarily disapproved. He did not press the matter, however: Philip McMahon was nearing seventy, and his sister a well-preserved sixty, he thought, and then confirmed it among the parish records. But even if the McMahons were longer-lived than himself, the church was the natural heir to an Irish estate without Irish beneficiaries. He reminded Elizabeth of this and was content in having fulfilled the mission assigned him.

It was while walking along the Coast Road on a summer day so clear she felt she could reach across the water and touch Scottish soil that Elizabeth thought first of going up to London to see Jonathan Hogan. He had not come to visit her and Philip that summer, and he was no longer teaching. When last Philip had seen him, he had taken rooms within walking distance of the British Museum, devoting himself entirely to research on his book. She wondered if she should write him first and decided against it. A little obstacle, if she allowed herself to contemplate it, could become a great barrier. She had not been out of Ireland in over thirteen years. Her brother phoned his London housekeeper to open the flat for her and Elizabeth brought her wardrobe somewhat up to date in Belfast.

Philip drove her to Dublin and chided her on what sort of a rendezvous she was going to have with Hogan to be getting herself up this way.

"It's with an old, old, man, I'm afraid," she said, and yet there was a curious gaiety in her heart.

"For the love of God, Elizabeth, don't you know any young ones? I'm sick to death of sitting down opposite myself to a glass of port and a game of chess."

"But you do like Jonathan," she said.

"So that's how it is," Philip said, and got the car up a kilometer or two faster.

It was a moment later that Elizabeth said, "That's how what is?"

Philip took his gloved hand from the wheel long enough to remove the empty pipe from his mouth. He set it in the ashtray, a suction-cupped American import that could be fastened atop the dashboard. "I'd rather he was a man who liked to hunt a bit."

"I remember he loved to garden," Elizabeth said. "I remember Martha coming home and telling me the first time she met him."

Philip grunted and drove on a distance before he asked, "Will I have the cottage aired? Or will you want the south wing opened up for him?"

Elizabeth looked around at him, startled. "Whatever gave you an idea like that?"

"My dear Elizabeth, I know you well enough by now, sister of mine. You've never gone on a mission and come home to me empty-handed yet."

"Once I did, Philip," she said, and looked ahead at the road they were about to climb, ribbed with ruts, but hedged along by the fragrant honeysuckle. "When I first came home."

"Empty-handed! You brought me yourself, didn't you? And little I knew all that was coming with you."

"Has it been that bad truly?"

"That bad or that good. It depends on which side of Parliament you're sitting." He shifted gears and concentrated on getting the car up the hill. Going down he said, "You haven't told me yet which rooms to have opened."

"I think none." But presently she added, "We shall have to see."

· 10

THE shawl fell from Jonathan's knees but he let it lie, for the sun was warm and there was scarcely any breeze. The scent of the freshly scythed hay was in the air, and from his chair at the cottage door he could see the farmer forking it into cocks. There was a timelessness to the scene which would not be so much longer. Even in Ireland in another generation what farmers were left would do their work entirely by machinery, and he who had said "shame" for all his lifetime on those who cherished the past above the present was glad that there was still a solitary gleaner on the land. He was reminded of Isak Dinesen's story, *Sorrow Acre*, which if he were to have to choose from seventy years of reading he would call the greatest short story ever written. But at seventy-seven one did not have to choose. One knew. He lifted a blue-veined, loose-skinned hand to shade his eyes and watched the swallows swoop and soar, two by two.

They also seemed to know. For all of the uncertainties of youth, court-ship never wavered in its goal. He lifted his face to the sun then and closed his eyes. "What is so rare as a day in June? Then if ever come perfect days . . ." He always felt that an Englishman should have written those lines, a Lake poet, Wordsworth probably. But it was an American, a Massachusetts Lowell.

He had himself married a Massachusetts woman, high-born as they came in America, and in a way it had prospered both his sons —in a democracy. He had courted her in Boston while he was in graduate school there. He could remember the striped coat he wore on the afternoon he first took her boating. It seemed, even from this distance, to have been as loud as Joseph's. What was a man that he remembered his own coat before he could remember the girl, and then only a whispering smile of her while he could still feel the texture of the coat?

"Jonathan, are you sleeping?"

"I'm dreaming." He turned his head only and, squinting from the after-glare of the sun, saw Elizabeth with her basket and flower shears. "What kind of a man is it who can remember the coat he wore on his first date and can't remember the girl?"

"It probably fit you badly."

How she indulged him! Now she was even making excuses for his youth.

"Well, the girl fit me better, I shall say that. That was in Boston about 1900. I don't suppose you were born yet."

"I was already gathering rosebuds where I might," Elizabeth said, and picked up the shawl from where it had fallen at his feet. She must have been an absolutely stunning beauty, he thought, for she was a handsome woman still, her head high, the gray-streaked black hair drawn tightly away from the patrician forehead. "Jonathan, do you know what day it is?"

"I do. They'll be getting on the boat today. I'm glad they're not flying, you know. And not for their sake especially. For my own. I want them to come soon, but not suddenly. That's an old man's distinction, I expect."

She lay the shawl over the arm of his chair. "Tad looks like Marcus, you know."

She was trying to prepare him, he thought, and it made him feel a bit like an invalid. "My heart is sound, Elizabeth. It's only the structure that needs to be shored up now and then."

She smiled down at him. "God knows, I've tried to put some flesh on those bones."

"As cook says, you couldn't do it with butter." He could hear the carpenters at work then, the hammering starting again at the big house. "What are you doing now up there?"

"I dare say that's the bathroom on the third floor. There's a great deal to be done, you know. We shall not have had so many rooms occupied since my refugees."

"From all directions," Jonathan said. He had at some time or other—though he could not remember when—met Sylvia's brother, Tony, who was coming from France with his French bride. And from America were coming Sylvia, Martha and Tad. "Which of the children around here are twelve, do you know, Elizabeth?"

She shook her head, and picked up the basket again from where she had set it down to fold the shawl. "It won't do, Jonathan. There's no one around here a fit comparison. Tad is precocious, I'm sure. He finished the eighth grade this year."

"He probably wets the bed, you had better take care."

"For shame, Jonathan."

"I don't approve the forced intellectual feeding of bright children. They're social, physical beings—not merely heads on sticks."

"He goes to one of the best schools in the country, one, if I'm not mistaken, you had something to do with the founding of yourself."

But Jonathan's mind had strayed ahead, or rather back: "I entered Rodgers University at the age of sixteen myself," he said. "So did Trent." He chuckled. "Marcus was the slow one among the Hogans. He was seventeen before he could make it."

Elizabeth threw open the door of the cottage. "Shall we let some sun in there for a while?" The sunlight seemed to fall on the whole of his thousand books: they looked to be that many. He had come over the year following her invitation, sending along a thousand books for a thousand days, as he had put it, and she had said at the time, "A thousand, you'll see, won't be near enough books." Now she asked, "What time is Mary coming up today?"

"Not till noon. She has to give dinner to the family."

"That's unfair," Elizabeth said. "They'll drive her away, taking advantage."

Mary did Jonathan's typing and secretarial work. She had gone to commercial school in Belfast, and was virtually the only girl on the coast who had found such work north of Larne.

"I was thinking of that myself," Jonathan said, slowly getting out of the chair. He stretched himself to the best height he was ever going to reach again. "I just sent young Tom Brennan up there on an errand for me. If he goes about it right, he'll get a free lunch, and they can smooch on their own time instead of mine."

"Aren't you the cunning one, Jonathan."

He did not like the way she sometimes had of treating him like a small child. That was the curse of age: people were not ashamed to look through you and tell you what they thought they saw. He made a rude joke to oblige her concept of him: "Well, I'd rather have her pregnant than not have her at all."

He went indoors and settled in the cushioned chair at the large table he used for a desk. He drew the lamp down from the ceiling and lit it, opened his notebook. He sucked on an empty pipe for he was not allowed tobacco until after lunch. There was a question that sorely troubled him almost every day. To give it a negative answer had the virtue at least of setting him to work. The question: Was he ever again to know the company of his peers?

They came, the American visitors, in a rented car, luggage piled atop it and canvassed over like a gypsy caravan. The farmer's youngest—and there was always one, barefooted, young enough to call the youngest—ran down from his lookout above the Coast Road, scattering dust and chickens, and singing out like a crier of old: "They be rounding the turn below the pump!" Elizabeth and Jonathan went out on the flagstone walk and waited, and Elizabeth remembered mutely, deeply, Marcus's coming that way, too. Jonathan looked at her sharply and knew by the sudden lift of her chin what she was remembering for they had often talked of it. Neither of them spoke until the car was bumping along at the bottom of the meadow and Elizabeth said, "We must get some fill for the hollow in the road."

Sylvia was driving, and with the car a right-hand drive, she got out the side nearer to Jonathan and Elizabeth. Jonathan remarked that there was still the loose-limbed swing to her of a woman dismounting a horse.

"Welcome home," Elizabeth said, looking only at her daughter. There was a long, slow shyness in the movement of Martha and her toward one another and almost a clash when finally they came together in a hard embrace. Afterwards they stood and looked at each other and wept in the midst of laughter.

Sylvia mediated the moment of diffidence between Tad and Jonathan.

"Ha!" Jonathan said, the boy already the height of the old man's shoulder, "it's a good thing you didn't wait any longer. I'd have had to look up to you."

"Wouldn't you know him anywhere?" Sylvia said.

Jonathan tugged at his own ear, a habit that went with his shyness. "Well, I'll say this: I'd like to!"

Tad smiled, a bright, sudden smile on so serious a mien, and Jonathan drew him close to kiss his forehead, and then hugged him.

Martha and Jonathan did not embrace. He put his hands upon her arms and felt her tremble as she leaned close and brushed his cheek with her lips, and that in itself hurt him, that and the flight of her eyes from his. He sensed a reserve far too deep for an old man to plumb. He was past his days of courting. People had to come to him.

Thaddeus Marcus Hogan, Jr., might not have been his grandfather's peer, but he was better intellectual company, the old man thought, discovering him day by day, than he had known in quite some time. One of his first questions, looking around the cottage, was, "Do you read all these books?"

"Perhaps not," the old man said.

"It's just that you think you might," the boy said, explaining more to himself than to Jonathan.

"I don't suppose you still take teddy-bears—or things like that—to bed with you?"

"No."

"Well, it's something like that." Jonathan thought he had moved their conversation back several years with that comparison.

Tad pushed it ahead: "I should think it would be easier to understand a book than a teddy-bear."

"Mmmmm. I think you have something there," his grandfather said.

Tad had the dark brown hair and the very blue eyes of his father, and sometimes Jonathan skipped a generation in his own mind talking with him. When on one occasion Tad said he thought he would like to be a diplomat, Jonathan said, "I thought you were going to be a doctor?"

"No. Nathan's a doctor. I used to think I'd like to be a veteri-narian, but I don't any more. I was just being sentimental, I guess."

"And what's wrong with that?"

Tad shrugged and drew a treble staff in the dust on the table with his finger. "My father was also a doctor," Tad said.

"Yes, I seem to remember putting him through medical school," the old man said dryly.

Tad said, "I'll be going to Rodgers in four years if they'll take me."

"Why shouldn't they take you?"

"Maybe I'll be too dumb." He said the nonsense and grinned impishly.

He seemed sometimes a little old man and then suddenly a boy. And he was likely at such a moment, without forewarning, to run outdoors, and perhaps clear across the meadow, scattering the sheep, and he might not come back for an hour or two, or for the whole afternoon sometimes. He had been brought up with a curious lack of discipline in some areas. Jonathan would have thought that Martha would be more likely to over-protect him than to let him go wild like that.

In the late afternoon of such a day, Jonathan might be giving Mary dictation when suddenly she would giggle in a suppressed way —rather as though she had hiccoughs, and he would know the mis-chiefer was back and at the cottage window making faces in at them. The old gentleman was never fast enough himself to see him.

Jonathan planned a trick. It was three days in the making and he needed Sylvia's help. They rigged up a square of unbreakable mir-ror on a pulley so that it would fall like a window shade when Jona-than released the string fastened under his desk. On the day that it worked Mary very nearly had hysterics, for Tad let out a shriek at the sudden sight of his own grimacing face.

"Would the gift the gods had gi' us," Jonathan said when Mary had got Tad in, "to see oursils as ithers see us."

That led him to getting down a volume of Robert Burns' poems and dismissing Mary for the day. Adjusting his glasses, he read Tad "Tam O'Shanter." He was again mixing generations, for he could quite literally believe that he was reading to Marcus and the quiet ache he felt within himself was because it seemed that Marcus's mother had died but recently. "Now, that's a tale for Hallowe'en," he said, finishing.

"I was born on Hallowe'en," Tad said.

"Were you? Yes, of course you were."

"The kids all call me 'Spooky'."

"Mmmmm. It could be worse, I suppose. In my day it was Stinky, or something like that."

"Grandpa Jon, could you and I take the ferry to Scotland and go and see the Robert Burns country?"

The old man put away his glasses. "You know about that, do you?"

"Papa used to read "Tam O'Shanter" to me. Now mother does—every Hallowe'en."

"Yes, they would," Jonathan murmured.

"Could we?"

"Eh?"

"Could we go across the channel to Ayre? I have the travel brochure in my room, pictures and maps and everything."

"Why not?" Jonathan said. "Why not indeed?"

After the Fields had come and gone and Sylvia returned to France with Tony and his wife—Sylvia still poking at Bohemia as though there were something in it she had lost in her own youth and hoped still to find—Martha tried at last to take some calculation of herself. Hearing of Jonathan's mirror trick on Tad she had thought: that's what I need. But one didn't see oneself looking in a mirror: that was only the person other people also saw, or the person one hoped other people saw. Always at the end of such self-seeking she asked if the quest was worth the effort. Was she not to others—to Tad, the only one who really mattered—all right as she was? The trouble with living outside oneself, never going inside, as it were, was that whatever there had been inside got more and more grown round as with some spiritual wisteria, and would in time, without ever showing itself again, die altogether. And, more troublous still, it must be assumed that then the outside person would die also, for however much she tried to pretend otherwise, a human being was only one person: one soul, one heart, one body. What duality there was was in the mind only. The essence was one.

Sometimes in the early mornings, especially on Sundays when Tad would oblige his grandmother by going to Mass with her, Martha would walk out among the hills alone following the paths of sheep and shepherds. She could see the wide blue of the channel waters and, on very clear days, the coast of Scotland like a cloudbank on the horizon. Inland she could see the summer greens, early grain the palest, the hay clover-spotted with purple, and the dark scrubby green of gorse on the hillsides. The cottages sat hither and yon, each of them beneath a twist of smoke, serene as only a North of Ireland Sabbath can be. And she would say to herself: this is what Marcus saw and loved. He might have stayed here by his own inclination, and staying, might have lived.

Erich had said he was wrong in his nostalgia for the primitive. But Erich was not always right, as he now well knew himself. She did not often see Erich, he and Nathan having quarrelled, but they shared a rare understanding—akin to that she had once had with Jonathan—and a somewhat similar purpose in life: the control of something to the formation of which each had, in his own case, contributed.

She had not thought Nathan a particularly good man, marrying him, but neither had she thought him evil. A fair question was what had she ever thought evil? The word to her had always been an abstraction, believing as she did, all mortal acts to be subject to mitigation: the catechismic definition of a mortal sin: a serious matter given sufficient reflection and full consent of the will. The closest she had ever come to a personal sense of evil had been emotional, her reaction as a girl to Genevieve Revere. She did not think Nathan evil now: if she thought that she would have been able to choose between her responsibilities: for him and to Tad. Nathan was in some ways a strong force for good—as Marcus had once called him, an instinctively good doctor—so long as it did not conflict with what he wanted. It had become her mission, her vigil, to guide and persuade his wants—even as she did Tad's—and sometimes to oppose them. Nathan had wanted to quit the Rehabilitation Plan when the threat of scandal over Sylvia's politics arose, and he had been quite capable, she had realized then, of doing it with all the publicity attendant on the Communist issue. Nor had he seen anything wrong in his contemplated action: he had yielded because she persuaded him. To this day Sylvia knew nothing of it, for the matter passed entirely with Alexander's death and the subsequent merging of the *Star* with the *Evening Post*. But from then on, Martha had taken up her vigil on him. Sometimes he even thanked her when she intervened, and sometimes he would then proceed to find another way of doing the very thing she had forestalled.

Now, away from him for the first time, she could get some perspective on herself, something she had neither wanted nor dared to do since Marcus's death. She was startled to discover the extent of her spiritual withdrawal. Never once, she supposed, had she and Nathan touched souls. In the beginning it had been involuntary on her part, Marcus too strong within her to admit any other influence. Now, she held herself consciously apart from him—not physically, spiritually only. She had managed that separation. She doubted very much that Nathan had any notion of it at all. But now it had got beyond Nathan, her withdrawal. She looked out from within herself and then closed up if there were a chance of anyone's looking in. Thus she could not admit even Jonathan. And she would have liked to let him know about her affinity with Erich. He would understand it—if she could make him understand how she had come to marry Nathan Reiss. For her it was impossible even to try.

Elizabeth thought she understood her daughter better than Martha understood herself. She had, after all, lived many years in duplicity, but her deception had not been of herself: she had contrived to understand everything. Martha, she feared, was deliberately contriving not to understand some things. She walked out one Sunday morning and waited atop the first ridge to see which way Martha would come through the valley. By the time she appeared the church bells all were silent.

"I'd have come further," Elizabeth said when they met, "if only I'd known the way you'd gone."

Their eyes met. Martha smiled briefly and said nothing.

"But I don't suppose you wanted that."

"You were at church," Martha said, choosing a literal interpretation of her mother's words.

"I wonder if you ever miss going to church. I must say I never did—until I didn't have anything else . . . Except you."

"I didn't come till much later," Martha said, a trace of humor in her voice.

Elizabeth did not deny it: it was so. What she had given to Alexander she had not taken as she then believed from an all but willing husband, but from her daughter. "Did it hurt you very much?"

"Nothing hurts very much, mother, when you get used to it."

Elizabeth drew back for the words cut deeply. They walked in silence for a time, the bleating of sheep and the scuffle of their own footsteps the only intrusion on the stillness. They came to a pond where two boys were wading, their short pants hitched up to the crotch and their Sunday white shirt sleeves rolled to the armpits.

Three other boys watched from the shore, sedately dressed and making not a sound.

"What are they doing?" Martha asked.

"They're looking for duck eggs." The boys in the water were stepping gingerly as though they were already walking on them.

"And the others?" Martha indicated the watchers.

"They're the Protestant lads. Theirs is a Presbyterian Sunday. Look now. Kevin has one."

The boy shot his long bare arm into the water, the motion reminding Martha of a swan's dive. And indeed his shirttail popped out behind even as a swan's tail.

"Will they share with the others?"

"They will not. Sunday is the only advantage they have over the Protestants. Otherwise, they're outnumbered."

"There are times when I enjoy my present perspective on religion," Martha said as they walked on.

"Did you leave the church because Nathan asked it?"

"No."

"Don't answer me if you don't want to. I see I've asked a question without meaning to."

"I left the church because I did not want someone who did not believe in it to join it for my sake."

"I suppose he would have had to be baptized in some Christian faith, wouldn't he?"

"He offered to be."

"How ironic!" Elizabeth said, thinking that Nathan Reiss might have embraced the excuse to become a Christian.

"I had given up the Sacraments after Marcus's death anyway. I wanted to hold him but I couldn't, and I didn't want anything else." She said it flatly, matter-of-factly.

She had been right about the demon love in her dark Irish understanding, Elizabeth thought. "You'll come back to the church in time," she said.

"I don't know. But I am glad now things are as they are. Tad will have the choice of his father's way—or the religion he was baptized in—or God knows." She touched her foot to a toadstool and toppled it, white on top and green as bile underneath. "He's been a very good boy since we are here."

"Isn't he generally?"

"Not always. He wants to know—too much. Which I don't mean is bad. That part is only difficult."

Elizabeth said, "Didn't you want to know at his age? You must have felt that something was wrong."

"We can't get away from that, can we, mother? The sin in the family: I don't see why you're so proud of it."

"I don't know that I am," Elizabeth said coldly.

"You carry it in front of you like a processional cross."

"Blasphemy is scarcely necessary. Or is it? Did you have to leave the church before you could tell your mother what you thought of her?"

They paused in the grove of trees at the bottom of the meadow for they were alone there. Martha said, "You've asked me to compare Tad to myself at his age and I'm trying to. I worshiped you and that's what you wanted. You didn't want me to love you, not really. You would have had to let me in then. I don't want Tad to worship me, I want him to love me. I want to be there when he needs me, not when I need him."

"I don't think that is something you are going to be able to determine, however you may think so now. And what of your husband? Can you categorize that love also?"

"I have loved one man only," Martha said quietly.

"Then why did you marry again? Why?" Elizabeth persisted.

"Because I needed him and he wanted me."

Her mother caught hold of her wrist. "Are you sure you needed him? Or was it the other way around? Didn't you want him, and didn't he need you?"

"I am sure," Martha said, the vein standing out on her forehead.

"It is time for questions and I will ask them," Elizabeth said. "I do not want happening to you what happened to your father, the pleasure of his life was in his persecution of himself. Do you sleep with Nathan?"

"Yes!"

"And die at every act."

Martha did not answer.

"You are in danger, child, not only of losing the power to love, but of losing your immortal soul."

"Mother, I do not give a damn about my immortal soul. If there is such a thing and I'd had my way, I'd have given it to the devil myself long ago. Nathan saved me from suicide. I used to look out at the garden, at the grape arbor where the tool shed used to be, and I wished the tool shed back. Then Nathan came one day and persuaded me I was alive. I felt him when he touched me. I knew that if life were forced upon me I could live. We were married that very day by a justice of the peace. And if there is anything for which I ever hope Tad to be grateful to him, it is that. And that is as close as I shall come to salvation."

Elizabeth let go her hand, suddenly realizing that she held it. "It is a greater burden you place on your son than ever I should have placed on you, for all my selfishness," she said, and walked alone up to the house.

Only Jonathan and Tad in the end discovered satisfaction in re-union, in their exploration of each other. He and Martha could not even reminisce. They could talk of friends, the Muellers, but not of one another. After all, Jonathan thought, remembering their photograph in the *Star,* at their finest moment together he had had to go and throw up against the Stadium wall. But he and Tad were a different matter. He could see the boy absorbing certain interests from him, and one day, during their trip to Scotland, he realized there was an important area in the boy's values which he would never need influence. Tad had found a postcard, a mountain scene, the legend written entirely in Gaelic.

"I want to send it to Nathan," Tad explained.

"I can walk as far as the post office with you."

"I don't want to send it from here. From France or some place like that."

"Why?"

Tad weighed the wisdom of confiding in his grandfather. "I want him to think it's written in Hebrew."

"The character resemblance between the languages," Jonathan said, "is very superficial."

The boy looked up at him and smiled, saying nothing, but quite as though to say, Jonathan was sure, that so was Nathan very super-ficial. The cunning disturbed him, but he felt the instinct to be true, and that to Jonathan had always been enough in any man.

· 11

ON THE flight back to New York from Paris Sylvia observed what good company Tad had become. His summer with Jonathan had made him both grave and courtly, the habit of solicitousness he had acquired for the aging man staying with him. The two of them had crossed from Scotland down into the Lake country, Jonathan's—and Tad's—favorite part of all England. More than fifty years before, Jonathan had gone from Keswick to Windermere in a horse drawn coach on his own first trip to England. All this Tad retold with a touching sense of the old gentleman's nostalgia, and gently miming his way now of carefully counting out his money from a change purse and murmuring: "Well spent, well spent." Having managed that much of England together, the two of them had gone on to London, each in the other's care. Tad had idled many hours among the Elgin marbles and other antiquities of the British Museum while Jonathan worked in the library. Tad was now thinking that he would like to be an archeologist.

Thank God for Tad, Sylvia thought. For her own part, she had found it difficult to stay out her appointed time, and she ended up visiting the D.P. camps, the memory of which even now disturbed her, the desolate becoming dissolute, the homeless despairingly at home in their homelessness. One could not even take the children out of this for care. To where do you return a stateless child? She was fleeing home herself with a sense of urgency to extend the work of her own project. After Alex' death she had leaned heavily on the Children's Plan. She had felt it the one thing she cared to salvage out of her life till then. Not a whit cared she any longer for politics or publications. She had arranged the sale of the *Star* to the first bidder, and when George Bergner was out of a job thereupon, she had been persuaded by Reiss to make him public relations council for the Children's Rehabilitation Plan. She had not thought in the beginning of the Plan's ever needing public relations. She had yielded. The important thing, she had told herself was to know that she was yielding.

"Mother," Tad said, thinking Martha asleep.

Martha opened her eyes. The signal was flickering and the loud-speaker system in the plane had been turned on. The stewardess was waiting, smiling, for the announcement that they were approaching International Airport.

Tad's eyes were dancing.

Sylvia drew a deep breath and another: her moment of fear. One wanted to live. Oh, yes, and the more the older one got. Thus, she thought, was made a conservative. She said to Martha: "Are you afraid?"

"A little," Martha said, but her eyes were on Tad. "I wonder if Nathan will meet us here. He said he would if it were possible."

"It's so damned far down," Sylvia said, "from up here."

Martha smiled broadly at her. "Courage."

"That's what we need—courage and a paper bag."

Tad looked round at her. "You're kidding, Syl."

"I hope so."

Nathan waved to them from beyond the glass partition as soon as they came into Customs. While they waited their turns for baggage inspection he pantomimed pleasure, affection, what-did-you-bring-me to whomever of them looked his way.

"What a ham," Sylvia said, but it occurred to her that you always felt good, seeing Nathan. He looked so vigorous, self-confident. It was a good thing to see in a doctor, in any human being in this shaky world. Proclaim yourself a savior and you've got a congregation.

He kissed them all, Tad on both cheeks. You could see all the American dream in him, Sylvia thought. He might have come from Brooklyn or up from New York's East Side. Instead he had come from the playgrounds of Europe which had also bred the festering camps she had just seen there. She could not blame him that he was not there. As soon could she blame herself. She asked immediately about the farm, how many new children, who, where, and particulars about one and another's of their progress.

"I will tell you everything," Nathan said. He took their baggage checks. "We shall send the luggage in a taxi. I have a surprise for you." The luggage arranged, he led the way through the terminal. "Someone you have not seen in many years, Martha," he said as they reached the curb where a limousine was waiting, a chauffeur coming to attention as they approached. "Nor I until this summer."

That much preparation Sylvia had before the car door was opened and the Baroness Schwarzbach leaned forward in the seat, her hand extended.

"Martha, dear child, do you remember me?"

"I remember you very well," Martha said, and took her hand.

The Baroness looked round Martha to Sylvia. "Mrs. Winthrop, one meets many places in a lifetime."

Sylvia also took the hand offered her and murmured: "How nice to see you again, Baroness Schwarzbach."

Nathan brought Tad close to the Baroness. "And this is Thaddeus, whom we call Tad. Your Aunt Johanna, Tad."

An aunt to end all aunts, Sylvia thought. Nathan had arranged for them to spend the night as the Baroness' houseguests before flying on to Traders City. Sylvia declined, saying she always stayed at the Sulgate in New York.

The Baroness was gracious. "We shall take you there on our way. I believe it is near to my house. John will know." She indicated the chauffeur. "But you will come to dinner and for the evening, please, Mrs. Winthrop. I have not forgotten your hospitality in Naples, and I have arranged a small gathering."

Sylvia acquiesced, and settled in the luxurious car on one side of Martha while the Baroness, on the other, took Martha's hand and gently patted it now and then, talking of their last meeting. She was as plump as when she had last seen her, Sylvia thought, but a little younger looking. Nathan and Tad sat on what, in Sylvia's childhood, she had called the monkey seats. Everyone became quite gay.

"It is the city of the modern world, New York," the Baroness said as the car moved smoothly, grooving its way into the sludge of traffic toward Manhattan.

Sylvia eased herself a little to the side, the better to see the profile of the man at the wheel, John. If he knew the city so well as the Baroness implied, he would be new to her employ, an American acquisition. John was young and dark, a strapping fellow with a ruddy glow to his cheeks. Sylvia leaned back in the seat and was mirthful within herself remembering a story Tony had told her: it concerned an old gentleman in Paris, a roué in his declining years and the bane of his numerous and proper family whom he nonetheless ruled with patriarchal tyranny. Then one day his doctor told him that he must give up the activity for which he was notorious. Whereupon, he hired a girl to come to his rooms every day at the usual hour. She was paid her fee just to sit with him the hour and to hold her tongue thereafter. The family remained in awe of his virility and submissive to his law to the day he died.

Tad, having seen within the year the film *Gone With the Wind,* was inclined to call the Baroness Aunt Pittypat, he confided to Martha, not that she was flustery in her manner, but she resembled her physically, like an animate doll, and was much concerned for everyone's comfort. Martha did not think the Baroness would be especially charmed by the comparison.

"I'm not going to say it to her," Tad said, and then speaking conspiratorially: "She must have tons of money."

The expression was Annie's. Martha laughed. "I dare say."

Tad was given the blue room at the top floor of the East Side house. He thought the house resembled a French hotel. There was a tiny elevator in which there was room for no more than two people at once. He could look out his window to the building across the way where he could see the boxed shrubbery of a penthouse garden, and beyond it a façade of New York buildings like a patchwork of glass. The bathroom between his room and his mother and Nathan's was walled in mirrors, something which at once fascinated and discomfited him.

"I remember the Baroness' house in Paris," Martha said. "I was much older than you, but I'd never been in a place like it, not that people lived in. But Nathan was very much at home there and that made it easier. She and her husband, you see, had sort of adopted him. They were his patrons in the way people do in Europe with artists or writers or doctors."

"Who was Pépé?" Tad asked, having heard the Baroness inquire if Martha remembered him.

"A toy French poodle the Baroness carried around rather like a baby."

"Ugh."

"I remember feeling that way, too," Martha said. "It was all very strange—but it's vivid to me still in the way dreams sometimes are. My father had just died and I was terribly lonesome for Marcus. Then on New Year's Day I got a cablegram from him asking me to come home at once and marry him."

Tad was looking over the books which had been placed on his bedside table: *Tom Brown's School Days, The Mystery of Sanders' Cave, Space Cadet.*

"I'll bet Nathan was mad," he said.

Martha laughed. "Perhaps. But he didn't show it."

"He smiled," Tad said, and drew his own lips wide across his teeth in mimicry.

"I don't much like that, Tad," she said.

"I'm sorry." He looked restlessly about the exquisite room. He toured the lithographs hanging on the walls, French caricatures of the courts of law. "When are we going home?"

"Tomorrow," Martha said.

"What kind of books are there in your room?"

"Come and see," Martha said.

Nathan was dressing for dinner. Martha's gown hung at a closet door, freshly pressed and brought upstairs by a pretty young servant who batted her eyes at Dr. Reiss.

Nathan said: "We have not had a chance to talk, Martha." He watched them in the mirror before which he was adjusting his black tie. "I have become very interested in Zionism while you were away this summer. I never was before, you know. There are some very interesting people . . ."

Tad said: "Did you get the postcard I sent you, Nathan—the one in Hebrew?"

"I was just thinking about it," Reiss said. "That was very thoughtful of you, Tad, to send it to me."

Tad examined the half-dozen books on the table between the beds and selected one to his liking, *The Plague* by Camus. "May I take this one, mother?"

Martha glanced at it. "Do you think you will understand it?"

Tad shrugged. "I liked *L'Etranger.*"

When Tad had returned to his room Nathan said: "A boy his age should not be allowed to read everything, do you think?"

"I think he should be allowed to read what he wants to read."

"Then you will have to explain it to him."

"I generally try," Martha said. She could not remember Nathan's having read a book since they were married.

After a moment Nathan said: "Do you mind very much coming to this house, Martha?"

She looked at him in the mirror, her own brows arched in wry humor. "Not if you don't, Nathan."

He finished bowing his tie before asking: "What do you mean, Martha?"

"I have always remembered the Baroness with affection. She was very kind to me, and she gave me something I might not otherwise have got—a respect for my father and how he died. When last you and I spoke of her, you were concerned that she thought you had betrayed her."

"It was all a misunderstanding, a confusion," Nathan said. "But I have explained and she has accepted. When she wrote to me that she was coming to New York I did not tell you, and I was very glad you were not here. I can tell you that now. You do not like to see me humiliate myself. And when one has to explain, it is humiliating, is it not?"

"I shouldn't think so. But that's the difference between us."

"Are you not glad to see me?" he said reproachfully.

"I am glad to see you, Nathan. And I shall be very glad to get home."

"This was a mistake—is that what you are saying? I'm sorry Martha. I thought you would be pleased—for just one day. And it is very important to me in many ways."

"I understand," she said and began to dress.

He watched her with critical satisfaction and when she had finished her make-up and tucked the last strand of her hair into the braided bun, he brought from his pocket a pearl and diamond chip pendant. Watching her in the mirror he fastened the clasp at the back of her neck. "Always I have tried to give you jewels," he said, "and always you have tried to give me a book."

"Wouldn't it be dreadful the other way around?" Martha said with gentle humor.

She wore the jewelry with reluctant grace.

Martha, meeting the distinguished company the Baroness had gathered for the evening, began to understand the ways in which it was important to Nathan. The Baroness was building—indeed seemed to have built—an American salon probably the match of that which Martha remembered with such awe in Paris. Philanthropy would be in common among most of the guests—some in the arts, some in medicine, and in the course of the evening she was able to trace the associations by which she assumed Nathan to have become interested in Zionism. She had not seen him so voluble and attentive to so numerous an audience since the days of his arrival in Lakewood. The difference here, however, was that he could move with the ease of belonging: the Baroness' prestige was behind him: there was a certain hauteur in his manner that Lakewod would have much

admired could he have managed it for them. Perhaps now he would
be able to carry it over. That particular vision of the future gave
her no great cheer. She felt herself removed to an even more distant
observation point of the life in which she presumably participated.

It was late in the evening when dancing had started in the first
floor gallery that the Baroness took Martha by the arm and drew
her apart. "Now, my dear, you and I may talk. In all my houses
I have always insisted on little coves of privacy." The Baroness
looked amused, glancing up at Martha, and Martha wondered if she
had been aware at the time of the cove of privacy into which Nathan
Reiss had led her on the night of the New Year's ball in Paris. "This
will do," the Baroness said.

The room was a small solarium, its double doors open upon the
dance, its opaque glass ceiling veiling them from the eyes presumably
in the adjoining building. Gold, brown and white chrysanthemums
banked the walls, their pungent sweetness pervasive in the room.

"Almost twenty years," the Baroness said as they sat side by side
in chairs of Danish leather. "We did not know then what lay between
us and our next meeting, and isn't it well not to know?"

The Baroness arranged her plump jeweled hands in the shape of
a cupola in her lap. "Now it is you I wish to talk about. You have a
beautiful son. His father must have been a splendid person. Such
a tragedy. I wish you would tell me about him. Once before I tried
to coax you. You were too shy. But oh, I remember your eyes the
morning you received the cablegram. It was the only time in my life
I was ever jealous of a woman, if you will believe me."

"It was a very great moment," Martha said. "I've even been jealous
of it myself."

The Baroness collapsed her hands and folded them. "You are en-
chanting still! I tried to learn about you from your friend, Mrs. Winthrop. She did not tell you? I knew that she would not. Nor did she
come tonight, you see. I knew that, too. She has no understanding
of women. I do not know really what she understands—not as much
I expect as she thinks she does. Mind now, I liked her, but she is
the sort of woman I always like to provoke. Do you know what I
mean? To shock."

Martha smiled.

The Baroness drew a deep breath. "But it was all a more serious
matter. I knew she felt I was . . . unclean. Perhaps she was right.
Where one survives and many perish, there are stories. And part of

a story is always the truth. Fire is a great purgative—which is why the Christians invented purgatory.

"But we were going to talk about you."

"I don't mind that we're not," Martha said.

"Ah, but I do. I want to talk about the good things. His name was Marcus?"

"Thaddeus Marcus Hogan, Senior," Martha said.

Some time after they had returned to Traders City Martha brought herself to ask Nathan outright how the Baroness had escaped the Nazis.

"You must not think unkindly of her if I tell you, Martha. One survives as one can at such a moment. The Nazis were corrupt and sometimes available to bribery . . ."

It occurred to Martha, his speaking so earnestly, explicitly, to wonder just for a fleeting instant, whether he was justifying the Baroness before her—or her captors.

"She persuaded a lieutenant, I believe—I am not sure and you can understand I would not press her for more than she wished to tell me—to take flight with her over international waters." Nathan made a slight adjustment in his own pride, telling the next part of the story, and Martha remembered Sylvia's saying to him at the dinner table, of the Baroness: she has other interests now. "I suppose she took him as her lover for they lived at her villa in Ischia throughout the war. But it came to the attention of the Italian partisans, and after their insurrection, they took the man and executed him."

Violence for violence, Martha thought. But she could understand now why Sylvia was not able to talk about her meeting with the Baroness Schwarzbach in Naples in the autumn of 1945.

PART
FOUR

1950

• 1

It was almost inevitable that a boy like Tad, given the circumstances of his childhood, should on reading *Hamlet* at the age of sixteen become obsessed by the parallels he could draw to his own condition. He spent the summer before he was to enter Rodgers University with Sylvia on the farm. He was to have gone to Ireland by himself to visit old Jonathan, but Jonathan died that spring quickly and quietly of a cerebral hemorrhage. Jonathan, whose health had always been a matter of concern to others, rarely to himself, had lived to the age of eighty-one.

Sylvia, inviting the boy, knew she was to have her hands full. He did not disappoint her. There were times he would not sleep in his bed at night. Out walking all night long. Miles along the river and back, he would say, and she believed him. Even as a small boy he had loved to go off great distances by himself. But Mr. Walker, the manager of the farm, got the fright of his life one dawn when he went to the far pasture to bring the cows in for milking: he heard Tad declaiming in the woods. "Talking to himself at the top of his lungs. That boy's not right." His own son could let the clock alarm run down without turning over in his bed.

There was also the matter of girls. It was Sylvia's practice to use student nurses from Lakewood among the crippled or recuperating children where she could. Tad needed to have nothing to do with the Rehabilitation house: Sylvia's own cottage was far enough away. But Tad fell into the practice of intercepting one or another of the nurses after work, teasing her, and making outrageous proposals: to one that she go swimming with him in the nude after dark. "He said things that made me blush," she told Sylvia, which, Sylvia, thought, was no easy accomplishment.

"What shall we do with you, Tad?" she said on the night she decided to finally have it out with him. "You're all flame and no hearth. You can't go wild like this, you know."

"I haven't hurt anyone. I haven't *done* anything. You know that." He glanced at her and then down at the fingers he had woven through one another. "I wouldn't know how." And after a few seconds: "I wonder who's going to teach me that."

373

"There's time enough," Sylvia said.

"They have dirty minds," Tad said, "and if they'd thought I was serious, they wouldn't have come to you about it at all."

My God, sixteen! Sylvia thought. He was tall, but thin as a flagpole, and with the crew or mohawk or whatever kind of haircut he had, his head looked smaller than it actually was. He had been much handsomer as a child. He was managing while she watched him to interlace his legs as well as his fingers.

"Most people do have dirty minds, I think," he went on.

"Sometimes," Sylvia admitted.

"I don't see how it can be a sometimes thing. Either you have or you don't have."

He had trapped her in that lawyerish way of his. This was what drove Nathan Reiss to fury about him. He made the otherwise graceful Nathan stampede like a baited bull, beguiling him into an untenable position—often on a moral issue. One might think the boy raised by the Jesuits from the precision of his mind. It was when he began again on a favorite recent subject of his, George Bergner, that Sylvia suddenly realized the model his fantasy was following. She always tried to answer his questions honestly: indeed she had little choice. Tad could spot a lie, she thought, even before the liar himself was sure of having told one.

"He wasn't really a very good newspaper man, was he, Syl?"

"He wasn't trained as a newspaper man at all. Alexander at least had written a column for a number of years. But George did very well as long as Alex was alive. He's one of those people you meet now and then who can't be on their own. Somebody told me once— I've forgotten who, maybe it was your father—that that was what the Depression did to some people."

"And now he's got Nathan to hang onto," Tad said with the relentlessness of a terrier.

"I suppose you could say that." It was true, she knew, George deferred entirely to Nathan in his public relations work for the Plan, although in the line of responsibility, it should have been to her. And Nathan used him, sometimes like a personal servant.

"Good old Polonius," Tad said. "May I have one of your cigarets, Syl?"

"No."

"I shall bum them from the nurses."

"Take one."

He lit her cigaret and his own. The maid came in and cleared

the coffee things on a tray and Sylvia was pleased to see the boy un-
tangle himself and gallop to the door to hold it open for her.

"I suppose you'd like a brandy now, too?"

It was said in jest, but he responded seriously. "No, thanks. I've
promised mother, you know. Only wine. I hope I'll have the guts to
stand up to it at Rodgers . . . Syl, do I look as young as I am?"

"My boy, you don't look half as old as you are."

Tad grinned with pleasure.

"I'd kill anybody who said that to me," Sylvia said.

Tad puffed elaborately at his cigaret. "How old were you when
you first slept with a man?"

"Forty-seven," Sylvia said without expression.

Tad looked at her, his eyes bulging.

"Which serves you damned right for asking a question like that.
I don't think your mother has ever asked a personal question in her
life."

"That's because she doesn't care about other people. She'd rather
not know—in case somebody might ask her a question or two." He
re-weighed his speculation on his mother. "You know, I think that's
true. She doesn't have any friends except you that she cares about
really. That crowd of Nathan's—I can tell how she feels. Me too.
They're a bunch of squares. Cadillacs and caviar."

"Both very good in small doses," Sylvia said.

"I'll take pigs' feet, thank you, and small beer."

"You're a peasant."

"A knave in peasant's clothes . . . Syl . . ."

She interrupted him: "How long have you been playing Hamlet,
Tad?"

He stuck the tip of his tongue between his teeth and she could
see by his eyes that he was excited, pleased to have been discovered.
She wished instantly she had not asked him.

"You see it, don't you?" he said.

"I can see some adolescent nonsense brewing," she said.

"A toy in blood," Tad said, having got his Hamlet down well.
For a moment he fixed his eyes upon her, weighing whether or not
to confide his elaborate projection. Sylvia would have given a great
deal to divert him. His confidences flattered her but they also dis-
mayed her. Intuitively she knew the turns his mind must now be
taking. Tad drew his chair up close to hers, jockeying it—and her—
into position.

"Don't you think it's weird that Nathan was right there when my father tumbled down the elevator shaft? I know he smashed his hand. But that made him a real hero, didn't it?"

"It happened, Tad. That's all . . . I think you're playing a very dangerous game with yourself."

"Why—if it's with myself?" he said sharply, and in a way that made her feel she must let him go on aloud, involving her, involving someone at least to answer him in ways not necessarily to his liking.

"I was there at the time," she said. "Your father was upset, disturbed when he left the office."

"Then why didn't you go after him?"

It was a question she had asked herself too many times. "I couldn't know what was going to happen, Tad."

"But Nathan could!"

"He could not and did not!"

"All right, Syl," he said placatingly. "But what happened to him: it set him up with mother, didn't it? Tell me, what can I do? That's what he always says to her—and then he goes on and does whatever he wants and she doesn't even know it."

"She knows it," Sylvia said quietly. "I know it when he does it to me." In that Tad was quite right: Reiss always consulted and then proceeding as he had wanted to in the first place, he was likely to say: But Sylvia, I thought we decided . . .

"Then why don't you stop him?"

"Because it's always too late. By then he has made whatever it was work."

The boy threw up his hands wildly. "You're all crazy!"

And for a soon vanished second Sylvia saw it that way too. Nathan Reiss took everyone he could use exactly where he wanted to go himself. The Plan had grown to something far beyond what Sylvia had anticipated: but was that bad? She would not say so. There was a center in New York now, a Long Island estate converted into such a convalescent home as she had made of the farm. Another was contemplated in San Francisco and among its benefactors was Alberto Gemini. Ironic, but she could not say it was bad.

"Everybody's crazy but thee and me," she said, "and there are times I think even thee's a bit teched."

But Tad said: "Remember when Grandpa Jon and I went to Scotland? I found a postcard that was written in Gaelic. I mailed it to Nathan from Holland and when I got home I asked him if he'd got the Hebrew card I'd sent him. He said: that was very thoughtful of you, Tad."

"So?"

"He's a phony, Syl," the boy said passionately, begging for confirmation. "Now he claims he's a Zionist and he doesn't know as much about it as I do. And he doesn't care as much!"

Sylvia took the boy's hands in hers. "Tad, you must understand there's a good deal of pretense in all of us. I know, Nathan's got more than most of us. But we like people to see us as we'd like to be, not as we are. I don't doubt for a moment that Nathan's causes aren't always idealistic. It's done to impress somebody—to enhance his own prestige. I don't know. But this is not unusual practice in church or charity. It is fairly common practice."

"But why do they take people like him? Don't they know what he's doing it for?"

"They may. But it's not a point easily established. Sometimes the line between sincerity and—illusion is very thin. I can only say that a great deal of good is often done in this world out of dubious motive."

Tad shook his head. "I don't dig it. I don't."

"You will—in time, but when you do, I hope you won't like it any more than you do now," Sylvia said.

The Hamlet fantasy having waxed then waned as other interests urged themselves upon him. He and Sylvia went twice a week to the music festival and Ravens' Park, a few miles south of Lakewood. He played a rather noisy piano himself and loved to break up classical themes into a jazz beat. He invited two friends out for a week who had finished at the Barker School with him the previous spring, and they gave Sylvia a recital one night on the veranda, the three of them on piano, drums and milk cans that Sylvia swore woke every chicken in the coop a quarter of a mile away.

The day it was time for him to go home, Sylvia took him to Lakewood where he waited to drive back to Traders City with Nathan. She put the accelerator to the floor, returning to the farm, and drove directly to the Rehabilitation house where the children came flocking as soon as they saw her.

Nathan on the way into town talked about how wonderful it was going to be for Tad in the University. "I wanted you to have a car, but your mother does not think you should, and she is probably right. She would worry. You will be able to rent one sometimes. You must take your driver's license."

"I'm not worried about it," Tad said. The fact was, and he wasn't sure Nathan did not know it, too, that cars were not permitted on the campus of Rodgers University.

"What athletics will you take?"

"None if I can get out of it," Tad said.

"None?"

"I'll ride if I can, and swim. Maybe some tennis. No football, Nathan."

"It is a shame. Competitive athletics are very good. When you were a child, you were very competitive. You kept me on my toes, let me tell you. I do not know. Sometimes I think the Barker School is not as well balanced as it could be."

Tad was tempted to suggest that military school for him would have been more to Nathan's tastes, but the fact was that baiting Nathan gave him no pleasure. Sometimes Nathan did not even know it, and sometimes when he found out, he would complain to Martha of it. Tad wondered suddenly: if I called him "father" would it please him? He hadn't been an easy kid to bring up, he thought now of himself. Sylvia was right when she had said to him that he'd never given Nathan a chance. There were two sides, etc. etc. He fell to thinking then of what it would be like to try for the rest of his time at home to be really decent to Nathan.

Nathan said, coming out of a reverie of his own: "I am thinking of getting a sports car—a Jaguar, perhaps. What do you think your mother will say?"

"Just get her a fish net for her hair at the same time," Tad said.

Nathan smiled. "She will say it is undignified. Do you think it is?"

"No. I think it's a fine idea," Tad said, making a beginning on agreeability.

"May I quote you?" Nathan said half-jokingly.

"Sure. She'll just say we're both square."

"I have never heard your mother use the word. What kind of an automobile would you prefer?"

"A Dusenberg," Tad said.

Nathan glanced at him. "You're pulling my leg."

"No. I'm serious. I like old cars."

"But did you know I drove one in a race once?"

Tad seemed to have heard the story before, but he could not remember the circumstances. "Did you win?"

"Yes. It was very exciting. . . . Tad, in New York when you are East, sometimes perhaps the Baroness Schwarzbach will invite you to visit her. Will you go?"

Tad thought about it .He did not care very much for the Baroness. She had a way, talking to a person, of trying to look down inside him. He was intrigued by her foreignness and the fact that she was rich in a way that no one else he knew was—except Sylvia. Sylvia didn't show it. The Baroness did. Tad had actually visited but three times altogether, the last time in the spring when he had gone out with Nathan and his mother to be interviewed at Rodgers. That was the time she had really got to him, sitting on the side of his bed and saying: "Tell me, mein Tad, what does it feel like to become a man?"

Nathan, he assumed, visited her whenever he went East.

"I don't expect I'll have much time for visiting," he said finally in answer to Nathan's question.

"But if you do, I want to ask a favor of you: do not confide in her all the things you do not like about me. She has known me for a long time. But in a way it is with her like your mother is about you. You can be a very difficult boy sometimes, but in the end your mother will always defend you. Do you understand what I mean?"

"I understand," Tad said.

· 2

TAD was observed early by his teachers at Rodgers University to have the makings of a scholar. He contrived to keep his bookish predilection from his fellow students and largely succeeded. They knew him to have a sharp tongue, a good allowance, and an indifference to authority just short of insubordination—assets all in a community of college freshmen. He roomed alone, ate in the less fashionable places, but occasionally stood a feast that won him favor with both gourmet and glutton, a distinction not always possible among lower classmen.

The campus of Rodgers was vast and uncrowded, the school heavily endowed especially in land. The agricultural college and experimental farm adjoined the main grounds adding miles of comparatively secluded walks. Tad was reminded, exploring the well-hedged pastures and fields, of England. He could have gone quite a long time without striking up particular friendships within his college: he supposed until winter. He did not repulse overtures of other boys, but he was slow to make them himself and tended to be suspicious of anyone who sought his company. He was slower still to accept the friendliness of one or another of his teachers. There he could see the cliques forming. He came very soon to understand that a teacher was measured among other teachers by the quality of the boys he attracted. Too much camaraderie among faculty and students was not approved; too little was disapproved.

Tad, from his first day in modern European history, was the follower of one man at Rodgers although it was some time before the man himself became aware of it.

Lawrence Covington was starting his first year as a full professor and was for the first time in his life earning a salary beyond his needs. He was not in as much awe of his new position when among the students as when in the faculty lounge. Certain men spoke to him there by name for the first time and not once during registration week did he hear himself referred to as "Young Covington." But in the classroom the change was barely perceptible. Nor did he change much his opening lecture to the predominantly freshman class.

And this was the lecture that won him Tad's devotion.

He started off, after a slow silent appraisal of the new faces, his gray eyes humorous as he took off his glasses: "Gentlemen, history is about people. First of all, it is about people. Remember that. We are not going to be able to understand what happened at, shall we say, the Congress of Vienna, unless we get to know M. Talleyrand, his aches and pains, his vanities, even a little about his love life: just a little. After all, we shan't be making a movie. We can afford perspective. So then, we shall study men, statesmen and generals, possibly their mistresses, occasionally their wives. And if I seem to suggest to you that women had more influence on history before they had the vote than since having it, believe me, it is not because I am a bachelor—which I am. It is rather because I believe suppression to be the beginning of all history. When women were politically suppressed, they moved men. In some cases, mountains might have been easier. But when man moves, history begins . . ."

Covington was the only person about whom Tad wrote home in

any detail. There were a lot of "bloaters" in the class, he wrote, and explained that bloaters were fellows who blew hard when they didn't know the answer. In that way some of the teachers were persuaded to blame themselves for not having been clear. Not "Cov". "You know, I've never heard it explained that way before," he would say. "I wish you'd write it up for me—say three or four hundred words."

Covington's students gathered occasionally in his rooms and all the talk did not run to history. He was good for advice on the girls at the "female academy" in the next town, on wines, vintage cars, omelets and poetic meter. On special occasions he would loan records. But he was one of those rare and fortunate people who did not have to call a halt to things, even with freshmen. "He never laughs out loud," Tad wrote again, "but you can see in his eyes that he got the joke, maybe a little ahead of everybody else. Maybe that's why he doesn't laugh aloud."

But for all that Tad was writing home about him, it was not until a football Saturday in early November that Covington first saw him as other than a reserved youngster with a good head on him. He was sitting in front of Hogan and his family at the Homecoming game. Hogan was one of 480 freshmen, and conspicuous in the grandstand only in that he looked even younger than a college freshman, and Covington had begun to feel that there was nothing younger. What came to recommend him to the teacher's attention was his apparent indifference to the game of football.

After the welcoming roar when the team came on the field everyone stood in silence for the band's playing of the Rodgers alma mater. Then Covington heard the man he presumed to be Hogan's father say: "No college spirit, Tad? Martha, I do not understand your son."

The boy said: "Team, team, team! How's that?"

His mother gave him a weary reproach.

"Such beautiful men," the older man said. "Graceful. Take the glasses, Martha. Look at number seventy-two. Look how he runs! A ballet dancer."

"He'd rather be dead," Tad said.

Covington cast him an amused glance over his shoulder. The boy looked at him blandly, unconspiratorially. His was a lone game.

"I do not yet understand American prejudices."

Covington had been trying to place the older man's accent. A bit guttural, but rather precise in pronunciation.

"Young men are jealous of their masculinity, I suppose," the woman said.

"Why, if they are men?"

Throughout the first half of the game Covington amused himself by speculating on the man's origins and business. Prosperous, athletic, possibly an importer. Covington hoped of French wines! He made himself available for an introduction at half time.

"Mother, may I present Professor Covington? My mother, sir: Mrs. Reiss."

Mrs. Reiss' beauty struck Covington as being so deeply feminine as to suggest an inwardness, a sort of self-cloistering one often associated with the women in early Renaissance painting. Demure was perhaps the word, and truly he could not remember having applied it before. Yet she spoke with utter ease.

"My husband, Dr. Reiss, Mr. Covington."

Covington shook hands and wondered why he had not surmised the man to be a doctor. He knew instantly: doctors were not supposed to look so prosperous!

"Football is a great athletic, Mr. Covington. American to the shoestrings. I like it."

"Is this your first game, doctor?"

"Except for television."

"Hot dogs, anyone?" Tad said.

"He doesn't like it," the doctor said, "and him an American born boy. He should want to carry the water bucket."

"I'm subversive," Tad said. "Have a hot dog, Nathan."

"Thank you, no."

"It's American."

"I wish you would not be so flippant, Tad," his mother said quietly.

Covington did not like the boy's attitude toward his stepfather. It was more than a little insolent to a man who, Covington would have said on first observance, did his best to please everyone. That would get to be pretty cloying in time, of course. But a man close to twenty years older than his wife had to do a lot of pleasing.

A moment came when Martha was able to speak to the teacher out of Tad's hearing. "My son often mentions you in his letters, Mr. Covington. He admires you very much."

"I'd never have known it," Covington said gravely.

"I suspected that—which is why I've told you."

Her simple directness further intrigued the teacher. Nor did she

follow up by pressing for information about the boy as would virtually every mother he knew having paid him a mother's highest
compliment. Instead, she asked: "Are you a Rodgers alumnus yourself, Mr. Covington?"

"Harvard, I'm afraid."

"It will do," she said, her eyes humorous. "I was thinking you
might have known Tad's father."

"So Tad is second generation Rodgers?"

"Third," Martha said. "His grandfather Jonathan went here, too.
And then to Harvard."

"The economist?" Covington asked.

"Yes. Did you know him?" Her face became vivid with the sudden
smile.

"I attended a number of his lectures at London University after
the war. A very fine gentleman, God rest him."

Again with Martha Reiss the unexpected happened: she did not,
turning almost at once to involve Tad and her husband in the conversation, mention the association she and Covington had just discovered.

It fell to Covington himself to tell the boy of it some time afterwards when they had become friends. Their friendship did develop
out of that afternoon, or the quicker for it. And one of the things
Covington first tried to understand was Tad's resentment of Nathan
Reiss. He was surprised himself to discover that Reiss had been in
this country for so long, an Austrian refugee. Something in his manner suggested a more recent arrival. Tad, when Covington mentioned
it, said it was part of his phoniness: something he put on for
strangers to impress them with his differentness.

"Don't you see, sir," the boy said, "he really loathes Americans.
That's his snobbism, pretending to love football. It really sticks him
that I won't fit in, that I won't cheer like a rooster and strut with the
team."

"You're mixing metaphors—among other things," Covington said.
"Don't you think you're a little young to judge a man?"

"No. It's time somebody did."

Another surprising thing he learned about the Hogan-Reiss relationship was that Tad was only five years old at the time of his
father's death. He could have known him scarcely at all, yet he spoke
of him quite often. Suddenly he realized that the boy's notion of his
father was actually a composite of father and grandfather, and Cov-

ington wondered if just possibly his mother did not entertain a similar admixture of memory.

Speaking of his father one day, Tad said: "It's funny, you know, what you once said about judging a man? Nobody ever hesitates to pronounce it on a good man, do they? When he dies they think only of the good in his life and sing him hallelujahs. That way his death doesn't have any meaning because there was so much meaning in his life."

"Don't you think your father's life had meaning, Tad?"

"I'm not so almighty sure it had a lot, if you want to know, sir." He looked at him suddenly. "Do you think a man can do evil, doing good?"

"I think the good a man does can be turned to evil purpose."

"I knew you'd say that."

"Why ask it then?" Covington said testily.

"I mean a teacher would have to say that, wouldn't he?"

"I try to rarely say things that have to be said, Tad. More often than not they're the very things that should not have been said at the moment."

Presently the boy asked: "Do you know anything about Judaism?"

"A little."

"Are you Jewish?" The question was sudden and with the brightness of hoped-for discovery.

"No . . . but I once wanted to marry a girl who was."

"Why didn't you?"

"It's a long story—with a short ending. She wouldn't have me."

"Because of your religion?"

Covington laughed. "Because of hers. And I wouldn't call it religion actually. It was after the war and there was Israel in which she was much more interested." Covington found himself then telling the boy quite a lot about that time in his life, his involvement in a cause and a culture which had sounded a response at the very core of his New England heart.

"I wish I had a cause like that," Tad said, "something I believed in with all my heart."

"It can't be manufactured," Covington said. "It's got to grow from seed. I found that out."

"Yes!" Tad said, and then confirmed what Covington already suspected, his turning back to the same old obsession: "Nathan's a Zionist."

"So?"

Tad said: "Mr. Covington, do you know Hebrew?"

"A smattering of it."

"Will you teach it to me?"

"If you're interested in the language, why don't you take it as one of your electives next year?"

"I'd have to do it under the Divinity School."

"Contiguous but not necessarily contagious," Covington said.

"Maybe I will."

"To make more sport of your stepfather? It's not good, Tad."

"No. I don't think it's for that." He fell silent for a few moments. They were sitting in Covington's study at the time, the logs in the fireplace sending up an orange-red glow that illumined their faces while the winter daylight faded leaving the rest of their bodies, the furniture, the books, the whole room in shadow. Tad bent down, untied and retied his shoelaces. Finally he said, trying to make it sound off-hand, "Nathan isn't the only Jew in the world."

Covington understood then, and was moved in a way he had not been before by this deep, if sometimes devious boy. Tad, from trying to find the worst in one man, he realized, had set himself to trying to find the best in others of his kind. There was a sort of anguished splendor in the youngster that made the teacher feel humble, glad to be a teacher. He wanted to pay him some casual compliment that would commend without embarrassing him, which Covington decided would satisfy himself more than the boy. He held his peace and let the fire make the only spangled noise in the room.

But more credit was due Covington for the social as well as the intellectual balance in Tad's development that year than the teacher would have presumed to accept. It was his custom, going into New York on free days to research a book set in Holland, to take three or four of the boys with him. Whenever possible he included Tad among them. They would catch an early train, separate at the Pennsylvania Station, Covington to work at the library, the boys to go to the U.N., a museum or library, or just to be on their own for a few hours in the city. They would meet again for a late lunch generally downtown, for Covington's fondness for lower Manhattan was contagious among his students. Tad loved to walk the old streets, Pearl, for example, still the shipwrights' market place; Fulton Street—fish and cheese; Elizabeth Street on an Italian festival; Chinatown; old cemeteries, St.

Paul's and Trinity, St. Mark's in-the-Bouwerie. On Saturdays the Broadway and Wall Street skyscrapers, all but deserted, seemed like spiraling ghosts of a city built upon a city and abandoned while a more primitive life went on at the level of their foundations.

Sometimes Covington and his charges stayed in town for theater or a concert and caught the last train back to Rodgers.

Twice during that winter Tad met Nathan in town for dinner, and once he stayed overnight, having a room adjoining Nathan's at the Imperial Hotel. On these occasions they got on well: they always seemed to get along better alone. Tad suspected this to be part of his mother's reason for not coming East. She often promised but never arrived. It was not until late spring that Tad received the invitation that Nathan promised he was likely to have from Madame Schwarzbach, as the Baroness preferred to be called in America.

Tad read her note aloud to Covington: "I have invited your mother and Nathan to spend the week-end. I hope it will be convenient for you also to be my guest. If you wish, you may bring a friend . . ."

"It's a fabulous place, Mr. Covington," Tad told him of the mirrored bathroom. "You stand there, you know, looking at yourself like a Bernini fountain."

Covington grinned.

"She says I may bring a friend. How about it? Mother's going to be there."

"Thanks very much, chum, but I'm not the sort of friend your hostess has in mind." It was never dominant in Covington's thought, but he was aware of a small self-cautioning voice where Tad's mother was concerned. It was not a matter of self-flattery to see a possible flight the boy's imagination could take, feeling as he did about his stepfather.

Tad himself had, at least since mid-year, been looking forward to an invitation to Madame Schwarzbach's: a week-end in New York. He laid out a daytime schedule for his mother and himself—the Frick Museum, the Museum of Modern Art, theater: a week would have scarcely sufficed it. Then a letter came from Martha.

"I have badly hurt my ankle," she wrote a few days before she was due, "and Nathan thinks it better that I do not travel just now . . ."

Tad showed the letter to Covington. "Do you believe it?"

"I believe it," the teacher said matter-of-factly. "I don't see that there's any choice but to believe it."

"What kind of logic is that?" Tad turned on him, furious with disappointment. "That's my mother's logic. I do have a choice and I don't believe it. There's some other reason. There has to be."

Covington could see the boy's progress toward social stability abruptly bogging down. He would have liked at that moment to have been able to say a few words to his mother. He persuaded Tad with some difficulty to go anyway, his hostess having telegraphed that he was still expected.

Tad went into town after his last class on Friday. He woke Covington out of a sound sleep at seven o'clock Saturday morning with a phone call. "I was afraid you might get off on the first train," he apologized.

"Afraid is not the word," Covington said.

"Mr. Covington, I was talking to Madame Schwarzbach about you last night. She's having one of her affairs tonight—you know, I told you—all kinds of people."

"Like whom?"

"I don't know, painters, theater people. Will you come? She said she would have called you herself, but she couldn't very well do it at seven o'clock in the morning, could she?"

"I don't like to think so," Covington said.

"Will you come? There's a Vermeer painting in the library and a Kalf in the dining room. And she knows a lot of people in Holland."

"What time?" Covington said.

"Seven. Wear your dinner jacket. And Mr. Covington, you're invited to stay over. Please do. It'll be late and we can talk. You'll find her very interesting."

Covington liked the idea even better after coffee. He was by no means a Scott Fitzgerald type, by his own calculation, but he agreed that rich people were different from himself . . . in more ways than having money. And looking forward as he was to spending a summer of work in Holland, he had been the more suspectible to Tad's cajolery. He packed his dinner clothes and in New York left them to be pressed at a tailor's shop while he did his day's work at the Forty-second Street Library.

·3

"I HAVE always felt, Mr. Covington," Madame Schwarzbach was saying, "that a person is known only by the consensus of many, never by one friend only. Or one enemy. We are discovered not by what we wish to reveal, but very often by what we wish not to reveal. Yet in the end we are knowable—all of us. And it is better to accept that, don't you think? Only God is an island, and even He expects the tribute of curiosity."

She had drawn him apart from the others to the sunroom off the downstairs gallery. A murmur of conversation and music came from the other room. Covington felt self-conscious, the more so because he was flattered by the particular attention. He kept thinking of her in the setting of Regency France although she was very much a woman of the modern world. He had observed at dinner where he was one of twenty guests, that certain of them were expected to provoke, accelerate—or when the time came—to modulate the conversation. She was its moderator. She knew whom to probe, he felt, for a timely witticism, and was rather loud in her own mirth. A lusty woman, without a doubt, who preferred the company of men but knew it was to be had only by inviting the proper women also. She had allowed him to pass untried conversationally through dinner, except in asides to the woman next to him, the wife of a newspaper publisher and herself a well-known columnist. But if his hostess had not tried him by direct address, Covington felt, she had nonetheless observed his performance. Her eyes had made her a party to every show of amusement he elicited from his companion.

"God Needs Men," Covington said, referring to the title of a Delannoy film, and prepared to speak of its theme if the Baroness were not familiar with it.

But she said, "Quite so. I know that coast of France very well. But such a story might have been set in certain of the Italian islands also —the mystique of the people. I understand you are to be in Holland this summer, Mr. Covington?"

"This summer and probably the next. God knows how many."

"You are a scholar?"

He rubbed the back of his neck. "I'm looking for something—if that makes me a scholar."

"You are too modest," she said, her eyes flashing with mockery of his humbleness. "If you find what you are looking for they will call you a scholar. Otherwise you must admit it of yourself. You will come to tea one of the Saturday afternoons Tad says you spend in New York, and tell me about your project. Perhaps I have friends to whom I can give you letters."

Covington recognized this as both a command performance and present dismissal. "You are very kind," he murmured and showed himself ready to leave her if she wished it.

She nodded and then detained him. "Is Tad interested in your . . . undertaking?"

"I shouldn't think especially," Covington said, "except that by coincidence, I attended some lectures of his grandfather which first got me onto it."

"I am entirely pleased," the Baroness said, a remark Covington was a long time understanding.

There was no one present at the party of Tad's own generation, a fact with which he was thoroughly satisfied. At dinner the Baroness had kept him next to her which he understood to be less a compliment to him than a courtesy to her other guests. She rarely spoke to him to be sure, attending more to the gentleman on her right. What fascinated him was that she had seemed to know what was going on up and down the table—even when the general conversation was suspended between courses and people fell to quiet talk among themselves. Once she had remarked half to him, half to herself: "Nathan will not carry that point very long, we shall see."

Tad, convinced that Nathan was the least informed person at the table, had answered: "Nathan never does carry any point very long." And having said it, he had blushed and added: "I beg your pardon, Madame Schwarzbach," for she had looked at him with mock severity. But just after that she reached across and pressed his hand.

Later she asked him a number of questions about Covington, and not once all evening had he had to talk with her about Nathan Reiss. He had eavesdropped on a number of conversations—openly; no one seemed to care—and as he told Covington when they went upstairs together toward midnight, what shocked him was the frankness with

12q

which people talked about, for example, a man very high in the United States government.

"What if such things got into the newspapers?"

"They won't."

"Why not?"

"Well, there are two levels of conspiracy, I suppose—and by no great stretch we could use the word decency instead of conspiracy—the people who know won't tell—and the people who don't know wouldn't believe it if it were told."

They sat for a long time and talked in Tad's room, Covington now curious about what Tad knew of Madame Schwarzbach's story. He was careful in his questions, for he suspected almost at once, calculating ages and relationships as a man of forty can and a boy of seventeen cannot, that far more than a patronal interest had existed at one time if it did not now exist between the Baroness and Nathan Reiss. He could see no other justification for her interest in so shallow a man. He was not himself, Covington supposed, her type: something that both amused and vaguely irritated him. But if his supposition about the Baroness and Reiss were true, it explained Martha Reiss' absence. He did not like to think of Tad's arriving at such an understanding.

A knock at the door interrupted them. The Baroness called: "I wish only to say good night."

Tad said: "Please come in, Madame Schwarzbach."

"I am sorry to interrupt," she said, seeing Covington. "Please do not disturb yourselves."

But he and Tad were already standing. Covington withdrew to the window while the Baroness crossed to the boy and taking his face in her hands kissed him on both cheeks. Tad was in his shirtsleeves, and Covington felt an uneasiness—squeamishness, no doubt—but he could not escape the feeling of sexuality about the woman. She seemed to be savoring of the boy. He had got himself into something, coming here, Covington thought. He was on the verge of becoming Tad's keeper. But if in fact he were that, he realized he would not let the boy come into this house again.

She turned to him more suddenly than he had supposed she could, a plump, no longer supple woman, with the consequence that the color leaped to his face. She both saw it and wanted him to know she saw it.

The awkward moment passed. He thanked her for her graciousness in inviting him. She lingered to speak of certain people she knew in Holland—or had known before the war. "I have not been entirely sociable since then," she said. "Context. So much is context, isn't it?"

Without knocking at the door the Baroness had left open, John, the servant of many tasks stepped into the room. "I've brought up your chocolate, Madame Schwarzbach. It's hot now, but it won't be for long."

Covington had been aware of the man until then only as he had been of the other servants in the house. He was under thirty, built like a weight-lifter, and he spoke American—New Yorkese. There was something insolent in his manner, something of letting down barriers. Covington refused to pursue his conjecture any further. But still the man stood.

"I'll come directly," the Baroness said, and then raising her voice: "Please check the locks before you go to bed."

At that directive, he left, closing the door.

The Baroness gave her hand to Covington. "I rise late in the morning," she said, "but cook will be in the kitchen by eight. You may have your breakfast sent up. You are a wise man, Mr. Covington. I am sure we understand one another."

When she was gone, Tad asked: "What did she mean by that?"

Covington decided instantly on a deliberate lie: "She means I ought to know my own place and stay in it."

"To hell with *her*," Tad said.

Which was exactly the response the teacher wanted.

·4

BUT where there is seeking there are many ways of learning.

Covington did not go to tea, nor did Tad again visit Madame Schwarzbach. Covington spent most of his summer in Holland and a part of it in London where a colleague of Jonathan's at the University was preparing Hogan's economic history of the Merchant Adventurers for publication.

Tad went on a walking tour of Kentucky and Tennessee. He filled three notebooks with observations, anecdotes and fragments of the hill country songs. At the end of summer he gave Sylvia and Martha a recital. Nathan, present for part of it, suggested that Tad repeat it for the visit of the trustees for the Children's Plan to the farm that week-end.

The suggestion and the repeat performance were well taken by all concerned. Tad also performed for the children. Everybody, he thought, seemed to be getting along just splendidly with everybody.

Martha was not aware of a change in Tad's attitude toward her: she was too well content in his apparent amity with Nathan. But it was now this contentment Tad was scrutinizing. Nothing, he thought, was so important to her as that the surface peace be kept: give her an umbrella and call her Lady Chamberlain. But now he did not talk even to Sylvia about such things. She was in Martha's camp. And there was Covington when he got back to Rodgers.

Tad put off to the last minute the physical check-up Nathan insisted he have before returning to school. Nathan would be looking for tuberculosis or God knows what, he suspected, from his having spent two months on mountain hospitality. It was Miss Kohler who took his chest X ray, Nathan seeing a patient at the time.

While he was waiting Miss Kohler chatted knowingly about his summer and his return to New York. She was a thin-lipped woman, not a girl in Tad's eyes though tolerably pretty. But she made up her face in a way he disliked: wearing her lipstick beyond the contour of her lips. It caused him to think of the Baroness who always made up highly, but never in contradiction to her own features.

"Rodgers is forty miles outside New York," he corrected Miss Kohler's impression of where he was going.

"I suppose it's harder to get to New York from there than from Traders City."

"Almost."

"Dr. Reiss doesn't think anything of going off to New York from here. But I suppose it all depends on what you're going for."

Tad was a few seconds catching a sort of insinuating sound to her voice, as though she had meaning beyond meaning in the words. She cast him a sidelong glance. That he caught.

"You mean the girls," he said nastily, being at once curious and disdainful.

She slapped an envelope into the typewriter. "You know everything, don't you?"

"I know what I know," he said.

"That makes two of us," she snapped.

Very few young men could be more feline than Tad when he chose. "Shall we swap stories?"

"Shame on you," she said. "I'll tell Dr. Reiss."

"Tell him," Tad said, impatient with her, with waiting, and with himself for having muffed the chance of hearing what she had in mind. Then he said: "I'll tell him you're jealous."

"Of whom?" she said sarcastically, lifting her chin.

Tad was non-plussed. "His wife," he said.

"Ha!"

"You bitch!" Tad said, and was impotent beyond the one word epithet in his sudden fury. He got away from her desk and went into the waiting room where he paced up and down until Nathan was ready for him. Gradually his temper abated: it was all so childish, their exchange, he thought, going over the words, like two children meeting and taking an instant dislike to each other and then tearing into one another.

But the burden of her "Ha!" lingered throughout the day with him and was still with him in the morning when it was almost time to go.

Martha watched him pack his own luggage. "I can't help feeling that two dozen pairs of socks are an extravagance. I'm sure you'll outgrow them before half of them wear out."

"I won't outgrow them, mother. My feet can't possibly get any bigger."

She wondered if he were as glad to be leaving the house as she had been going off to St. Cecilia's. "I think Nathan's allowance will be more than adequate." The moment she said it she thought of her own father: whenever a difficult moment had occurred between them he had bridged it with a question about whether she needed money.

"He's still trying to corrupt me," Tad said. "I thought after this summer he'd give me up for a peasant."

Martha went to the window. Across the way a Negro maid was taking in geraniums from the summer boxes, plucking off the dead leaves and dropping them below one by one.

"It was a bad joke, mother," Tad called to her. "I'm sorry."

Martha turned back. "I've forgotten what you said."

He put his suitcase on the floor and knelt on it to get it closed. "You're coming out in November, aren't you? You won't renege again?"

"I'll go East with Nathan on one of his trips. And I shall write to you—once a week."

"Don't!" He let the suitcase fly open. "If you've got to measure out your letters, don't bother writing at all."

They looked at one another mutely across the room.

"I'm sorry again," Tad said. "But I can just see you going into that paint room of yours and hiding—from him, from yourself, from me."

Martha said: "I've always been solitary by nature. I'm grateful that you take after Marcus in that respect."

"I'll bet you didn't have to force yourself to write him letters, did you?"

"Strangely, Tad, there was a time when he had to force himself to write to me. During the war. He was very troubled."

"But you're not," Tad said, again sarcastically.

Martha went on as though he had not spoken. "He seemed to have lost me—and you. You were here then, too."

"That's what I'm afraid of," Tad said. "One of these days we won't even know each other when I come home."

"He hadn't lost me. Nor I him. But separation can do that for a time. But when people love each other, Tad, nothing is lost—except time. And we don't ever know how much of that there is." She said it with the air of resignation Tad detested.

He went back to work on the suitcase and finished closing it.

"Mother, when you went away to Europe, to school, how did you remember Marcus? I mean did you remember the way he looked—something special about him you fastened onto, you know . . ."

"I know what you mean," Martha said. "There's one picture of him I have to this day whenever I suddenly think of him. It was the first time I was in his house—the day I met Jonathan. We were sitting across the table at dinner and suddenly our eyes met. Nothing in my life has been more vivid, more wonderful than that moment." Her face had come alive with the conjuring again of the moment. "That's what it's like to be in love," she said. "It will happen to you some day."

"Do you think you'll like the girl?" Tad said, feeling a sudden diffidence.

Martha laughed. "I'll have precious little choice in the matter."

"Or will you be like Annie? Every girl she sees me even look at: 'What an inferior creature!' " He mimicked the brogue, then added: "A creature yet!"

Martha looked about the room scattered with odd pieces of clothing. "How can you tell when you're packed?"

"Wouldn't you like to fall in love again yourself, mother?"

Martha said: "I've never fallen out of love."

"Not even married to Nathan?"

She went to the dresser and began to put it in order. "No," she said.

Tad had never got this close to an admission of what he wanted to know, of what he wanted to be the truth. But he knew her well enough not to pursue the matter directly. He plucked at the tufts of the quilt on his bed. "When you were in school in Europe, were you homesick?"

"Not homesick exactly. As you know, mother and my father did not get along very well together."

"Don't you think they should have got a divorce?"

"Yes, now I think so. I shoud have been horrified then. But no more than I was finding out about Alexander and mother. That was worse. Only I didn't know it at the time. But I remember I lost that intimate sense of Marcus for a time. I didn't even want to see him, I thought . . . until his cablegram came. I still have that. Also the Baroness Schwarzbach's invitation to spend the holiday with her . . ."

"And that was when you got to know Nathan." Tad pulled the tuft from the quilt.

"Mother and I had met him earlier that summer in Vienna. But he was in Paris then and came to see me at school. I remember that, too, the old nun, the portress, sitting just outside the parlor door, so that we could see her foot and hear the rattle of her beads . . . But I've told you all this before . . . about the New Year's ball."

"Did you go to the ball with Nathan?"

"It was in the Baroness' home. So that it wasn't a matter of going with anyone. But all that holiday he was very kind. He took me shopping for New Year's presents. And we went up to the Latin Quarter to look for some of Julie Mueller's friends, and bought cognac for all the artists."

"Did he make a pass at you?" Tad went to work loosening another tuft.

"I suppose you could call it that—on the night of the ball."

"The dog," Tad said. He got up and dug his hands into his pockets.

Martha said: "I didn't feel that way about it, Tad. I think I was flattered, and I suppose that's what he intended."

"Didn't you tell him you were in love with Marcus?"

"Yes. And that was how it ended."

"Oh," Tad said, disappointed.

Martha realized she had reached the point of dishonesty: Nathan had known of Marcus before. One always reached the point of dishonesty and either stopped or plunged ahead as though the point had not been reached and passed. But that was the night, she thought, by which her marriage to him was foresworn. She went to the window and opened it wide for a moment.

Tad, watching her, thought he had got on to something else. "Was Nathan ever married before?"

"No." But she hesitated before answering.

"You don't even know for sure, do you? Tell me the truth, mother. You don't even know."

"I suppose you're old enough now, Tad, to know what I was too young to realize then: he and the Baroness were—intimate friends."

"Lovers, you mean?" Tad burst out incredulously.

She had told him fearing he would hear it from someone else, visiting in New York. "Once long ago they were," she said quietly.

Tad's mind was aflame: "Did he leave her for you?" he persisted. "Is that what's making you feel guilty now, mother? Is that why you don't go there?"

"No. I just don't like leaving home," she said. But she felt utterly ineffectual. She was sick of defending Nathan and the part of herself that had become part of him. She could feel despair like a giant hand closing down upon her. With a great effort she turned away from it. "Should I have told you so much, Tad?" She took his hands in hers to still them. "I've often thought you understood too much, knowing too little. It's been the other way around with me: I've known too much for the little of it I was able to understand. I've tried to be honest with you today, but I haven't altogether managed it. I don't know what total honesty is. Perhaps there is no such thing. We are conditioned by so many things—our childhood, our faith or lack of it, those whom we love and hurt seeking to hurt ourselves hurting them: you do that sometimes. There is a twist and tangle to all of us. I haven't learned much in my almost forty years, but this I think is true: without love, without sacrificial love, the potential for evil in us is very great. I don't think I could live if you were in danger and I couldn't save you—you, Annie, Nathan, I'm almost sure a stranger— if I saw death approaching, I should have to try. And I think that's about the best of me. I'm by no means sure it's enough in a human being."

She let go of his hands and began rubbing her own together as though to bring warmth into them.

"But Marcus and your grandfather Jonathan were quite something else. Their souls were not pinched up like mine. Even when they were wrong, they were good men with vision and humility, and what I can only call a sort of cosmic charity. Dr. Mueller has it. Mother St. John whom I've told you about, the dean at St. Cecilia's. She had faith. My religion, I've come to think now never got beyond credulity. And it might have been enough. I expect it is for most people." She stopped abruptly and smiled at him. "Now, do you think we'll know each other when you come home again?"

"Mother, if Nathan were unfaithful to you now, would you divorce him?"

Martha stared at him, her smile slowly diminishing. "What did you say, Tad?"

He tried to stand his ground, but he knew from the pallor of his mother's face that he should not have said it after all. But he could only repeat: "If you thought Nathan . . ."

Martha cut him off. "I have never thought of the possibility. And if my speaking frankly this afternoon has put that idea in your mind, I regret it with all my heart."

Tad looked at her and away. Her eyes were green and angry and the vein showed on her forehead.

"You do not play with emotions, Tad. You don't improvise things like that to gratify your own fancy."

"I said IF," the boy retreated.

"I know you said IF. That's what I'm talking about."

He went to the dresser and gathered his wallet, his nail clippers and his watch. "That isn't any worse than some other things I've thought about him. And it didn't happen just today. I was able to say it to you today, that's all."

Martha went to the door. There she paused, waiting. For the same old apology, he supposed.

"Tad, I don't like your leaving with this blackness in your heart."

"You don't like my staying either," he said, looking at her only through the mirror. "Peace at any price. I can't apologize, mother. I would if I could. But I just can't any more."

"I understand," Martha said. "Bring your things when you're ready." And going out, she closed the door behind her.

· 5

TAD returned to school with somewhat less than a scholar's enthusiasm. Nor was he in any of Professor Covington's classes that semester. Their first meeting of any length occurred when Covington suggested an hour's walk one afternoon in mid-October. They set out across the farm along the stubbled corn field where the stalks were cocked, row upon row like Indian teepees. Tad asked if the teacher knew the McCutcheon cartoon called "Injun Summer." It did not seem to mean much to Covington who was not a Midwesterner. They exchanged accounts of the summer, neither of them striking fire to the other's imagination, and both of them had thought from time to time during those months of this exchange as being one of its rewards.

Covington asked whose classes Tad was in.

Tad said: "I want to learn more French and some Italian. Maybe I'll go abroad next year."

"Add a little Dutch and I'll give you a job," Covington said.

"Do you mean it, Mr. Covington?"

"Well, I hadn't meant it literally, but I can think about it."

Gusts of wind blew up as they walked, the raw east wind from the ocean which at the farmland's edge bowed the trees and stripped them early of their leaves. The taste of the sea was in it that day, and overhead the clouds rode faster and faster across the sky as though racing to be off the horizon before the sun's setting.

"Did you like Grandpa Jon's book? Did it help you?"

"More in its sources, I'm afraid, than in its summary."

"Isn't it any good?"

"I shouldn't say that. I just didn't find it as good as I had hoped. I got the feeling it was the work of a man who set out to prove something—not to find something. Will you want to go into the city when we get organized this year? I suppose not since most of my gang will be freshmen."

"I expect to be going in on my own quite a lot this year, sir. But thanks."

Covington picked up an oak tree twig, two empty acorn cups at the end of it. He broke one off. "We used to make pipes of these as kids and stuff them with corn silk."

"Mr. Covington, do you remember who the woman was sitting next to Nathan at dinner that night at Madame Schwarzbach's?"

"It seems to me she was a designer," Covington said. It gave him no cheer to see where Tad's mind was again. Indeed the more he thought of it, the more uneasy he became. "I recall her husband sat across the table from them."

Tad smiled.

"Why?"

"I met her on the street the other day. That's all."

Covington suspected that to be a lie, but nothing was to be gained by challenging it. He threw the bit of oak away.

They climbed a gate rather than open its complicated latch, and walked through a glade of bent pines. The wind made the sound among them of constant sighing. The only other sound was that of crows, loud, desolate and unrelieved. Covington wished that they had gone into the village for coffee instead. Only when they came out of the grove and stood on the high ridge from where they could see the ocean—a mile beyond the flatland that lay in a steep drop below them—did either of them speak again, Covington proposing that they return by way of the road.

"It's a bleak day," Tad said. "I like it."

"Wuthering—that's the word for it. There are times it would suit me better," Covington said.

"Mr. Covington, if I call on Madame Schwarzbach now and then, you won't consider it disloyal of me, will you?"

"I'd be curious to know to whom you are being loyal," the teacher said.

"To myself."

"A better man I never knew," Covington said with attempted levity. Then: "I don't suppose you want to tell me any more about it than that."

"There isn't anything to tell much . . . yet. She and Nathan once were lovers. Would you have thought so?"

"It crossed my mind," Covington said. "But I'm sure it's not so now."

"So am I," Tad said.

Covington's relief was brief.

Tad added: "I think she must loathe him as much as I do . . . but I want to be sure."

Covington sucked in a deep breath of the cold, raw air. "All right, Tad, even if it's so and you find out—what purpose will it serve?"

"I've got to know," the boy said.

On their way back to the campus, going by the highway, they had to wait at the railway tracks for the passing of the train to New York City. Tad remarked: "I wish I were on that."

Covington said: "You might as well be for all the good it's going to do you to be in school in your frame of mind." Before they parted he said: "Come and see me whenever you have a chance, Tad. I promise that I won't interfere."

"Thank you, sir." They shook hands.

Tad wrote what he considered an ingratiating letter to the Baroness that night asking if he might come to tea when next he was in New York. In a week's time he had not received a reply. He wrote again, suggesting this time that he wished to talk with her on an important matter. Having not heard from her by the following Saturday, he went into New York and while there telephoned her. A maid answered and then John came to the phone to say that Madame Schwarzbach was not feeling well and therefore was not accepting calls or callers.

Tad passed his eighteenth birthday that Hallowe'en, and came very close to failing his first quarter's examination. He did so poorly for one who had stood second in a class of 480 at the end of his freshman year that when Nathan Reiss came East and Tad asked permission to stay overnight in New York with him, he was refused. He was allowed to go in town for dinner, but expected to sign on campus before midnight.

The dean of studies called Covington in to discuss the problem of the boy.

It was a day of heavy fog and Tad hurried to get off campus lest all permissions be canceled because of the weather. When Nathan had called, he said that George Bergner had come East with him to be present at a testimonial luncheon. "I had hoped Sylvia might also come. After all, she too is responsible. It is for The Plan I am being honored."

"And mother?" Tad had asked.

"She is not well. And considering the weather, I am pleased she did not come."

So was Tad this time.

In his haste to catch the first train, he chanced the shortcut which took him close to Covington's quarters. His luck did not hold: he ran almost into the teacher's arms.

Covington had but an hour before come from the dean of studies' office.

"What are you going in town for, Tad?"

The boy's eyes were glittering. "To pay my homage to the great man. This is the day he's crowned king of the Jews."

"Let's have the translation for that," Covington said irritably.

"The Conference of Jewish Women gave him a testimonial luncheon. I've got to hurry, sir."

Covington caught his arm. "I have a good notion to campus you for the day. Your marks are disgraceful, the weather is filthy, and I don't like anything about this trip."

"If you do," the boy said in quiet insubordination, "I shall go A.W.O.L."

· 6

GEORGE BERGNER and Tad were not likely to have been friends under any circumstance. George detested brilliance, having felt himself its victim in so many ways, and there was, he sensed, about the youngster the unmistakable mark of it. But George was no longer the friend of any man: he was one man's servant. When Tad arrived at the Imperial Hotel in the late afternoon it was George who was waiting for him in Reiss' room.

"I'm sorry to be late," Tad said, "but I couldn't get a cab in this weather."

"So is Nathan late," Bergner said. "He hasn't time to pack for himself, but he has time to be late."

The room was muggy with a sort of body warmth as though a man had been sweating in it for a long time. George himself looked untidy, his suit wrinkled and there was the glisten of sweat on his bald head. But Nathan's luggage, open on the rack, was neatly packed. The room was hung with heavy draperies, furnished ornately, and decorated with pictures of pasturelands and seascapes weightily framed in gilt. A bottle of brandy, a third empty stood open on the writing desk. The Gideon Bible there was also open, and when Tad paused, noticing it, Bergner said:

"Couldn't find another damn thing to read. Have a drink?"

"No thanks," Tad said. He took off his raincoat. George's coat lay over a chair beside the door, his hat atop it. "How was the testimonial?"

"Stupendous. Absolutely stupendous. The ladies gave him an ovation—and that." He gestured toward the dresser, spilling the drink, a few drops, over himself.

"They're a corny outfit." Tad went to the dresser where a case lined with white satin stood open. It held, each piece fitted into its own slot, a set of surgical instruments. "How come this? I thought they came with the hospital. Or are they giving him one of those, too?"

George guffawed. "A symbol, my boy. Rehabilitation. Or it might just be that somebody on the board of Jewish ladies has a friend a manufacturer of surgical instruments."

Tad did not like the remark, and Bergner was a little drunk and for it the more offensive. But neither did Tad care very much for the Conference of Jewish Women when they gave Nathan Reiss a testimonial luncheon.

"The Jewish people are very sentimental. Don't you think so?" George sat down carefully on the edge of the bed, this time shepherding the glass in his hand.

But Tad, catching the aroma of brandy, plunged back in memory to the scene on the dock when Dr. Winthrop died. He remembered Louise Bergner taking the brandy Sylvia had brought and spilling it over her husband who lay gasping like a guppy, otherwise unattended while Nathan tried to resuscitate the dead. Tad's own heart began to pound.

"He saved your life once, didn't he, Mr. Bergner?"

"Yes," George said, "one of the chosen."

Nothing he could have said would have been more likely to fire Tad's imagination. He moistened his lips. "But he couldn't save my father's life—or Dr. Winthrop's. They weren't among the chosen."

Bergner opened his mouth and then closed it again without saying what had come into his mind.

"Mr. Bergner, did you know the boat was going to tip that day—I mean just before it happened, didn't you know it was going to happen?"

Bergner did not understand the preciseness of the distinction in time Tad was trying to make. "My boy, if I'd known that, I wouldn't have been aboard it, not even for Nathan Reiss."

Tad had reached the place of taking the meanings he wanted from the man's words. He felt himself exhilarated, in command, and almost cruelly superior at the moment to George Bergner. Nor had he ever felt so alert: memory and the present vividly merged. He could relive his very feeling on the dock, his chagrin at being excluded, his loss of the opportunity to show off his nautical skill to Dr. Winthrop. Nathan had seen to it he was not aboard, presumably to make room for Mr. Bergner. "You didn't want to go at all, did you?" he said, attempting to make his voice casual, even as the hunter might disarm his prey.

And George, looking at his glass, was diverted. "I didn't," he said. "That's the truth. And now I wish to Christ I hadn't gone."

"Why?"

Bergner took a long swallow of the brandy. The color rose in blotches to his face with the impact of the drink. "It's the story of my life," he said between choking coughs. "I don't think you want to hear it any more than I want to hear it. Where the hell is Nathan?" He looked at his watch.

"I knew you were going over," Tad said. "I knew it the minute Nathan let the boom swing free."

Bergner grunted his disparagement. "You were a child."

"I knew how to sail that boat," Tad said, "and I was watching. I had the field glasses and I could see everything."

Bergner wiped the tears brought on by the coughing from the corners of his eyes. His eyelids were so puffy Tad could scarcely see his eyes. "Just what could you see?"

"That Nathan was smiling and that you were scared."

Bergner laughed. "A blind man could have seen that."

Tad blurted out the words purposely, lest the opportunity to say them be lost, the words that would commit him beyond retreat: "Nathan deliberately tipped that boat, Mr. Bergner."

Very slowly the look of sour amusement faded from George's face.

He sat a few seconds as though in a stupor. Then he got up and trundled across the room to the writing desk where he poured himself another drink. With it in hand, he turned to the boy who stood clutching the back of a chair on which he sometimes leaned, and sometimes pushed about, the activity an unconscious compliment to the manipulations of his mind.

Bergner said: "I'm going to give you a small piece of advice, my boy, just two words of it: shut up. If you don't, you may wind up like me, drinking this stuff."

"Or like my father—another accident?"

"What are you saying this to me for? I didn't like your father. But he didn't like me either. And I did him no more harm than he did me. I'd have been his friend if he'd let me. When decent people turn you down, you run after dogs." George began to whine, a self-pitying stream of irrelevant invective against his own father, against Marcus Hogan, his wife, himself. Only when he touched on Nathan Reiss could Tad attend him with patience. But he was powerless to stem the half-drunken, maudlin ramblings. "You know what I am?" George said finally. "Another cripple. A broken reed. So don't lean on me. I don't hear anything, I don't know anything, I don't do anything. I belch and I break wind. That way I know I'm alive."

Tad's excitement fell almost as quickly as it had risen. He had taken his plunge—into blubber.

He went to the writing table and picked up the Bible, reading at random where the book was open: "Wherefore the sin of the young men was very great before the Lord: for men abhorred the offering of the Lord.

"But Samuel ministered before the Lord, being a child, girded with a linen ephod.

"Moreover his mother made him a little coat, and brought it to him from year to year, when she came up with her husband to offer the yearly sacrifice."

Tad read the paragraphs again, taking from them a special understanding. He closed the book and hugged it to him.

George, watching him, grew philosophic. "Bible, bed and bottle . . . as it was in the beginning, is now and ever shall be, world without end, amen."

Nathan Reiss let himself into the room, looked about it as though to see who was there, and then without speaking to either Tad or Bergner closed the door and took off his hat and coat. Tad had not heard the key in the door and he thought there was something different about Nathan as he came in, a preoccupation whereby he forgot to put on the smiling mask. But in his own far from normal state he was in no position to judge the normalcy of Nathan.

"So, George. What are you drinking to this time?"

"I hadn't thought of it, Nathan." He lifted his glass. "Your health and long life."

Reiss glared at him from under drawn brows. "I should have as many lives as you drink toasts to me." Finally he acknowledged the boy's presence. His smile was quick but brief, a shot of teeth. "Hello, Tad." He went toward the bathroom. At the door he paused. "George, did you make the reservation?"

"Jacques' Restaurant at seven," George said.

"Will you go down please and arrange a cab to be waiting for us?" He closed the door behind him.

"Your obedient servant," George said in self-mocking humility. He drained his glass, and on sudden impulse, cried to Tad: "Catch." He tossed the glass underhand to the boy who had to lunge in order to catch it. George picked up his own coat and hat. "He must be back here by eleven o'clock. We are taking the train since there are no flights."

Reiss opened the bathroom door, and made no secret of the fact that he had been listening. "No flights, did you say, George?"

"That's what they tell me downstairs. All planes grounded in the fog."

"For how long?"

George said gravely: "I'll try and find out for you, Nathan."

Tad grinned, but Reiss returned to the bathroom without knowing the mockery in George's subservient response.

"Have fun," Bergner said to Tad, and went out.

Tad, waiting, took up the Bible again and tried to find the page in Samuel, but before he found it, his mind shot restlessly elsewhere. He put down the book and moved to the dresser where he gazed down on the glittering display of steel, cold as the snow-white satin in which they were shrouded. He had never wanted to be a doctor, only a veterinarian as a small child, and that because he was fonder then of animals than people. He ventured to draw from its sheathing one of the knives, and put it back at once: the sight of it made him nauseous for he could imagine its incision into the flesh. He went to the window, unlocked, and tried to open it.

Nathan came from the bathroom. "What are you doing?"

"Trying to open the window."

"For what reason?"

"Fresh air," Tad said. "The room stinks of brandy."

"It stinks of more than that," Reiss said, and passing the dresser on his way across the room, he asked: "Aren't you going to congratulate me?"

Tad was a moment remembering the occasion. "Yes, of course."

Reiss looked at him. "You look feverish, dissipated. Like him." He jerked his head, indicating the door by which George had gone out. He opened the window with very little difficulty. "It is a fine evening for fresh air," he said sarcastically.

Tad had observed in awe the ease with which Reiss had managed the window. Outside the fog hugged the building like a dirty sheet. Instinctively he drew away from the window.

"Are you afraid of heights?" Reiss said. "I think your father was."

"I am not afraid," Tad said, but he moistened his lips, and was aware that something very like fear was overtaking him.

"Sometimes it is better to be afraid."

"Nathan, why won't the Baroness see me?"

Reiss smiled in his old fashion for the first time since he had come. "For whatever reason, it is not because she is afraid. Go and put some cold water on your face. You look sick."

"I'm not sick!"

"Do as I say. Look at yourself in the mirror."

Tad obeyed him, but out of the need to move, to lift his feet, to counter the sudden, self-shaming weakness that had come on him. Nor did the vision of his own face in the mirror, the flushed cheeks, the pale lips, the staring eyes, restore him. He felt himself utterly inadequate. More than ever he had loathed Nathan Reiss he loathed himself at that moment. He washed his face and drew several deep breaths before rejoining his stepfather who was at the dresser gazing down at the instruments.

Voices grew loud in the hallway as people approached and passed their doorway. Someone shouted: "Hold it!" presumably to the elevator operator and the voices faded.

Reiss closed the display of instruments with a contemptuous flick of his wrist. "Are you ready?"

Tad said: "Nathan, I told George this afternoon that I thought you deliberately tipped the *Lorna Doone* when and he and Dr. Winthrop . . . when Dr. Winthrop died."

Reiss looked at him, a curious gaze, but not one of surprise. Having said the words, Tad could say no more. He required all his strength to stand up straight and keep his head steady.

Reiss said: "You have a long memory. What, may I ask, did George say?" Reiss waited, but the boy did not answer, and he went on. "I should not be surprised if he agreed with you. Ah, but I would be surprised. George has the fat tongue of a coward. Do you know what I thought, Tad, when I saw you trying so desperately to open that window? I was afraid you were contemplating suicide."

Tad calculated the few steps between himself and the hall door. Hit and run. But by the calculation he was able to say: "So you opened it for me . . . and didn't even hurt your hand."

"Poor boy," Reiss said, and then rather crossly: "Take your coat and let us go. This room is reeking of malignancy."

Tad, out of an old training, waited at the door for the man to precede him. He knew an instant of terror in the brief interlude of darkness when Nathan snapped off the room lights before they moved into the hall. But in the flood of light and space to which they passed that terror, too, became a part of a larger chagrin. Reiss went back and tried the door to be sure that it was locked. Returning and leading the way he said: "Many people would have believed your father a suicide if I had not been there."

"I don't believe it," Tad said.

Reiss shrugged. "I am only telling what was said to everyone except your mother." At the elevator he smiled, his reproachful, lower lip-hanging smile. "Perhaps you had better press the signal yourself."

Tad merely stared at the man as though with his eyes he hoped to penetrate to the inside of him. Reiss touched the signal button and waiting, adjusted his tie, which at another time Tad would have thought a ridiculous gesture of indifference. Now he was steeped in his own frustration. "It doesn't matter what I think now, does it, Nathan? You've got everything the way you want it—and all the old answers. It's too late for new ones, isn't it?"

"Shall I tell you the truth?" Reiss said. "If it mattered more to me just now, Tad, I should feel very sorry for you. Why not pretend a little longer that we enjoy each other? Let us try to make the best of this expensive dinner I am proposing—as the climax, let us say, of the father and son ceremony."

The elevator stopped and Reiss got in. The operator said testily to Tad: "Down, sir?"

He got in mutely.

Bergner was waiting for them at the Park Avenue entrance to the hotel, his hand on a cab door as though he were prepared to run alongside the vehicle if that were necessary to hold it. As soon as Tad and Reiss were inside, the driver thrust them back in their seats with the violence of his start from the curb. Reiss spoke sharply to him and a moment later they were engaged in an acrimonious exchange. "I'm not your private chauffeur, see?" the driver said. "If I get a ticket, I'm the guy what's got to pay for it. It says 'no standing' and me they don't let stand."

Tad was grateful for the diversion, numb as were his own senses. You could answer a curse, but cursing a smile turned back the curses on yourself. Once he had been able to infuriate his stepfather—like a small stinging gnat. In his rashness, he had lost even that measly strength.

When they reached Greenwich Village the driver had to stop to get his bearings in the fog.

"Schlaacht's," Nathan said, observing the sign as they started up again. He sat forward in his seat. The restaurant sign gleamed within a halo of mist. "That will suit us quite as well as the French tonight. We will stop here, driver."

The driver stepped on his brakes. A car, too close behind them, came to a screaming stop.

In the restaurant the head waiter asked if Reiss had a reservation.

"I do not need a reservation," Reiss said. His and the waiter's eyes met, and after the slightest further hesitation, the waiter seated them at an excellent table in an uncrowded part of the room.

When he was gone, Reiss said: "That is how it is done, even in America. You will have a drink, Tad? I prescribe it."

"Only wine."

"Champagne, perhaps?"

"If you like."

"And why not?" Reiss said, "since we are celebrating your maturity —and my discovery. So. The mouse nibbles and the lion claws." He ordered the wine, and waiting, looked around the room of heavy dark beams and voluptuous panelings. "I am glad they do not bring in manufactured music." When the wine came he supervised its chilling himself. He read the menu aloud, translating the English into German, and thereby enjoying himself. He called the headwaiter back to inquire particularly about the *pâté*.

"I remember recommending a certain *pâté* to your mother once in Vienna—such a long time ago. Who would have supposed?"

With the first sip of wine, he said: "So. You and the Baroness have become friends, do I understand?"

Tad wondered if the Baroness had given him that impression. He said nothing, doubting it.

"And of course you discussed your prognosis concerning your father and Dr. Winthrop?"

Tad resolved to do so at the first opportunity, and he would make his own opportunity.

Reiss was smiling, amused, tolerant, hypocritical. "Believe me, Tad, she is a melodramatic woman."

Throughout the elaborate service of the first course, Nathan talked in Nathan's way—smoothly-spoken ambiguities, in which Tad discovered, trying to attend him, to understand him if not his meanderings, there was a sort of glancing relevancy. Tad's own mind grew keener as he realized this. Nathan was playing with the truth as a child plays on ice he knows to be dangerous, skating ever closer to trouble and growing ecstatic with the crackling of the ice beneath him. Tad began to participate, and with the strain, further exhausted his nerves, trying to provoke the man to the disaster he fervently believed lay beyond the edge.

Suddenly Reiss leaned across the table and said: "Suppose, Tad, I admitted to you that it was sometimes within my power to save—where I have deliberately not saved: if I were to admit that to you now, how would you profit yourself of such an admission? In other words, who would believe you?"

"The Baroness," Tad said cunningly.

"Very good," Reiss said, as though Tad had given a correct answer in recitation. "But not your mother."

"I'm not so damned sure of that, Nathan."

"I am so damned sure of it. And so, my dear boy, is the Baroness who knows a good deal more about human nature than you or I. I am going to tell you something about your mother, Tad: some day she will go into a nunnery. Mark my having told you. It is the prison to which people like her commit themselves when there is no other way to expiate their guilt—or the guilt of others."

"I would rather she was in one now than married to you," Tad said.

"Would you? Shall I tell you the truth? So would I. I am revolted by her patience, her forebearance. It is like an act of contrition every time she takes me to her bed."

The words went through Tad like so many stabs. He blurted out: "Why don't you leave her then?"

Reiss shrugged. "She would not permit it. She is Mrs. Nathan Reiss, part and bond of me. Rather she would die than give me up. Do you not believe it?"

Tad fell back in his chair, faint and damp with a cold perspiration. He struggled with himself to hold consciousness, to focus on something to save him from that degradation: hatred—if only he could hate enough. Then, for the first time in fact—or fantasy—he thought: I must kill this man. It is the only way. He said the words to himself and with them, with their challenge, was revived, even presently exhilarated. He was able to sit up straight and ask out boldly for more wine. He even managed the bravura of eating a morsel of bread. He was able then to eat a shrimp.

Reiss scraped the last of his *pâté* from the plate and spread it on a cracker. He ate it, sipped his champagne and signaled the waiter to refill his glass. "I have not been in a German restaurant in America," he said. "So foolish of me."

Tad's one thought was to get away as quickly as he could, to walk the streets, to think, to plan. If he could go out now and make his way to the haunts of the city's hunted, among the degraded, the degenerates and the vicious, if he could go among them and yet remain himself apart, unsullied—where better learn the art of killing and the ease to practice it? To kill, but not to die: that was his wish; to live free and strong, in some distant place if necessary, and to be the kinder to all God's creatures for having done so dreadful but inescapable a duty. There was no other freedom possible for him until he freed his mother and himself from this obsessive man. While his thoughts ran thusly, he toyed with the food set before him, and pretended to attend Nathan's new tirade.

Had he been less involved in his own dire dream, he might have realized that Nathan Reiss—in his revelation of his true feeling about Martha and now in his derision of the Conference of Jewish Women—had skated far beyond the edge of safety. But Tad was himself beyond that state of comprehension.

Abruptly, as though testing his power to act, he laid his silver down neatly on the plate, and rose from the table.

"Good night, Nathan," he said, and with the exuberance born of freedom he walked buoyantly from the room.

Everything now was a test. Nathan had their coat checks, but Tad demanded of the check-room girl the right to find his own coat and was given it.

But once he was upon the street everything changed. He found the fog a wall into which he seemed constantly about to crash, and he would draw up suddenly, even throwing up his arm in self-protection. Other people came through it, but they came at him like spirits which disappeared as soon as he was sure that they were real. The foghorns groaned incessantly, complaints from the shores of hell. Loneliness enveloped him and he became afraid, even of himself. He groped his way toward light, the company of neon nobodies on drugstore stools, at bookstore stalls, who nonetheless were flesh and blood and voices. Where he was—what street—he did not know. He thought he had been walking in the angled straightness of the Greenwich Village streets for a long time. And when he found himself once more within a few feet of Schlaacht's he was confounded. Fear abated. How ironic that he should have walked so boldly—in a circle. Self-contempt returned. Where could he turn to ease this agony of self-derision? He thought again of the Baroness who he believed, as did Nathan, knew more of human nature than anyone he had ever known. Had the cab drawing up to the restaurant at that moment not been caught by emerging diners, he would have taken it directly to her house.

Nathan Reiss came out of the restaurant. Tad moved instinctively into the shadows at the corner of the building. Reiss walked past him within touching distance and on into the fog, his step sure, his direction set. The few seconds Tad hesitated, uncertain whether to follow Nathan or to try to call the Baroness from the phone inside the restaurant door were sufficient for Reiss to disappear. A car drove close to the curb and went on in the direction Reiss had taken, but it was not a taxi. Tad went into the restaurant, looked up the number and dialed. He got a busy signal. The bartender was mixing drinks in manual expertise, the hat-check girl chewing gum, reading a magazine as fast as she could chew: all New York was a busy signal. He dialed again, and again got a busy signal.

He went out then and walked in the direction Nathan had gone. He did not expect to catch up with him, he did not want to, and yet he began to run. He was not aware of passing a soul within the block. He almost stumbled over the feet of a man slumped against a building whom he thought at the instant to be groaning drunk. He was startled, slowed down, shying away from the figure, and then glanced back, for something lay on the ground that caught and reflected light. Tad hesitated and went back knowing, he afterwards thought, before he had seen what it was: a surgical knife smeared all but a small star-bright part of it with blood. He would not remember touching Nathan except that he became aware of the warmth and blood-wetness of him, and his sudden dead limpness and the silence when the moaning had ceased. Nothing else of those few moments was ever clear again to him until the hat-check girl's scream when he returned to Schlaacht's Restaurant.

·7

MUCH of the conversation in the faculty lounge that night turned upon the weather. One man or another would rise every few minutes and go to a window. The mists rolled in from the East, surge upon surge across the green, like the swells of a slow sea. It was not Covington's habit to linger so late among his fellows—an hour after dinner perhaps before settling down to the night's work. But he knew that he was not able to work and he knew that he would meet the last train from New York if Hogan had not reported in before midnight. He had left a message with Tad's house mother to have the boy call him when he came in.

At a few minutes after eleven he was called to the telephone. Person to person, the operator said, and Covington wondered if Tad were calling him from New York, perhaps having purposely missed the last train.

Covington identified himself.

"Go ahead, Traders City," the operator said.

"Mr. Covington, this is Martha Reiss, Tad Hogan's mother." Her voice was quite clear but a slight tremor ran through it.

"Yes, Mrs. Reiss."

"You have not heard . . . from Tad?"

"Not since he went off campus at four this afternoon."

She was a few seconds going on as though waiting for him to say something further. Then: "Doctor Reiss was murdered in New York tonight. The police have arrested Tad."

Over and over again going back to the moment afterwards Covington would feel that he had known what she was going to say before he heard the words. He said only: "God Almighty."

"I can't get transportation to New York except the train at midnight. Will you go to him, Mr. Covington?"

"Of course."

"Don't let him talk too much."

Covington began to recover his senses. "Shall I get a lawyer?"

"Please do. I am most beholden to you." And she hung up.

Someone from the president's office was waiting for him when he got off the phone. The news of the murder had been broadcast at eleven o'clock. Covington called the dean of the law school at home and got the name and phone number of Thomas Andrew Dobbs, one of the foremost criminal lawyers in the country and an alumnus of Rodgers University. Covington was fortunate in reaching Dobbs at once.

"They'll have to arraign him in night court if we get onto it immediately," Dobbs said, and from his competent matter-of-factness, Covington supposed that was good. "They'll try for a confession first, of course." He was thinking aloud. "Redmond will be our man for it, I think. He's got the connections."

It was almost dawn when Covington reached the city, his nerves taut, his eyes strained from concentration on the Turnpike road. He reached the court before Tad had been called. He saw him sitting on a bench between two policemen—an undistinguished looking trio among the discoverers and perpetrators of one night's crime on the city streets. The low-ceilinged room was fairly crowded still. Beneath the naked light bulbs and against the green, sweating walls of Magistrate's Court, all men and women, black or white, bore a greenish tinge. The monotonous hum of charges, dismissals, remands, was constant as was the scraping and shuffle of feet on the cement floor. Tad did not see the teacher, not looking to see anyone, just staring straight ahead.

But almost at once Redmond spotted him and came up to introduce himself: Dennis P. Redmond. The two men shook hands. P. for Patrick, surely. He had the smile of a politician, the hand shake of a hurler, and the moment Tad was called up, Covington was grateful he had such counsel. When they stood before the magistrate, they seemed the very caricature of lawyer and client, the one confident, vigorous, a champion, and Tad, his narrow shoulders slumped, only his head defiant, a small, close-cropped knob shooting up as though telescoped out of his collar.

The charge against Thaddeus Marcus Hogan was read in a quick monotone, much of which Covington could not hear. He heard enough, however, to understand that Tad was alleged to have assaulted his stepfather on a lightly trafficked street in Greenwich Village a few minutes after they had quarreled and parted at the restaurant where they had dined. The weapon was a surgical knife, part of a set given to Dr. Reiss at a testimonial luncheon that day.

Hogan pleaded "Not guilty." But that was the instant when Covington was first able to see the boy's eyes. He looked sullenly, almost defiantly at Redmond before he said the words.

Hogan was ordered held without bail on suspicion of murder, and remanded to the custody of the police. Covington was shocked at the dispatch with which so portentous a thing was accomplished.

Covington was shocked also at the undisguised satisfaction the uniformed police showed in taking charge of the prisoner. Hogan had never been a boy for making obeisance to authority, and the authoritarians here were going to have it one way or the other. Covington asked the lawyer if he could be allowed to talk to Hogan.

It was so easily accomplished by Redmond's affable persuasion Covington wished the boy might take notice and example: a vain wish. If Hogan were more of that character he might have made the compromises long ago that would have halted him far short of this disaster. And it was, perhaps, his uncompromising nature which had recommended him to the teacher's affection. On all sides that day was the prevalence of such friendly persuasion as Redmond's. Unfriendly witnesses automatically bore testimony against themselves.

Redmond arranged that both he and the teacher ride downtown in the police van with the prisoner and his guards. It was one of the strangest rides in Covington's experience: the half-light within the wagon illuminating faces beneath which the bodies were lost in a murky darkness, the springless seats; the dawn to be glimpsed beyond the barred windows, a dawn that gave light but defined none of the objects one expects to see in daylight, for the fog persisted though the sun was burning through it. He was taken back in memory to wartime Holland, the springless vans jolting along the shell-pocked roads. Even the light was such as he remembered, the sun obscured by the restless dust after the night's bombardment.

No one in the police van spoke for a long time. The bell sometimes clanged and Tad would grin a little at the sound. It pleased Covington to see manifest some stirring of the boy's imagination; no matter whether the grin was mocking or ironic.

And mocking it was, alas, for he jerked his head in the direction of the driver and said, purposely slurring his usually careful speech: "That's doin' his dooty."

The policeman to whom he was manacled wrenched the boy's wrist by giving a sudden twist to the chain between them. Tad winced, then cast him a venomous glance and said: "You son of a bitch."

Covington, sitting opposite him, looked at his own hands. He had never heard Tad use language like it before. The night had wrought much change in him. Redmond, next to Covington, softly whistled a few phrases from something operatic.

"This is what they're coddling in the universities of the country nowadays," the policeman said, and leaning sidewise, he spat expertly between the bars of the back window.

Oh, yes. Tad would get on marvelously with the police.

There was not much time left. Covington tried to find a way to put his question that would not provoke some bitter, self-injurious retort from the boy. He had not yet acknowledged even the presence of the teacher. Finally he asked simply: "Is there anything you want me to do, Tad? To say to your mother when she gets here?"

The boy lifted his eyes, the wide dark blue eyes that met Covington's frankly and then narrowed as he withdrew again into isolated misery. Covington had held his own gaze steady, trying to convey a little understanding at least. And a little was all he had, for such a hatred as this boy had cherished for Nathan Reiss was beyond the teacher's reckoning. There was nothing in his own life by which he could relate to it.

Hogan turned his head away as though he would have hid his face if that were possible, and Covington saw the quick movement in the boy's throat, the thrust of pain without tears, and he assumed that something of his unworded message had got across. He rode out the rest of the interminable journey in aching suspense himself. One of the cops said it was clearing up, and the other said he was glad because he had promised to take his kids to the zoo that afternoon. "If it don't clear up," he said, "I'll have to take them to the Museum of Natural History. The dead zoo, my kid calls it. Ain't that something, the dead zoo!"

Covington had been staring at the window. In the afterglow he could see nothing but striped patches of light wherever he tried to focus his vision. His sight was still bleared when the vehicle slowed down. That and the tires' rubbing against the curb, indicated their arrival at the city prison. He laid his hand on the boy's knee. "Anything, Tad?"

The boy shook his head, but murmured, "Thanks."

The van door was opened from the outside, and then in the instant they stood all of them together, the men getting their legs steady beneath them, Tad said: "Mr. Covington, if you would tell my mother . . ." By his own choice, the boy left off the sentence there.

·8

Covington met Assistant District Attorney Reginald Tripp in his office at a little before noon. Redmond had told him he was likely to be called and advised him to be cooperative without volunteering anything, above all opinions. But with Mr. Tripp himself, Covington thought after a very few minutes in his company, fact and opinion were hardly distinguishable.

Tripp was a tough, but soft spoken man with the crisp manner of being able to get things done. He was well under fifty, and Covington had no doubt, ambitious. But then, one was always likely to think of a prosecutor as ambitious, and sharp. This fellow was sharper than most. And Covington realized just where he was trying to go very early in the interrogation.

"Did Hogan tell you why he was going into New York?"

"To have dinner with his stepfather."

"Was there anything special about the occasion?" the lawyer asked.

"About their having dinner, not to my knowledge."

"You didn't know Doctor Reiss was in town for a testimonial luncheon?"

"Yes, I knew that."

Tripp smiled a little and said casually: "Hogan didn't think much of the Conference of Jewish Women, did he?"

"I don't think I could answer that."

"He called them a corny outfit," Tripp said.

"I suppose," Covington said, "I would say the same thing about most fraternal—or benevolent organizations."

"Would you," the lawyer murmured, and Covington realized he had volunteered an opinion.

"Have you ever heard him make any other anti-Semitic remarks?"

"That, sir, was not an anti-Semitic remark. Nor is the boy anti-Semitic." Covington was not a quick-tempered man, but the lawyer had come very near to making him one then.

Tripp himself merely drew a line across the blank piece of paper before him as though striking a question. "In other words, professor, you don't think that's an issue in this case?"

"I do not."

"Then let's try and clear up a couple of thing if we can," the lawyer said, and scratched his ear. "Ever have your ear go numb on you? Maybe I get it from the telephone . . . Schlaacht's Restaurant. That's as German as Hitler. As a matter of fact it was a Bundist hangout back in the thirties. What do you suppose persuaded Reiss, a Jewish refugee to have dinner there?" Covington did not answer. "Especially when he himself had had a reservation made at Jacques'."

"From my knowledge of Hogan, I know that he would have preferred Jacques'," the teacher said.

"You know, professor," Tripp said, "according to you, the boy and his stepfather should have got along beautifully. But we both know that isn't so, don't we?"

"I know that Hogan did not like his stepfather," Covington said coldly.

"What do you know about this character, Bergner?"

Covington was aware again of being led, the word "character" would be meant to disarm him. "Practically nothing," Covington said. All he did know of Bergner was Tad's contempt for him: "Nathan's broom."

"A friend of the family, would you say?"

"Probably a friend of Doctor Reiss'."

"Not a likely confidant of the boy's?"

"I shouldn't think so," Covington said.

"And yet Hogan seems to have confided to him yesterday afternoon that he thought Nathan Reiss was responsible for his father's death . . . In fact, Hogan himself admits saying it. And he goes further: he claims to have said it to Reiss—and that at dinner in a restaurant called Schlaacht's—Reiss refused to deny it. You know, professor, it would take very little persuasion to get that boy to plead guilty, and I'm not at all sure it wouldn't be in his own best interests."

The lawyer raised his hand to forestall Covington's protest. "Let me go over with you just for a few minutes the way it looks to this office right now:

"First there's the matter of physical evidence and the findings of the medical examiner's office. I assure you, everything in that is going to be checked out. Our job right now is looking to motive. We have to go back a ways for that, I think.

"Doctor Reiss came to this country, a refugee, in '39 or '40, according to Bergner. He got out, we may assume, with enough money, enough of everything to take care of him until he was established. He was a man, shall we say, not ostensibly Jewish—despite his subsequent activities in this country. I say all of this because he shared a practice which probably wasn't Jewish at all with Doctor Hogan at one time. He was affiliated with three hospitals at the time of his death. None of them is Jewish sponsored. His wife is not Jewish. All that is one side of the man. The other side is something else. He became active in the Zionist movement, he was honored yesterday by a Jewish organization. It's my feeling, Mr. Covington, that a man does not survive handily where several million like him perished without carrying the burden of their martyrdom for the rest of his natural life. And it gets heavier all the time. Such a man, I propose, might literally beg for persecution. I mean he'd want it—like food, like sex, deeply, pathologically, trying to provoke people into it. I think you and I know enough of human nature to realize that if anybody asks for a beating, he's going to find someone to give it to him."

Covington sat, determined to hear the man out. He could not deny the ring of truth in the theory he was sounding: and Tad responded always where Nathan Reiss was concerned as though deliberately goaded into some new expression of hatred.

"And so we come to young Hogan: he grew up in the house with this strong-willed man, this—masochist. I don't deny for a minute, Covington, that Reiss was a bastard where this boy was concerned. I shouldn't be surprised if he deliberately turned him into an anti-Semite. That's what I meant by saying it might be better for the boy to plead guilty: his lawyers could expose Reiss for what he was —and save the boy's life." Tripp leaned across his desk. "I'm not trying to shock you into anything, Covington. I assure you that if you were to read Bergner's and the boy's own testimony as to what he went through last night you would understand our line of reasoning."

Covington said: "But he pleaded 'not guilty', Mr. Tripp."

"I think he will change that plea . . . voluntarily. Because I think he's proud of what he did."

"I swear to God, sir, that boy is not anti-Semitic. No!" Covington pushed himself away from Tripp's desk and got up. "No, sir. You're wrong there and you've got to be wrong in the rest of it. Whatever happened last night, I tell you, Nathan Reiss did not, could not brainwash that boy. You've come closer doing that to me than ever he did to Hogan."

"All right," Tripp said placatingly. "I'm not going to argue it with you. There's not much point, is there? Would you like some coffee?"

"No thanks."

"Sure?" He picked up the phone and ordered two cartons of it sent up anyway.

Covington, given the moment's respite, began to contemplate why the lawyer had put him through that gambit: he was hoping, Covington came to suspect, that the teacher might persuade the boy and his lawyers to change the plea: that was what he wanted. And realizing it, Covington suspected that the District Attorney did not actually have sufficient evidence on which to hold Hogan otherwise.

Covington's whole line of reasoning must have shone in his face, for as soon as Tripp hung up the phone, he said: "He's going to be arraigned soon, you know. And we're going to charge him with first-degree murder . . . So if there's any way in which you think can help him, it ought to be now."

"God knows, I want to," Covington said.

The lawyer studied him for a moment. "Have y

he should have wanted to telephone a woman named Madame Johanna Schwarzbach at twenty minutes to nine last night?"

"Why he should have wanted to, I don't know," Covington said slowly.

The lawyer sighed. "That makes two of you. He doesn't seem to know either."

"Have you asked Madame Schwarzbach?"

"Do you know her?"

"I know who she is," Covington said.

"Then you know why I haven't asked her. I'm waiting for the boss' okay."

There were some things, some people on whom the city of New York could wait apparently. Covington said: "She used to be Doctor Reiss' mistress, Mr. Tripp. Perhaps that should enhance her privilege even more."

Tripp was a few seconds before he spoke. Then: "Does young Hogan know that?"

Too late Covington turned his bitterness on himself. He answered truthfully: "That's where I found it out."

·9

THAT same noon came for Martha as the train on which she rode pulled out of Albany, down along the widening Hudson River. The mist lay in patches sometimes severing a bright sky from a clouded landscape. Heaven and earth were never joined, she thought. She sat at the window of the compartment in much the same position as she had sat the night, not even having had the bed lowered. She moved her lips now and then, the habit of prayer no less strong than the need for it.

Nathan is dead, Nathan is dead, Nathan is dead. The words had long since set themselves to the rhythm of wheels on rails. And Marcus was dead. Longer dead, yet dead more recently. She allowed her ump against the window more and more violently as though ight go away with pain. God knew what violence she his memory and herself in marrying Nathan Reiss.

There are darkness within into which one cannot go even during the eclipse of day. The burden of that violence now lay on Tad, and the terror of it was he had in all the years of his precocity been trying to embrace it.

The porter brought her coffee. She could not drink it having a mouth of gall. She could only wait to be taken to one who could not come to meet her.

The afternoon tabloid was put aboard at Harmon. The train floor and seats were strewn with copies when at last she left the compartment as the train pulled into Grand Central Station. She tried not to look at them. But Tad's face stared up at her, startled and angry as though it were himself that even she was treading on.

George Bergner met her at the station, unshaven, his eyes bloodshot. Nor was his speech coherent as he wobbled alongside her bumping into people with her suitcase. "I've made a reservation for you at the Imperial. The police. Nathan's things are there. All night, all day, nothing but questions. I can go, they say now. I'm going." In the ramp he put her into the first taxi. "I'm going home, Martha. The lawyers, they'll do everything."

To Martha's shock, he closed the cab door between them and directed the driver to take her to the Imperial Hotel. The vision of him on the curb, limp and gaping, as she was driven off did much to help Martha take hold for herself. Sylvia had put her on the train. For years till now, it seemed, she had not acted of her own volition. Now she was on her own, her son to find.

At the hotel, Lawrence Covington and the attorney, Redmond, were waiting for her.

It was Covington who asked her as soon as he had introduced the lawyer: "Where's Bergner? Didn't he meet you?"

"He put me in the taxi," Martha said, "and then he said that he was going home."

Covington and Redmond exchanged glances. Redmond said: "I knew we weren't going to get at him, not till cross-examination."

Which, Martha thought without specifically understanding, portended ill for Tad.

"It will probably be easier for you," the lawyer said, "if we talk here."

"I do not want things made easier for me, Mr. Redmond. I want only to do what I can quickly—and I want to see my son."

"I want you to see him, too," Redmond said. "Maybe he'll tell you things he won't tell me."

"Or Mr. Covington?" Martha said.

"The fact is," Covington said. "He doesn't want to see either you or me."

They moved quickly out of the hotel lobby to Martha's room, Redmond aware of the sudden presence of newsmen. Between them he and Covington told Martha as much as they felt she should be told. Redmond had requested the switchboard to withhold all calls. When the room phone rang despite this order Redmond answered it. Martha and Covington waited.

Redmond said to Martha: "Madame Johanna Schwarzbach wishes to speak with you. I think you'd better take it."

"So do I," Martha said, and crossed the room with a firm, quick step.

· 10

THE sifting of such evidence as was available by noon of the day following the crime enabled the Manhattan District Attorney's office to set up such a pattern of motivation as Reginald Tripp had indicated to Covington. And there was upon the investigators the pressure of having either to charge Hogan or to release him: he could not be held long on suspicion of murder. Each item, however, had to be checked out.

If Hogan could have taken the murder weapon from the hotel room, so also could Bergner or Reiss himself. Bergner had not left his hotel room, going to it directly after putting Reiss and Hogan in a taxi. A woman had spent the evening in the room with him. If Reiss had carried the weapon, his assailant needed to take it from him before using it. This was possible according to the medical examiner, but only for a person much stronger than Thaddeus Hogan.

The driver of the taxi was located. He corroborated the boy's story that the choice of restaurant was actually Reiss'. When asked if he thought his car might have been followed to the restaurant, the driver recalled the screeching of brakes of a car behind him when

423

he stopped suddenly at Schlaacht's. Not much, but in combination with Hogan's recollection of a car driving slowly past the restaurant as soon as Reiss left it, a car Hogan said he would have hailed himself had it been a taxi, needed to be noted.

A precinct detective turned up a bookstore proprietor who thought he could identify Hogan as the boy at his outdoor stall who had asked for a Bible and then disappeared when the man went indoors to look for one. (Even Tad did not remember the Bible part of it: he had remembered the bookstall which was why the detective was checking it.)

There was also the question of Bergner's reliability as a witness, and it was primarily his testimony that had set the line of inquiry as to motivation. Tripp, who had questioned him most severely, had a sneaking suspicion that he was the kind of man who saw his own faults in other people. Yet his testimony was sworn.

Lawrence Covington, a professor at one of the country's leading universities, was another matter.

And the possible involvement of a woman as socially prominent as Madame Johanna Schwarzbach brought the District Attorney himself into the case. Before he moved, however, a possibly significant piece of information was turned up by the homicide detective checking out her household staff: she had in her employ a man named John Ferrari. On a hunch the detective had the name searched in the police files. John Ferrari had served a good part of his youth in a state detention prison, having been twice convicted of robbery. Ferrari had been missing since eleven o'clock the night before.

· 11

THE lights were coming on throughout Manhattan when Martha and Covington parted with Redmond to catch a cab in front of the Imperial Hotel. The fog was gone entirely. Evening traffic moved in surges across town released at measured intervals from every intersection.

Several cars were double-parked in front of the elegant old mansion, so that Covington and Martha were forced to leave the cab a few doors away from it and walk back. It allowed them to observe the arrival and departure of men who by their gait and bearing suggested police business. Covington could not help construing it as a good sign. But he was not yet able to throw off the oppression of his interview with Tripp.

A maid opened the door to them, a pale and somewhat frightened looking girl, by no means as sure of herself as were the servants he had hitherto observed in the employ of Madame Schwarzbach. Her eyes fairly leaped when Martha gave her name.

The Baroness received them in the library. She did not rise from the couch where she was propped up in pillows as though recuperating from an illness. Nor was she alone. Three men in business suits arose when Martha entered. The Baroness extended both her hands.

"My dearest Martha. I am sorry I could not have come to you."

Martha crossed the room and gave her hands into the Baroness', allowing herself to be drawn down to the chair beside her couch.

"Yes," the Baroness said, "it would be Mr. Covington. I cannot say I would not have expected him."

"I asked him to come," Martha said.

The Baroness said: "I like to think he would have come anyway." She was gowned in silk, an afghan covering her legs. There was very little make-up on her face. She was at the moment, Covington thought, an acknowledged old woman. "May I present Mr. Forester who is the District Attorney of New York?" She barely looked toward the other men, but said: "I am sorry I have forgotten the other gentlemen's names."

It did not matter to anyone. Nor did they bother to identify themselves.

"Mr. Forester has been kind enough to spend much of his afternoon with me," the Baroness said, with irony. She said to him: "I should suppose it must be near your dinner time?"

"I have no special engagement," Forester said blandly. He was a lean, balding man in his early fifties. Not without humor, Covington thought, observing the lines at his eyes and mouth.

"And the other gentlemen?" the Baroness said.

"I think we might get along without their company for now," Forester said. "They can wait in another room."

"Since you are so considerate, I am sure my cook can arrange dinner for them downstairs." She rang a small silver bell and gave instructions to the girl. The two detectives left with her.

moment in her whole story, Covington thought afterwards, that she participated in what she told.

"I was in love with him and he was my equal thereafter."

Her voice grew listless again, raspy with the effort of talk. "What do I need to tell of the intervening years? He succeeded in doing the most difficult, for he wanted to play almost as much as he wanted to be a doctor, but not quite. I was one part of his life, the Baron another: and we each understood. If anything is to be said of our world, it is that we all understood one another. The Baron died and Nathan grieved—in his fashion. And I in mine. Alone, we were no longer to one another what we had been when we were three of us. And then suddenly—in our world at least—there was Hitler . . . and poor Nathan had to cope with his patriotic soul. That, I do believe, was his darkest hour."

The Baroness sat a moment in bitter, amused contemplation.

"I am not entirely Jewish myself, you know? That has never mattered to my friends . . . or to my enemies.

"But you see, Martha, it did not happen quite as Nathan told it, either of our escapes from the Nazis. He did not wait for me. He tried to stay himself, but when he could not, I proposed to save him and went back across the border to do it, having already left Austria. *I* was the price he had promised to pay the Nazis for his own freedom. It must been a very great shock to him to discover afterwards I had never reached a concentration camp.

"I must tell you something else which you may have heard not quite as it happened: there was a German soldier who risked his life to help me escape when he was supposed to take me into custody. I rightly supposed that such a man wished also himself to escape for his own reasons. We crossed with much travail, you may imagine, through Switzerland and Vichy France and finally to Ischia. There we lived alone and remote. But he paid a dreadful price in the end to the Italian partisans who heard but did not know . . . who perhaps did not want to know. Vengeance does not always ask on whom it is avenged. Is that not so, Mr. Forester?"

Forester merely uncrossed and recrossed his knees.

The Baroness rested her head back for a moment. "I am tired," she said. "I have been tired always since then. But I knew what I had to do.

"I came to New York and sought out Nathan. I could not go to him since he was married to you. I had to bring him to me. And sometimes, I could not believe what I knew. Maybe you can understand that, Martha. One could not believe what one knew about him. It is so?"

Martha did not look up.

"I did not admit to him I knew of his betrayal of me to the Nazis. He told me he had tried to reach our rendezvous—and arrived too late, like all his heroic failures . . . escaping alone afterwards. I gave him my pity for his failure: it is the easiest emotion to simulate before those who are themselves without it.

"It was interesting to see what Nathan had become in America . . . I was remembering, you see, what my husband, the Baron, had made of him. And when I saw how distinguished a person he had become in his own right: I told him of my knowledge of his collaboration. It was at this point, I should say, I had hired John Ferrari as my . . . servant.

"I am not a good person, Martha, in any way. And in your own mind you must not make excuses for me—ever. But I do not think you will be so tempted.

"I wanted only my own kind of vengeance. I opened to Nathan a new door, and proposed that he enter it: It is very easy for someone like me to open doors. It was to a world I mocked, mocking him. But that I did not see at the time. It was only he I wished to watch behaving like a Jew. Who would believe Nathan Reiss was a Zionist? Only those who did not know him. I doubt he could spell the word Israel. No more could I. But who denied him? I ask you: who denied him?"

For the first time Martha spoke: "My son."

"Your son," the Baroness repeated. She fell back upon her cushions and was a long moment silent. Footsteps could be heard upon a stair, a bell rang in another part of the house, and the clock on the mantel ticked.

"You are right. If that were not so I should not have had to tell this monstrous tale. There is a blame even beyond my own that I will mention, for if it were not so, what has happened could not have happened. There are people who justify themselves in a cause sufficient to the burden of their conscience, and therefore to them lip service and heart service make very little difference. Only the forms matter, and there was no form ever devised by God or man to which Nathan Reiss could not accommodate himself.

"What else must be told? Before my arrival in this country I had determined that Nathan must be destroyed. I have told you of my procrastinations. But I made my arrangements. I hired a man in my house capable of protecting me—and of killing for me. And yet, I could not say the word . . . until yesterday. When Nathan began to deride to me the women who had gathered to pay him tribute, it was enough. Fools I do not doubt some of them are. But from Nathan Reiss I could not tolerate any longer such arrogance and cruelty. He brought even a souvenir of the occasion: the small surgical knife. And to Mr. Forester I could only say when he asked me, this afternoon: Oh, yes! I had indeed seen it before."

The District Attorney got up, and very neatly put his chair back from where he had drawn it round the better to see them.

The Baroness said: "Will you find John, Mr. Forester? I do not think so."

He stood a moment looking down at her. Then he said coldly: "I don't think it will be difficult to find a man who enjoyed his work as much as he did." He turned. "Mrs. Reiss."

He said only the name, but by the little gesture of his head, both Martha and Covington understood that they were to follow him as he left the room.

The Baroness closed her eyes and did not re-open them until she was alone.

By the activity in the vestibule, the self-assured presence there of several detectives and uniformed police, Covington realized that Madame Schwarzbach had been already under arrest when he and Martha arrived.

· 12

TAD's ordeal was over.

For Martha a new one began that night: she suffered a nervous collapse and was hospitalized for several months. But by the end of the school year she was able—with Tad and Sylvia—to go abroad again, and in Ireland that summer she began a sure and steady recuperation.

Tad was able to spend a part of the summer with Covington in

Holland. He was accepted, starting with the fall term, at London University.

Madame Johanna Schwarzbach died by her own hand and in her own house. In time, John Ferrari was extradited from Venezuela. He is now waiting trial for the murder of Nathan Reiss.